EVERYMAN,

I WILL GO WITH THEE,

AND BE THY GUIDE,

IN THY MOST NEED

TO GO BY THY SIDE

EVERYMAN'S POCKET CLASSICS

GARDEN STORIES

EDITED BY DIANA SECKER TESDELL

EVERYMAN'S POCKET CLASSICS
Alfred A. Knopf New York London Toronto

This selection by Diana Secker Tesdell first published in
Everyman's Library, 2022
Copyright © 2022 by Everyman's Library

A list of acknowledgments to copyright owners appears at
the back of this volume.

everymanslibrary.com
www.everymanslibrary.co.uk

ISBN 978-0-593-32130-0 (US)
978-1-84159-632-7 (UK)

A CIP catalogue reference for this book is available from the
British Library

Typography by Peter B. Willberg

Typeset in the UK by Input Data Services Ltd, Isle Abbotts, Somerset

Printed and bound in Germany by GGP Media GmbH, Pössneck

GARDEN STORIES

Contents

AVID GARDENERS

GARDEN PLEASURES AND SORROWS

WILD GARDENS

HUMOR IN THE GARDEN

GARDENS OF THE
IMAGINATION

AVID GARDENERS

"And some can pot begonias, and some can bud a rose,
And some are hardly fit to trust with anything that grows."

– Rudyard Kipling, "The Glory of the Garden"

JAMAICA KINCAID

THE GARDEN I HAVE IN MIND

I KNOW GARDENERS well (or at least I think I do, for I am a gardener, too, but I experience gardening as an act of utter futility). I know their fickleness, I know their weakness for wanting in their own gardens the thing they have never seen before, or never possessed before, or saw in a garden (their friends'), something which they do not have and would like to have (though what they really like and envy – and especially that, envy – is the entire garden they are seeing, but as a disguise they focus on just one thing: the Mexican poppies, the giant butter burr, the extremely plump blooms of white, purple, black, pink, green, or the hellebores emerging from the cold, damp, and brown earth).

I would not be surprised if every gardener I asked had something definite that he or she liked or envied. Gardeners always have something they like intensely and in particular, right at the moment you engage them in the reality of the borders they cultivate, the space in the garden they occupy; at any moment, they like in particular this, or they like in particular that, nothing in front of them (that is, in the borders they cultivate, the space in the garden they occupy) is repulsive and fills them with hatred, or this thing would not be in front of them. They only love, and they only love in the moment; when the moment has passed, they love the memory of the moment, they love the memory of that particular plant or that particular bloom, but the plant of the bloom itself they have moved on from, they have left it behind for something else, something new, especially something from far away, and from so far away, a place where they will never live (occupy, cultivate; the Himalayas, just for an example).

Of all the benefits that come from having endured childhood (for it is something to which we must submit, no matter how beautiful we find it, no matter how enjoyable it has been), certainly among them will be the garden and the desire to be involved with gardening. A gardener's grandmother will have grown such and such a rose, and the smell of that rose at dusk (for flowers always seem to be most fragrant at the end of the day, as if that, smelling, was the last thing to do before going to sleep), when the gardener was a child and walking in the grandmother's footsteps as she went about her business in her garden – the memory of that smell of the rose combined with the memory of that smell of the grandmother's skirt will forever inform and influence the life of the gardener, inside or outside the garden itself. And so in a conversation with such a person (a gardener), a sentence, a thought that goes something like this – "You know, when I was such and such an age, I went to the market for a reason that is no longer of any particular interest to me, but it was there I saw for the first time something that I have never and can never forget" – floats out into the clear air, and the person from whom these words or this thought emanates is standing in front of you all bare and trembly, full of feeling, full of memory. Memory is a gardener's real palette; memory as it summons up the past, memory as it shapes the present, memory as it dictates the future.

I have never been able to grow *Meconopsis betonicifolia* with success (it sits there, a green rosette of leaves looking at me, with no bloom. I look back at it myself, without a pleasing countenance), but the picture of it that I have in my mind, a picture made up of memory (I saw it some time ago), a picture made up of "to come" (the future, which is the opposite of remembering), is so intense that whatever happens between me and this plant will never satisfy the picture I have of it (the past remembered, the past to come). I first saw it (*Meconopsis betonicifolia*) in Wayne Winterrowd's garden (a garden he shares with that other garden eminence Joe Eck), and I shall never see this plant (in flower or not, in the wild or cultivated) again without thinking of him (of them, really – he and Joe Eck) and saying to myself, It shall never look quite like this (the way I saw it in their garden), for in their garden it was itself and beyond comparison (whatever that amounts to right now, whatever that might ultimately turn out to be), and I will always want it to look that way, growing comfortably in the mountains of Vermont, so far away from the place to which it is endemic, so far away from the place in which it was natural, unnoticed, and so going about its own peculiar ways of perpetuating itself (perennial, biannual, monocarpic, or not).

I first came to the garden with practicality in mind, a real beginning that would lead to a real end: where to get this, how to grow that. Where to get this was always nearby, a nursery was never too far away; how to grow that led me to acquire volume upon volume, books all with the same advice (likes shade, does not tolerate lime, needs staking), but in the end I came to know how to grow the things I like to grow through looking – at other people's gardens. I imagine they acquired knowledge of such things in much the same way – looking and looking at somebody else's garden.

But we who covet our neighbor's garden must finally return to our own, with all its ups and downs, its disappointments, its rewards. We come to it with a blindness, plus a jumble of feelings that mere language (as far as I can see) seems inadequate to express, to define an attachment that is so ordinary: a plant loved especially for something endemic to it (it cannot help its situation: it loves the wet, it loves the dry, it reminds the person seeing it of a wave or a waterfall or some event that contains so personal an experience as when my mother would not allow me to do something I particularly wanted to do and in my misery I noticed that the frangipani tree was in bloom).

I shall never have the garden I have in my mind, but that for me is the joy of it; certain things can never be realized and so all the more reason to attempt them. A garden, no matter how good it is, must never completely satisfy. The world as we know it, after all, began in a very good garden, a completely satisfying garden – Paradise – but after a while the owner and the occupants wanted more.

ELIZABETH VON ARNIM

FROM ELIZABETH
AND HER GERMAN
GARDEN

May 7th. – I LOVE MY garden. I am writing in it now in the late afternoon loveliness, much interrupted by the mosquitoes and the temptation to look at all the glories of the new green leaves washed half an hour ago in a cold shower. Two owls are perched near me, and are carrying on a long conversation that I enjoy as much as any warbling of nightingales. The gentleman owl says ♪♪♪, and she answers from her tree a little way off, ♪♪♪, beautifully assenting to and completing her lord's remark, as becomes a properly constructed German she-owl. They say the same thing over and over again so emphatically that I think it must be something nasty about me; but I shall not let myself be frightened away by the sarcasm of owls.

This is less a garden than a wilderness. No one has lived in the house, much less in the garden, for twenty-five years, and it is such a pretty old place that the people who might have lived here and did not, deliberately preferring the horrors of a flat in a town, must have belonged to that vast number of eyeless and earless persons of whom the world seems chiefly composed. Noseless too, though it does not sound pretty; but the greater part of my spring happiness is due to the scent of the wet earth and young leaves.

I am always happy (out of doors be it understood, for indoors there are servants and furniture), but in quite different ways, and my spring happiness bears no resemblance to my summer or autumn happiness, though it is not more intense, and there were days last winter when I danced for sheer joy out in my frost-bound garden in spite of my years and children. But I did it behind a bush, having a due regard for the decencies.

There are so many bird-cherries round me, great trees with branches sweeping the grass, and they are so wreathed just now with white blossoms and tenderest green that the garden looks like a wedding. I never saw such masses of them; they seem to fill the place. Even across a little stream that bounds the garden on the east, and right in the middle of the cornfield beyond, there is an immense one, a picture of grace and glory against the cold blue of the spring sky.

My garden is surrounded by cornfields and meadows, and beyond are great stretches of sandy heath and pine forests, and where the forests leave off the bare heath begins again; but the forests are beautiful in their lofty, pink-stemmed vastness, far overhead the crowns of softest grey-green, and underfoot a bright green whortleberry carpet, and every-where the breathless silence; and the bare heaths are beautiful too, for one can see across them into eternity almost, and to go out on to them with one's face towards the setting sun is like going into the very presence of God.

In the middle of this plain is the oasis of bird-cherries and greenery where I spend my happy days, and in the middle of the oasis is the grey stone house with many gables where I pass my reluctant nights. The house is very old, and has been added to at various times. It was a convent before the Thirty Years' War, and the vaulted chapel, with its brick floor worn by pious peasant knees, is now used as a hall. Gustavus Adolphus and his Swedes passed through more than once, as is duly recorded in archives still preserved, for we are on what was then the high-road between Sweden and Brandenburg the unfortunate. The Lion of the North was no doubt an estimable person and acted wholly up to his convictions, but he must have sadly upset the peaceful nuns, who were not without convictions of their own, sending them out on to the wide, empty plain to piteously seek some life to replace the life of silence here.

From nearly all the windows of the house I can look out across the plain, with no obstacle in the shape of a hill, right away to a blue line of distant forest, and on the west side uninterruptedly to the setting sun – nothing but a green, rolling plain, with a sharp edge against the sunset. I love those west windows better than any others, and have chosen my bedroom on that side of the house so that even times of hair-brushing may not be entirely lost, and the young woman who attends to such matters has been taught to fulfil her duties about a mistress recumbent in an easy-chair before an open window, and to not profane with chatter that sweet and solemn time. This girl is grieved at my habit of living almost in the garden, and all her ideas as to the sort of life a respectable German lady should lead have got into a sad muddle since she came to me. The people round about are persuaded that I am, to put it as kindly as possible, exceedingly eccentric, for the news has travelled that I spend the day out of doors with a book, and that no mortal eye has ever yet seen me sew or cook. But why cook when you can get some one to cook for you? And as for sewing, the maids will hem the sheets better and quicker than I could, and all forms of needlework of the fancy order are inventions of the evil one for keeping the foolish from applying their hearts to wisdom.

We had been married five years before it struck us that we might as well make use of this place by coming down and living in it. Those five years were spent in a flat in a town, and during their whole interminable length I was perfectly miserable and perfectly healthy, which disposes of the ugly notion that has at times disturbed me that my happiness here is less due to the garden than to a good digestion. And while we were wasting our lives there, here was this dear place with dandelions up to the very door, all the paths grass-grown and completely effaced, in winter so lonely, with nobody but the north wind taking the least notice of it, and in May – in all those five lovely Mays – no one to look at the wonderful bird-cherries and still more wonderful masses of lilacs, everything glowing and blowing, the virginia creeper madder every year until at last, in October, the very roof was wreathed with blood-red tresses, the owls and the squirrels and all the blessed little birds reigning supreme, and not a living creature ever entering the empty house except the snakes, which got into the habit during those silent years of wriggling up the south wall into the rooms on that side whenever the old housekeeper opened the windows. All that was here – peace, and happiness, and a reasonable life, and yet it never struck me to come and live in it. Looking back I am astonished, and can in no way account for the tardiness of my discovery that here, in this far-away corner, was my kingdom of heaven. Indeed, so little did it enter my head to even use the place in summer, that I submitted to weeks of seaside life with all its horrors every year; until at last, in the early spring of last year, having come down for the opening of the village school, and wandering out afterwards into the bare and desolate garden, I don't know what smell of wet earth or rotting leaves brought back my childhood with a rush and all the happy days I had spent in a garden. Shall I ever forget that day? It was the beginning of my real life, my coming of age as it were, and entering into my kingdom. Early March, gray, quiet skies, and brown, quiet earth; leaf-less and sad and lonely enough out there in the damp and silence, yet there I stood feeling the same rapture of pure delight in the first breath of spring that I used to as a child, and the five wasted years fell from me like a cloak, and the world was full of hope, and I vowed myself then and there to nature and have been happy ever since.

My other half being indulgent, and with some faint thought perhaps that it might be as well to look after the place, consented to live in it at any rate for a time; whereupon followed six specially blissful weeks from the end of April into June, during which I was here alone, supposed to be superintending the painting and papering, but as a matter of fact only going into the house when the workmen had gone out of it.

How happy I was! I don't remember any time quite so perfect since the days when I was too little to do lessons and was turned out with sugar on my eleven o'clock bread and butter on to a lawn closely strewn with dandelions and daisies. The sugar on the bread and butter has lost its charm, but I love the dandelions and daisies even more passionately now than then, and never would endure to see them all mown away if I were not certain that in a day or two they would be pushing up their little faces again as jauntily as ever. During those six weeks I lived in a world of dandelions and delights. The dandelions carpeted the three lawns – they used to be lawns, but have long since blossomed out into meadows filled with every sort of pretty weed – and under and among the groups of leafless oaks and beeches were blue hepaticas, white anemones, violets, and celandines in sheets. The celandines in particular delighted me with their clean, happy brightness, so beautifully trim and newly varnished, as though they too had had the painters at work on them. Then, when the anemones went, came a few stray periwinkles and Solomon's Seal, and all the bird-cherries blossomed in a burst. And then, before I had a little got used to the joy of their flowers against the sky, came the lilacs – masses and masses of them, in clumps on the grass, with other shrubs and trees by the side of walks, and one great continuous bank of them half a mile long right past the west front of the house, away down as far as one could see, shining glorious against a background of firs. When that time came, and when, before it was over, the acacias all blossomed too, and four great clumps of pale, silvery-pink peonies flowered under the south windows, I felt so absolutely happy, and blest, and thankful, and grateful, that I really cannot describe it. My days seemed to melt away in a dream of pink and purple peace.

There were only the old housekeeper and her handmaiden in the house, so that on the plea of not giving too much trouble I could indulge what my other half calls my *fantaisie déréglée* as regards meals – that is to say, meals so simple that they could be brought out to the lilacs on a tray; and I lived, I remember, on salad and bread and tea the whole time, sometimes a very tiny pigeon appearing at lunch to save me, as the old lady thought, from starvation. Who but a woman could have stood salad for six weeks, even salad sanctified by the presence and scent of the most gorgeous lilac masses? I did, and grew in grace every day, though I have never liked it since. How often now, oppressed by the necessity of assisting at three dining-room meals daily, two of which are conducted by the functionaries held indispensable to a proper maintenance of the family dignity, and all of which are pervaded by joints of meat, how often do I think of my salad days, forty in number, and of the blessedness of being alone as I was then alone!

And then the evenings, when the workmen had all gone and the house was left to emptiness and echoes, and the old housekeeper had gathered up her rheumatic limbs into her bed, and my little room in quite another part of the house had been set ready, how reluctantly I used to leave the friendly frogs and owls, and with my heart somewhere down in my shoes lock the door to the garden behind me, and pass through the long series of echoing south rooms full of shadows and ladders and ghostly pails of painters' mess, and humming a tune to make myself believe I liked it, go rather slowly across the brick-floored hall, up the creaking stairs, down the long whitewashed passage, and with a final rush of panic whisk into my room and double lock and bolt the door!

There were no bells in the house, and I used to take a great dinner-bell to bed with me so that at least I might be able to make a noise if frightened in the night, though what good it would have been I don't know, as there was no one to hear. The housemaid slept in another little cell opening out of mine, and we two were the only living creatures in the great empty west wing. She evidently did not believe in ghosts, for I could hear how she fell asleep immediately after getting into bed; nor do I believe in them, "*mais je les redoute*," as a French lady said, who from her books appears to have been strong-minded.

The dinner-bell was a great solace; it was never rung, but it comforted me to see it on the chair beside my bed, as my nights were anything but placid, it was all so strange, and there were such queer creakings and other noises. I used to lie awake for hours, startled out of a light sleep by the cracking of some board, and listen to the indifferent snores of the girl in the next room. In the morning, of course, I was as brave as a lion and much amused at the cold perspirations of the night before; but even the nights seem to me now to have been delightful, and myself like those historic boys who heard a voice in every wind and snatched a fearful joy.

I would gladly shiver through them all over again for the sake of the beautiful purity of the house, empty of servants and upholstery.

How pretty the bedrooms looked with nothing in them but their cheerful new papers! Sometimes I would go into those that were finished and build all sorts of castles in the air about their future and their past. Would the nuns who had lived in them know their little whitewashed cells again, all gay with delicate flower papers and clean white paint? And how astonished they would be to see cell No. 14 turned into a bathroom, with a bath big enough to ensure a cleanliness of body equal to their purity of soul! They would look upon it as a snare of the tempter; and I know that in my own case I only began to be shocked at the blackness of my nails the day that I began to lose the first whiteness of my soul by falling in love at fifteen with the parish organist, or rather with the glimpse of surplice and Roman nose and fiery moustache which was all I ever saw of him, and which I loved to distraction for at least six months; at the end of which time, going out with my governess one day, I passed him in the street, and discovered that his unofficial garb was a frock-coat combined with a turn-down collar and a "bowler" hat, and never loved him any more.

The first part of that time of blessedness was the most perfect, for I had not a thought of anything but the peace and beauty all round me. Then he appeared suddenly who has a right to appear when and how he will and rebuked me for never having written, and when I told him that I had been literally too happy to think of writing he seemed to take it as a reflection on himself that I could be happy alone. I took him round the garden along the new paths I had had made, and showed him the acacia and lilac glories, and he said that it was the purest selfishness to enjoy myself when neither he nor the offspring were with me, and that the lilacs wanted thoroughly pruning. I tried to appease him by offering him the whole of my salad and toast supper which stood ready at the foot of the little verandah steps when we came back, but nothing appeased that Man of Wrath, and he said he would go straight back to the neglected family. So he went; and the remainder of the precious time was disturbed by twinges of conscience (to which I am much subject) whenever I found myself wanting to jump for joy. I went to look at the painters every time my feet were for taking me to look at the garden; I trotted diligently up and down the passages; I criticised and suggested and commanded more in one day than I had done in all the rest of the time; I wrote regularly and sent my love; but I could not manage to fret and yearn. What are you to do if your conscience is clear and your liver in order and the sun is shining?

May 10th. – I knew nothing whatever last year about gardening and this year know very little more, but I have dawnings of what may be done, and have at least made one great stride – from ipomæa to tea-roses.

The garden was an absolute wilderness. It is all round the house, but the principal part is on the south side and has evidently always been so. The south front is one-storied, a long series of rooms opening one into the other, and the walls are covered with virginia creeper. There is a little verandah in the middle, leading by a flight of rickety wooden steps down into what seems to have been the only spot in the whole place that was cared for. This is a semicircle cut into the lawn and edged with privet, and in this semicircle are eleven beds of different sizes bordered with box and arranged round a sun-dial, and the sun-dial is very venerable and moss-grown, and greatly beloved by me. These beds were the only sign of any attempt at gardening to be seen (except a solitary crocus that came up all by itself each spring in the grass, not because it wanted to, but because it could not help it), and these I had sown with ipomæa, the whole eleven, having found a German gardening book, according to which ipomæa in vast quantities was the one thing needful to turn the most hideous desert into a paradise. Nothing else in that book was recommended with anything like the same warmth, and being entirely ignorant of the quantity of seed necessary, I bought ten pounds of it and had it sown not only in the eleven beds but round nearly every tree, and then waited in great agitation for the promised paradise to appear. It did not, and I learned my first lesson.

Luckily I had sown two great patches of sweet-peas which made me very happy all the summer, and then there were some sunflowers and a few hollyhocks under the south windows, with Madonna lilies in between. But the lilies, after being transplanted, disappeared to my great dismay, for how was I to know it was the way of lilies? And the hollyhocks turned out to be rather ugly colours, so that my first summer was decorated and beautified solely by sweet-peas.

At present we are only just beginning to breathe after the bustle of getting new beds and borders and paths made in time for this summer. The eleven beds round the sun-dial are filled with roses, but I see already that I have made mistakes with some. As I have not a living soul with whom to hold communion on this or indeed on any matter, my only way of learning is by making mistakes. All eleven were to have been carpeted with purple pansies, but finding that I had not enough and that nobody had any to sell me, only six have got their pansies, the others being sown with dwarf mignonette. Two of the eleven are filled with Marie van Houtte roses, two with Viscountess Folkestone, two with Laurette Messimy, one with Souvenir de la Malmaison, one with Adam and Devoniensis, two with Persian Yellow and Bicolour, and one big bed behind the sun-dial with three sorts of red roses (seventy-two in all), Duke of Teck, Cheshunt Scarlet, and Prefet de Limburg. This bed is, I am sure, a mistake, and several of the others are, I think, but of course I must wait and see, being such an ignorant person. Then I have had two long beds made in the grass on either side of the semicircle, each sown with mignonette, and one filled with Marie van Houtte, and the other with Jules Finger and the Bride; and in a warm corner under the drawing-room windows is a bed of Madame Lambard, Madame de Watteville, and Comtesse Riza du Parc; while farther down the garden, sheltered on the north and west by a group of beeches and lilacs, is another large bed, containing Rubens, Madame Joseph Schwartz, and the Hon. Edith Gifford. All these roses are dwarf; I have only two standards in the whole garden, two Madame George Bruants, and they look like broomsticks. How I long for the day when the teas open their buds! Never did I look forward so intensely to anything; and every day I go the rounds, admiring what the dear little things have achieved in the twenty-four hours in the way of new leaf or increase of lovely red shoot.

The hollyhocks and lilies (now flourishing) are still under the south windows in a narrow border on the top of a grass slope, at the foot of which I have sown two long borders of sweet-peas facing the rose beds, so that my roses may have something almost as sweet as themselves to look at until the autumn, when everything is to make place for more tea-roses. The path leading away from this semicircle down the garden is bordered with China roses, white and pink, with here and there a Persian Yellow. I wish now I had put teas there, and I have misgivings as to the effect of the Persian

Yellows among the Chinas, for the Chinas are such wee little baby things, and the Persian Yellows look as though they intended to be big bushes.

There is not a creature in all this part of the world who could in the least understand with what heart-beatings I am looking forward to the flowering of these roses, and not a German gardening book that does not relegate all teas to hot-houses, imprisoning them for life, and depriving them for ever of the breath of God. It was no doubt because I was so ignorant that I rushed in where Teutonic angels fear to tread and made my teas face a northern winter; but they did face it under fir branches and leaves, and not one has suffered, and they are looking to-day as happy and as determined to enjoy themselves as any roses, I am sure, in Europe.

May 14th. – To-day I am writing on the verandah with the three babies, more persistent than mosquitoes, raging round me, and already several of the thirty fingers have been in the ink-pot and the owners consoled when duty pointed to rebukes. But who can rebuke such penitent and drooping sunbonnets? I can see nothing but sunbonnets and pinafores and nimble black legs.

These three, their patient nurse, myself, the gardener, and the gardener's assistant, are the only people who ever go into my garden, but then neither are we ever out of it. The gardener has been here a year and has given me notice regularly on the first of every month, but up to now has been induced to stay on. On the first of this month he came as usual, and with determination written on every feature told me he intended to go in June, and that nothing should alter his decision. I don't think he knows much about gardening, but he can at least dig and water, and some of the things he sows come up, and some of the plants he plants grow, besides

32

which he is the most unflaggingly industrious person I ever saw, and has the great merit of never appearing to take the faintest interest in what we do in the garden. So I have tried to keep him on, not knowing what the next one may be like, and when I asked him what he had to complain of and he replied "Nothing," I could only conclude that he has a personal objection to me because of my eccentric preference for plants in groups rather than plants in lines. Perhaps, too, he does not like the extracts from gardening books I read to him sometimes when he is planting or sowing something new. Being so helpless myself I thought it simpler, instead of explaining, to take the book itself out to him and let him have wisdom at its very source, administering it in doses while he worked. I quite recognise that this must be annoying, and only my anxiety not to lose a whole year through some stupid mistake has given me the courage to do it. I laugh sometimes behind the book at his disgusted face, and wish we could be photographed, so that I may be reminded in twenty years' time, when the garden is a bower of loveliness and I learned in all its ways, of my first happy struggles and failures.

All through April he was putting the perennials we had sown in the autumn into their permanent places, and all through April he went about with a long piece of string making parallel lines down the borders of beautiful exactitude and arranging the poor plants like soldiers at a review. Two long borders were done during my absence one day, and when I explained that I should like the third to have plants in groups and not in lines, and that what I wanted was a natural effect with no bare spaces of earth to be seen, he looked even more gloomily hopeless than usual; and on my going out later on to see the result, I found he had planted two long borders down the sides of a straight walk with little lines of five plants in a row – first five pinks, and next to them five rockets, and behind the rockets five pinks, and behind the pinks five rockets, and so on with different plants of every sort and size down to the end. When I protested, he said he had only carried out my orders and had known it would not look well; so I gave in, and the remaining borders were done after the pattern of the first two, and I will have patience and see how they look this summer, before digging them up again; for it becomes beginners to be humble.

If I could only dig and plant myself! How much easier, besides being so fascinating, to make your own holes exactly where you want them and put in your plants exactly as you choose instead of giving orders that can only be half understood from the moment you depart from the lines laid down by that long piece of string! In the first ecstasy of having a garden all my own, and in my burning impatience to make the waste places blossom like a rose, I did one warm Sunday in last year's April during the servants' dinner hour, doubly secure from the gardener by the day and the dinner, slink out with a spade and a rake and feverishly dig a little piece of ground and break it up and sow surreptitious ipomæa and run back very hot and guilty into the house and get into a chair and behind a book and look languid just in time to save my reputation. And why not? It is not graceful, and it makes one hot; but it is a blessed sort of work, and if Eve had had a spade in Paradise and known what to do with it, we should not have had all that sad business of the apple.

What a happy woman I am living in a garden, with books, babies, birds, and flowers, and plenty of leisure to enjoy them! Yet my town acquaintances look upon it as imprisonment, and burying, and I don't know what besides, and would rend the air with their shrieks if condemned to such a life. Sometimes I feel as if I were blest above all my

34

fellows in being able to find my happiness so easily. I believe I should always be good if the sun always shone, and could enjoy myself very well in Siberia on a fine day. And what can life in town offer in the way of pleasure to equal the delight of any one of the calm evenings I have had this month sitting alone at the foot of the verandah steps, with the perfume of young larches all about, and the May moon hanging low over the beeches, and the beautiful silence made only more profound in its peace by the croaking of distant frogs and the hooting of owls?

DORIS LESSING

FLAVOURS OF EXILE

AT THE FOOT of the hill, near the well, was the vegetable garden, an acre fenced off from the Big Field where the earth was so rich that mealies grew there, year after year, ten feet tall. Nursed from that fabulous soil, carrots, lettuces, beets, tasting as I have never found vegetables taste since, loaded our table and the tables of our neighbours. Sometimes, if the garden boy was late with the supply for lunch, I would run down the steep pebbly path through the trees at the back of the hill and along the red dust of the waggon road until I could see the windlass under its shed of thatch. There I stopped. The smell of manure, of sun on foliage, of evaporating water, rose to my head; two steps farther, and I could look down into the vegetable garden enclosed within its tall pale of reeds – rich chocolate earth studded emerald green, frothed with the white of cauliflowers, jewelled with the purple globes of eggplant and the scarlet wealth of tomatoes. Around the fence grew lemons, pawpaws, bananas – shapes of gold and yellow in their patterns of green.

In another five minutes I would be dragging from the earth carrots ten inches long, so succulent they snapped between two fingers. I ate my allowance of these before the cook could boil them and drown them in the white flour sauce without which – and unless they were served in the large china vegetable dishes brought from that old house in London – they were not carrots to my mother.

For her, that garden represented a defeat.

When the family first came to the farm, she built vegetable beds on the *kopje* near the house. She had in her mind, perhaps, a vision of the farmhouse surrounded by outbuildings and gardens like a hen sheltering its chicks.

The *kopje* was all stone. As soon as the grass was cleared off its crown where the house stood, the fierce rains beat the soil away. Those first vegetable beds were thin sifted earth walled by pebbles. The water was brought up from the well in the water-cart.

"Water is gold," grumbled my father, eating peas which, he reckoned, must cost a shilling a mouthful. "Water is gold!" he came to shout at last, as my mother toiled and bent over those reluctant beds. But she got more pleasure from them than she ever did from the exhaustless plenty of the garden under the hill.

At last, the spaces in the bush where the old beds had been were seeded by wild or vagrant plants, and we children played there. Someone must have thrown away gooseberries, for soon the low spreading bushes covered the earth. We used to creep under them, William MacGregor and I, lie flat on our backs, and look through the leaves at the brilliant sky, reaching around us for the tiny sharp sweet yellow fruits in their jackets of papery white. The smell of the leaves was spicy. It intoxicated us. We would laugh and shout, then quarrel; and William, to make up, shelled a double-handful of the fruit and poured it into my skirt, and we ate together, pressing the biggest berries on each other. When we could eat no more, we filled baskets and took them to the kitchen to be made into that rich jam, which, if allowed to burn just the right amount on the pan, is the best jam in the world – clear sweet amber, with lumps of sticky sharpness in it, as if the stings of bees were preserved in honey.

But my mother did not like it. "Cape gooseberries!" she

said bitterly. "They aren't gooseberries at all. Oh, if I could let you taste a pie made of real English gooseberries."

In due course, the marvels of civilisation made this possible; she found a tin of gooseberries in the Greek store at the station and made us a pie.

My parents and William's ate the pie with a truly religious emotion.

It was this experience with the gooseberries that made me cautious when it came to Brussels sprouts. Year after year my mother yearned for Brussels sprouts, whose name came to represent to me something exotic and forever unattainable. When at last she managed to grow half a dozen spikes of this plant in one cold winter that offered us sufficient frost, she of course sent a note to the MacGregors, so that they might share the treat. They came from Glasgow, they came from Rome, and they could share the language of nostalgia. At the table the four grownups ate the bitter little cabbages and agreed that the soil of Africa was unable to grow food that had any taste at all. I said scornfully that I couldn't see what all the fuss was about. But William, three years older than myself, passed the plate up and said he found them delicious. It was like a betrayal; and afterwards I demanded how he could like such flavourless stuff. He smiled at me and said it cost us nothing to pretend, did it?

That smile, so gentle, a little whimsical, was a lesson to me; and I remembered it when it came to the affair of the cherries. She found a tin of cherries at the store, we ate them with cream; and while she sighed over memories of barrows loaded with cherries in the streets of London, I sighed with her, ate fervently, and was careful not to meet her eyes.

And when she said: "The pomegranates will be fruiting soon," I offered to run down and see how they progressed.

41

I returned from the examination saying: "It won't be long now, really it won't – perhaps next year."

The truth was, my emotion over the pomegranates was not entirely due to the beautiful lesson in courtesy given me by William. Brussels sprouts, cherries, English goose-berries – they were my mother's; they recurred in her talk as often as "a real London pea-souper," or "chestnuts by the fire," or "cherry blossom at Kew." I no longer grudged these to her; I listened and was careful not to show that my thoughts were on my own inheritance of veld and sun. But pomegranates were an exotic for my mother; and therefore more easily shared with her. She had been in Persia, where, one understood, pomegranate juice ran in rivers. The wife of a minor official, she had lived in a vast stone house cooled by water trickling down a thousand stone channels from the mountains; she had lived among roses and jasmine, walnut trees and pomegranates. But, unfortunately, for too short a time.

Why not pomegranates here, in Africa? Why not?

The four trees had been planted at the same time as the first vegetable beds; and almost at once two of them died. A third lingered on for a couple of seasons and then succumbed to the white ants. The fourth stood lonely among the Cape gooseberry bushes, bore no fruit, and at last was forgotten.

Then one day my mother was showing Mrs. MacGregor her chickens; and as they returned through tangles of grass and weed, their skirts lifted high in both hands, my mother exclaimed: "Why, I do believe the pomegranate is fruiting at last. Look, look, it is!" She called to us, the children, and we went running, and stood around a small thorny tree, and looked at a rusty-red fruit the size of a child's fist. "It's ripe," said my mother, and pulled it off.

Inside the house we were each given a dozen small seeds

42

on saucers. They were bitter, but we did not like to ask for sugar. Mrs. MacGregor said gently: "It's wonderful. How you must miss all that!"

"The roses!" said my mother. "And sacks of walnuts . . . and we used to drink pomegranate juice with the melted snow water . . . nothing here tastes like that. The soil is no good."

I looked at William, sitting opposite to me. He turned his head and smiled. I fell in love.

He was then fifteen, home for the holidays. He was a silent boy, thoughtful; and the quietness in his deep grey eyes seemed to me like a promise of warmth and understanding I had never known. There was a tightness in my chest, because it hurt to be shut out from the world of simple kindness he lived in. I sat there, opposite to him, and said to myself that I had known him all my life and yet until this moment had never understood what he was. I looked at those extraordinarily clear eyes, that were like water over grey pebbles; I gazed and gazed, until he gave me a slow, direct look that showed he knew I had been staring. It was like a warning, as if a door had been shut.

After the MacGregors had gone, I went through the bushes to the pomegranate tree. It was about my height, a tough, obstinate-looking thing; and there was a round yellow ball the size of a walnut hanging from a twig.

I looked at the ugly little tree and thought, Pomegranates! Breasts like pomegranates and a belly like a heap of wheat! The golden pomegranates of the sun, I thought . . . pomegranates like the red of blood.

I was in a fever, more than a little mad. The space of thick grass and gooseberry bushes between the trees was haunted by William, and his deep, calm, grey eyes looked at me across the pomegranate tree.

Next day I sat under the tree. It gave no shade, but the acrid sunlight was barred and splotched under it. There was hard, cracked, red earth beneath a covering of silvery dead grass. Under the grass I saw grains of red and half a hard brown shell. It seemed that a fruit had ripened and burst without our knowing it – yes, everywhere in the soft old grass lay the tiny crimson seeds. I tasted one; warm sweet juice flooded my tongue. I gathered them up and ate them until my mouth was full of dry seeds. I spat them out and thought that a score of pomegranate trees would grow from that mouthful.

As I watched, tiny black ants came scurrying along the roots of the grass, scrambling over the fissures in the earth, to snatch away the seeds. I lay on my elbow and watched. A dozen of them were levering at a still unbroken seed. Suddenly the frail tissue split as they bumped it over a splinter, and they were caught in a sticky red ooze.

The ants would carry these seeds for hundreds of yards; there would be an orchard of pomegranates. William MacGregor would come visiting with his parents and find me among the pomegranate trees; I could hear the sound of his grave voice mingled with the tinkle of camel bells and the splashing of falling water.

I went to the tree every day and lay under it, watching the single yellow fruit ripening on its twig. There would come a moment when it must burst and scatter crimson seeds; I must be there when it did; it seemed as if my whole life was concentrated and ripening with that single fruit.

It was very hot under the tree. My head ached. My flesh was painful with the sun. Yet there I sat all day, watching the tiny ants at their work, letting them run over my legs, waiting for the pomegranate fruit to ripen. It swelled slowly; it seemed set on reaching perfection, for when it was the size that the other had been picked, it was still a bronzing yellow, and the rind was soft. It was going to be a big fruit, the size of both my fists.

Then something terrifying happened. One day I saw that the twig it hung from was splitting off the branch. The wizened, dry little tree could not sustain the weight of the fruit it had produced. I went to the house, brought down bandages from the medicine chest, and strapped the twig firm and tight to the branch, in such a way that the weight was supported. Then I wet the bandage, tenderly, and thought of William, William, William. I wet the bandage daily, and thought of him.

What I thought of William had become a world, stronger than anything around me. Yet, since I was mad, so weak, it vanished at a touch. Once, for instance, I saw him, driving with his father on the waggon along the road to the station. I remember I was ashamed that that marvellous feverish world should depend on a half-grown boy in dusty khaki, gripping a piece of grass between his teeth as he stared ahead of him. It came to this – that in order to preserve the dream, I must not see William. And it seemed he felt something of the sort himself, for in all those weeks he never came near me, whereas once he used to come every day. And yet I was convinced it must happen that William and the moment when the pomegranate split open would coincide.

I imagined it in a thousand ways, as the fruit continued to grow. Now, it was a clear bronze yellow with faint rust-coloured streaks. The rind was thin, so soft that the swelling seeds within were shaping it. The fruit looked lumpy and veined, like a nursing breast. The small crown where the stem fastened on it, which had been the sheath of the flower, was still green. It began to harden and turn back into iron-grey thorns.

Soon, soon, it would be ripe. Very swiftly, the skin lost its smooth thinness. It took on a tough, pored look, like the skin of an old weather-beaten countryman. It was a ruddy scarlet now, and hot to the touch. A small crack appeared, which in a day had widened so that the packed red seeds within were visible, almost bursting out. I did not dare leave the tree. I was there from six in the morning until the sun went down. I even crept down with the candle at night, although I argued it could not burst at night, not in the cool of the night; it must be the final unbearable thrust of the hot sun that would break it.

For three days nothing happened. The crack remained the same. Ants swarmed up the trunk, along the branches, and into the fruit. The scar oozed red juice in which black ants swarmed and struggled. At any moment it might happen. And William did not come. I was sure he would; I watched the empty road helplessly, waiting for him to come striding along, a piece of grass between his teeth, to me and the pomegranate tree. Yet he did not. In one night, the crack split another half-inch. I saw a red seed push itself out of the crack and fall. Instantly it was borne off by the ants into the grass.

I went up to the house and asked my mother when the MacGregors were coming to tea.

"I don't know, dear. Why?"

"Because. I just thought. . . ."

She looked at me. Her eyes were critical. In one moment, she would say the name "William." I struck first. To have William and the moment together, I must pay fee to the family gods. "There's a pomegranate nearly ripe, and you know how interested Mrs. MacGregor is. . . ."

She looked sharply at me. "Pick it, and we'll make a drink of it."

"Oh, no, it's not quite ready. Not altogether. . . ."

"Silly child," she said at last. She went to the telephone and said: "Mrs. MacGregor, this daughter of mine, she's got it into her head – you know how children are."

I did not care. At four that afternoon I was waiting by the pomegranate tree. Their car came thrusting up the steep road to the crown of the hill. There was Mr. MacGregor in his khaki, Mrs. MacGregor in her best afternoon dress – and William. The adults shook hands, kissed. William did not turn round and look at me. It was not possible, it was monstrous, that the force of my dream should not have had the power to touch him at all, that he knew nothing of what he must do.

Then he slowly turned his head and looked down the slope to where I stood. He did not smile. It seemed he had not seen me, for his eyes travelled past me, and back to the grownups. He stood to one side while they exchanged their news and greetings; and then all four laughed, and turned to look at me and my tree. It seemed for a moment they were all coming. At once, however, they went into the house, William trailing after them, frowning.

In a moment he would have gone in; the space in front of the old house would be empty. I called "William!" I had not known I would call. My voice sounded small in the wide afternoon sunlight.

He went on as if he had not heard. Then he stopped, seemed to think, and came down the hill towards me while I anxiously examined his face. The low tangle of the goose-berry bushes was around his legs, and he swore sharply.

"Look at the pomegranate," I said. He came to a halt beside the tree, and looked. I was searching those clear grey eyes now for a trace of that indulgence they had shown my mother over the Brussels sprouts, over that first unripe

47

pomegranate. Now all I wanted was indulgence; I abandoned everything else.

"It's full of ants," he said at last.

"Only a little, only where it's cracked."

He stood, frowning, chewing at his piece of grass. His lips were full and thin-skinned; and I could see the blood, dull and dark around the pale groove where the grass stem pressed.

The pomegranate hung there, swarming with ants.

"Now," I thought wildly, "now – crack now."

There was not a sound. The sun came pouring down, hot and yellow, drawing up the smell of the grasses. There was, too, a faint sour smell from the fermenting juice of the pomegranate.

"It's bad," said William, in that uncomfortable, angry voice. "And what's that bit of dirty rag for?"

"It was breaking, the twig was breaking off – I tied it up."

"Mad," he remarked, aside, to the afternoon. "Quite mad." He was looking about him in the grass. He reached down and picked up a stick.

"No," I cried out, as he hit at the tree. The pomegranate flew into the air and exploded in a scatter of crimson seeds, fermenting juice, and black ants.

The cracked empty skin, with its white, clean-looking inner skin faintly stained with juice, lay in two fragments at my feet.

He was poking sulkily with the stick at the little scarlet seeds that lay everywhere on the earth.

Then he did look at me. Those clear eyes were grave again, thoughtful, and judging. They held that warning I had seen in them before.

"That's your pomegranate," he said at last.

"Yes," I said.

48

He smiled, "We'd better go up, if we want any tea."

We went together up the hill to the house, and as we entered the room where the grownups sat over the teacups, I spoke quickly, before he could. In a bright, careless voice I said: "It was bad, after all; the ants had got at it. It should have been picked before."

HENRY DAVID THOREAU

FROM WALDEN

MEANWHILE MY BEANS, the length of whose rows, added together, was seven miles already planted, were impatient to be hoed, for the earliest had grown considerably before the latest were in the ground; indeed, they were not easily to be put off. What was the meaning of this so steady and self-respecting, this small Herculean labour, I knew not. I came to love my rows, my beans, though so many more than I wanted. They attached me to the earth, and so I got strength like Antæus. But why should I raise them? Only Heaven knows. This was my curious labour all summer, – to make this portion of the earth's surface, which had yielded only cinquefoil, blackberries, johnswort, and the like, before, sweet wild fruits and pleasant flowers, produce instead this pulse. What shall I learn of beans or beans of me? I cherish them, I hoe them, early and late I have an eye to them; and this is my day's work. It is a fine broad leaf to look on. My auxiliaries are the dews and rains which water this dry soil, and what fertility is in the soil itself, which for the most part is lean and effete. My enemies are worms, cool days, and most of all woodchucks. The last have nibbled for me a quarter of an acre clean. But what right had I to oust johnswort and the rest, and break up their ancient herb garden? Soon, however, the remaining beans will be too tough for them, and go forward to meet new foes.

When I was four years old, as I well remember, I was brought from Boston to this my native town, through these very woods and this field, to the pond. It is one of the oldest scenes stamped on my memory. And now to-night my flute has waked the echoes over that very water. The pines still stand here, older than I; or, if some have fallen, I have cooked my supper with their stumps, and a new growth is rising all around, preparing another aspect for a new infant eyes. Almost the same johnswort springs from the same perennial root in this pasture, and even I have at length helped to clothe that fabulous landscape of my infant dreams, and one of the results of my presence and influence is seen in these bean leaves, corn blades, and potato vines.

I planted about two acres and a-half of upland; and as it was only about fifteen years since the land was cleared, and I myself had got out two or three cords of stumps, I did not give it any manure; but in the course of the summer it appeared by the arrow-heads which I turned up in hoeing, that an extinct nation had anciently dwelt here and planted corn and beans ere white men came to clear the land, and so, to some extent, had exhausted the soil for this very crop.

Before yet any woodchuck or squirrel had run across the road, or the sun had got above the shrub oaks, while all the dew was on, though the farmers warned me against it, – I would advise you to do all your work if possible while the dew is on, – I began to level the ranks of haughty weeds in my bean-field and throw dust upon their heads. Early in the morning I worked barefooted, dabbling like a plastic artist in the dewy and crumbling sand, but later in the day the sun blistered my feet. There the sun lighted me to hoe beans, pacing slowly backward and forward over that yellow gravelly upland, between the long green rows, fifteen rods, the one end terminating in a shrub oak copse where I could rest in the shade, the other in a blackberry field where the green berries deepened their tints by the time I had made another bout. Removing the weeds, putting fresh soil about the bean stems, and encouraging this weed which I had sown, making the yellow soil express its summer thought in bean leaves and blossoms rather than in wormwood and piper and millet grass, making the earth say beans instead of grass, – this was my daily work. As I had little aid from horses or cattle, or hired men or boys, or improved implements of husbandry, I was much slower, and became much more intimate with my beans than usual. But labour of the hands, even when pursued to the verge of drudgery, is perhaps never the worst form of idleness. It has a constant and imperishable moral, and to the scholar it yields a classic result. A very *agricola laboriosus* was I to travellers bound westward through Lincoln and Wayland to nobody knows where; they sitting at their ease in gigs, with elbows on knees, and reins loosely hanging in festoons; I the home-staying, laborious native of the soil. But soon my homestead was out of their sight and thought. It was the only open and cultivated field for a great distance on either side of the road, so they made the most of it; and sometimes the man in the field heard more of travellers' gossip and comment than was meant for his ear: "Beans so late! peas so late!" – for I continued to plant when others had began to hoe, – the ministerial husbandman had not suspected it. "Corn, my boy, for fodder; corn for fodder." "Does he *live* there?" asks the black bonnet of the grey coat; and the hard-featured farmer reins up his grateful dobbin to inquire what you are doing when he sees no manure in the furrow, and recommends a little chip dirt, or any little waste stuff, or it may be ashes or plaster. But here were two acres and a-half of furrows, and only a hoe for cart and two hands to draw it, – there being an aversion to other carts and horses, – and chip dirt far away. Fellow-travellers as they rattled by compared it aloud with the fields which they had passed, so that I came to know how I stood in the agricultural world. This was one field not in Mr. Coleman's report. And, by the way, who estimates the value of the crop which Nature yields in the still wilder fields unimproved by man? The crop of *English* hay is carefully weighed, the moisture calculated, the silicates and the potash; but in all dells and pond holes in the woods and pastures and swamps grows a rich and various crop only unreaped by man. Mine was, as it were, the connecting link between wild and cultivated fields; as some states are civilised, and others half-civilised, and others savage or barbarous, so my field was, though not in a bad sense, a half-cultivated field. They were beans cheerfully returning to their wild and primitive state that I cultivated, and my hoe played the *Rans des Vaches* for them.

Near at hand, upon the topmost spray of a birch, sings the brown-thrasher – or red mavis, as some love to call him – all the morning, glad of your society, that would find out another farmer's field if yours were not here. While you are planting the seed, he cries, – "Drop it, drop it, – cover it up, cover it up, – pull it up, pull it up, pull it up." But this was not corn, and so it was safe from such enemies as he. You may wonder what his rigmarole, his amateur Paganini performances on one string or on twenty, have to do with your planting, and yet prefer it to leached ashes or plaster. It was a cheap sort of top-dressing in which I had entire faith.

As I drew a still fresher soil about the rows with my hoe, I disturbed the ashes of unchronicled nations who in primeval years lived under these heavens, and their small implements of war and hunting were brought to the light of this modern day. They lay mingled with other natural stones, some of which bore the marks of having been burned by Indian fires, and some by the sun, and also bits of pottery and glass brought hither by the recent cultivators of the soil. When my hoe tinkled against the stones, that music echoed to the woods and the sky, and was an accompaniment to my labour which yielded an instant and immeasurable crop. It was no longer beans that I hoed nor I that hoed beans; and I remembered with as much pity as pride, if I remembered at all, my acquaintances who had gone to the city to attend the oratorios. The night-hawk circled overhead in the sunny afternoons – for I sometimes made a day of it – like a mote in the eye, or in heaven's eye, falling from time to time with a swoop and a sound as if the heavens were rent, torn at last to very rags and tatters, and yet a seamless cope remained; small imps that fill the air and lay their eggs on the ground on bare sand or rocks on the tops of hills, where few have found them; graceful and slender like ripples caught up from the pond, as leaves are raised by the wind to float in the heavens; such kindredship is in Nature. The hawk is aerial brother of the wave which he sails over and surveys, those his perfect air-inflated wings answering to the elemental unfledged pinions of the sea. Or sometimes I watched a pair of hen-hawks circling high in the sky, alternately soaring and descending, approaching and leaving one another, as if they were the embodiment of my own thoughts. Or I was attracted by the passage of wild pigeons from this wood to that, with a slight quivering winnowing sound and carrier haste; or from under a rotten stump my hoe turned up a sluggish, portentous, and outlandish salamander, a trace of Egypt and the Nile, yet our contemporary. When I paused to lean on my hoe, these sounds and sights I heard and saw anywhere in the row, a part of the inexhaustible entertainment which the country offers. . . .

It was a singular experience that long acquaintance which I cultivated with beans, what with planting and hoeing, and harvesting, and threshing, and picking over, and selling them, – the last was the hardest of all, – I might add eating, for I did taste. I was determined to know beans. When they were growing, I used to hoe from five o'clock in the morning till noon, and commonly spent the rest of the day about other affairs. Consider the intimate and curious acquaintance one makes with various kinds of weeds, – it will bear some iteration in the account, for there is no little iteration in the labour, – disturbing their delicate organisations so ruthlessly, and making such invidious distinctions with his hoe, levelling whole ranks of one species, and sedulously cultivating another. That's Roman wormwood, – that's pigweed, – that's sorrel, – that's piper-grass, – have at him, chop him up, turn his roots upward to the sun, don't let him have a fibre in the shade; if you do, he'll turn himself t'other side up and be as green as a leek in two days. A long war, not with cranes, but with weeds, those Trojans who had sun, and rain, and dews on their side. Daily the beans saw me come to their rescue armed with a hoe, and thin the ranks of their enemies, filling up the trenches with weedy dead. Many a lusty crest-waving Hector, that towered a whole foot above his crowding comrades, fell before my weapon.

Those summer days which some of my contemporaries devoted to the fine arts in Boston or Rome, and others to contemplation in India, and others to trade in London or New York, I thus, with the other farmers of New England, devoted to husbandry. Not that I wanted beans to eat, for I am by nature a Pythagorean, so far as beans are concerned, whether they mean porridge or voting, and exchanged them for rice; but, perchance, as some must work in fields if only for the sake of tropes and expression, to serve a parable-maker one day. It was on the whole a rare amusement, which, continued too long, might have become a dissipation. Though

I gave them no manure, and did not hoe them all once, I hoed them unusually well as far as I went, and was paid for it in the end, "there being in truth," as Evelyn says, "no compost or lætation whatsoever comparable to this continual motion, repastination, and turning of the mould with the spade." "The earth," he adds elsewhere, "especially if fresh, has a certain magnetism in it, by which it attracts the salt, power, or virtue (call it either) which gives it life, and is the logic of all the labour and stir we keep about it, to sustain us; all dungings and other sordid temperings being but the vicars succedaneous to this improvement." Moreover, this being one of those "worn-out and exhausted lay fields which enjoy their Sabbath," had perchance, as Sir Kenelm Digby thinks likely, attracted "vital spirits" from the air. I harvested twelve bushels of beans.

L. P. HARTLEY

UP THE GARDEN PATH

I WAS SURPRISED to get a letter from Christopher Fenton with a Rome postmark, for I did not know that he had gone abroad. I was surprised to get a letter from him at all, for we had not been on letter-writing terms for some time.

"My dear Ernest," he began, and the opening, conventional as it was, gave me a slight twinge; "How are you getting on? I've never had to ask you this before – I've always known! But it's my fault, I've let myself drop out of things, and it's a good deal thanks to all this gardening. Gardening was to have been the solace of my middle age, but it's become a tyrant, and holds me in a kind of spell while you have been forging ahead. Well, now I am punished because I've had to go abroad just as the rhododendrons and azaleas were coming out. They should have been nearly over, if they had obeyed the calendar, and I timed my departure accordingly, but, as you may have noticed, spring this year is three weeks late, and they have let me down. I promised R. M. I would pay him this visit and I can't possibly get out of it. All unwillingly I have made myself 'the angel with the flaming sword'.

"In a world bursting with sin and sorrow I oughtn't to make a grievance of such a small matter, but I can't bear to think of all my flowers (very good ones some of them) blooming without me. And this is where you come in, or where I hope you will. I know you're not much interested in gardens, you have more important fish to fry, but you used to quite enjoy them in the old days, so perhaps you would do me a kindness now. Will you spend a week-end – the week-end after next would be the best from the flowers' point of view – at Crossways? My couple are in charge. You were always one of their favourite visitors and I know they will do their best to make you comfortable. Please get what you like out of the cellar, I still have left a few bottles of the Mouton Rothschild 1929 that you used to like. Make yourself thoroughly at home – but I know you will. I always think that a host's first duty is to absent himself as much as possible; I shall be with you in spirit, though not in the flesh. There's just one thing – I won't call it a condition or a stipulation, because in these days the burden of hospitality (if one can call it that) falls more heavily on the guest than on the host – what with tips, train-fares, the discomforts of travelling, etc., and, in your case, loss of valuable time. It is really for the host to write a Collins. So I will only say that if you consent to do this it will increase my sense of obligation. I know how tiresome other people's hobbies can be – lucky you, you never needed any, your career has always been your hobby. I don't suppose you will really want to look at the flowers very much – they toil not neither do they spin! – and a glance from the dining-room window may be all you will want to give my Eden. But all the same, I *do* want the flowers to be seen, even more urgently, perhaps, than I want *you* to see them. Somehow I feel that if no one sees them except the gardeners (who don't care much for flowers anyhow and just take them for granted) they might as well not exist. Perhaps, if Ronald Knox's limerick is true, they *don't* exist! All that glorious colour lost, as if it had never been, and the scent of the azaleas just fading into the sky! It is the only beauty I have ever created and I should like to think it was preserved in someone's mind. I really ought to have had the garden 'thrown open' (ridiculous expression) to the public, but it needed more arranging than I now feel equal to. So would you, my dear Ernest, at four o'clock on the Sunday afternoon, stroll down what I magniloquently call the Long Walk, from the fountain at one end to what you once called the *temple d'amour* at the other? (The fountain is new, you haven't seen it.) And as you go, give the flowers a good look and don't hesitate to tread on the beds to read the names of anything that specially takes your fancy (but I don't suppose anything will). And try to keep me in mind at the time, as though you were looking through my eyes as well as yours.

"Will you do this for the sake of our old friendship? Will you even promise to do it?

"I know how busy you are, but perhaps you would send me a line to say yes or no.

"Yours ever, Christopher."

Christopher was right. I was busy and though I didn't happen to have any engagement for the week-end he suggested, I didn't want to travel all the way down to the New Forest to spend a lonely Sunday. And I didn't want to get drawn again into what I felt to be the unreality of Christopher's life, of which this proposal was such an excellent example. He had never outgrown his adolescence or improved his adolescent gift for painting. He had allowed himself to become a back number. A private income had enabled him to indulge a certain contempt for the world where men strove, but he was jealous of it really; hence the digs and scratches in his letter. I had got on at the Bar, whereas he had not been even a successful dilettante. I imagine that he did not know the way that people talked about him, but perhaps he guessed. At Oxford he had been a leading figure in a group of which I was an inconspicuous member; we looked up to him then, and foretold a future for him, but I doubt if he would have achieved it, even without the handicap of his silver spoon. Except in what pertained to hospitality he was out of touch, *à côté de la vie*. He was good at pouring out drinks, and his friends, myself among them, appreciated this talent long after it was clear to most of us that his other talents would come to nothing. And though a drink is a drink, the satisfaction it gives one varies with whom one takes it with. At one time Christopher could afford drinks when we couldn't. Later, we would buy our own drinks and consume them in circumstances and in company which he couldn't attain to. There is a freemasonry of the successful which we shared and he did not. This he must have realized, for mine was not the only defection from his circle. I didn't dislike him – one couldn't dislike him – but equally one couldn't take him quite seriously as a human being.

So my first impulse was to say no, for I hate prolonging any relationship that the meaning has gone out of. But then I remembered Constantia and I thought again. I hadn't forgotten her but I had pushed her out of my mind while reading Christopher's letter.

Christopher hadn't mentioned Constantia in his letter but she was there all the same, in the wistful tone of it and the scarcely concealed bitterness. Yet he had no right to feel bitter; she told me that at one time she would have married him gladly if he had asked her. She was thirty-two and wanted to get married. But he didn't ask her. She hadn't told me, but I am sure that their relationship was never more than an *amitié amoureuse*. It was a sentimental attachment with the same unreality about it that there was in everything he did, and I felt no qualms about taking her from him. It is true that I met her through him – at Crossways, as a matter of fact, at a week-end party – and to that extent I owed her to him. But that is an unreal way of looking at things, and I did not think I was betraying his hospitality or anything of that sort, when I persuaded her that I could give her more than he could. He had no right to keep her indefinitely paddling in the shallows in which his own life was passing. But though we were lovers she hadn't said that she would marry me and I guessed it was some scruple about Christopher that stopped her.

I suppose some of her tenderness for him must have entered into me for when I read the letter again I felt that I ought to humour him, as much for her sake as for his. After all, she was the last, the only person who cared for him in the way he wanted to be cared for – whatever that was. I should get through the week-end somehow. I wrote to Christopher and I wrote to the Hancocks, Christopher's married couple, telling them the train that I should come by.

What surprised me, when I got there, was the familiarity of it all. I had forgotten what a frequent visitor I used to be.

"Why, Mr. Gretton," Hancock said, "you've deserted us, you're quite a stranger!" But I didn't feel one; I could have found my way about the house blindfolded.

"It's over a year since you came to us," he reproached me. "We often used to ask Mr. Fenton what had become of you."

"And what did he say?" I asked.

"Oh, he said you were too busy, but as I said, you couldn't be too busy to get away at the week-end."

"Oh, but I expect you have plenty of visitors without me," I said.

"No, sir, we don't, not like we used to have. Of course it's a nuisance, food being what it is, but Mr. Fenton likes having, them, and it's always a real treat to see you, sir. The new faces aren't the same by any means, not the same class of people either." I took up the Visitors' Book and saw several names that were strange to me. Christopher had been trying out some new friends. But there weren't many names at all; to turn back a page was to turn back a year, and I soon found my own.

"It does seem too bad that you should be here when Mr. Fenton isn't," Hancock prattled on. "He always looks forward particularly to you coming, sir. Though now, of course, he's a good deal taken up with his garden. Often he works in it quite late. He's got to be terrible fond of flowers. Those rhododendrons he's so set on, sir, of course they looks after themselves, as you might say. But gardeners are all alike, sir, you can't get them to weed the flower-beds. Now this herbaceous border, sir, you can see it from the window –" His glance invited me to go to the window, but for some reason I didn't want to go. "Often of an evening I go to the window and see him stooping and call out to him that dinner's ready. Would you like to see the garden, sir? He was ever so anxious you should see it."

"Well, not just now," I said. "Of course I shall go and see it to-morrow. Now I think I shall have a bath. Dinner's at eight, I suppose?"

"Yes, sir, that's Mr. Fenton's hour, though there's many in these times has put it earlier. The wife she sometimes has a moan about it, but of course we have to respect Mr. Fenton's wishes."

A question that had absurdly been nagging me all day now demanded utterance. "I've brought my dinner-jacket, Hancock," I said, "because I know Mr. Fenton likes one to change for dinner. But as I'm going to be alone, do you suppose he would mind?"

"Well, sir, it's just as you like, of course, but you won't be alone because there's a lady coming."

"A lady?"

"Yes, sir, didn't you know? But perhaps Mr. Fenton forgot to tell you. He's been very forgetful lately, we've both remarked on it. Yes, sir, Miss Constantia Corwen, you know her, don't you, you've stayed with her here several times. A tall lady."

"Yes," I said, "I know her quite well. I wonder if Mr. Fenton told her I was going to be here."

"Oh yes, sir, I expect so. He wouldn't forget the same thing twice."

It was six o'clock. I went to my room, meaning to stay there till dinner-time, but when I heard the crunch of wheels curiosity overcame me and I tiptoed out on to the landing above the hall and listened.

"Yes, Miss," I heard Hancock say, "the master was dreadfully cut up about missing the flowers and all on account of spring being so late."

I could understand Constantia making sympathetic noises, but there were tears in her voice as she said, "Yes, it was terribly bad luck. I *am* so sorry. Is there time to go out and see the garden now?"

"Well, Miss, it's just as you like but dinner's at eight and there's a soufflé."

"I shall only be a moment and I think I won't change for dinner as I shall be alone."

There was quite a long pause and then Hancock said, in a puzzled, different voice, "You won't be altogether alone, Miss, because you see Mr. Gretton's here."

"Mr. Gretton?"

"Yes, Miss. Didn't Mr. Fenton tell you?"

"No, he must have forgotten. I think I'll go up to my room now."

"Yes, Miss, it's the usual one. I'll bring your things."

We were sitting together in the drawing-room after dinner, still a little in the shadow of our first embarrassed greeting. When we met in public we often didn't smile; but never until now had we not smiled when we met in private.

"Should we take a turn in the garden?" Constantia asked.

I demurred. "It's too late, don't you think? Probably all the flowers are shut up for the night."

"I don't think rhododendrons shut up," Constantia said.

"Well, there isn't enough light to see them by."

"Let's make sure," said Constantia, and unwillingly I followed her to the bay window. It was a house of vaguely Regency date and the drawing-room was on the first floor. The Long Walk ran at right angles to it, nearly a hundred yards away. It made the southern boundary of the garden. We could see the tops of the rhododendrons, they were like a line of foam crowning a long dark billow; and in front of and below them the azaleas, a straggling line, hardly a line at all, gave an effect of sparseness and delicacy and fragility. But the colour hardly showed at all.

"You see," I said. "You can't see."

She smiled. "Perhaps you're right, but we'll go first thing in the morning."

I laughed. "First thing with you isn't very early."

We went back into the room and sat one on each side of the fireplace, trying to look and feel at home; but the constraint had not left us and the house resisted us. It would not play the host. I felt an intruder, almost a trespasser, and caught myself listening for Christopher's footstep on the stairs.

"Christopher's absence is more potent than his presence," I said as lightly as I could.

"Ah, poor Christopher," Constantia said. "I wish I could feel we were doing what he wanted us to do."

"What did he want us to do," I asked, "besides look at the flowers?"

"I wish I knew," Constantia answered.

I was glad to find myself growing annoyed. Christopher had somehow turned the tables on us; he had got us into his world of make-believe, his emotional climate of self-stultifying sentimentalism. He had becalmed us with his spell of inaction, which made the ordinary pursuits of life seem not worth-while. He had put us into an equivocal position; even in the conventional sense of the term it was equivocal. Well, I must get us out.

"Are you sure you wouldn't like me to go?" I said. "The Tyrrel Arms is only a mile away."

"No, no," she answered. "He wouldn't want you to, nor do I."

"Listen," I said. "If it was a practical joke it was a damn bad one. You don't really think he forgot to warn us both that the other would be there?"

"Warn us?"

"Well, would you have come if you'd known I was to be here?"

"Would you?" she parried.

"Certainly," I said, with more decision than I felt. "I would go anywhere where you were, Constantia. It would be a plain issue to me. All the issues are plain where you are concerned. I don't have to dress them up in flowers."

"Ah, the flowers," she said, and turned again to the window.

"If he meant to make us doubt our feelings for each other," I argued, "he will be disappointed, as far as I'm concerned. He has thrown us together by a trick. He has arranged for us to be alone together in his house. He has put us into the position of an illicit couple. Why don't we accept the challenge?"

Constantia frowned. "He wanted us to see the flowers," she said, and she was still saying it, in effect if not in word, when the time came for week-end visitors to separate for the night.

I am usually a good sleeper but I could not sleep and was the more annoyed because I felt that Christopher's influence was gaining – it had spread from the emotional into the physical sphere. First he had surprised and kept me guessing; now he was keeping me awake. I had a shrewd idea that Constantia too was wakeful; and the irony and futility of our lying sleepless in separate rooms all because of some groundless scruple that Christopher had insinuated into our minds enraged me and made me more than ever wakeful, as anger will. About two o'clock I rose and, turning on the light, I stole along the passage towards Constantia's room. To reach it I had to pass the head of the staircase where it disappeared into the thick darkness of the hall below. Accentuated by the stillness of the night, the blackness seemed to come up at me, as though it was being brewed in a vat and given off like vapour; and though I wasn't frightened I felt that Christopher was trying to frighten me and this made me still more angry. I listened at Constantia's door and if I had heard a movement I should have gone in, but there was none, and I would not risk waking her; my love for her was intensified by my irritation against Christopher, and I could not bear to do her a disservice. So I turned away and deliberately bent my steps towards Christopher's room, for I knew that he left his letters lying about and I thought I might find something that would let me into the secret of his intentions – if intentions he had; but more and more I felt that the conception of the visit was an idle whim, with hardly enough purpose behind it to be mischievous.

I like a bedroom to be a bedroom, a place for sleeping in, not an extra sitting-room arranged for the display of modish and chi-chi-objects. Christopher's bedroom was even less austere than I remembered it; there were additions in the shape of fashionable Regency furniture, which I never care for. The bed looked as if it never had been and never could be slept in. And in contrast to this luxury were vases full of withered flowers, lilac and iris; the soup-green water they stood in smelt decidedly unpleasant. The Hancocks were not such perfect servants as Christopher liked to make out. Nothing looks so dead as a dead flower, and the bright light gave these a garish look as though they had been painted. But there was nothing to my purpose; no letters, sketches, no books even; only a tall pile of flower catalogues, topped by a Government pamphlet on pest control.

Pest control! It was the pamphlet, no less than the shrivelled flowers, which gave me the idea that burst into full bloom as soon as I was back in bed. The flowers, I felt, represented that part of Christopher with which I was least in sympathy; his instinct to substitute for life something that was apart from life – something that would prettify it, aromatize it, falsify it, enervate and finally destroy it. These flowers were pests and must, in modern parlance, be controlled and neutralized. Thinking how to do it I soon fell asleep.

I was sitting at Christopher's writing-table drafting an opinion when, at the hour at which well-to-do women usually make their first appearance, that is to say about half-past eleven, Constantia came in. She was dressed in grey country clothes the severity of which was relieved by a few frivolous touches here and there, and she was wearing a hat, or the rudiments of a hat. I kissed her and asked how she had slept.

"Not very well," she said.

"Oh?" I said. "Why not?"

"I was thinking about Christopher's flowers," she said. "I couldn't get them out of my head. I nearly went down to them in the watches of the night. But I'm going now. Will you come with me, Ernest, or are you too busy?"

"I am rather busy," I said, "and to tell you the truth, Constantia, I think this flower business is rather a bore."

Constantia opened her grey eyes wide. "Oh, why?" she said.

I pulled a chair towards the writing-table as if she was a client come to interview me, and sat down in Christopher's place.

"Because they distract you from me," I replied. "That's one thing. And another is, I have reasons for thinking they are not very good flowers."

"Not?" queried Constantia, puzzled. "But Christopher has spent so much time and money on them."

"I know," I said. "But I also know that Christopher never gets anything quite right. You must have noticed that yourself."

Constantia smiled. "Poor Christopher, I suppose he doesn't quite, but still – Ernest, let's go out and look at them."

"I hate the second-rate," I said. "My motto is, don't touch it."

Constantia shifted in her chair and gave her dress a little pat. "Oh well, if you don't want to, I'll –" she began.

"But I don't want you to, either," I said, pointing my pen at her. "You'll only regret it if you do."

"Regret it?" she repeated. "Ernest, darling, I quite understand if you don't want to go into the garden now, but please

74

don't try to stop me." She began to get up, but I motioned her to be seated.

"Yes, regret it," I said, firmly. "Do you know why Christopher played this trick on us?"

"But was it a trick?" Constantia asked doubtfully.

"Of course it was! He was leading us, if I may say so, up the garden path. I think he had two ideas in his mind, an upper and a lower one, and both were meant to separate us."

She looked at me reproachfully and without speaking.

"The first was, frankly, to compromise us."

"Oh, my dear Ernest!" Constantia protested.

"Yes, it was. He may not have put it to himself as crudely as that. He may not have meant to publish it abroad; that would have been the natural thing to do and he doesn't like the natural. No; the satisfaction he would get – will get – is from knowing that we know that he knows. It will enable him to practise a kind of gentle blackmail on us. We shall never be quite alone together any more; he will always be there, watching our thoughts. He will be like an agent – Cupid's agent – taking a ten per cent commission on our love. He will expect us to feel guilty and grateful at the same time and it will act like a poison – it will come between us."

Constantia made a grimace of distaste. "Really, Ernest, I don't think he meant anything of the sort."

But I saw I had impressed her. "He did, he did," I said. "You have no idea what fancies people get when they live alone and play at life."

Constantia sighed but she did not meet my eye. "What was the other idea?" she asked.

"I'll tell you," I said. "But first I must ask you a question which I think our relationship entitles me to ask. He was never your lover, was he?"

After a pause Constantia said, "What do you want me to say?"

"No need for you to say anything," I said. "By shielding him you have answered my question. He was not. He kept you for years – where? In his enchanted garden, among the loves of the plants, despising this trivial act of union, infecting you with his unreality; and now he means us to meet in his Eden (he called it Eden in his letter) exposed to this same beauty of flowers, like Adam and Eve before the Fall, with this difference" – here I tapped the table with my pen and it gave out a sharp, dry sound – "that *we* shall have been warned. We shan't dare to eat of the tree of knowledge; we shall be trapped for life in a labyrinth of false values, captives of a memory too gracious and delicate to be contaminated by such an ugly fact as man and wife. Yes," I went on, for I saw that against herself she was being convinced, "if you went out into that garden now you might well find a snake and what would it be? An incarnation of our old friend Christopher, luring us back to his eunuch's paradise!"

With frightened eyes Constantia looked about her; but I noticed that her glance avoided the window, through which I could see the rhododendrons stirring in the gentle summer breeze.

"Very well," she said. "I think you are more fanciful than poor Christopher ever was, but if you like I'll go and write some letters until lunch-time."

"And you promise not to go into the garden?"

"Yes, since you're so childish."

"And you won't even speak of going?"

"No, not till four o'clock."

"All right," I said. I knew that Constantia would be as good as her word.

* * *

After luncheon we decided that our morning's hard work entitled us to a siesta. Constantia had kept her promise, she had not even mentioned the garden; but she stipulated that Hancock should rouse us at a quarter to four, in case either of us over-slept.

I did not sleep, however. The watch ticking on my wrist was not more careful of the minutes than I was. After half an hour of this I got up (it was just on three) and decided to take a walk. Where? I knew the walks round Crossways, of course, quite well. Two of them, the best two, were reached by the garden gate that opened on the lane. What of it? The flowers were dangerous to Constantia, but not to me. Anyhow, I needn't look. But as I started out my steps came slower; I stopped and glanced back at the house. "Confound it!" I thought. "Confound Christopher and all his works!" I found myself walking back to the house and my rage against him redoubled. Then I had an idea. I had brought a pair of dark glasses with me, sun-glasses, so strong they turned day into night. I put them on and started out with firmer tread. Such colours as I saw were wholly falsified by an admixture of dark sepia tints. I was not looking at Christopher's flowers. But indeed I kept my eyes fixed on the broad path, I did not have to look about me, and here was the gate, the door rather, that led into the lane; and according to Christopher's custom the key had been left in it, for the convenience of guests bent on exercise. The key out of Eden! I unlocked the door, locked it on the other side, put the key in my pocket, and drew a deep breath.

I had been walking for some time when my first plan occurred to me, and I wondered why I had not thought of it before, for it was such an obvious one. I would not go back; I would leave Constantia to keep her tryst with Christopher's

77

spirit, for she would keep it: I had shaken her mind, but not her resolution. She would go through the silly ritual by herself and it would mean to her – well, whatever it did mean. It could not fail to be something of an anti-climax. She would wait, toeing the line like a runner, and looking round for me; she would give me a minute or two, and then she would start off. And as she went through that afternoon blaze of flowers, very slowly, drinking it in and thinking of Christopher, as no doubt he had enjoined her to – what would her reactions be? What would any woman's reactions be? Would she think less kindly of Christopher and more kindly of me? She would remember the many times she had walked there with him, wishing, no doubt, that he was other than he was, but indulgent to his faults, as women are, perhaps half liking him for them, not minding his ineffectualness. And the flowers would plead for him. She would not care if they were poor specimens (I had invented that), it would only make her feel sorry for him, and protective.

No, it would not do to let her go down the Long Walk alone. And nor would I escort her, for that would be the ultimate surrender to all that I was saving her from.

It was time to turn back and I still had formed no plan. I stopped and as I put my hands in my pockets the key of the garden door jingled and seemed to speak to me. At once the peace of decision, unknown to men of Christopher's type, descended on me. I felt that the problem of the garden was already solved. I had plenty of time to get back by a quarter to four, so I did not hurry, indeed I loitered. Suddenly I wondered why the familiar landscape looked so odd, and I remembered I was still wearing my dark glasses. I took them off and immediately felt interested in the wayside flowers, the dog-roses and honeysuckle of the hedgerows. In spite of what Christopher said I am really quite fond of flowers, and it gave me an intimate sense of power and freedom to examine these, which he had not asked me to examine. What plainer proof could I have that I was free of him and that my will was uncontaminated by his?

But when I reached the lane that bordered his garden wall I stopped botanizing and put on my sun-glasses again, for I still judged it better not to take risks. And I had thought out all my actions during the next twenty minutes so carefully that it came as a great surprise when I found that something had happened outside my calculations.

The garden door was open.

There could only be one explanation and it disturbed me: Constantia must have opened the door, and to do so must have passed through the garden. She must have asked Hancock for one of the several duplicate keys that Christopher had had made (the key of the garden door was always getting lost) and gone for a walk as I had. I did not want to disturb the rest of my plan so I left the door as it was and went towards the house. I did not return by the Long Walk; I went another way, invisible from the house, for I did not want to be seen by anyone just then.

But Constantia had not gone out; she was sitting by the drawing-room window. She jumped up. "Oh," she said, "thank goodness, here you are. I was afraid you were going to be late. But I have a bone to pick with you. You stole a march on me."

"How?" I challenged her.

"You've been to see the flowers already."

"What makes you think so?"

"I saw you in the Long Walk, don't tell me it wasn't you!"

"When?"

"About ten minutes ago."

79

"What was I doing?"

"Oh, Ernest, don't be so mysterious! You were looking at the flowers, of course."

I joined her at the window.

"You couldn't see from here," I said.

"Of course I could! And you were ashamed – you didn't want to be seen, you dodged in and out of the bushes, and pretended to be a rhododendron. But I knew you by your hat."

Nothing she said made any sense to me; I hadn't gone out in a hat; but I said quickly, "I think you're imagining things, but afterwards I'll explain." It was like being back on the main road after a traffic diversion. "Now what is our plan of campaign? At the stroke of four we are to walk from the fountain to the temple?"

Constantia hurriedly searched in her bag and brought out a letter. "No, no, Ernest," she said in agitation. "He says from the temple to the fountain."

"Are you sure?"

"Quite sure."

"Did you promise him to do it?"

"Yes, did you?"

"Well, I suppose I did. But my instructions were the other way round. He means us to meet in the middle, then."

"Yes. What time is it, Ernest? We mustn't be late."

"Three minutes to four. Just let me get my stick."

"Stick, you won't want a stick. What do you want a stick for?"

"To beat you with," I said.

She smiled. "Be quick, then."

I hurried out, shutting the door behind me and turning the key in the lock. Suddenly feeling tired I sat down on a chair on the landing.

In the hall below me the grandfather clock struck four.

Oh, the ecstasy of that moment! It seemed to me that my whole life was being fulfilled in it. I heard Constantia's voice calling "Ernest! Ernest!" But I could not move, I could not even think, for the waves of delight that were surging through me. I heard the rattle of the door-handle; I could see it stealthily turning, backwards and forwards, in a cramped semi-circle. Soon she began to beat upon the door. "Her little fists will soon get tired of that," I thought. "And she can't get out through the window: there's a drop of twenty feet into the garden."

As distinctly as if there had been no door between us I saw her face clenched in misery and fury. Ah, but this was real! This was no sentimental saunter down a garden-path! Presently the hammering ceased and another sound began. Constantia was crying: she did not do it prettily: she did not know she had a listener: she coughed her tears out. That, too, ministered to my ecstasy; I was the king of pain. I sat on, savouring it till all sounds ceased, except the ticking of the clock below.

How long my drowse lasted I cannot tell, but it was broken by the crack of a shot. It seemed to be inside me, it hurt me so much. I jumped up as if it was I who had been hit. I pressed the key against the lock too hard: it turned unwillingly, but at last I was in the room.

She was sitting bent forward with her face in her hands, blood was trickling from her broken knuckles, and for a moment I believed that she was dead. But she raised her face and looked at me unrecognizingly.

"Ernest?" she said, as if it was a question. "Ernest?"

"I'm sorry, Constantia," I said. "Something delayed me. Shall we go into the garden now?"

She rose without a word and followed me downstairs, and

81

we went out through the french windows in Christopher's room.

"Here we divide," I said. "You go to the temple and I'll go to the fountain, and we'll meet in the middle, Constantia." She obeyed me like a child.

I looked at the flowers as Christopher wished me to. I did not look at anything else, though when I raised my eyes I could see Constantia, very small and far away, coming towards me. The afternoon sunshine lay thick on all these thousands of blooms. Not a single one seemed to be in shadow: all were displayed for us to look at, as Christopher had wished them to be. Constantia and I were representing the public, the great public, in fact the world, to whom Christopher had felt this strange obligation to make known the beauty he had helped to create. And now I was not only willing but eager to fall in with his plan. Methodically I zigzagged from one side of the grass path to the other, from the rhododendrons to the azaleas, from the Boucher-like luxuriance of the one to the Chinese delicacy and tenuousness of the other. I went on the flower-beds; I lifted the brown labels, trying to decipher rain-smudged names; I stooped to the earth, yes, from time to time I knelt, to read the inscriptions on the leaden markers. Nothing that he would have wished me to see escaped me; the smallest effect was as clear to me as the largest; I found no faults – no dissonance, even, between the prevailing pink of the rhododendrons and the prevailing orange of the azaleas, which had hitherto always offended my eye when these flowers were juxtaposed. Yes, I thought, he has brought it off, he has established a harmony; the flowers all sing together an anthem to his glory.

I was approaching the middle of the Long Walk and my journey's end when I heard Constantia scream. Instantly the garden was in ruins, its spell broken.

I did not see her at first. Like me, she had been going to and fro among the flower-beds, and it was there, under the shadow of a towering rhododendron that I found her, bending over Christopher. Something or someone – perhaps Christopher, perhaps Constantia in the shock of her discovery, had shaken the bush, for the body was covered with rose-pink petals, and his forehead, his damaged forehead, was adrift with them. Even the revolver in his hand had petals on it, softening its steely gleam. But for that, and for something in his attitude that suggested he was defying Nature, not obeying her, one might have supposed that he had fallen asleep under his own flowers.

In his pocket we afterwards found a letter. It was addressed to both of us and dated Sunday 4.30. "I had meant to join you at the garden-party," it said, "but now I feel it's best I shouldn't. Only half an hour, but long enough to be convinced that I have messed things up. And yet I can't quite understand it, for I felt so differently at four o'clock. Was it too much to ask, that you should keep your promise to me, or too little? All my life I have been asking myself this question, in one form or another, and perhaps this is the only answer. Bless you, my children, be happy. – Christopher."

"But don't you *see*," I said to Constantia, 'it all proves what I said? He couldn't come to terms with life, he didn't know how to live, and so he had to die?"

"You may be right," she answered listlessly. "But I shall never forgive myself for failing him – or you."

I argued with her – I even got angry with her – but she would not see reason, and after the inquest we never met again.

WILLIAM MAXWELL

THE FRENCH
SCARECROW

I spied John Mouldy in his cellar
  Deep down twenty steps of stone;
In the dusk he sat a-smiling,
  Smiling there alone.
                    – Walter de la Mare

DRIVING PAST THE Fishers' house on his way out to the public road, Gerald Martin said to himself absentmindedly, "There's Edmund working in his garden," before he realized that it was a scarecrow. And two nights later he woke up sweating from a dream, a nightmare, which he related next day, lying tense on the analyst's couch.

"I was in this house, where I knew I oughtn't to be, and I looked around and saw there was a door, and in order to get to it I had to pass a dummy – a dressmaker's dummy without any head."

After a considerable silence the disembodied voice with a German accent said, "Any day remnants?"

"I can't think of any," Gerald Martin said, shifting his position on the couch. "We used to have a dressmaker's dummy in the sewing room when I was a child, but I haven't thought of it for years. The Fishers have a scarecrow in their garden, but I don't think it could be that. The scarecrow looks like Edmund. The same thin shoulders, and his clothes, of course, and the way it stands looking sadly down at the ground. It's a caricature of Edmund. One of those freak

87

accidents. I wonder if they realize it. Edmund is not sad, exactly, but there was a period in his life when he was neither as happy or as hopeful as he is now. Dorothy is a very nice woman. Not at all maternal, I would say. At least, she doesn't mother Edmund. And when you see her with some woman with a baby, she always seems totally indifferent. Edmund was married before, and his first wife left him. Helena was selfish but likable, the way selfish people sometimes are. And where Edmund was concerned, completely heartless. I don't know why. She used to turn the radio on full blast at two o'clock in the morning, when he had to get up at six-thirty to catch a commuting train. And once she sewed a ruffle all the way around the bed he was trying to sleep in. Edmund told me that her mother preferred her older sister, and that Helena's whole childhood had been made miserable because of it. He tried every way he could think of to please her and make her happy, and with most women that would have been enough, I suppose, but it only increased her dissatisfaction. Maybe if there had been any children . . . She used to walk up and down the road in a long red cloak, in the wintertime when there was snow on the ground. And she used to talk about New York. And it was as if she was under a spell and waiting to be delivered. Now she blames Edmund for the divorce. She tells everybody that he took advantage of her. Perhaps he did, unconsciously. Consciously, he wouldn't take advantage of a fly. I think he needs analysis, but he's very much opposed to it. Scared to death of it, in fact . . ."

Step by step, Gerald Martin had managed to put a safe distance between himself and the dream, and he was beginning to breathe easier in the complacent viewing of someone else's failure to meet his problems squarely when the voice said, "Well – see you again?"

"I wish to Christ you wouldn't say that! As if I had any choice in the matter."

His sudden fury was ignored. A familiar hypnotic routine obliged him to sit up and put his feet over the side of the couch. The voice became attached to an elderly man with thick glasses and a round face that Gerald would never get used to. He got up unsteadily and walked toward the door. Only when he was outside, standing in front of the elevator shaft, did he remember that the sewing room had a door opening into his mother and father's bedroom, and at one period of his life he had slept there, in a bed with sides that could be let down, a child's bed. This information was safe from the man inside – unless he happened to think of it while he was lying on the couch next time.

That evening he stopped when he came to the Fishers' vegetable garden and turned the engine off and took a good look at the scarecrow. Then, after a minute or two, afraid that he would be seen from the house, he started the car and drove on.

The Fishers' scarecrow was copied from a scarecrow in France. The summer before, they had spent two weeks as paying guests in a country house in the Touraine, in the hope that this would improve their French. The improvement was all but imperceptible to them afterward, but they did pick up a number of ideas about gardening. In the *potager*, fruit trees, tree roses, flowers, and vegetables were mingled in a way that aroused their admiration, and there was a more than ordinarily fanciful scarecrow, made out of a blue peasant's smock, striped morning trousers, and a straw hat. Under the hat the stuffed head had a face painted on it; and not simply two eyes, a nose, and a mouth but a face with a sly expression. The scarecrow stood with arms upraised, shaking its white-gloved fists at the sky. Indignant, self-centered, half crazy, it seemed to be saying: *This is what it means to be exposed to experience.* The crows were not taken in.

Effects that had needed generations of dedicated French gardeners to bring about were not, of course, to be imitated successfully by two amateur gardeners in Fairfield County in a single summer. The Fishers gave up the idea of marking off the paths of their vegetable garden with espaliered dwarf apple and pear trees, and they could see no way of having tree roses without also having to spray them, and afterward having to eat the spray. But they did plant zinnias, marigolds, and blue pansies in with the lettuce and the peas, and they made a very good scarecrow. Dorothy made it, actually. She was artistic by inclination, and threw herself into all such undertakings with a childish pleasure.

She made the head out of a dish towel stuffed with hay, and was delighted with the blue stripe running down the face. Then she got out her embroidery thread and embroidered a single eye, gathered the cloth in the middle of the face into a bulbous nose, made the mouth leering. For the body she used a torn pair of Edmund's blue jeans she was tired of mending, and a faded blue workshirt. When Edmund, who was attached to his old clothes, saw that she had also helped herself to an Army fatigue hat from the shelf in the hall closet, he exclaimed, "Hey, don't use that hat for the scarecrow! I wear it sometimes."

"*When* do you wear it?"

"I wear it to garden in."

"You can wear some other old hat to garden in. He's got to have something on his head," she said lightly, and made the hat brim dip down over the blank eye.

"When winter comes, I'll wear it again," Edmund said to

himself, "if it doesn't shrink too much, or fall apart in the rain."

The scarecrow stood looking toward the house, with one arm limp and one arm extended stiffly, ending in a gloved hand holding a stick. After a few days the head sank and sank until it was resting on the straw breastbone, and the face was concealed by the brim of the hat. They tried to keep the head up with a collar of twisted grass, but the grass dried, and the head sank once more, and in that attitude it remained.

The scarecrow gave them an eerie feeling when they saw it from the bedroom window at twilight. A man standing in the vegetable garden would have looked like a scarecrow. If he didn't move. Dorothy had never lived in the country before she married Edmund, and at first she was afraid. The black windows at night made her nervous. She heard noises in the basement, caused by the steam circulating through the furnace pipes. And she would suddenly have the feeling – even though she knew it was only her imagination – that there was a man outside, looking through the windows at them. "Shouldn't we invite him in?" Edmund would say when her glance strayed for a second. "Offer him a drink and let him sit by the fire? It's not a very nice night out."

He assumed that The Man Outside represented for her all the childish fears – the fear of the dark, of the burglar on the stairs, of what else he had no way of knowing. Nor she either, probably. The Man Outside was simply there, night after night, for about six weeks, and then he lost his power to frighten, and finally went away entirely, leaving the dark outside as familiar and safe to her as the lighted living room. It was Edmund, strangely, who sometimes, as they were getting ready for bed, went to the front and back doors and locked them. For he was aware that the neighborhood was changing, and that things were happening – cars stolen, houses broken into in broad daylight – that never used to happen in this part of the world.

The Fishers' white clapboard house was big and rambling, much added onto at one time or another, but in its final form still plain and pleasant-looking. The original house dated from around 1840. Edmund's father, who was a New York banker until he retired at the age of sixty-five, had bought it before the First World War. At that time there were only five houses on this winding country road, and two of them were farmhouses. When the Fishers came out from town for the summer, they were met at the railroad station by a man with a horse and carriage. The surrounding country was hilly and offered many handsome views, and most of the local names were to be found on old tombstones in the tiny Presbyterian churchyard. Edmund's mother was a passionate and scholarly gardener, the founder of the local garden club and its president for twenty-seven years. Her regal manner was quite unconscious, and based less on the usual foundations of family, money, etc., than on the authority with which she could speak about the culture of delphinium and lilies, or the pruning of roses. The house was set back from the road about three hundred yards, and behind it were the tennis courts, the big three-story barn, a guest house overlooking the pond where all the children in the neighborhood skated in winter, and, eventually, a five-car garage. Back of the pond, a wagon road went off into the woods and up onto higher ground. In the late twenties, when Edmund used to bring his school friends home for spring and fall weekends and the Easter vacation, the house seemed barely large enough to hold them all. During the last war, when the taxes began to be burdensome, Edmund's father sold off the back land, with the guest house, the barn, and the pond, to a Downtown lawyer, who shortly afterward sold it to a manufacturer of children's underwear. The elder Mr. and Mrs. Fisher started to follow the wagon road back into the woods one pleasant Sunday afternoon, and he ordered them off his property. He was quite within his rights, of course, but nevertheless it rankled. "In the old days," they would say whenever the man's name was mentioned, "you could go anywhere, on anybody's land, and no one ever thought of stopping you."

Edmund's father, working from his own rough plans and supervising the carpenters and plumbers and masons himself, had converted the stone garage into a house, and he had sold it to Gerald Martin, who was a bachelor. The elder Fishers were now living in the Virgin Islands the year round, because of Mrs. Fisher's health. Edmund and Dorothy still had ten acres, but they shared the cinder drive with Gerald and the clothing manufacturer, and, of course, had less privacy than before. The neighborhood itself was no longer the remote place it used to be. The Merritt Parkway had made all the difference. Instead of five houses on the two-and-a-half-mile stretch of dirt road, there were twenty-five, and the road was macadamized. Cars and delivery trucks cruised up and down it all day long.

In spite of all these changes, and in spite of the considerable difference between Edmund's scale of living and his father's – Dorothy had managed with a part-time cleaning woman where in the old days there had been a cook, a waitress, an upstairs maid, a chauffeur, and two gardeners – the big house still seemed to express the financial stability and social confidence and belief in good breeding of the Age of Trellises. Because he had lived in the neighborhood longer than anyone else, Edmund sometimes felt the impulses of a host, but he had learned not to act on them. His mother always used to pay a call on new people within a month of their settling in, and if she liked them, the call was followed by an invitation to the Fishers' for tea or cocktails, at which time she managed to bring up the subject of the garden club. But in the last year or so that she had lived there, she had all but given this up. Twice her call was not returned, and one terribly nice young couple accepted an invitation to tea and blithely forgot to come. Edmund was friendly when he met his neighbors on the road or on the station platform, but he let them go their own way, except for Gerald Martin, who was rather amusing, and obviously lonely, and glad of an invitation to the big house.

"I am sewed to this couch," Gerald Martin said. "My sleeves are sewed to it, and my trousers. I could not move if I wanted to. Oedipus is on the wall over me, answering the spink-spank-sphinx, and those are pussy willows, and I do not like bookcases with glass sides that let down, and the scarecrow is gone. I don't know what they did with it, and I don't like to ask. And today *I* might as well be stuffed with straw. The dream I had last night did it. I broke two plates, and woke up unconfident and nervous and tired. I don't know what the dream means. I had three plates and I dropped two of them, and it was so vivid. It was a short dream but very vivid. I thought at first that the second plate – why *three* plates? – was all right, but while I was looking at it, the cracks appeared. When I picked it up, it gave; it came apart in my hands. It was painted with flowers, and it had openwork, and I was in a hurry, and in my hurry I dropped the plates. And I was upset. I hardly ever break anything. Last night while I was drying the glasses, I thought how I never break any of them. They're Swedish and very expensive. The plates I dreamed about were my mother's. Not actually; I *dreamed* that they were my mother's plates. I broke two things of hers when I was little. And both times it was something she had warned me about. I sat in the tea cart playing house, and forgot and raised my head suddenly, and it went right through the glass tray. And the other was an etched-glass hurricane lamp that she prized very highly. I climbed up on a chair to reach it. And after she died, I could have thought – I don't ever remember thinking this, but I could have thought that I did something I shouldn't have, and she died. . . . Thank you, I have matches. . . . I can raise my arm. I turned without thinking. I can't figure out that dream. My stepmother was there, washing dishes at the sink, and she turned into Helena Fisher, and I woke up thinking, Ah, that's it. They're *both* my stepmothers! My stepmother never broke anything that belonged to my mother, so she must have been fond of her. They knew each other as girls. And I never broke anything that belonged to my stepmother. I only broke something that belonged to my mother. . . . Did I tell you I saw her the other day?"

"You saw someone who reminded you of your mother?"

"No, I saw Helena Fisher. On Fifth Avenue. I crossed over to the other side of the street, even though I'm still fond of her, because she hasn't been very nice to Dorothy, and because it's all so complicated, and I really didn't have anything to say to her. She was very conspicuous in her country clothes." He lit another cigarette and then said, after a prolonged silence, "I don't seem to have anything to say now, either." The silence became unbearable, and he said, "I can't think of anything to talk about."

"Let's talk about you – about this dream you had," the voice said, kind and patient as always, the voice of his father (at $20 an hour).

*   *   *

95

The scarecrow had remained in the Fishers' vegetable garden, with one arm limp and one arm stiffly extended, all summer. The corn and the tomato vines grew up around it, half obscuring it during the summer months, and then, in the fall, there was nothing whatever around it but the bare ground. The blue workshirt faded still more in the sun and rain. The figure grew frail, the straw chest settled and became a middle-aged thickening of the waist. The resemblance to Edmund disappeared. And on a Friday afternoon in October, with snow flurries predicted, Edmund Fisher went about the yard carrying in the outdoor picnic table and benches, picking up stray flowerpots, and taking one last look around for the pruning shears, the trowel, and the nest of screwdrivers that had all disappeared during the summer's gardening. There were still three or four storm windows to put up on the south side of the house, and he was about to bring them out and hang them when Dorothy, on her hands and knees in the iris bed, called to him.

"What about the scarecrow?"

"Do you want to save it?" he asked.

"I don't really care."

"We might as well," he said, and was struck once more by the lifelike quality of the scarecrow, as he lifted it out of the soil. It was almost weightless. "Did the doctor say it was all right for you to do that sort of thing?"

"I didn't ask him," Dorothy said.

"Oughtn't you to ask him?"

"No," she said, smiling at him. She was nearly three months pregnant. Moonfaced, serenely happy, and slow of movement (when she had all her life been so quick about everything), she went about now doing everything she had always done but like somebody in a dream, a sleepwalker. The clock had been replaced by the calendar. Like the gardeners in France, she was dedicated to making something grow. As Edmund carried the scarecrow across the lawn and around the corner of the house, she followed him with her eyes. Why is it, she wondered, that he can never bear to part with anything, even though it has ceased to serve its purpose and he no longer has any interest in it?

It was as if sometime or other in his life he had lost something, of such infinite value that he could never think of it without grieving, and never bear to part with anything worthless because of the thing he had had to part with that meant so much to him. But what? She had no idea, and she had given some thought to the matter. She was sure it was not Helena; he said (and she believed him) that he had long since got over any feeling he once had for her. His parents were both still living, he was an only child, and death seemed never to have touched him. Was it some early love, that he had never felt he dared speak to her about? Some deprivation? Some terrible injustice done to him? She had no way of telling. The attic and the basement testified to his inability to throw things away, and she had given up trying to do anything about either one. The same with people. At the end of a perfectly pleasant evening he would say "Oh no, it's early still. You mustn't go home!" with such fervor that even though it actually was time to go home and the guests wanted to, they would sit down, confused by him, and stay a while longer. And though the Fishers knew more people than they could manage to see, he would suddenly remember somebody he hadn't thought of or written to in a long time, and feel impelled to do something about them. Was it something that happened to him in his childhood, Dorothy asked herself. Or was it something in his temperament, born in him, a flaw in his horoscope, Mercury in an unsympathetic relation to the moon?

She resumed her weeding, conscious in a way that she hadn't been before of the autumn day, of the end of the summer's gardening, of the leaf-smoke smell and the smell of rotting apples, the hickory tree that lost its leaves before all the other trees, the grass so deceptively green, and the chill that had descended now that the sun had gone down behind the western hill.

Standing in the basement, looking at the hopeless disorder ("A place for everything," his father used to say, "and nothing in its place"), Edmund decided that it was more important to get at the storm windows than to find a place for the scarecrow. He laid it on one of the picnic-table benches, with the head toward the oil burner, and there it sprawled, like a man asleep or dead-drunk, with the line of the hipbone showing through the trousers, and one arm extended, resting on a slightly higher workbench, and one shoulder raised slightly, as if the man had started to turn in his sleep. In the dim light it could have been alive. I must remember to tell Dorothy, he thought. If she sees it like that, she'll be frightened.

The storm windows were washed and ready to hang. As Edmund came around the corner of the house, with IX in one hand and XI in the other, the telephone started to ring, and Dorothy went in by the back door to answer it, so he didn't have a chance to tell her about the scarecrow. When he went indoors, ten minutes later, she was still standing by the telephone, and from the fact that she was merely contributing a monosyllable now and then to the conversation, he knew she was talking to Gerald Martin. Gerald was as dear as the day was long – everybody liked him – but he had such a ready access to his own memories, which were so rich in narrative detail and associations that dovetailed into further narratives, that if you were busy it was a pure and simple misfortune to pick up the telephone and hear his cultivated, affectionate voice.

Edmund gave up the idea of hanging the rest of the storm windows, and instead he got in the car and drove to the village; he had remembered that they were out of cat food and whiskey. When he walked into the house, Dorothy said, "I've just had such a scare. I started to go down in the cellar –"

"I knew that would happen," he said, putting his hat and coat in the hall closet. "I meant to tell you."

"The basement light was burnt out," she said, "and so I took the flashlight. And when I saw the scarecrow I thought it was a man."

"Our old friend," he said, shaking his head. "The Man Outside."

"And you weren't here. I knew I was alone in the house . . ."

Her fright was still traceable in her face as she described it.

On Saturday morning, Edmund dressed hurriedly, the alarm clock having failed to go off, and while Dorothy was getting breakfast, he went down to the basement, half asleep, to get the car out and drive to the village for the cleaning woman, and saw the scarecrow in the dim light, sprawling by the furnace, and a great clot of fear seized him and his heart almost stopped beating. It lay there like an awful idiot, the realistic effect accidentally encouraged by the pair of work shoes Edmund had taken off the night before and tossed carelessly down the cellar stairs. The scarecrow had no feet – only two stumps where the trouser legs were tied at the bottom – but the shoes were where, if it had been alive, they might have been dropped before the person lay down on the bench. I'll have to do something about it, Edmund thought.

We can't go on frightening ourselves like this. . . . But the memory of the fright was so real that he felt unwilling to touch the scarecrow. Instead, he left it where it was, for the time being, and backed the car out of the garage.

On the way back from the village, Mrs. Ryan, riding beside him in the front seat of the car, had a story to tell. Among the various people she worked for was a family with three boys. The youngest was in the habit of following her from room to room, and ordinarily he was as good as gold, but yesterday he ran away, she told Edmund. His mother was in town, and the older boys, with some of the neighbors' children, were playing outside with a football, and Mrs. Ryan and the little boy were in the house. "Monroe asked if he could go outside, and I bundled him up and sent him out. I looked outside once, and saw that he was laying with the Bluestones' dog, and I said, 'Monroe, honey, don't pull that dog's tail. He might turn and bite you.' " While she was ironing, the oldest boy came inside for a drink of water, and she asked him where Monroe was, and he said, "Oh, he's outside." But when she went to the door, fifteen minutes later, the older boys were throwing the football again and Monroe was nowhere in sight. The boys didn't know what had happened to him. He disappeared. All around the house was woods, and Mrs. Ryan, in a panic, called and called.

"Usually when I call, he answers immediately, but this time there was no answer, and I went into the house and telephoned the Bluestones, and they hadn't seen him. And then I called the Hayeses and the Murphys, and they hadn't seen him either, and Mr. Hayes came down, and we all started looking for him. Mr. Hayes said only one car had passed in the last half hour – I was afraid he had been kidnapped, Mr. Fisher – and Monroe wasn't in it. And I thought, When his mother comes home and I have to tell her what I've done

". . . And just about that time, he answered, from behind the hedge!"

"Was he there all the time?" Edmund asked, shifting into second as he turned in to his own driveway.

"I don't know where he was," Mrs. Ryan said. "But he did the same thing once before – he wandered off on me. Mr. Ryan thinks he followed the Bluestones' dog home. His mother called me up last night and said that he knew he'd done something wrong. He said, 'Mummy, I was bad today. I ran off on Sadie. . . .' But Mr. Fisher, I'm telling you, I was almost out of my mind."

"I don't wonder," Edmund said soberly.

"With woods all around the house, and as Mr. Hayes said, climbing over a stone wall a stone could fall on him and we wouldn't find him for days."

Ten minutes later, she went down to the basement for the scrub bucket, and left the door open at the head of the stairs. Edmund heard her exclaim, for their benefit, "God save us, I've just had the fright of my life!"

She had seen the scarecrow.

The tramp that ran off with the child, of course, Edmund thought. He went downstairs a few minutes later, and saw that Mrs. Ryan had picked the dummy up and stood it in a corner, with its degenerate face to the wall, where it no longer looked human or frightening.

Mrs. Ryan is frightened because of the nonexistent tramp. Dorothy is afraid of The Man Outside. What am I afraid of, he wondered. He stood there waiting for the oracle to answer, and it did, but not until five or six hours later. Poor Gerald Martin called, after lunch, to say that he had the German measles.

"I was sick as a dog all night," he said mournfully. "I thought I was dying. I wrote your telephone number on a slip of paper and put it beside the bed, in case I *did* die."

"Well, for God's sake, why didn't you call us?" Edmund exclaimed.

"What good would it have done?" Gerald said. "All you could have done was say you were sorry."

"Somebody could have come over and looked after you."

"No, somebody couldn't. It's very catching. I think I was exposed to it a week ago at a party in Westport."

"I had German measles when I was a kid," Edmund said. "We've both had it."

"You can get it again," Gerald said. "I still feel terrible. . . ."

When Edmund left the telephone, he made the mistake of mentioning Gerald's illness to Mrs. Ryan, forgetting that it was the kind of thing that was meat and drink to her.

"Has Mrs. Fisher been near him?" she asked, with quickened interest.

He shook his head.

"There's a great deal of it around," Mrs. Ryan said. "My daughter got German measles when she was carrying her first child, and she lost it."

He tried to ask if it was a miscarriage or if the child was born dead, and he couldn't speak; his throat was too dry.

"She was three months along when she had it," Mrs. Ryan went on, without noticing that he was getting paler and paler. "The baby was born alive, but it only lived three days. She's had two other children since. I feel it was a blessing the Lord took that one. If it had lived, it might have been an imbecile. You love them even so, because they belong to you, but it's better if they don't live, Mr. Fisher. We feel it was a blessing the child was taken."

Edmund decided that he wouldn't tell Dorothy, and then five minutes later he decided that he'd better tell her. He went upstairs and into the bedroom where she was resting, and sat down on the edge of the bed, and told her about Gerald's telephone call. "Mrs. Ryan says it's very bad if you catch it while you're pregnant. . . . And she said some more."

"I can see she did, by the look on your face. You shouldn't have mentioned it to her. What did she say?"

"She said –" He swallowed. "She said the child could be born an imbecile. She also said there was a lot of German measles around. You're not worried?"

"We all live in the hand of God."

"I tell myself that every time I'm really frightened. Unfortunately that's the only time I do think it."

"Yes, I know."

Five minutes later, he came back into the room and said, "Why don't you call the doctor? Maybe there's a shot you can take."

The doctor was out making calls, and when he telephoned back, Dorothy answered, on the upstairs extension. Edmund sat down on the bottom step of the stairs and listened to her half of the conversation. As soon as she had hung up, she came down to tell him what the doctor had said.

"The shot only lasts three weeks. He said he'd give it to me if I should be exposed to the measles anywhere."

"Did he say there was an epidemic of it?"

"I didn't ask him. He said that it was commonly supposed to be dangerous during the first three months, but that the statistics showed that it's only the first two months, while the child is being formed, that you have to worry." Moonfaced and serene again, she went to put the kettle on for tea.

Edmund got up and went down to the basement. He carried the dummy outside, removed the hat and then the head, unbuttoned the shirt, removed the straw that filled it and the trousers, and threw it on the compost pile. The hat, the head, the shirt and trousers, the gloves that were hands, he rolled into a bundle and put away on a basement shelf, in case Dorothy wanted to make the scarecrow next summer. The two crossed sticks reminded him of the comfort that Mrs. Ryan, who was a devout Catholic, had and that he did not have. The hum of the vacuum cleaner overhead in the living room, the sad song of a mechanical universe, was all the reassurance he could hope for, and it left so much (it left the scarecrow, for example) completely unexplained and unaccounted for.

GARDEN PLEASURES AND SORROWS

"How could such sweet and wholesome hours
Be reckoned but with herbs and flowers?"

– Andrew Marvell, "The Garden"

COLETTE

BYGONE SPRING

Translated by Una Vicenzo Troubridge and Enid McLeod

THE BEAK OF a pruning shears goes clicking all down the rose-bordered paths. Another clicks in answer from the orchard. Presently the soil in the rose garden will be strewn with tender shoots, dawn-red at the tips but green and juicy at the base. In the orchard the stiff, severed twigs of the apricot trees will keep their little flames of flower alight for another hour before they die, and the bees will see to it that none of them is wasted.

The hillside is dotted with white plum trees like puffs of smoke, each of them filmy and dappled as a round cloud. At half past five in the morning, under the dew and the slanting rays of sunrise, the young wheat is incontestably blue, the earth rust-red, and the white plum trees coppery pink. It is only for a moment, a magic delusion of light that fades with the first hour of day. Everything grows with miraculous speed. Even the tiniest plant thrusts upward with all its strength. The peony, in the flush of its first month's growth, shoots up at such a pace that its scapes and scarcely unfolded leaves, pushing through the earth, carry with them the upper covering of it so that it hangs suspended like a roof burst asunder.

The peasants shake their heads. "April will bring us plenty of surprises." They bend wise brows over this folly, this annual imprudence of leaf and flower. They grow old, borne helplessly along in the wake of a terrible pupil who learns nothing from their experience. In the tilled valley, still crisscrossed with parallel rivulets, lines of green emerge above the inundation. Nothing can now delay the mole-like ascent of the asparagus, or extinguish the torch of the purple iris. The furious breaking of bonds infects birds, lizards, and insects. Greenfinch, goldfinch, sparrow, and chaffinch behave in the morning like farmyard fowl gorged with brandy-soaked grain. Ritual dances and mock battles, to the accompaniment of exaggerated cries, are renewed perpetually under our eyes, almost under our very hands. Flocks of birds and mating grey lizards share the same sun-warmed flagstones, and when the children, wild with excitement, run aimlessly hither and thither, clouds of mayfly rise and hover around their heads.

Everything rushes onward, and I stay where I am. Do I not already feel more pleasure in comparing this spring with others that are past than in welcoming it? The torpor is blissful enough, but too aware of its own weight. And though my ecstasy is genuine and spontaneous, it no longer finds expression. "Oh, look at those yellow cowslips! And the soapwort! And the unicorn tips of the lords and ladies are showing! . . ." But the cowslip, that wild primula, is a humble flower, and how can the uncertain mauve of the watery soapwort compare with a glowing peach tree? Its value for me lies in the stream that watered it between my tenth and fifteenth years. The slender cowslip, all stalk and rudimentary in blossom, still clings by a frail root to the meadow where I used to gather hundreds to straddle them along a string and then tie them into round balls, cool projectiles that struck the cheek like a rough, wet kiss.

I take good care nowadays not to pick cowslips and crush them into a greenish ball. I know the risk I should run if I did. Poor rustic enchantment, almost evaporated now, I cannot even bequeath you to another me: "Look,

Bel-Gazou, like this and then like that; first you straddle them on the string and then you draw it tight." "Yes, I see," says Bel-Gazou. "But it doesn't bounce; I'd rather have my India-rubber ball."

The shears click their beaks in the gardens. Shut me into a dark room and that sound will still bring in to me April sunshine, stinging the skin and treacherous as wine without a bouquet. With it comes the bee scent of the pruned apricot trees, and a certain anguish, the uneasiness of one of those slight preadolescent indispositions that develop, hang about for a time, improve, are cured one morning, and reappear at night. I was ten or eleven years old but, in the company of my foster-mother, who had become our cook, I still indulged in nursling whims. A grown girl in the dining-room, I would run to the kitchen to lick the vinegar off the salad leaves on the plate of Mélie, my faithful watchdog, my fair-haired, fair-skinned slave. One April morning I called out to her, "Come along, Mélie, let's go and pick up the clippings from the apricot trees, Milien's at the espaliers."

She followed me, and the young housemaid, well named Marie-la-Rose, came too, though I had not invited her. Milien, the day labourer, a handsome, crafty youth, was finishing his job, silently and without haste.

"Mélie, hold out your apron and let me put the clippings in it."

I was on my knees collecting the shoots starred with blossom. As though in play, Mélie went "Hou!" at me and, flinging her apron over my head, folded me up in it and rolled me gently over. I laughed, thoroughly enjoying making myself small and silly. But I began to stifle and came out from under it so suddenly that Milien and Marie-la-Rose, in the act of kissing, had not time to spring apart, nor Mélie to hide her guilty face.

Click of the shears, harsh chatter of hard-billed birds! They tell of blossoming, of early sunshine, of sunburn on the forehead, of chilly shade, of uncomprehended repulsion, of childish trust betrayed, of suspicion, and of brooding sadness.

VIRGINIA WOOLF

KEW GARDENS

FROM THE OVAL-SHAPED flower-bed there rose perhaps a hundred stalks spreading into heart-shaped or tongue-shaped leaves half way up and unfurling at the tip red or blue or yellow petals marked with spots of colour raised upon the surface; and from the red, blue or yellow gloom of the throat emerged a straight bar, rough with gold dust and slightly clubbed at the end. The petals were voluminous enough to be stirred by the summer breeze, and when they moved, the red, blue and yellow lights passed one over the other, staining an inch of the brown earth beneath with a spot of the most intricate colour. The light fell either upon the smooth, grey back of a pebble, or the shell of a snail with its brown, circular veins, or, falling into a raindrop, it expanded with such intensity of red, blue and yellow the thin walls of water that one expected them to burst and disappear. Instead, the drop was left in a second silver grey once more, and the light now settled upon the flesh of a leaf, revealing the branching thread of fibre beneath the surface, and again it moved on and spread its illumination in the vast green spaces beneath the dome of the heart-shaped and tongue-shaped leaves. Then the breeze stirred rather more briskly overhead and the colour was flashed into the air above, into the eyes of the men and women who walk in Kew Gardens in July.

The figures of these men and women straggled past the flower-bed with a curiously irregular movement not unlike that of the white and blue butterflies who crossed the turf in zigzag flights from bed to bed. The man was about six inches in front of the woman, strolling carelessly, while she bore on with greater purpose, only turning her head now and then to see that the children were not too far behind. The man kept this distance in front of the woman purposely, though perhaps unconsciously, for he wished to go on with his thoughts.

"Fifteen years ago I came here with Lily," he thought. "We sat somewhere over there by a lake and I begged her to marry me all through the hot afternoon. How the dragon-fly kept circling round us; how clearly I see the dragon-fly and her shoe with the square silver buckle at the toe. All the time I spoke I saw her shoe and when it moved impatiently I knew without looking up what she was going to say: the whole of her seemed to be in her shoe. And my love, my desire, were in the dragon-fly; for some reason I thought that if it settled there, on that leaf, the broad one with the red flower in the middle of it, if the dragon-fly settled on the leaf she would say 'Yes' at once. But the dragon-fly went round and round: it never settled anywhere – of course not, happily not, or I shouldn't be walking here with Eleanor and the children – Tell me, Eleanor. D'you ever think of the past?"

"Why do you ask, Simon?"

"Because I've been thinking of the past. I've been thinking of Lily, the woman I might have married . . . Well, why are you silent? Do you mind my thinking of the past?"

"Why should I mind, Simon? Doesn't one always think of the past, in a garden with men and women lying under the trees? Aren't they one's past, all that remains of it, those men and women, those ghosts lying under the trees, . . . one's happiness, one's reality?"

"For me, a square silver shoe-buckle and a dragon-fly –"

"For me, a kiss. Imagine six little girls sitting before their easels twenty years ago, down by the side of a lake, painting the water-lilies, the first red water-lilies I'd ever seen. And suddenly a kiss, there on the back of my neck. And my hand shook all the afternoon so that I couldn't paint. I took out my watch and marked the hour when I would allow myself to think of the kiss for five minutes only – it was so precious – the kiss of an old grey-haired woman with a wart on her nose, the mother of all my kisses all my life. Come Caroline, come Hubert."

They walked on past the flower-bed, now walking four abreast, and soon diminished in size among the trees and looked half transparent as the sunlight and shade swam over their backs in large trembling irregular patches.

In the oval flower-bed the snail whose shell had been stained red, blue, and yellow for the space of two minutes or so, now appeared to be moving very slightly in its shell, and next began to labour over the crumbs of loose earth which broke away and rolled down as it passed over them. It appeared to have a definite goal in front of it, differing in this respect from the singular high-stepping angular green insect who attempted to cross in front of it, and waited for a second with its antennae trembling as if in deliberation, and then stepped off as rapidly and strangely in the opposite direction.

Brown cliffs with deep green lakes in the hollows, flat blade-like trees that waved from root to tip, round boulders of grey stone, vast crumpled surfaces of a thin crackling texture – all these objects lay across the snail's progress between one stalk and another to his goal. Before he had decided whether to circumvent the arched tent of a dead leaf or to breast it there came past the bed the feet of other human beings.

This time they were both men. The younger of the two wore an expression of perhaps unnatural calm; he raised his eyes and fixed them very steadily in front of him while his companion spoke, and directly his companion had done speaking he looked on the ground again and sometimes opened his lips only after a long pause and sometimes did not open them at all. The elder man had a curiously uneven and shaky method of walking, jerking his hand forward and throwing up his head abruptly, rather in the manner of an impatient carriage horse tired of waiting outside a house; but in the man these gestures were irresolute and pointless. He talked almost incessantly; he smiled to himself, and again began to talk, as if the smile had been an answer.

He was talking about spirits – the spirits of the dead, who, according to him, were even now telling him all sorts of odd things about their experiences in Heaven.

"Heaven was known to the ancients as Thessaly, William, and now, with this war, the spirit matter is rolling between the hills like thunder." He paused, seemed to listen, smiled, jerked his head and continued: –

"You have a small electric battery and a piece of rubber to insulate the wire – isolate? – insulate? – well, we'll skip the details, no good going into details that wouldn't be understood – and in short the little machine stands in any convenient position by the head of the bed, we will say, on a neat mahogany stand. All arrangements being properly fixed by workmen under my direction, the widow applies her ear and summons the spirit by sign as agreed, Women! Widows! Women in black – "

Here he seemed to have caught sight of a woman's dress in the distance, which in the shade looked a purple black. He took off his hat, placed his hand upon his heart, and hurried towards her muttering and gesticulating feverishly.

But William caught him by the sleeve and touched a flower with the tip of his walking-stick in order to divert the old man's attention. After looking at it for a moment in some confusion the old man bent his ear to it and seemed to answer a voice speaking from it, for he began talking about the forests of Uruguay which he had visited hundreds of years ago in company with the most beautiful young woman in Europe. He could be heard murmuring about forests of Uruguay blanketed with the wax petals of tropical roses, nightingales, sea beaches, mermaids, and women drowned at sea, as he suffered himself to be moved on by William, upon whose face the look of stoical patience grew slowly deeper and deeper.

Following his steps so closely as to be slightly puzzled by his gestures came two elderly women of the lower middle class, one stout and ponderous, the other rosy-cheeked and nimble. Like most people of their station they were frankly fascinated by any signs of eccentricity betokening a disordered brain, especially in the well-to-do; but they were too far off to be certain whether the gestures were merely eccentric or genuinely mad. After they had scrutinised the old man's back in silence for a moment and given each other a queer, sly look, they went on energetically piecing together their very complicated dialogue:

"Nell, Bert, Lot, Cess, Phil, Pa, he says, I says, she says, I says, I says, I says —"

"My Bert, Sis, Bill, Grandad, the old man, sugar,

Sugar, flour, kippers, greens,

Sugar, sugar, sugar."

The ponderous woman looked through the pattern of falling words at the flowers standing cool, firm and upright in the earth, with a curious expression. She saw them as a sleeper waking from a heavy sleep sees a brass candlestick reflecting the light in an unfamiliar way, and closes his eyes and opens them, and seeing the brass candlestick again, finally starts wide awake and stares at the candlestick with all his powers. So the heavy woman came to a standstill opposite the oval-shaped flower-bed, and ceased even to pretend to listen to what the other woman was saying. She stood there letting the words fall over her, swaying the top part of her body slowly backwards and forwards, looking at the flowers. Then she suggested that they should find a seat and have their tea.

The snail had now considered every possible method of reaching his goal without going round the dead leaf or climbing over it. Let alone the effort needed for climbing a leaf, he was doubtful whether the thin texture which vibrated with such an alarming crackle when touched even by the tip of his horns would bear his weight; and this determined him finally to creep beneath it, for there was a point where the leaf curved high enough from the ground to admit him. He had just inserted his head in the opening and was taking stock of the high brown roof and was getting used to the cool brown light when two other people came past outside on the turf. This time they were both young, a young man and a young woman. They were both in the prime of youth, or even in that season which precedes the prime of youth, the season before the smooth pink folds of the flowers have burst their gummy case, when the wings of the butterfly, though fully grown, are motionless in the sun.

"Lucky it isn't Friday," he observed.

"Why? D'you believe in luck?"

"They make you pay sixpence on Friday."

"What's sixpence anyway? Isn't it worth sixpence?"

"What's 'it' – what do you mean by 'it'?"

"O, anything – I mean – you know what I mean."

Long pauses came between each of these remarks; they were uttered in toneless and monotonous voices. The couple stood still on the edge of the flower-bed, and together pressed the end of her parasol deep down into the soft earth.

The action and the fact that his hand rested on the top of hers expressed their feelings in a strange way, as these short insignificant words also expressed something, words with short wings for their heavy body of meaning, inadequate to carry them far and thus alighting awkwardly upon the very common objects that surrounded them, and were to their inexperienced touch so massive; but who knows (so they thought as they pressed the parasol into the earth) what precipices aren't concealed in them, or what ridges of ice don't shine in the sun on the other side? Who knows? Who has ever seen this before? Even when she wondered what sort of tea they gave you at Kew, he felt that something loomed up behind her words and stood vast and solid behind them; and the mist very slowly rose and uncovered – O heavens! – what were those shapes? – little white tables, and waitresses who looked first at her and then at him; and there was a bill that he would pay with a real two shilling piece, and it was real, all real, he assured himself, fingering the coin in his pocket, real to everyone except to him and to her; even to him it began to seem real; and then – but it was too exciting to stand and think any longer, and he pulled the parasol out of the earth with a jerk and was impatient to find the place where one had tea with other people, like other people.

"Come along, Trissie; it's time we had our tea."

"Wherever *does* one have one's tea?" she asked with the oddest thrill of excitement in her voice, looking vaguely round and letting herself be drawn on down the grass path, trailing her parasol, turning her head this way and that way, forgetting her tea, wishing to go down there and then down there, remembering orchids and cranes among wild flowers, a Chinese pagoda and a crimson-crested bird; but he bore her on.

Thus one couple after another with much the same irregular and aimless movement passed the flower-bed and were enveloped in layer after layer of green-blue vapour, in which at first their bodies had substance and a dash of colour, but later both substance and colour dissolved in the green-blue atmosphere. How hot it was! So hot that even the thrush chose to hop, like a mechanical bird, in the shadow of the flowers, with long pauses between one movement and the next; instead of rambling vaguely the white butterflies danced one above another, making with their white shifting flakes the outline of a shattered marble column above the tallest flowers; the glass roofs of the palm house shone as if a whole market full of shiny green umbrellas had opened in the sun; and in the drone of the aeroplane the voice of the summer sky murmured its fierce soul.

Yellow and black, pink and snow white, shapes of all these colours, men, women, and children were spotted for a second upon the horizon, and then, seeing the breadth of yellow that lay upon the grass, they wavered and sought shade beneath the trees, dissolving like drops of water in the yellow and green atmosphere, staining it faintly with red and blue. It seemed as if all gross and heavy bodies had sunk down in the heat motionless and lay huddled upon the ground, but their voices went wavering from them as if they were flames lolling from the thick waxen bodies of candles. Voices, yes, voices, wordless voices, breaking the silence suddenly with such depth of contentment, such passion of desire, or, in the voices of children, such freshness of surprise; breaking the silence? But there was no silence; all the time the motor omnibuses were turning their wheels and changing their gear; like a vast nest of Chinese boxes all of wrought steel turning ceaselessly one within another the city murmured; on the top of which the voices cried aloud and the petals of myriads of flowers flashed their colours into the air.

KATHERINE MANSFIELD

THE GARDEN-PARTY

AND AFTER ALL the weather was ideal. They could not have had a more perfect day for a garden-party if they had ordered it. Windless, warm, the sky without a cloud. Only the blue was veiled with a haze of light gold, as it is sometimes in early summer. The gardener had been up since dawn, mowing the lawns and sweeping them, until the grass and the dark flat rosettes where the daisy plants had been seemed to shine. As for the roses, you could not help feeling they understood that roses are the only flowers that impress people at garden-parties; the only flowers that everybody is certain of knowing. Hundreds, yes, literally hundreds, had come out in a single night; the green bushes bowed down as though they had been visited by archangels.

Breakfast was not yet over before the men came to put up the marquee.

"Where do you want the marquee put, mother?"

"My dear child, it's no use asking me. I'm determined to leave everything to you children this year. Forget I am your mother. Treat me as an honoured guest."

But Meg could not possibly go and supervise the men. She had washed her hair before breakfast, and she sat drinking her coffee in a green turban, with a dark wet curl stamped on each cheek. Jose, the butterfly, always came down in a silk petticoat and a kimono jacket.

"You'll have to go, Laura; you're the artistic one."

Away Laura flew, still holding her piece of bread-and-butter. It's so delicious to have an excuse for eating out of doors, and besides, she loved having to arrange things; she always felt she could do it so much better than anybody else.

Four men in their shirt-sleeves stood grouped together on the garden path. They carried staves covered with rolls of canvas, and they had big tool-bags slung on their backs. They looked impressive. Laura wished now that she had not got the bread-and-butter, but there was nowhere to put it, and she couldn't possibly throw it away. She blushed and tried to look severe and even a little bit short-sighted as she came up to them.

"Good morning," she said, copying her mother's voice. But that sounded so fearfully affected that she was ashamed, and stammered like a little girl, "Oh – er – have you come – is it about the marquee?"

"That's right, miss," said the tallest of the men, a lanky, freckled fellow, and he shifted his tool-bag, knocked back his straw hat and smiled down at her. "That's about it."

His smile was so easy, so friendly that Laura recovered. What nice eyes he had, small, but such a dark blue! And now she looked at the others, they were smiling too. "Cheer up, we won't bite," their smile seemed to say. How very nice workmen were! And what a beautiful morning! She mustn't mention the morning; she must be business-like. The marquee.

"Well, what about the lily-lawn? Would that do?"

And she pointed to the lily-lawn with the hand that didn't hold the bread-and-butter. They turned, they stared in the direction. A little fat chap thrust out his under-lip, and the tall fellow frowned.

"I don't fancy it," said he. "Not conspicuous enough. You see, with a thing like a marquee," and he turned to Laura in his easy way, "you want to put it somewhere where it'll give you a bang slap in the eye, if you follow me."

Laura's upbringing made her wonder for a moment whether it was quite respectful of a workman to talk to her of bangs slap in the eye. But she did quite follow him.

"A corner of the tennis-court," she suggested. "But the band's going to be in one corner."

"H'm, going to have a band, are you?" said another of the workmen. He was pale. He had a haggard look as his dark eyes scanned the tennis-court. What was he thinking?

"Only a very small band," said Laura gently. Perhaps he wouldn't mind so much if the band was quite small. But the tall fellow interrupted.

"Look here, miss, that's the place. Against those trees. Over there. That'll do fine."

Against the karakas. Then the karaka-trees would be hidden. And they were so lovely, with their broad, gleaming leaves, and their clusters of yellow fruit. They were like trees you imagined growing on a desert island, proud, solitary, lifting their leaves and fruits to the sun in a kind of silent splendour. Must they be hidden by a marquee?

They must. Already the men had shouldered their staves and were making for the place. Only the tall fellow was left. He bent down, pinched a sprig of lavender, put his thumb and forefinger to his nose and snuffed up the smell. When Laura saw that gesture she forgot all about the karakas in her wonder at him caring for things like that – caring for the smell of lavender. How many men that she knew would have done such a thing? Oh, how extraordinarily nice workmen were, she thought. Why couldn't she have workmen for her friends rather than the silly boys she danced with and who came to Sunday night supper? She would get on much better with men like these.

129

It's all the fault, she decided, as the tall fellow drew something on the back of an envelope, something that was to be looped up or left to hang, of these absurd class distinctions. Well, for her part, she didn't feel them. Not a bit, not an atom . . . And now there came the chock-chock of wooden hammers. Someone whistled, someone sang out, "Are you right there, matey?" "Matey!" The friendliness of it, the – the – Just to prove how happy she was, just to show the tall fellow how at home she felt, and how she despised stupid conventions, Laura took a big bite of her bread-and-butter as she stared at the little drawing. She felt just like a work-girl.

"Laura, Laura, where are you? Telephone, Laura!" a voice cried from the house.

"Coming!" Away she skimmed, over the lawn, up the path, up the steps, across the veranda, and into the porch. In the hall her father and Laurie were brushing their hats ready to go to the office.

"I say, Laura," said Laurie very fast, "you might just give a squiz at my coat before this afternoon. See if it wants pressing."

"I will," said she. Suddenly she couldn't stop herself. She ran at Laurie and gave him a small, quick squeeze. "Oh, I do love parties, don't you?" gasped Laura.

"Ra-ther," said Laurie's warm, boyish voice, and he squeezed his sister too, and gave her a gentle push. "Dash off to the telephone, old girl."

The telephone. "Yes; yes; oh yes. Kitty? Good morning, dear. Come to lunch? Do, dear. Delighted of course. It will only be a very scratch meal – just the sandwich crusts and broken meringue-shells and what's left over. Yes, isn't it a perfect morning? Your white? Oh, I certainly should. One moment – hold the line. Mother's calling." And Laura sat back. "What, mother? Can't hear."

Mrs. Sheridan's voice floated down the stairs. "Tell her to wear that sweet hat she had on last Sunday."

"Mother says you're to wear that sweet hat you had on last Sunday. Good. One o'clock. Bye-bye."

Laura put back the receiver, flung her arms over her head, took a deep breath, stretched and let them fall. "Huh," she sighed, and the moment after the sigh she sat up quickly. She was still, listening. All the doors in the house seemed to be open. The house was alive with soft, quick steps and running voices. The green baize door that led to the kitchen regions swung open and shut with a muffled thud. And now there came a long, chuckling absurd sound. It was the heavy piano being moved on its stiff castors. But the air! If you stopped to notice, was the air always like this? Little faint winds were playing chase, in at the tops of the windows, out at the doors. And there were two tiny spots of sun, one on the inkpot, one on a silver photograph frame, playing too. Darling little spots. Especially the one on the inkpot lid. It was quite warm. A warm little silver star. She could have kissed it.

The front door bell pealed, and there sounded the rustle of Sadie's print skirt on the stairs. A man's voice murmured; Sadie answered, careless, "I'm sure I don't know. Wait. I'll ask Mrs. Sheridan."

"What is it, Sadie?" Laura came into the hall.

"It's the florist, Miss Laura."

It was, indeed. There, just inside the door, stood a wide, shallow tray full of pots of pink lilies. No other kind. Nothing but lilies – canna lilies, big pink flowers, wide open, radiant, almost frighteningly alive on bright crimson stems.

"O-oh, Sadie!" said Laura, and the sound was like a little moan. She crouched down as if to warm herself at that blaze of lilies; she felt they were in her fingers, on her lips, growing in her breast.

"It's some mistake," she said faintly. "Nobody ever ordered so many. Sadie, go and find mother."

But at that moment Mrs. Sheridan joined them.

"It's quite right," she said calmly. "Yes, I ordered them. Aren't they lovely?" She pressed Laura's arm. "I was passing the shop yesterday, and I saw them in the window. And I suddenly thought for once in my life I shall have enough canna lilies. The garden-party will be a good excuse."

"But I thought you said you didn't mean to interfere," said Laura. Sadie had gone. The florist's man was still outside at his van. She put her arm round her mother's neck and gently, very gently, she bit her mother's ear.

"My darling child, you wouldn't like a logical mother, would you? Don't do that. Here's the man."

He carried more lilies still, another whole tray.

"Bank them up, just inside the door, on both sides of the porch, please," said Mrs. Sheridan. "Don't you agree, Laura?"

"Oh, I *do*, mother."

In the drawing-room Meg, Jose and good little Hans had at last succeeded in moving the piano.

"Now, if we put this chesterfield against the wall and move everything out of the room except the chairs, don't you think?"

"Quite."

"Hans, move these tables into the smoking-room, and bring a sweeper to take these marks off the carpet and – one moment, Hans –" Jose loved giving orders to the servants, and they loved obeying her. She always made them feel they were taking part in some drama. "Tell mother and Miss Laura to come here at once."

"Very good, Miss Jose."

She turned to Meg. "I want to hear what the piano sounds like, just in case I'm asked to sing this afternoon. Let's try over 'This Life is Weary'."

Pom! Ta-ta-ta *Tee*-ta! The piano burst out so passionately that Jose's face changed. She clasped her hands. She looked mournfully and enigmatically at her mother and Laura as they came in.

> This Life is *Wee*-ary,
> A Tear – a Sigh.
> A Love that *Chan*-ges,
> This Life is *Wee*-ary,
> A Tear – a Sigh.
> A Love that *Chan*-ges,
> And then . . . Goodbye!

But at the word "Goodbye," and although the piano sounded more desperate than ever, her face broke into a brilliant, dreadfully unsympathetic smile.

"Aren't I in good voice, mummy?" she beamed.

> This Life is *Wee*-ary,
> Hope comes to Die.
> A Dream – a *Wa*-kening.

But now Sadie interrupted them. "What is it, Sadie?"

"If you please, m'm, cook says have you got the flags for the sandwiches?"

"The flags for the sandwiches, Sadie?" echoed Mrs. Sheridan dreamily. And the children knew by her face that she hadn't got them. "Let me see." And she said to Sadie firmly, "Tell cook I'll let her have them in ten minutes."

Sadie went.

"Now, Laura," said her mother quickly, "come with me

133

into the smoking-room. I've got the names somewhere on the back of an envelope. You'll have to write them out for me. Meg, go upstairs this minute and take that wet thing off your head. Jose, run and finish dressing this instant. Do you hear me, children, or shall I have to tell your father when he comes home tonight? And – and, Jose, pacify cook if you do go into the kitchen, will you? I'm terrified of her this morning."

The envelope was found at last behind the dining-room clock, though how it had got there Mrs. Sheridan could not imagine.

"One of you children must have stolen it out of my bag, because I remember vividly – cream cheese and lemon-curd. Have you done that?"

"Yes."

"Egg and –" Mrs. Sheridan held the envelope away from her. "It looks like mice. It can't be mice, can it?"

"Olive, pet," said Laura, looking over her shoulder.

"Yes, of course, olive. What a horrible combination it sounds. Egg and olive."

They were finished at last, and Laura took them off to the kitchen. She found Jose there pacifying the cook, who did not look at all terrifying.

"I have never seen such exquisite sandwiches," said Jose's rapturous voice. "How many kinds did you say there were, cook? Fifteen?"

"Fifteen, Miss Jose."

"Well, cook, I congratulate you."

Cook swept up crusts with the long sandwich knife, and smiled broadly.

"Godber's has come," announced Sadie, issuing out of the pantry. She had seen the man pass the window.

That meant the cream puffs had come. Godber's were

famous for their cream puffs. Nobody ever thought of making them at home.

"Bring them in and put them on the table, my girl," ordered cook.

Sadie brought them in and went back to the door. Of course Laura and Jose were far too grown-up to really care about such things. All the same, they couldn't help agreeing that the puffs looked very attractive. Very. Cook began arranging them, shaking off the extra icing sugar.

"Don't they carry one back to all one's parties?" said Laura.

"I suppose they do," said practical Jose, who never liked to be carried back. "They look beautifully light and feathery, I must say."

"Have one each, my dears," said cook in her comfortable voice. "Yer ma won't know."

Oh, impossible. Fancy cream puffs so soon after breakfast. The very idea made one shudder. All the same, two minutes later Jose and Laura were licking their fingers with that absorbed inward look that only comes from whipped cream.

"Let's go into the garden, out by the back way," suggested Laura. "I want to see how the men are getting on with the marquee. They're such awfully nice men."

But the back door was blocked by cook, Sadie, Godber's man and Hans.

Something had happened.

"Tuk-tuk-tuk," clucked cook like an agitated hen. Sadie had her hand clapped to her cheek as though she had tooth-ache. Hans's face was screwed up in the effort to understand. Only Godber's man seemed to be enjoying himself; it was his story.

"What's the matter? What's happened?"

"There's been a horrible accident," said cook. "A man killed."

"A man killed! Where? How? When?"

But Godber's man wasn't going to have his story snatched from under his very nose.

"Know those little cottages just below here, miss?" Know them? Of course, she knew them. "Well, there's a young chap living there, name of Scott, a carter. His horse shied at a traction-engine, corner of Hawke Street this morning, and he was thrown out on the back of his head. Killed."

"Dead!" Laura stared at Godber's man.

"Dead when they picked him up," said Gober's man with relish. "They were taking the body home as I come up here." And he said to the cook, "He's left a wife and five little ones."

"Jose, come here." Laura caught hold of her sister's sleeve and dragged her through the kitchen to the other side of the green baize door. There she paused and leaned against it. "Jose!" she said, horrified, "however are we going to stop everything?"

"Stop everything, Laura!" cried Jose in astonishment. "What do you mean?"

"Stop the garden-party, of course." Why did Jose pretend?

But Jose was still more amazed. "Stop the garden-party? My dear Laura, don't be so absurd. Of course we can't do anything of the kind. Nobody expects us to. Don't be so extravagant."

"But we can't possibly have a garden-party with a man dead just outside the front gate."

That really was extravagant, for the little cottages were in a lane to themselves at the very bottom of a steep rise that led up to the house. A broad road ran between. True, they were far too near. They were the greatest possible eyesore, and they had no right to be in that neighbourhood at all. They were little mean dwellings painted a chocolate brown. In the garden patches there was nothing but cabbage stalks, sick hens and tomato cans. The very smoke coming out of their chimneys was poverty-stricken. Little rags and shreds of smoke, so unlike the great silvery plumes that uncurled from the Sheridans' chimneys. Washerwomen lived in the lane and sweeps and a cobbler, and a man whose house-front was studded all over with minute bird-cages. Children swarmed. When the Sheridans were little they were forbidden to set foot there because of the revolting language and of what they might catch. But since they were grown up, Laura and Laurie on their prowls sometimes walked through. It was disgusting and sordid. They came out with a shudder. But still one must go everywhere; one must see everything. So through they went.

"And just think of what the band would sound like to that poor woman," said Laura.

"Oh, Laura!" Jose began to be seriously annoyed. "If you're going to stop a band playing every time someone has an accident, you'll lead a very strenuous life. I'm every bit as sorry about it as you. I feel just as sympathetic." Her eyes hardened. She looked at her sister just as she used to when they were little and fighting together. "You won't bring a drunken workman back to life by being sentimental," she said softly.

"Drunk! Who said he was drunk?" Laura turned furiously on Jose. She said, just as they had used to say on those occasions, "I'm going straight up to tell mother."

"Do, dear," cooed Jose.

"Mother, can I come into your room?" Laura turned the big glass door-knob.

"Of course, child. Why, what's the matter? What's given you such a colour?" And Mrs. Sheridan turned round from her dressing-table. She was trying on a new hat.

"Mother, a man's been killed," began Laura.

"Not in the garden?" interrupted her mother.

"No, no!"

"Oh, what a fright you gave me!" Mrs. Sheridan sighed with relief, and took off the big hat and held it on her knees.

"But listen, mother," said Laura. Breathless, half-choking, she told the dreadful story. "Of course, we can't have our party, can we?" she pleaded. "The band and everybody arriving. They'd hear us, mother; they're nearly neighbours!"

To Laura's astonishment her mother behaved just like Jose; it was harder to bear because she seemed amused. She refused to take Laura seriously.

"But, my dear child, use your common sense. It's only by accident we've heard of it. If someone had died there normally – and I can't understand how they keep alive in those poky little holes – we should still be having our party, shouldn't we?"

Laura had to say "yes" to that, but she felt it was all wrong. She sat down on her mother's sofa and pinched the cushion frill.

"Mother, isn't it terribly heartless of us?" she asked.

"Darling!" Mrs. Sheridan got up and came over to her, carrying the hat. Before Laura could stop her she had popped it on. "My child!" said her mother, "the hat is yours. It's made for you. It's much too young for me. I have never seen you look such a picture. Look at yourself!" And she held up her hand-mirror.

"But, mother," Laura began again. She couldn't look at herself; she turned aside.

This time Mrs. Sheridan lost patience just as Jose had done.

"You are being very absurd, Laura," she said coldly. "People like that don't expect sacrifices from us. And it's not very sympathetic to spoil everybody's enjoyment as you're doing now."

"I don't understand," said Laura, and she walked quickly out of the room into her own bedroom. There, quite by chance, the first thing she saw was this charming girl in the mirror, in her black hat trimmed with gold daisies, and a long black velvet ribbon. Never had she imagined she could look like that. Is mother right? she thought. And now she hoped her mother was right. Am I being extravagant? Perhaps it was extravagant. Just for a moment she had another glimpse of that poor woman and those little children, and the body being carried into the house. But it all seemed blurred, unreal, like a picture in the newspaper. I'll remember it again after the party's over, she decided. And somehow that seemed quite the best plan . . .

Lunch was over by half-past one. By half-past two they were all ready for the fray. The green-coated band had arrived and was established in a corner of the tennis-court.

"My dear!" trilled Kitty Maitland, "aren't they too like frogs for words? You ought to have arranged them round the pond with the conductor in the middle on a leaf."

Laurie arrived and hailed them on his way to dress. At the sight of him Laura remembered the accident again. She wanted to tell him. If Laurie agreed with the others, then it was bound to be all right. And she followed him into the hall.

"Laurie!"

"Hallo!" He was half-way upstairs, but when he turned round and saw Laura he suddenly puffed out his cheeks and goggled his eyes at her. "My word, Laura! You do look stunning," said Laurie. "What an absolutely topping hat!"

Laura said faintly "Is it?" and smiled up at Laurie, and didn't tell him after all.

Soon after that people began coming in streams. The band struck up; the hired waiters ran from the house to the marquee. Wherever you looked there were couples strolling, bending to the flowers, greeting, moving on over the lawn. They were like bright birds that had alighted in the Sheridans' garden for this one afternoon, on their way to – where? Ah, what happiness it is to be with people who all are happy, to press hands, press cheeks, smile into eyes.

"Darling Laura, how well you look!"

"What a becoming hat, child!"

"Laura, you look quite Spanish. I've never seen you look so striking."

And Laura, glowing, answered softly, "Have you had tea? Won't you have an ice? The passion-fruit ices really are rather special." She ran to her father and begged him. "Daddy darling, can't the band have something to drink?"

And the perfect afternoon slowly ripened, slowly faded, slowly its petals closed.

"Never a more delightful garden-party . . ." "The greatest success . . ." "Quite the most . . ."

Laura helped her mother with the goodbyes. They stood side by side in the porch till it was all over.

"All over, all over, thank heaven," said Mrs. Sheridan. "Round up the others, Laura. Let's go and have some fresh coffee. I'm exhausted. Yes, it's been very successful. But oh, these parties, these parties! Why will you children insist on giving parties!" And they all of them sat down in the deserted marquee.

"Have a sandwich, daddy dear. I wrote the flag."

"Thanks." Mr. Sheridan took a bite and the sandwich was gone. He took another. "I suppose you didn't hear of a beastly accident that happened today?" he said.

"My dear," said Mrs. Sheridan, holding up her hand, "we

did. It nearly ruined the party. Laura insisted we should put it off."

"Oh, mother!" Laura didn't want to be teased about it.

"It was a horrible affair all the same," said Mr. Sheridan. "The chap was married too. Lived just below in the lane, and leaves a wife and half a dozen kiddies, so they say."

An awkward little silence fell. Mrs. Sheridan fidgeted with her cup. Really, it was very tactless of father . . .

Suddenly she looked up. There on the table were all those sandwiches, cakes, puffs, all uneaten, all going to be wasted. She had one of her brilliant ideas.

"I know," she said. "Let's make up a basket. Let's send that poor creature some of this perfectly good food. At any rate, it will be the greatest treat for the children. Don't you agree? And she's sure to have neighbours calling in and so on. What a point to have it all ready prepared. Laura!" She jumped up. "Get me the big basket out of the stairs cupboard."

"But, mother, do you really think it's a good idea?" said Laura.

Again, how curious, she seemed to be different from them all. To take scraps from their party. Would the poor woman really like that?

"Of course! What's the matter with you today? An hour or two ago you were insisting on us being sympathetic, and now –"

Oh well! Laura ran for the basket. It was filled, it was heaped by her mother.

"Take it yourself, darling," said she. "Run down just as you are. No, wait, take the arum lilies too. People of that class are so impressed by arum lilies."

"The stems will ruin her lace frock," said practical Jose.

So they would. Just in time. "Only the basket, then. And,

Laura!" – her mother followed her out of the marquee – "don't on any account –"

"What mother?"

No, better not put such ideas into the child's head! "Nothing! Run along."

It was just growing dusky as Laura shut their garden gates. A big dog ran by like a shadow. The road gleamed white, and down below in the hollow the little cottages were in deep shade. How quiet it seemed after the afternoon. Here she was going down the hill to somewhere where a man lay dead, and she couldn't realise it. Why couldn't she? She stopped a minute. And it seemed to her that kisses, voices, tinkling spoons, laughter, the smell of crushed grass were somehow inside her. She had no room for anything else. How strange! She looked up at the pale sky, and all she thought was, "Yes, it was the most successful party."

Now the broad road was crossed. The lane began, smoky and dark. Women in shawls and men's tweed caps hurried by. Men hung over the palings; the children played in the doorways. A low hum came from the mean little cottages. In some of them there was a flicker of light, and a shadow, crab-like, moved across the window. Laura bent her head and hurried on. She wished now she had put on a coat. How her frock shone! And the big hat with the velvet streamer – if only it was another hat! Were the people looking at her? They must be. It was a mistake to have come; she knew all along it was a mistake. Should she go back even now?

No, too late. This was the house. It must be. A dark knot of people stood outside. Beside the gate an old, old woman with a crutch sat in a chair, watching. She had her feet on a newspaper. The voices stopped as Laura drew near. The group parted. It was as though she was expected, as though they had known she was coming here.

Laura was terribly nervous. Tossing the velvet ribbon over her shoulder, she said to a woman standing by, "Is this Mrs. Scott's house?" and the woman, smiling queerly, said, "It is, my lass."

Oh, to be away from this! She actually said, "Help me, God," as she walked up the tiny path and knocked. To be away from those staring eyes, or to be covered up in anything, one of those women's shawls even. I'll just leave the basket and go, she decided. I shan't even wait for it to be emptied.

Then the door opened. A little woman in black showed in the gloom.

Laura said, "Are you Mrs. Scott?" But to her horror the woman answered, "Walk in please, miss," and she was shut in the passage.

"No," said Laura, "I don't want to come in. I only want to leave this basket. Mother sent –"

The little woman in the gloomy passage seemed not to have heard her. "Step this way, please, miss," she said in an oily voice, and Laura followed her.

She found herself in a wretched little low kitchen, lighted by a smoky lamp. There was a woman sitting before the fire.

"Em," said the little creature who had let her in. "Em! It's a young lady." She turned to Laura. She said meaningly, "I'm 'er sister, miss. You'll excuse 'er, won't you?"

"Oh, but of course!" said Laura. "Please, please don't disturb her. I – I only want to leave –"

But at that moment the woman at the fire turned round. Her face, puffed up, red, with swollen eyes and swollen lips, looked terrible. She seemed as though she couldn't understand why Laura was there. What did it mean? Why was this stranger standing in the kitchen with a basket? What was it all about? And the poor face puckered up again.

"All right, my dear," said the other. "I'll thenk the young lady."

And again she began, "You'll excuse her, miss, I'm sure," and her face, swollen too, tried an oily smile.

Laura only wanted to get out, to get away. She was back in the passage. The door opened. She walked straight through into the bedroom, where the dead man was lying.

"You'd like a look at 'im, wouldn't you?" said Em's sister, and she brushed past Laura over to the bed. "Don't be afraid, my lass," – and now her voice sounded fond and sly, and fondly she drew down the sheet – "'e looks a picture. There's nothing to show. Come along, my dear."

Laura came.

There lay a young man, fast asleep – sleeping so soundly, so deeply, that he was far, far away from them both. Oh, so remote, so peaceful. He was dreaming. Never wake him up again. His head was sunk in the pillow, his eyes were closed; they were blind under the closed eyelids. He was given up to his dream. What did garden-parties and baskets and lace frocks matter to him? He was far from all those things. He was wonderful, beautiful. While they were laughing and while the band was playing, this marvel had come to the lane. Happy . . . happy . . . All is well, said that sleeping face. This is just as it should be. I am content.

But all the same you had to cry, and she couldn't go out of the room without saying something to him. Laura gave a loud childish sob.

"Forgive my hat," she said.

And this time she didn't wait for Em's sister. She found her way out of the door, down the path, past all those dark people. At the corner of the lane she met Laurie.

He stepped out of the shadow. "Is that you, Laura?"

"Yes."

"Mother was getting anxious. Was it all right?"

"Yes, quite. Oh, Laurie!" She took his arm, she pressed up against him.

"I say, you're not crying, are you?" asked her brother.

Laura shook her head. She was.

Laurie put his arm round her shoulder. "Don't cry," he said in his warm, loving voice. "Was it awful?"

"No," sobbed Laura. "It was simply marvellous. But Laurie –" She stopped, she looked at her brother. "Isn't life," she stammered, "isn't life –" But what life was she couldn't explain. No matter. He quite understood.

"*Isn't* it, darling?" said Laurie.

D. H. LAWRENCE

THE SHADOW IN THE ROSE GARDEN

A RATHER SMALL young man sat by the window of a pretty seaside cottage trying to persuade himself that he was reading the newspaper. It was about half-past eight in the morning. Outside, the glory roses hung in the morning sunshine like little bowls of fire tipped up. The young man looked at the table, then at the clock, then at his own big silver watch. An expression of stiff endurance came on to his face. Then he rose and reflected on the oil-paintings that hung on the walls of the room, giving careful but hostile attention to "The Stag at Bay". He tried the lid of the piano, and found it locked. He caught sight of his own face in a little mirror, pulled his brown moustache, and an alert interest sprang into his eyes. He was not ill-favoured. He twisted his moustache. His figure was rather small, but alert and vigorous. As he turned from the mirror a look of self-commiseration mingled with his appreciation of his own physiognomy.

In a state of self-suppression, he went through into the garden. His jacket, however, did not look dejected. It was new, and had a smart and self-confident air, sitting upon a confident body. He contemplated the Tree of Heaven that flourished by the lawn, then sauntered on to the next plant. There was more promise in a crooked apple tree covered with brown-red fruit. Glancing round, he broke off an apple and, with his back to the house, took a clean, sharp bite. To his surprise the fruit was sweet. He took another. Then again he turned to survey the bedroom windows overlooking

149

the garden. He started, seeing a woman's figure; but it was only his wife. She was gazing across to the sea, apparently ignorant of him.

For a moment or two he looked at her, watching her. She was a good-looking woman, who seemed older than he, rather pale, but healthy, her face yearning. Her rich auburn hair was heaped in folds on her forehead. She looked apart from him and his world, gazing away to the sea. It irked her husband that she should continue abstracted and in ignorance of him; he pulled poppy fruits and threw them at the window. She started, glanced at him with a wild smile, and looked away again. Then almost immediately she left the window. He went indoors to meet her.

She had a fine carriage, very proud, and wore a dress of soft white muslin.

"I've been waiting long enough," he said.

"For me or for breakfast?" she said lightly. "You know we said nine o'clock. I should have thought you could have slept after the journey."

"You know I'm always up at *five*, and I couldn't stop in bed after six. You might as well be in pit as in bed, on a morning like this."

"I shouldn't have thought the pit would occur to you, here."

She moved about examining the room, looking at the ornaments under glass covers. He, planted on the hearth-rug, watched her rather uneasily, and grudgingly indulgent. She shrugged her shoulders at the apartment.

"Come," she said, taking his arm, "let us go into the garden till Mrs. Coates brings the tray."

"I hope she'll be quick," he said, pulling his moustache. She gave a short laugh, and leaned on his arm as they went. He had lighted a pipe.

Mrs. Coates entered the room as they went down the steps. The delightful, erect old lady hastened to the window for a good view of her visitors. Her china-blue eyes were bright as she watched the young couple go down the path, he walking in an easy, confident fashion, with his wife on his arm. The landlady began talking to herself in a soft, Yorkshire accent.

"Just of a height they are. She wouldn't ha' married a man less than herself in stature, I think, though he's not her equal otherwise." Here her granddaughter came in, setting a tray on the table. The girl went to the old woman's side.

"He's been eating the apples, Gran'," she said.

"Has he, my pet? Well, if he's happy, why not?"

Outside, the young, well-favoured man listened with impatience to the chink of the tea-cups. At last, with a sigh of relief, the couple came in to breakfast. After he had eaten for some time, he rested a moment and said:

"Do you think it's any better place than Bridlington?"

"I do," she said, "infinitely! Besides, I am at home here – it's not like a strange sea-side place to me."

"How long were you here?"

"Two years."

He ate reflectively.

"I should ha' thought you'd rather go to a fresh place," he said at length.

She sat very silent, and then, delicately, put out a feeler. "Why?" she said. "Do you think I shan't enjoy myself?" He laughed comfortably, putting the marmalade thick on his bread. "I hope so," he said.

She again took no notice of him.

"But don't say anything about it in the village, Frank," she said casually. "Don't say who I am, or that I used to live here. There's nobody I want to meet, particularly, and we should never feel free if they knew me again."

"Why did you come, then?"

"Why? Can't you understand why?"

"Not if you don't want to know anybody."

"I came to see the place, not the people."

He did not say any more.

"Women," she said, "are different from men. I don't know why I wanted to come – but I did."

She helped him to another cup of coffee, solicitously.

"Only," she resumed, "don't talk about me in the village." She laughed shakily. "I don't want my past brought up against me, you know." And she moved the crumbs on the cloth with her finger-tip.

He looked at her as he drank his coffee; he sucked his moustache, and putting down his cup, said phlegmatically:

"I'll bet you've had a lot of past."

She looked with a little guiltiness, that flattered him, down at the table-cloth.

"Well," she said, caressive, "you won't give me away, who I am, will you?"

"No," he said, comforting, laughing, "I won't give you away." He was pleased.

She remained silent. After a moment or two she lifted her head, saying:

"I've got to arrange with Mrs. Coates, and do various things. So you'd better go out by yourself this morning – and we'll be in to dinner at one."

"But you can't be arranging with Mrs. Coates all morning," he said.

"Oh, well – then I've some letters to write, and I must get that mark out of my skirt. I've got plenty of little things to do this morning. You'd better go out by yourself."

He perceived that she wanted to be rid of him, so that

when she went upstairs, he took his hat and lounged out on to the cliffs, suppressedly angry.

Presently she too came out. She wore a hat with roses, and a long lace scarf hung over her white dress. Rather nervously, she put up her sunshade, and her face was half hidden in its coloured shadow. She went along the narrow track of flagstones that were worn hollow by the feet of the fishermen. She seemed to be avoiding her surroundings, as if she remained safe in the little obscurity of her parasol.

She passed the church, and went down the lane till she came to a high wall by the wayside. Under this she went slowly, stopping at length by an open doorway, which shone like a picture of light in the dark wall. There in the magic beyond the doorway, patterns of shadow lay on the sunny court, on the blue and white sea-pebbles of its paving, while a green lawn glowed beyond, where a bay tree glittered at the edges. She tiptoed nervously into the courtyard, glancing at the house that stood in shadow. The uncurtained windows looked black and soulless, the kitchen door stood open. Irresolutely she took a step forward, and again forward, leaning, yearning, towards the garden beyond.

She had almost gained the corner of the house when a heavy step came crunching through the trees. A gardener appeared before her. He held a wicker tray on which were rolling great, dark red gooseberries, over-ripe. He moved slowly.

"The garden isn't open to-day," he said quietly to the attractive woman, who was poised for retreat.

For a moment she was silent with surprise. How should it be public at all?

"When is it open?" she asked, quick-witted.

"The rector lets visitors in on Fridays and Tuesdays."

She stood still, reflecting. How strange to think of the rector opening his garden to the public!

"But everybody will be at church," she said coaxingly to the man. "There'll be nobody here, will there?"

He moved, and the big gooseberries rolled.

"The rector lives at the new rectory," he said.

The two stood still. He did not like to ask her to go. At last she turned to him with a winning smile.

"Might I have *one* peep at the roses?" she coaxed, with pretty wilfulness.

"I don't suppose it would matter," he said, moving aside; "you won't stop long –"

She went forward, forgetting the gardener in a moment. Her face became strained, her movements eager. Glancing round, she saw all the windows giving on to the lawn were curtainless and dark. The house had a sterile appearance, as if it were still used, but not inhabited. A shadow seemed to go over her. She went across the lawn towards the garden, through an arch of crimson ramblers, a gate of colour. There beyond lay the soft blue sea within the bay, misty with morning, and the farthest headland of black rock jutting dimly out between blue and blue of the sky and water. Her face began to shine, transfigured with pain and joy. At her feet the garden fell steeply, all a confusion of flowers, and away below was the darkness of tree-tops covering the beck.

She turned to the garden that shone with sunny flowers around her. She knew the little corner where was the seat beneath the yew tree. Then there was the terrace where a great host of flowers shone, and from this, two paths went down, one at each side of the garden. She closed her sunshade and walked slowly among the many flowers. All round were rose bushes, big banks of roses, then roses hanging and tumbling from pillars, or roses balanced on the standard bushes. By the open earth were many other flowers. If she lifted her head, the sea was upraised beyond, and the Cape.

Slowly she went down one path, lingering, like one who has gone back into the past. Suddenly she was touching some heavy crimson roses that were soft as velvet, touching them thoughtfully, without knowing, as a mother sometimes fondles the hand of her child. She leaned slightly forward to catch the scent. Then she wandered on in abstraction. Sometimes a flame-coloured, scentless rose would hold her arrested. She stood gazing at it as if she could not understand it. Again the same softness of intimacy came over her, as she stood before a tumbling heap of pink petals. Then she wondered over the white rose, that was greenish, like ice, in the centre. So, slowly, like a white, pathetic butterfly, she drifted down the path, coming at last to a tiny terrace all full of roses. They seemed to fill the place, a sunny, gay throng. She was shy of them, they were so many and so bright. They seemed to be conversing and laughing. She felt herself in a strange crowd. It exhilarated her, carried her out of herself. She flushed with excitement. The air was pure scent.

Hastily, she went to a little seat among the white roses, and sat down.

Her scarlet sunshade made a hard blot of colour. She sat quite still, feeling her own existence lapse. She was no more than a rose, a rose that could not quite come into blossom, but remained tense. A little fly dropped on her knee, on her white dress. She watched it, as if it had fallen on a rose. She was not herself.

Then she started cruelly as a shadow crossed her and a figure moved into her sight. It was a man who had come in slippers, unheard. He wore a linen coat. The morning was shattered, the spell vanished away. She was only afraid of being questioned. He came forward. She rose. Then, seeing him, the strength went from her and she sank on the seat again.

He was a young man, military in appearance, growing slightly stout. His black hair was brushed smooth and bright, his moustache was waxed. But there was something rambling in his gait. She looked up, blanched to the lips, and saw his eyes. They were black, and stared without seeing. They were not a man's eyes. He was coming towards her.

He stared at her fixedly, made an unconscious salute, and sat down beside her on the seat. He moved on the bench, shifted his feet, saying, in a gentlemanly, military voice:

"I don't disturb you – do I?"

She was mute and helpless. He was scrupulously dressed in dark clothes and a linen coat. She could not move. Seeing his hands, with the ring she knew so well upon the little finger, she felt as if she were going dazed. The whole world was deranged. She sat unavailing. For his hands, her symbols of passionate love, filled her with horror as they rested now on his strong thighs.

"May I smoke?" he asked intimately, almost secretly, his hand going to his pocket.

She could not answer, but it did not matter, he was in another world. She wondered, craving, if he recognised her – if he could recognise her. She sat pale with anguish. But she had to go through it.

"I haven't got any tobacco," he said thoughtfully.

But she paid no heed to his words, only she attended to him. Could he recognise her, or was it all gone? She sat still in a frozen kind of suspense.

"I smoke John Cotton," he said, "and I must economise with it, it is expensive. You know, I'm not very well off while these law-suits are going on."

"No," she said, and her heart was cold, her soul kept rigid.

He moved, made a loose salute, rose, and went away. She sat motionless. She could see his shape, the shape she had loved with all her passion: his compact, soldier's head, his fine figure now slackened. And it was not he. It only filled her with horror too difficult to know.

Suddenly he came again, his hand in his jacket pocket.

"Do you mind if I smoke?" he said. "Perhaps I shall be able to see things more clearly."

He sat down beside her again, filling a pipe. She watched his hands with the fine strong fingers. They had always inclined to tremble slightly. It had surprised her, long ago, in such a healthy man. Now they moved inaccurately, and the tobacco hung raggedly out of the pipe.

"I have legal business to attend to. Legal affairs are always so uncertain. I tell my solicitor exactly, precisely what I want, but I can never get it done."

She sat and heard him talking. But it was not he. Yet those were the hands she had kissed, there were the glistening, strange black eyes that she had loved. Yet it was not he. She sat motionless with horror and silence. He dropped his tobacco-pouch, and groped for it on the ground. Yet she must wait to see if he would recognise her. Why could she not go! In a moment he rose.

"I must go at once," he said. "The owl is coming." Then he added confidentially: "His name isn't really the owl, but I call him that. I must go and see if he has come."

She rose too. He stood before her, uncertain. He was a handsome, soldierly fellow, and a lunatic. Her eyes searched him, and searched him, to see if he would recognise her, if she could discover him.

"You don't know me?" she asked, from the terror of her soul, standing alone.

He looked back at her quizzically. She had to bear his

157

eyes. They gleamed on her, but with no intelligence. He was drawing nearer to her.

"Yes, I do know you," he said, fixed, intent, but mad, drawing his face nearer hers. Her horror was too great. The powerful lunatic was coming too near to her.

A man approached, hastening.

"The garden isn't open this morning," he said.

The deranged man stopped and looked at him. The keeper went to the seat and picked up the tobacco-pouch left lying there.

"Don't leave your tobacco, sir," he said, taking it to the gentleman in the linen coat.

"I was just asking this lady to stay to lunch," the latter said politely. "She is a friend of mine."

The woman turned and walked swiftly, blindly, between the sunny roses, out from the garden, past the house with the blank, dark windows, through the sea-pebbled courtyard to the street. Hastening and blind, she went forward without hesitating, not knowing whither. Directly she came to the house she went upstairs, took off her hat, and sat down on the bed. It was as if some membrane had been torn in two in her, so that she was not an entity that could think and feel. She sat staring across at the window, where an ivy spray waved slowly up and down in the sea wind. There was some of the uncanny luminousness of the sunlit sea in the air. She sat perfectly still, without any being. She only felt she might be sick, and it might be blood that was loose in her torn entrails. She sat perfectly still and passive.

After a time she heard the hard tread of her husband on the floor below, and, without herself changing, she registered his movement. She heard his rather disconsolate footsteps go out again, then his voice speaking, answering, growing cheery, and his solid tread drawing near.

He entered, ruddy, rather pleased, an air of complacency about his alert, sturdy figure. She moved stiffly. He faltered in his approach.

"What's the matter?" he asked, a tinge of impatience in his voice. "Aren't you feeling well?"

This was torture to her.

"Quite," she replied.

His brown eyes became puzzled and angry.

"What is the matter?" he said.

"Nothing."

He took a few strides, and stood obstinately, looking out of the window.

"Have you run up against anybody?" he asked.

"Nobody who knows me," she said.

His hands began to twitch. It exasperated him, that she was no more sensible of him than if he did not exist. Turning on her at length, driven, he asked:

"Something has upset you, hasn't it?"

"No, why?" she said, neutral. He did not exist for her, except as an irritant.

His anger rose, filling the veins of his throat.

"It seems like it," he said, making an effort not to show his anger, because there seemed no reason for it. He went away downstairs. She sat still on the bed, and with the residue of feeling left to her, she disliked him because he tormented her. The time went by. She could smell the dinner being served, the smoke of her husband's pipe from the garden. But she could not move. She had no being. There was a tinkle of the bell. She heard him come indoors. And then he mounted the stairs again. At every step her heart grew tight in her. He opened the door.

"Dinner is on the table," he said.

It was difficult for her to endure his presence, for he would

159

interfere with her. She could not recover her life. She rose stiffly and went down. She could neither eat nor talk during the meal. She sat absent, torn, without any being of her own. He tried to go on as if nothing were the matter. But at last he became silent with fury. As soon as it was possible, she went upstairs again, and locked the bedroom door. She must be alone. He went with his pipe into the garden. All his suppressed anger against her who held herself superior to him filled and blackened his heart. Though he had not known it, yet he had never really won her, she had never loved him. She had taken him on sufferance. This had foiled him. He was only a labouring electrician in the mine, she was superior to him. He had always given way to her. But all the while, the injury and ignominy had been working in his soul because she did not hold him seriously. And now all his rage came up against her.

He turned and went indoors. The third time, she heard him mounting the stairs. Her heart stood still. He turned the catch and pushed the door – it was locked. He tried it again, harder. Her heart was standing still.

"Have you fastened the door?" he asked quietly, because of the landlady.

"Yes. Wait a minute."

She rose and turned the lock, afraid he would burst in. She felt hatred towards him, because he did not leave her free. He entered, his pipe between his teeth, and she returned to her old position on the bed. He closed the door and stood with his back to it.

"What's the matter?" he asked determinedly.

She was sick with him. She could not look at him.

"Can't you leave me alone?" she replied, averting her face from him.

He looked at her quickly, fully, wincing with ignominy. Then he seemed to consider for a moment.

"There's something up with you, isn't there?" he asked definitely.

"Yes," she said, "but that's no reason why you should torment me."

"I don't torment you. What's the matter?"

"Why should you know?" she cried, in hate and desperation.

Something snapped. He started and caught his pipe as it fell from his mouth. Then he pushed forward the bitten-off mouthpiece with his tongue, took it from off his lips, and looked at it. Then he put out his pipe, and brushed the ash from his waistcoat. After which he raised his head.

"I want to know," he said. His face was greyish pale, and set uglily.

Neither looked at the other. She knew he was fired now. His heart was pounding heavily. She hated him, but she could not withstand him. Suddenly she lifted her head and turned on him.

"What right have you to know?" she asked.

He looked at her. She felt a pang of surprise for his tortured eyes and his fixed face. But her heart hardened swiftly. She had never loved him. She did not love him now.

But suddenly she lifted her head again swiftly, like a thing that tries to get free. She wanted to be free of it. It was not him so much, but it, something she had put on herself, that bound her so horribly. And having put the bond on herself, it was hardest to take it off. But now she hated everything and felt destructive. He stood with his back to the door, fixed, as if he would oppose her eternally, till she was extinguished. She looked at him. Her eyes were cold and hostile. His workman's hands spread on the panels of the door behind him.

"You know I used to live here?" she began, in a hard voice, as if wilfully to wound him. He braced himself against her, and nodded.

"Well, I was companion to Miss Birch of Torill Hall – she and the rector were friends, and Archie was the rector's son." There was a pause. He listened without knowing what was happening. He stared at his wife. She was squatted in her white dress on the bed, carefully folding and re-folding the hem of her skirt. Her voice was full of hostility.

"He was an officer – a sub-lieutenant – then he quarrelled with his colonel and came out of the army. At any rate" – she plucked at her skirt hem, her husband stood motionless, watching her movements which filled his veins with madness – "he was awfully fond of me, and I was of him – awfully."

"How old was he?" asked the husband.

"When – when I first knew him? Or when he went away –?"

"When you first knew him."

"When I first knew him, he was twenty-six – he's thirty-one – nearly thirty-two – because I'm twenty-nine, and he is nearly three years older –"

She lifted her head and looked at the opposite wall.

"And what then?" said her husband.

She hardened herself, and said callously:

"We were as good as engaged for nearly a year, though nobody knew – at least – they talked – but – it wasn't open. Then he went away –"

"He chucked you?" said the husband brutally, wanting to hurt her into contact with himself. Her heart rose wildly with rage. Then "Yes," she said, to anger him. He shifted from one foot to the other, giving a "Pah!" of rage. There was silence for a time.

"Then," she resumed, her pain giving a mocking note to

her words, "he suddenly went out to fight in Africa, and almost the very day I first met you, I heard from Miss Birch he'd got sunstroke – and two months after, that he was dead –"

"That was before you took on with me?" said the husband. There was no answer. Neither spoke for a time. He had not understood. His eyes were contracted uglily.

"So you've been looking at your old courting places!" he said. "That was what you wanted to go out by yourself for this morning."

Still she did not answer him anything. He went away from the door to the window. He stood with his hands behind him, his back to her. She looked at him. His hands seemed gross to her, the back of his head paltry.

At length, almost against his will, he turned round, asking:

"How long were you carrying on with him?"

"What do you mean?" she replied coldly.

"I mean how long were you carrying on with him?"

She lifted her head, averting her face from him. She refused to answer. Then she said:

"I don't know what you mean, by carrying on. I loved him from the first days I met him – two months after I went to stay with Miss Birch."

"And do you reckon he loved you?" he jeered.

"I know he did."

"How do you know, if he'd have no more to do with you?"

There was a long silence of hate and suffering.

"And how far did it go between you?" he asked at length, in a frightened, stiff voice.

"I hate your not-straightforward questions," she cried, beside herself with his baiting. "We loved each other, and we *were* lovers – we were. I don't care what *you* think: what have you got to do with it? We were lovers before I knew you –"

"Lovers – lovers," he said, white with fury. "You mean you had your fling with an army man, and then came to me to marry you when you'd done –"

She sat swallowing her bitterness. There was a long pause.

"Do you mean to say you used to go – the whole hogger?" he asked, still incredulous.

"Why, what else do you think I mean?" she cried brutally.

He shrank, and became white, impersonal. There was a long, paralysed silence. He seemed to have gone small.

"You never thought to tell me all this before I married you," he said, with bitter irony, at last.

"You never asked me," she replied.

"I never thought there was any need."

"Well, then, you *should* think."

He stood with expressionless, almost child-like set face, revolving many thoughts, whilst his heart was mad with anguish.

Suddenly she added:

"And I saw him to-day," she said. "He is not dead, he's mad."

"Mad!" he said involuntarily.

"A lunatic," she said. It almost cost her her reason to utter the word. There was a pause.

"Did he know you?" asked the husband, in a small voice.

"No," she said.

He stood and looked at her. At last he had learned the width of the breach between them. She still squatted on the bed. He could not go near her. It would be violation to each of them to be brought into contact with the other. The thing must work itself out. They were both shocked so much, they were impersonal, and no longer hated each other. After some minutes he left her and went out.

WILLA CATHER

FROM MY ÁNTONIA

I DO NOT REMEMBER our arrival at my grandfather's farm sometime before daybreak, after a drive of nearly twenty miles with heavy work-horses. When I awoke, it was afternoon. I was lying in a little room, scarcely larger than the bed that held me, and the window-shade at my head was flapping softly in a warm wind. A tall woman, with wrinkled brown skin and black hair, stood looking down at me; I knew that she must be my grandmother. She had been crying, I could see, but when I opened my eyes she smiled, peered at me anxiously, and sat down on the foot of my bed.

"Had a good sleep, Jimmy?" she asked briskly. Then in a very different tone she said, as if to herself, "My, how you do look like your father!" I remembered that my father had been her little boy; she must often have come to wake him like this when he overslept. "Here are your clean clothes," she went on, stroking my coverlid with her brown hand as she talked. "But first you come down to the kitchen with me, and have a nice warm bath behind the stove. Bring your things; there's nobody about."

"Down to the kitchen" struck me as curious; it was always "out in the kitchen" at home. I picked up my shoes and stockings and followed her through the living-room and down a flight of stairs into a basement. This basement was divided into a dining-room at the right of the stairs and a kitchen at the left. Both rooms were plastered and white-washed – the plaster laid directly upon the earth walls, as it used to be in dugouts. The floor was of hard cement. Up under the wooden ceiling there were little half-windows with white curtains, and pots of geraniums and wandering Jew in the deep sills. As I entered the kitchen, I sniffed a pleasant smell of gingerbread baking. The stove was very large, with bright nickel trimmings, and behind it there was a long wooden bench against the wall, and a tin washtub, into which grandmother poured hot and cold water. When she brought the soap and towels, I told her that I was used to taking my bath without help.

"Can you do your ears, Jimmy? Are you sure? Well, now, I call you a right smart little boy."

It was pleasant there in the kitchen. The sun shone into my bath-water through the west half-window, and a big Maltese cat came up and rubbed himself against the tub, watching me curiously. While I scrubbed, my grandmother busied herself in the dining-room until I called anxiously, "Grandmother, I'm afraid the cakes are burning!" Then she came laughing, waving her apron before her as if she were shooing chickens.

She was a spare, tall woman, a little stooped, and she was apt to carry her head thrust forward in an attitude of attention, as if she were looking at something, or listening to something, far away. As I grew older, I came to believe that it was only because she was so often thinking of things that were far away. She was quick-footed and energetic in all her movements. Her voice was high and rather shrill, and she often spoke with an anxious inflection, for she was exceedingly desirous that everything should go with due order and decorum. Her laugh, too, was high, and perhaps a little strident, but there was a lively intelligence in it. She was then fifty-five years old, a strong woman, of unusual endurance.

After I was dressed, I explored the long cellar next the kitchen. It was dug out under the wing of the house, was plastered and cemented, with a stairway and an outside door by which the men came and went. Under one of the windows there was a place for them to wash when they came in from work.

While my grandmother was busy about supper, I settled myself on the wooden bench behind the stove and got acquainted with the cat – he caught not only rats and mice, but gophers, I was told. The patch of yellow sunlight on the floor travelled back toward the stairway, and grandmother and I talked about my journey, and about the arrival of the new Bohemian family; she said they were to be our nearest neighbours. We did not talk about the farm in Virginia, which had been her home for so many years. But after the men came in from the fields, and we were all seated at the supper table, then she asked Jake about the old place and about our friends and neighbours there.

My grandfather said little. When he first came in he kissed me and spoke kindly to me, but he was not demonstrative. I felt at once his deliberateness and personal dignity, and was a little in awe of him. The thing one immediately noticed about him was his beautiful, crinkly, snow-white beard. I once heard a missionary say it was like the beard of an Arabian sheik. His bald crown only made it more impressive.

Grandfather's eyes were not at all like those of an old man; they were bright blue, and had a fresh, frosty sparkle. His teeth were white and regular – so sound that he had never been to a dentist in his life. He had a delicate skin, easily roughened by sun and wind. When he was a young man his hair and beard were red; his eyebrows were still coppery.

As we sat at the table, Otto Fuchs and I kept stealing covert glances at each other. Grandmother had told me while she was getting supper that he was an Austrian who came to this country a young boy and had led an adventurous life in the Far West among mining-camps and cow outfits. His iron constitution was somewhat broken by mountain pneumonia, and he had drifted back to live in a milder country for a while. He had relatives in Bismarck, a German settlement to the north of us, but for a year now he had been working for grandfather.

The minute supper was over, Otto took me into the kitchen to whisper to me about a pony down in the barn that had been bought for me at a sale; he had been riding him to find out whether he had any bad tricks, but he was a "perfect gentleman," and his name was Dude. Fuchs told me everything I wanted to know: how he had lost his ear in a Wyoming blizzard when he was a stage-driver, and how to throw a lasso. He promised to rope a steer for me before sundown next day. He got out his "chaps" and silver spurs to show them to Jake and me, and his best cowboy boots, with tops stitched in bold design – roses, and true-lover's knots, and undraped female figures. These, he solemnly explained, were angels.

Before we went to bed, Jake and Otto were called up to the living-room for prayers. Grandfather put on silver-rimmed spectacles and read several Psalms. His voice was so sympathetic and he read so interestingly that I wished he had chosen one of my favourite chapters in the Book of Kings. I was awed by his intonation of the word "Selah." "He shall choose our inheritance for us, the excellency of Jacob whom He loved. Selah." I had no idea what the word meant; perhaps he had not. But, as he uttered it, it became oracular, the most sacred of words.

Early the next morning I ran out-of-doors to look about me. I had been told that ours was the only wooden house west of Black Hawk – until you came to the Norwegian settlement, where there were several. Our neighbours lived in sod houses and dugouts – comfortable, but not very roomy. Our white frame house, with a storey and half-storey above the basement, stood at the east end of what I might call the farmyard, with the windmill close by the kitchen door. From the windmill the ground sloped westward, down to the barns and granaries and pig-yards. This slope was trampled hard and bare, and washed out in winding gullies by the rain. Beyond the corncribs, at the bottom of the shallow draw, was a muddy little pond, with rusty willow bushes growing about it. The road from the post-office came directly by our door, crossed the farmyard, and curved round this little pond, beyond which it began to climb the gentle swell of unbroken prairie to the west. There, along the western skyline, it skirted a great cornfield, much larger than any field I had ever seen. This cornfield, and the sorghum patch behind the barn, were the only broken land in sight. Everywhere, as far as the eye could reach, there was nothing but rough, shaggy, red grass, most of it as tall as I.

North of the house, inside the ploughed fire-breaks, grew a thick-set strip of box-elder trees, low and bushy, their leaves already turning yellow. This hedge was nearly a quarter of a mile long, but I had to look very hard to see it at all. The little trees were insignificant against the grass. It seemed as if the grass were about to run over them, and over the plum-patch behind the sod chicken-house.

As I looked about me I felt that the grass was the country, as the water is the sea. The red of the grass made all the great prairie the colour of wine-stains, or of certain seaweeds when they are first washed up. And there was so much motion in it; the whole country seemed, somehow, to be running.

I had almost forgotten that I had a grandmother, when

she came out, her sunbonnet on her head, a grain-sack in her hand, and asked me if I did not want to go to the garden with her to dig potatoes for dinner.

The garden, curiously enough, was a quarter of a mile from the house, and the way to it led up a shallow draw past the cattle corral. Grandmother called my attention to a stout hickory cane, tipped with copper, which hung by a leather thong from her belt. This, she said, was her rattlesnake cane. I must never go to the garden without a heavy stick or a corn-knife; she had killed a good many rattlers on her way back and forth. A little girl who lived on the Black Hawk road was bitten on the ankle and had been sick all summer.

I can remember exactly how the country looked to me as I walked beside my grandmother along the faint wagon-tracks on that early September morning. Perhaps the glide of long railway travel was still with me, for more than anything else I felt motion in the landscape; in the fresh, easy-blowing morning wind, and in the earth itself, as if the shaggy grass were a sort of loose hide, and underneath it herds of wild buffalo were galloping, galloping. . . .

Alone, I should never have found the garden – except, perhaps, for the big yellow pumpkins that lay about unprotected by their withering vines – and I felt very little interest in it when I got there. I wanted to walk straight on through the red grass and over the edge of the world, which could not be very far away. The light air about me told me that the world ended here: only the ground and sun and sky were left, and if one went a little farther there would be only sun and sky, and one would float off into them, like the tawny hawks which sailed over our heads making slow shadows on the grass. While grandmother took the pitchfork we found standing in one of the rows and dug potatoes, while I picked them up out of the soft brown earth and put them into the bag, I kept looking up at the hawks that were doing what I might so easily do.

When grandmother was ready to go, I said I would like to stay up there in the garden awhile.

She peered down at me from under her sunbonnet. "Aren't you afraid of snakes?"

"A little," I admitted, "but I'd like to stay, anyhow."

"Well, if you see one, don't have anything to do with him. The big yellow and brown ones won't hurt you; they're bull-snakes and help to keep the gophers down. Don't be scared if you see anything look out of that hole in the bank over there. That's a badger hole. He's about as big as a big 'possum, and his face is striped, black and white. He takes a chicken once in a while, but I won't let the men harm him. In a new country a body feels friendly to the animals. I like to have him come out and watch me when I'm at work."

Grandmother swung the bag of potatoes over her shoulder and went down the path, leaning forward a little. The road followed the windings of the draw; when she came to the first bend, she waved at me and disappeared. I was left alone with this new feeling of lightness and content.

I sat down in the middle of the garden, where snakes could scarcely approach unseen, and leaned my back against a warm yellow pumpkin. There were some ground-cherry bushes growing along the furrows, full of fruit. I turned back the papery triangular sheaths that protected the berries and ate a few. All about me giant grasshoppers, twice as big as any I had ever seen, were doing acrobatic feats among the dried vines. The gophers scurried up and down the ploughed ground. There in the sheltered draw-bottom the wind did not blow very hard, but I could hear it singing its humming tune up on the level, and I could see the tall grasses wave. The earth was warm under me, and warm as I crumbled

173

it through my fingers. Queer little red bugs came out and moved in slow squadrons around me. Their backs were polished vermilion, with black spots. I kept as still as I could. Nothing happened. I did not expect anything to happen. I was something that lay under the sun and felt it, like the pumpkins, and I did not want to be anything more. I was entirely happy. Perhaps we feel like that when we die and become a part of something entire, whether it is sun and air, or goodness and knowledge. At any rate, that is happiness; to be dissolved into something complete and great. When it comes to one, it comes as naturally as sleep.

JANE GARDAM

BLUE POPPIES

MY MOTHER DIED with her hand in the hand of the Duchess. We were at Clere in late summer. It was a Monday. Clere opens on Mondays and Tuesdays only. It is not a great house and the Duke likes silence. It offers only itself. "No teas, no toilets!" I once heard a woman say on one of the few coaches that ever found its way there. "It's not much, is it?" Clere stands blotchy and moulding and its doves look very white against its peeling portico. Grass in the cobbles. If you listen hard you can still hear a stable clock thinly strike the quarters.

Mother had been staying with me for a month, sometimes knowing me, sometimes looking interestedly in my direction as if she ought to. Paddling here, paddling there. Looking out of windows, saying brightly, "Bored? Of course I'm not bored." Once or twice when I took her breakfast in bed she thought I was a nurse. Once after tea she asked if she could play in the garden and then looked frightened.

Today was showery. She watched the rain and the clouds blowing.

"Would you like to go to Clere?"

"Now what is that?"

"You know. You've been there before. It's the place with the blue poppies."

"Blue poppies?"

"You saw them last time."

"*Meconopsis?*" she asked. "I really ought to write letters."

My mother was ninety-one and she wrote letters every day. She had done so since she was a girl. She wrote at last to a very short list of people. Her address book looked like a tycoon's diary. Negotiations completed. Whole pages crossed out. The more recent crossings-off were wavery.

We set out for the blue poppies and she wore a hat and gloves and surveyed the rainy world through the car window. Every now and then she opened her handbag to look at her pills or wondered aloud where her walking stick had gone.

"Back seat."

"No," she said, "I like the front seat in a car. It was always manners to offer the front seat. It's the best seat, the front seat."

"But the stick is on the back seat."

"What stick is that?"

At Clere the rain had stopped, leaving the grass slippery and a silvery dampness hanging in the air. The Duchess was on the door, taking tickets. That is to say she was at the other side of a rickety trestle table working in a flower border. She was digging. On the table a black tin box stood open for small change and a few spotted postcards of the house were arranged beside some very poor specimens of plants for sale at exorbitant prices. The Duchess's corduroy behind rose beyond them. She straightened up and half turned to us, great gloved hands swinging, caked in earth.

The Duchess is no beauty. She has a beak of ivory and deep-sunken, hard blue eyes. Her hair is scant and colourless. There are ropes in her throat. Her face is weather-beaten and her haunches strong, for she has created the gardens at Clere almost alone. When she speaks, the voice of the razorbill is heard in the land.

The Duke. Oh, the poor Duke! We could see him under the portico seated alone at another rough table eating bread. There was a slab of processed cheese beside the bread and a small bottle of beer. He wore a shawl and his face was long and rueful. His near-side shoulder was raised at a defensive angle to the Duchess, as if to ward off blows. I saw the Duchess see me pity the neglected Duke as she said to us, "Could you hold on? Just a moment?" and turning back to the flower-bed she began to tug at a great, leaden root.

My mother opened her bag and began to scrabble in it. "Now, this is my treat."

"There!" cried the Duchess, heaving the root aloft, shaking off soil, tossing it down. "Two, is it?"

"*Choisya ternata*," said my mother. "One and a half."

A pause.

"For the house, is it? Are you going round the house as well as the garden?"

"We really came just for the poppies," I said, "and it's two, please."

"Oh, I should like to see the house," said my mother. "I saw the poppies when I stayed with Lilian last year."

I blinked.

"Lilian thinks I can't remember," my mother said to the Duchess. "This time I should like to see the house. And I shall pay."

"Two," I signalled to the Duchess, smiling what I hoped would be a collaborative smile above my mother's head. I saw the Duchess think, "A bully."

"One and a half," said my mother.

"Mother, I am over fifty. It is children who are half-price."

"And senior citizens," said my mother. "And I am one of those as I'm sure Her Grace will believe. I can prove it if I can only find my card."

179

"I'll trust you," said the Duchess. Her eyes gleamed on my mother. Then her icicle-wax face cracked into a smile drawing the thin skin taut over her nose. "I'm a Lilian, too," she said and gave a little cackle that told me she thought me fortunate.

We walked about the ground floor of the house, though many corridors were barred, and small ivory labels hung on hooks on many doors. They said "*PRIVATE*" in beautifully painted copperplate. In the drawing room, where my mother felt a little dizzy – nothing to speak of – there was nowhere to sit down. All the sofas and chairs were roped off, even the ones with torn silk or stuffing sprouting out. We were the only visitors and there seemed to be nobody in attendance to see that we didn't steal the ornaments.

"Meissen, I'd think, dear," said my mother, picking up a little porcelain box from a table. "Darling, oughtn't we to get this valued?" On other tables stood photographs in silver frames. On walls hung portraits in carved and gilded frames. Here and there across the centuries shone out the Duchess's nose.

"Such a disadvantage," said my mother, "poor dear. That photograph is a Lenare. He's made her very hazy. That was his secret, you know. The haze. He could make anybody look romantic. All the fat young lilies. It will be her engagement portrait."

"I'm surprised her mother let her have it done."

"Oh, she would have had to. It was very much the thing. Like getting confirmed. Well, with these people, more usual really than getting confirmed. She looks as though she'd have no truck with it. I agree. I think she seems a splendid woman, don't you?"

We walked out side by side and stood on the semicircular marble floor of the porch, among the flaking columns. The

Duke had gone. The small brown beer-bottle was on its side. Robins were pecking about among the crumbs of bread. The Duchess could be seen, still toiling in the shrubs. Mother watched her as I considered the wet and broken steps down from the portico and up again towards the gardens, and my fury at my mother's pleasure in the Duchess. I wondered if we might take the steps one by one, arm in arm, with the stick and a prayer. "Who is that person over there digging in that flower-bed?" asked Mother, looking towards the Duchess. "A gardener, I suppose. They often get women now. You know – I should like to have done that."

Down and up the steps we went and over the swell of the grass slope. There was a flint arch into a rose garden and a long white seat under a *gloire de Dijon* rose. "I think I'll sit," said my mother.

"The seat's wet."

"Never mind."

"It's sopping."

She sat and the wind blew and the rose shook drops and petals on her. "I'll just put up my umbrella."

"You haven't an umbrella."

"Don't be silly, dear, I have a beautiful umbrella. It was Margaret's. I've had it for years. It's in the hall-stand."

"Well, I can't go all the way home for it."

"It's not in your home, dear. You haven't got a hall-stand. It's in *my* home. I'm glad to say I still have a home of my own."

"Well, I'm not going there. It's a hundred miles. I'm not going a hundred miles for your umbrella."

"But of course not. I didn't bring an umbrella to *you*, Lilian. Not on holiday. I told you when you collected me: 'There's no need for me to bring an umbrella because I can always use one of yours.' Lilian, this seat is very wet."

"For heaven's sake then – Come with me to see the blue poppies."

The Duchess's face suddenly peered round the flint arch and disappeared again.

"Lilian, such a very strange woman just looked into this garden. Like a hawk."

"Mother. I'm going to see the poppies. Are you coming?"

"I saw them once before. I'm sure I did. They're very nice, but I think I'll just sit."

"Nice!"

"Yes, *nice*, dear. *Nice*. You know I can't enthuse like you can. I'm not very imaginative, I never have been."

"That is true."

"They always remind me of Cadbury's chocolates, but I can never remember why."

I thought, "senile." I must have said it.

I did say it.

"Well, yes. I dare say I am. Who is this woman approaching with a cushion? How very kind. Yes, I would like a cushion. My daughter forgot the umbrella. How thoughtful. She's *clever*, you see. She went to a university. Very clever, and *imaginative*, too. She insisted on coming all this way – such a wet day and, of course, most of your garden is over – because of the blue of the poppies. Children are so funny, aren't they?"

"I never quite see why everybody gets so worked up about the blue," said the Duchess.

"*Meconopsis Baileyi*," said my mother.

"Yes."

"*Betonicifolia*."

"Give me *Campanula carpatica*," said the Duchess.

"Ah! Or *Gentiana verna angulosa*," said my mother. "We sound as if we're saying our prayers."

The two of them looked at me. My mother regarded me with kindly attention, as if I were a pleasant acquaintance she would like to think well of. "You go off," said the Duchess. "I'll stay here. Take your time."

As I went I heard my mother say, "She's just like her father of course. You have to understand her; she hasn't much time for old people. And, of course, she is *no* gardener."

When I came back – and they were: they were just like Cadbury's chocolate papers crumpled up under the tall black trees in a sweep, the exact colour, lying about among their pale hairy leaves in the muddy earth, raindrops scattering them with a papery noise – when I came back, the Duchess was holding my mother's hand and looking closely at her face. She said, "Quick. You must telephone. In the study. Left of the portico. Says 'Private' on a disc. *Run!*" She let go the hand, which fell loose. Loose and finished. The Duchess seemed to be smiling. A smile that stretched the narrow face and stretched the lines sharper round her eyes. It was more a sneer than a smile. I saw she was sneering with pain. I said, "My mother is dead." She said, "Quick. Run. Be quick."

I ran. Ran down the slope, over the porch, and into the study, where the telephone was old and black and lumpen and the dial flopped and rattled. All done, I ran out again and stood at the top of the steps looking up the grassy slope. We were clamped in time. Round the corner of the house came the Duke in a wheelchair pushed by a woman in a dark-blue dress. She had bottle legs. The two of them looked at me with suspicion. The Duke said, "Phyllis?" to the woman and continued to stare. "Yes?" asked the woman. "Yes? What is it? Do you want something?" I thought, "I want this last day again."

I walked up the slope to the rose garden, where the

Duchess sat looking over the view. She said, "Now she has died."

She seemed to be grieving. I knew though that my mother had not been dead when I ran for the telephone, and if it had been the Duchess who had run for the telephone I would have been with my mother when she died. So then I hated the Duchess and all her works.

It was two years later that I came face to face with her again, at a luncheon party given in aid of the preservation of trees, and quite the other side of the country. There were the usual people – some eccentrics, some gushers, some hard-grained, valiant fund-raisers. No village people. The rich. All elderly. All, even the younger ones, belonging to what my children called "the old world". They had something of the ways of my mother's generation. But none of them was my mother.

The Duchess was over in a corner, standing by herself and eating hugely, her plate up near her mouth, her fork working away, her eyes swivelling frostily about. She saw me at once and went on staring as she ate. I knew she meant that I should go across to her.

I had written a letter of thanks of course and she had not only replied adequately – an old thick cream card inside a thick cream envelope and an indecipherable signature – but she had sent flowers to the funeral. And that had ended it.

I watched with interest as the Duchess cut herself a good half-pound cheese and put it in her pocket. Going to a side-table she opened her handbag and began to sweep fruit into it. Three apples and two bananas disappeared, and the people around her looked away. As she reached the door she looked across at me. She did not exactly hesitate, but there was something.

Then she left the house.

But in the car park, there she was in a filthy car, eating one of the bananas. Still staring ahead, she wound down a window and I went towards her.

She said, "Perhaps I ought to have told you. Your mother said to me, 'Goodbye, Lilian dear.'"

"Your name is Lilian," I said. "She was quite capable of calling you Lilian. She had taken a liking to you. Which she never did to me."

"No, no. She meant you," said the Duchess. "She said, 'I'm sorry, darling, not to have gone with you to the poppies.'"

WILD GARDENS

"A garden to walk in and immensity to dream in –
what more could he ask? A few flowers at his feet and
above him the stars."

– Victor Hugo, *Les Misérables*

FRANCES HODGSON BURNETT

FROM THE
SECRET GARDEN

FOR TWO OR three minutes he stood looking round him, while Mary watched him, and then he began to walk about softly, even more lightly than Mary had walked the first time she had found herself inside the four walls. His eyes seemed to be taking in everything – the grey trees with the grey creepers climbing over them and hanging from their branches, the tangle on the wall and among the grass, the evergreen alcoves with the stone seats and tall flower urns standing in them.

"I never thought I'd see this place," he said at last in a whisper.

"Did you know about it?" asked Mary.

She had spoken aloud and he made a sign to her.

"We must talk low," he said, "or someone'll hear us an' wonder what's to do in here."

"Oh! I forgot!" said Mary, feeling frightened and putting her hand quickly against her mouth. "Did you know about the garden?" she asked again when she had recovered herself.

Dickon nodded.

"Martha told me there was one as no one ever went inside," he answered. "Us used to wonder what it was like."

He stopped and looked round at the lovely grey tangle about him, and his round eyes looked queerly happy.

"Eh! The nests as'll be here come springtime," he said. "It'd be th' safest nestin' place in England. No one ever comin'

191

near an' tangles o' trees an' roses to build in. I wonder all th' birds on th' moor don't build here."

Mistress Mary put her hand on his arm again without knowing it.

"Will there be roses?" she whispered. "Can you tell? I thought perhaps they were all dead."

"Eh! No! Not them – not all of 'em!" he answered. "Look here!"

He stepped over to the nearest tree – an old, old one with grey lichen all over its bark, but upholding a curtain of tangled sprays and branches. He took a thick knife out of his pocket and opened one of its blades.

"There's lots o' dead wood as ought to be cut out," he said. "An' there's a lot o' old wood, but it made some new last year. This here's a new bit," and he touched a shoot which looked brownish-green instead of hard, dry grey.

Mary touched it herself in an eager, reverent way.

"That one?" she said. "Is that one quite alive – quite?"

Dickon curved his wide, smiling mouth.

"It's as wick as you or me," he said; and Mary remembered that Martha had told her that "wick" meant "alive" or "lively".

"I'm glad it's wick!" she cried out in her whisper. "I want them all to be wick. Let us go round the garden and count how many wick ones there are."

She quite panted with eagerness and Dickon was as eager as she was. They went from tree to tree and from bush to bush. Dickon carried his knife in his hand and showed her things which she thought wonderful.

"They're run wild," he said, "but th' strongest ones has fair thrived on it. The delicatest ones has died out, but the others has growed an' growed, an' spread an' spread, till they's a wonder. See here!" and he pulled down a thick, grey, dry-looking branch. "A body might think this was dead wood, but I don't believe it is – down to th' root. I'll cut it low down an' see."

He knelt and with his knife cut the lifeless-looking branch through, not far above the earth.

"There!" he said exultantly. "I told thee so. There's green in that wood yet. Look at it."

Mary was down on her knees before he spoke, gazing with all her might.

"When it looks a bit greenish an' juicy like that, it's wick," he explained. "When th' inside is dry an' breaks easy, like this here piece I've cut off, it's done for. There's a big root here as all this live wood sprung out of, an' if th' old wood's cut off an' it's dug round, an' took care of there'll be" – he stopped and lifted his face to look up at the climbing and hanging sprays about him – "there'll be a fountain o' roses here this summer."

They went from bush to bush and from tree to tree. He was very strong and clever with his knife and knew how to cut the dry and dead wood away, and could tell when an unpromising bough or twig had still green life in it. In the course of half an hour, Mary thought she could tell too, and when he cut through a lifeless-looking branch she would cry out joyfully under her breath when she caught sight of the least shade of moist green. The spade, and hoe, and fork were very useful. He showed her how to use a fork while he dug about the roots with the spade and stirred the earth and let the air in.

They were working industriously round one of the biggest standard roses when he caught sight of something which made him utter an exclamation of surprise.

"Why!" he cried, pointing to the grass a few feet away. "Who did that?"

It was one of Mary's own little clearings round the pale-green points.

"I did it," said Mary.

"Why, I thought tha' didn't know nothin' about garden-in'," he exclaimed.

"I don't," she answered, "but they were so little and the grass was so thick and strong, and they looked as if they had no room to breathe. So I made a place for them. I don't even know what they are."

Dickon went and knelt down by them, smiling his wide smile.

"Tha' was right", he said. "A gardener couldn't have told thee better. They'll grow now like Jack's bean-stalk. They're crocuses an' snowdrops, an' these here is narcissuses," turning to another patch, "an' here's daffydowndillys. Eh! They will be a sight."

He ran from one clearing to another.

"Tha' has done a lot o' work for such a little wench," he said, looking her over.

"I'm growing fatter," said Mary, "and I'm growing strong-er. I used always to be tired. When I dig I'm not tired at all. I like to smell the earth when it's turned up."

"It's rare good for thee," he said, nodding his head wisely. "There's naught as nice as th' smell o' good clean earth, except th' smell o' fresh growin' things when th' rain falls on 'em. I get out on th' moor many a day when it's rainin' an' I lie under a bush an' listen to th' soft swish o' drops on th' heather an' I just sniff an' sniff. My nose end fair quivers like a rabbit's, Mother says."

"Do you never catch cold?" inquired Mary, gazing at him wonderingly. She had never seen such a funny boy, or such a nice one.

"Not me," he said, grinning. "I never ketched cold since

I was born. I wasn't brought up nesh enough. I've chased about th' moor in all weathers, same as th' rabbits does. Mother says I've sniffed too much fresh air for twelve year' to ever get to sniffin' with cold. I'm as tough as a whitethorn knobstick."

He was working all the time he was talking and Mary was following him and helping him with her fork or the trowel.

"There's a lot of work to do here!" he said once, looking about quite exultantly.

"Will you come again and help me to do it?" Mary begged. "I'm sure I can help, too. I can dig and pull up weeds, and do whatever you tell me. Oh! do come, Dickon!"

"I'll come every day if tha' wants me, rain or shine," he answered stoutly. "It's th' best fun I ever had in my life – shut in here an' wakening' up a garden."

"If you will come," said Mary, "if you will help me to make it alive I'll – I don't know what I'll do," she ended helplessly. What could you do for a boy like that?

"I'll tell thee what tha'll do," said Dickon, with his happy grin. "Tha'll get fat an' tha'll get as hungry as a young fox an' tha'll learn how to talk to th' robin same as I do. Eh! We'll have a lot o' fun."

He began to walk about, looking up in the trees and at the walls and bushes with a thoughtful expression.

"I wouldn't want to make it look like a gardener's garden, all clipped an' spick an' span, would you?" he said. "It's nicer like this with things runnin' wild, an' swingin' an' catchin' hold of each other."

"Don't let us make it tidy," said Mary anxiously. "It wouldn't seem like a secret garden if it was tidy."

Dickon stood rubbing his rusty-red head with a rather puzzled look.

"It's a secret garden sure enough," he said, "but seems like someone besides th' robin must have been in it since it was shut up ten year' ago."

"But the door was locked and the key was buried," said Mary. "No one could get in."

"That's true," he answered. "It's a queer place. Seems to me as if there'd been a bit o' prunin' done here an' there, later than ten year' ago."

"But how could it have been done?" said Mary.

He was examining a branch of a standard rose and he shook his head.

"Aye! How could it!" he murmured. "With th' door locked an' th' key buried."

Mistress Mary always felt that however many years she lived she should never forget that first morning when her garden began to grow. Of course, it did seem to begin to grow for her that morning. When Dickon began to clear places to plant seeds, she remembered what Basil had sung at her when he wanted to tease her.

"Are there any flowers that look like bells?" she inquired.

"Lilies o' th' valley does," he answered, digging away with the trowel, "an' there's Canterbury bells, an' campanulas."

"Let us plant some," said Mary.

"There's lilies o' th' valley here already; I saw 'em. They'll have growed too close an' we'll have to separate 'em, but there's plenty. Th' other ones take two years to bloom from seed, but I can bring you some bits o' plants from our cottage garden. Why does tha' want 'em?"

Then Mary told him about Basil and his brothers and sisters in India and of how she had hated them, and of their calling her "Mistress Mary Quite Contrary".

"They used to dance round and sing at me. They sang:

Mistress Mary, quite contrary,
How does your garden grow?
With silver bells and cockle shells,
And marigolds all in a row.

I just remembered it and it made me wonder if there were really flowers like silver bells."

She frowned a little and gave her trowel a rather spiteful dig into the earth.

"I wasn't as contrary as they were."

But Dickon laughed.

"Eh!" he said, and as he crumpled the rich black soil she saw he was sniffing up the scent of it, "there doesn't seem to be no need for no one to be contrary when there's flowers an' such like, an' such lots o' friendly wild things running' about makin' homes for themselves, or buildin' nests an' singin' an' whistling, does there?"

Mary, kneeling by him holding the seeds, looked at him and stopped frowning.

"Dickon," she said. "You are as nice as Martha said you were. I like you, and you make the fifth person. I never thought I should like five people."

Dickon sat up on his heels as Martha did when she was polishing the grate. He did look funny and delightful, Mary thought, with his round blue eyes and red cheeks and happy-looking turned-up nose.

"Only five folks as tha' likes?" he said. "Who is th' other four?"

"Your mother and Martha," Mary checked them off on her fingers, "and the robin and Ben Weatherstaff."

Dickon laughed, so that he was obliged to stifle the sound by putting his arm over his mouth.

"I know tha' thinks I'm a queer lad," he said, "but I think tha' art th' queerest little lass I ever saw."

Then Mary did a strange thing. She leaned forward and asked him a question she had never dreamed of asking anyone before. And she tried to ask it in Yorkshire because that was his language, and in India a native was always pleased if you knew his speech.

"Does tha' like me?" she said.

"Eh!" he answered heartily, "that I does. I likes thee wonderful, an' so does th' robin, I do believe!"

"That's two, then," said Mary. "That's two for me."

And then they began to work harder than ever and more joyful. Mary was startled and sorry when she heard the big clock in the courtyard strike the hour of her midday dinner.

"I shall have to go," she said mournfully. "And you will have to go too, won't you?"

Dickon grinned.

"My dinner's easy to carry about with me," he said. "Mother always lets me put a bit o' somethin' in my pocket."

He picked up his coat from the grass and brought out of a pocket a lumpy little bundle tied up in a quite clean, coarse, blue and white handkerchief. It held two thick pieces of bread with a slice of something laid between them.

"It's oftenest naught but bread," he said, "but I've got a fine slice o' fat bacon with it today."

Mary thought it looked a queer dinner, but he seemed ready to enjoy it.

"Run on an' get thy victuals," he said. "I'll be done with mine first. I'll get some more work done before I start back home."

He sat down with his back against a tree.

"I'll call th' robin up," he said, "and give him th' rind o' th' bacon to peck at. They likes a bit o' fat wonderful."

Mary could scarcely bear to leave him. Suddenly it seemed as if he might be a sort of wood fairy who might be gone when she came into the garden again. He seemed too good to be true. She went slowly half-way to the door in the wall and then she stopped and went back.

"Whatever happens, you – you never would tell?" she said.

His poppy-coloured cheeks were distended with his first big bite of bread and bacon, but he managed to smile encouragingly.

"If tha' was a missel thrush an' showed me where thy nest was, does tha' think I'd tell anyone? Not me," he said. "Tha' art as safe as a missel thrush."

And she was quite sure she was.

SANDRA CISNEROS

THE MONKEY GARDEN

THE MONKEY DOESN'T live there anymore. The monkey moved – to Kentucky – and took his people with him. And I was glad because I couldn't listen anymore to his wild screaming at night, the twangy yakkety-yak of the people who owned him. The green metal cage, the porcelain table top, the family that spoke like guitars. Monkey, family, table. All gone.

And it was then we took over the garden we had been afraid to go into when the monkey screamed and showed its yellow teeth.

There were sunflowers big as flowers on Mars and thick cockscombs bleeding the deep red fringe of theater curtains. There were dizzy bees and bow-tied fruit flies turning somersaults and humming in the air. Sweet sweet peach trees. Thorn roses and thistle and pears. Weeds like so many squinty-eyed stars and brush that made your ankles itch and itch until you washed with soap and water. There were big green apples hard as knees. And everywhere the sleepy smell of rotting wood, damp earth and dusty holly-hocks thick and perfumy like the blue-blond hair of the dead.

Yellow spiders ran when we turned rocks over and pale worms blind and afraid of light rolled over in their sleep. Poke a stick in the sandy soil and a few blue-skinned beetles would appear, an avenue of ants, so many crusty lady bugs. This was a garden, a wonderful thing to look at in the spring.

But bit by bit, after the monkey left, the garden began to take over itself. Flowers stopped obeying the little bricks that kept them from growing beyond their paths. Weeds mixed in. Dead cars appeared overnight like mushrooms. First one and then another and then a pale blue pickup with the front windshield missing. Before you knew it, the monkey garden became filled with sleepy cars.

Things had a way of disappearing in the garden, as if the garden itself ate them, or, as if with its old-man memory, it put them away and forgot them. Nenny found a dollar and a dead mouse between two rocks in the stone wall where the morning glories climbed, and once when we were playing hide-and-seek, Eddie Vargas laid his head beneath a hibiscus tree and fell asleep there like a Rip Van Winkle until somebody remembered he was in the game and went back to look for him.

This, I suppose, was the reason why we went there. Far away from where our mothers could find us. We and a few old dogs who lived inside the empty cars. We made a clubhouse once on the back of that old blue pickup. And besides, we liked to jump from the roof of one car to another and pretend they were giant mushrooms.

Somebody started the lie that the monkey garden had been there before anything. We liked to think the garden could hide things for a thousand years. There beneath the roots of soggy flowers were the bones of murdered pirates and dinosaurs, the eye of a unicorn turned to coal.

This is where I wanted to die and where I tried one day but not even the monkey garden would have me. It was the last day I would go there.

Who was it that said I was getting too old to play the games? Who was it I didn't listen to? I only remember that when the others ran, I wanted to run too, up and down and through the monkey garden, fast as the boys, not like Sally who screamed if she got her stockings muddy.

I said, Sally, come on, but she wouldn't. She stayed by the curb talking to Tito and his friends. Play with the kids if you want, she said, I'm staying here. She could be stuck-up like that if she wanted to, so I just left.

It was her own fault too. When I got back Sally was pretending to be mad . . . something about the boys having stolen her keys. Please give them back to me, she said punching the nearest one with a soft fist. They were laughing. She was too. It was a joke I didn't get.

I wanted to go back with the other kids who were still jumping on cars, still chasing each other through the garden, but Sally had her own game.

One of the boys invented the rules. One of Tito's friends said you can't get the keys back unless you kiss us and Sally pretended to be mad at first but she said yes. It was that simple.

I don't know why, but something inside me wanted to throw a stick. Something wanted to say no when I watched Sally going into the garden with Tito's buddies all grinning. It was just a kiss, that's all. A kiss for each one. So what, she said.

Only how come I felt angry inside. Like something wasn't right. Sally went behind that old blue pickup to kiss the boys and get her keys back, and I ran up three flights of stairs to where Tito lived. His mother was ironing shirts. She was sprinkling water on them from an empty pop bottle and smoking a cigarette.

Your son and his friends stole Sally's keys and now they won't give them back unles she kisses them and right now they're making her kiss them, I said all out of breath from the three flights of stairs.

Those kids, she said, not looking up from her ironing.

That's all?

What do you want me to do, she said, call the cops? And kept on ironing.

I looked at her a long time, but couldn't think of anything to say, and ran back down the three flights to the garden where Sally needed to be saved. I took three big sticks and a brick and figured this was enough.

But when I got there Sally said go home. Those boys said leave us alone. I felt stupid with my brick. They all looked at me as if *I* was the one that was crazy and made me feel ashamed.

And then I don't know why but I had to run away. I had to hide myself at the other end of the garden, in the jungle part, under a tree that wouldn't mind if I lay down and cried a long time. I closed my eyes like tight stars so that I wouldn't, but I did. My face felt hot. Everything inside hiccupped.

I read somewhere in India there are priests who can will their heart to stop beating. I wanted to will my blood to stop, my heart to quit its pumping. I wanted to be dead, to turn into the rain, my eyes melt into the ground like two black snails. I wished and wished. I closed my eyes and willed it, but when I got up my dress was green and I had a headache.

I looked at my feet in their white socks and ugly round shoes. They seemed far away. They didn't seem to be my feet anymore. And the garden that had been such a good place to play didn't seem mine either.

DAPHNE DU MAURIER

FROM REBECCA

LAST NIGHT I dreamt I went to Manderley again. It seemed to me I stood by the iron gate leading to the drive, and for a while I could not enter, for the way was barred to me. There was a padlock and a chain upon the gate. I called in my dream to the lodge-keeper, and had no answer, and peering closer through the rusted spokes of the gate I saw that the lodge was uninhabited.

No smoke came from the chimney, and the little lattice windows gaped forlorn. Then, like all dreamers, I was possessed of a sudden with supernatural powers and passed like a spirit through the barrier before me. The drive wound away in front of me, twisting and turning as it had always done, but as I advanced I was aware that a change had come upon it; it was narrow and unkept, not the drive that we had known. At first I was puzzled and did not understand, and it was only when I bent my head to avoid the low swinging branch of a tree that I realized what had happened. Nature had come into her own again and, little by little, in her stealthy, insidious way had encroached upon the drive with long, tenacious fingers. The woods, always a menace even in the past, had triumphed in the end. They crowded, dark and uncontrolled, to the borders of the drive. The beeches with white, naked limbs leant close to one another, their branches intermingled in a strange embrace, making a vault above my head like the archway of a church. And there were other trees as well, trees that I did not recognize, squat oaks and tortured elms that straggled cheek by jowl with the beeches, and had thrust themselves out of the quiet earth, along with monster shrubs and plants, none of which I remembered.

The drive was a ribbon now, a thread of its former self, with gravel surface gone, and choked with grass and moss. The trees had thrown out low branches, making an impediment to progress; the gnarled roots looked like skeleton claws. Scattered here and again amongst this jungle growth I would recognize shrubs that had been landmarks in our time, things of culture and grace, hydrangeas whose blue heads had been famous. No hand had checked their progress, and they had gone native now, rearing to monster height without a bloom, black and ugly as the nameless parasites that grew beside them.

On and on, now east now west, wound the poor thread that once had been our drive. Sometimes I thought it lost, but it appeared again, beneath a fallen tree perhaps, or struggling on the other side of a muddied ditch created by the winter rains. I had not thought the way so long. Surely the miles had multiplied, even as the trees had done, and this path led but to a labyrinth, some choked wilderness, and not to the house at all. I came upon it suddenly; the approach masked by the unnatural growth of a vast shrub that spread in all directions, and I stood, my heart thumping in my breast, the strange prick of tears behind my eyes.

There was Manderley, our Manderley, secretive and silent as it had always been, the grey stone shining in the moonlight of my dream, the mullioned windows reflecting the green lawns and the terrace. Time could not wreck the perfect symmetry of those walls, nor the site itself, a jewel in the hollow of a hand.

The terrace sloped to the lawns, and the lawns stretched

to the sea, and turning I could see the sheet of silver placid under the moon, like a lake undisturbed by wind or storm. No waves would come to ruffle this dream water, and no bulk of cloud, wind-driven from the west, obscure the clarity of this pale sky. I turned again to the house, and though it stood inviolate, untouched, as though we ourselves had left but yesterday, I saw that the garden had obeyed the jungle law, even as the woods had done. The rhododendrons stood fifty feet high, twisted and entwined with bracken, and they had entered into alien marriage with a host of nameless shrubs, poor, bastard things that clung about their roots as though conscious of their spurious origin. A lilac had mated with a copper beech, and to bind them yet more closely to one another the malevolent ivy, always an enemy to grace, had thrown her tendrils about the pair and made them prisoners. Ivy held prior place in this lost garden, the long strands crept across the lawns, and soon would encroach upon the house itself. There was another plant too, some half-breed from the woods, whose seed had been scattered long ago beneath the trees and then forgotten, and now, marching in unison with the ivy, thrust its ugly form like a giant rhubarb towards the soft grass where the daffodils had blown.

Nettles were everywhere, the vanguard of the army. They choked the terrace, they sprawled about the paths, they leant, vulgar and lanky, against the very windows of the house. They made indifferent sentinels, for in many places their ranks had been broken by the rhubarb plant, and they lay with crumpled heads and listless stems, making a pathway for the rabbits. I left the drive and went on to the terrace, for the nettles were no barrier to me, a dreamer. I walked enchanted, and nothing held me back.

Moonlight can play odd tricks upon the fancy, even upon a dreamer's fancy. As I stood there, hushed and still, I could swear that the house was not an empty shell but lived and breathed as it had lived before.

Light came from the windows, the curtains blew softly in the night air, and there, in the library, the door would stand half open as we had left it, with my handkerchief on the table beside the bowl of autumn roses.

The room would bear witness to our presence. The little heap of library books marked ready to return, and the discarded copy of *The Times*. Ash-trays, with the stub of a cigarette; cushions, with the imprint of our heads upon them, lolling in the chairs; the charred embers of our log fire still smouldering against the morning. And Jasper, dear Jasper, with his soulful eyes and great, sagging jowl, would be stretched upon the floor, his tail a-thump when he heard his master's footsteps.

A cloud, hitherto unseen, came upon the moon, and hovered an instant like a dark hand before a face. The illusion went with it, and the lights in the windows were extinguished. I looked upon a desolate shell, soulless at last, unhaunted, with no whisper of the past about its staring walls.

The house was a sepulchre, our fear and suffering lay buried in the ruins. There would be no resurrection. When I thought of Manderley in my waking hours I would not be bitter. I should think of it as it might have been, could I have lived there without fear. I should remember the rose-garden in summer, and the birds that sang at dawn. Tea under the chestnut tree, and the murmur of the sea coming up to us from the lawns below.

I would think of the blown lilac, and the Happy Valley. These things were permanent, they could not be dissolved. They were memories that cannot hurt. All this I resolved in my dream, while the clouds lay across the face of the moon, for like most sleepers I knew that I dreamed. In reality I lay many hundred miles away in an alien land, and would wake, before many seconds had passed, in the bare little hotel bedroom, comforting in its very lack of atmosphere. I would sigh a moment, stretch myself and turn, and opening my eyes, be bewildered at that glittering sun, that hard, clean sky, so different from the soft moonlight of my dream. The day would lie before us both, long no doubt, and uneventful, but fraught with a certain stillness, a dear tranquillity we had not known before. We would not talk of Manderley, I would not tell my dream. For Manderley was ours no longer. Manderley was no more.

JEAN STAFFORD

THE LIPPIA LAWN

ALTHOUGH ITS ROOTS are clever, the trailing arbutus at Deer Lick had been wrenched out by the hogs. Only a few bruised and muddied blossoms still clung to the disordered stems. The old man and I, baskets over our arms, had come looking for good specimens to transplant. It had been a long walk, and Mr. Oliphant was fatigued. Oppressed also with his disappointment, he lowered himself carefully to the ground and sighed.

"They're carnivorous, you know," he said, speaking of the hogs. "They're looking for worms." Everywhere about us, the cloven hoofprints had bitten into the soil, and it was easy to imagine the sow and her retinue lumbering to this place on their preposterously shapely legs, huffing and puffing with incessant appetite. Mr. Oliphant, a man who loved nature in an immense yet ungenerous way, complained as he lay there, shading his eyes against the sunlight that was finely sifted through the hemlock above us. "In town the chickens come to spoil my jonquils, and here the hogs tear up the arbutus. But what good would it do to beg the mountain people to keep their stock at home?"

He was such a spirited and able man that he never seemed old until he commenced to fret, and then, when his deliberate voice became sibilant, I saw how white his hair was and how the flesh of his brown face had been twilled into hundreds of tiny pleats. His large hands, stained with the grime of garden earth, simultaneously became the uncertain, misshapen hands of an aged person. I stopped listening to him and plucked a cluster of trampled blossoms from among the leaves, hoping that my idle twirling of it would make him think I was following what he said. The unvarying tone of his voice made time seem absolute, and absolute, too, became my contemplation of the flower. Once I realized that he had paused. I found myself wanting him to continue, for I was distracted by the ragged petals which, in their revolutions between my fingers, assumed many shapes.

He had only stopped to choose a word, and, having found it, resumed his tirade. I ceased the flower's rotations, and abruptly my rambling daydreams were arrested as the arbutus began to resemble something I had seen before. Although I knew that Mr. Oliphant, a devout horticulturalist, could help me name its cousin, I hesitated to interrupt him lest I interrupt also my own tranquillity. The tenuous memory wove in and out of my thoughts, always tantalizingly just ahead of me. Like the butterfly whose yellow wings are camouflaged to look like sunlight, the flower I could not remember masqueraded as arbutus whenever I had almost discovered it in its native habitat. As I pursued it in the places where I had lived, a voice came back to me. It was not so elusive. Its unique timbre and its accent established it in a particular time, and with only a little research, I found its owner, Fräulein Ströck, my landlady in Heidelberg. She gave me German lessons in exchange for English, and afterward she served me coffee. Of a once fine set, all that remained was the tall pot of white china scattered with pink flowers and minute heart-shaped leaves. I must have complimented her on it, for I recalled her strenuous, elevated reply in English: "No, it makes me very sorry that I do not know the name of the bloom."

Slowly, like a shadow, the past seeped back. A wise scout

was reconnoitering for me and at last led me to a place where I never would have looked. The arbutus was larger, pinker, but was something like the lippia that had grown on the lawn when I was a child in California. It was as thick and close to the ground as clover, and it looked like a head of cropped and decorated hair. Under an umbrella tree, I used to sit waiting for the school bus bringing my sisters and my brothers and pretend that the lawn was the ocean at Redondo Beach, and that I could see them coming through the breakers after a long swim. Once, as I ran toward them, the springy earth cool to my feet, I was stung on the ankle by a bee at work in the brilliant sunlight.

Because I was only five years old when we went away, I have never been able to remember much about our ranch. Whenever I think of California, my impressions are confused and ramified with later ones apprehended in Santa Fe, Denver, Chicago, Toledo, and New Orleans. Only a few of my early memories are pure. I can still summon up the taste of oxalis, but whether I ate the stem or the leaf, I cannot say. I remember the day my grandmother came from Santa Barbara, bringing me a pink tatted handbag to carry to Sunday School, but beyond that, all I can reconstruct of my grandmother is her blackthorn walking stick which had belonged to my grandfather, an Irishman. Now and again a random recollection will swim vaguely across my mind, a wisp too ephemeral to detain: a dairy in Covina where we bought Schmierkäse from a German who frightened me by saying that the Bolsheviks would get me because bright red ribbons streamed from my sailor hat; a Mexican's house with a dried mud floor where a girl named Fuchsia made drawnwork doilies and where my brother and I went one Sunday afternoon, instructed by our mother, to say, "Muchas gracias, señorita," for she had sent us a lemon pie. Sometimes

I think of a dream I often had of a thousand new pennies heaped up beneath a fig tree. The more I picked up, the more there were, and I cried with impatience because the skirt of my dress was not big enough to hold them all. Sometimes I can see a green glass pig which my brother kept in the china closet, forbidding anyone to touch it. Or suddenly I am standing beside Hana, the Japanese washerwoman, as she lifts the lid of a trunk: the smell of camphor balls is strong as she holds up my mother's pin-striped hobble skirt.

But I remember nothing of the house. From photographs and conversation, I know that my father's den was hung with serapes from Tía Juana and that the floor was covered with deer-skins. I know that at the back of the house the grove stretched for eighty acres and that within a south field of chrysanthemums there was a frog pond. But I cannot recall how the fruit looks on an English walnut tree, and the feel and color of those chrysanthemums are spurious, come from later ones I bought or gathered. I can accomplish only a partial reconstruction even of the umbrella tree.

That day in the woods of the Cumberland plateau, the lippia returned unaltered. Tender, fragrant, lavender and white, it extended across a flat and limitless terrain upon which the tree and I, the only altitudes, cast our brief shadows.

"The ground was carpeted with it," said Mr. Oliphant. "Literally carpeted with it, before the mountaineers started digging it up to send off to New York. There used to be a place in the gorge where it grew right out of the rock, but I suppose that's gone too."

He grumbled on as monotonously as the waterfall to our right, reviewing the mountaineers' past offenses and those they would perpetrate in the future. He said it would be his bad luck to come after they had stripped the laurel thicket.

They had no respect for nature, he declared, no desire to conserve the beauty of the woods. Why, they were as ruthless as the Visigoths and it was unimaginable to Mr. Oliphant that they should devastate their native soil. "It is my native soil too!" he cried passionately. "They have no right to hurt my share of it!"

He came from city stock, but he had been born here in the mountains. Off and on for seventy years, with an occasional winter in Florida or France, he had lived alone in the flimsy yellow house in the summer resort where he had been born. From September until late May nearly every year, his was the only chimney in the grounds that regularly sent up a tendril of smoke. The village and houses of the mountain people were a mile away, and sometimes, for as long as a week, the only face he saw was his own reflected in the mirror as he shaved. This winter I had shared the settlement of empty cottages with him, but my house was so far from his that even on a clear day he could not hear my radio. Occasionally, he rambled up my front walk, bringing a packet of *tilleul* which he brewed himself on my electric plate.

Mr. Oliphant was not pitiful as friendless old bachelors often are. His innumerable interests and projects kept him perpetually busy. I had encountered him first in the autumn in the woods, where he was gathering mushrooms to dry for winter use. I joined him in the hunt and, as we scrambled over fallen trees and under low branches, he gave me a receipt for making mead and told me how he canned peas in long-necked wine bottles. A few weeks later he summoned me formally through the mail to dine with him. It was late in September and already so cold that we ate beside the fireplace in his cluttered sitting room. He painted in oils and water-colors for his own amusement, and canvases were stacked against every wall, and the room smelled of turpentine and the wood fire. He pointed out his pleasant, untalented pictures of grape hyacinth and wild azalea, and a wavering, ectoplasmic landscape in fog. A gourmet of sorts, he had such reverence for the broiled beefsteak mushrooms, the curried veal and the avocado salad and the home-made sauterne, that we ate in silence. Afterward, he addressed a fluent monologue to me on the repairs he planned for his flagstone walk, his summer house, his roofs and floors. And finally, he took me to his conservatory, as fragrant and luxuriant as a jungle, where all through the winter he nursed his plants. Just as I left the house, he gave me a tin of mingled herbs which he had taken from his glass-windowed cabinet, allowing the smell of basil and thyme to hover in the air a moment.

All winter I saw him roving through the grounds collecting kindling after a wind or an ice storm. Or I saw him, armed with shears and a basket, going to the woods for holly. On fine days, if I called on him, usually I found him working in the pit, fitted with a glass door, where he kept his hydrangeas through the cold months. Early in February he informed me that he had begun negotiating with the mountaineers for fertilizer and that his seed catalogues had arrived. In March, he heard the first flock of wild geese honking over his house, and knowing by this sign that spring was here to stay, he began to get up earlier in the mornings, making use of every hour of daylight to work in his garden.

Nevertheless, people often asked Mr. Oliphant how he put in his time. A look of bewilderment would invade his face and his lips would curve in a tentative smile like that of a child who does not know for a moment whether to laugh or cry. Once he had replied, "Why, I don't know. Seems like there never *is* enough time."

His character was not arresting, and his continual

murmuring, which amounted to a persecution mania, was tedious. He had done nothing noteworthy in his life; his religion was of the scantiest and most sentimental. He was not charming, and his information, beyond flowers and food and weather, was banal. But I admired him, for there was something deep about him, a subtle vitality that resided in his fingertips and his eyes which enabled him to make anything flourish in the sour mountain soil and to detect to the hour the coming of frost or rain or wind. I had wondered why he chose to live in a place so inimical to gardening, and he had replied, "If I moved, I'd lose all the years I've spent learning my land."

He was saying, "You might make out that I had no room to talk the way I dig up flowers myself to put in my garden. But I maintain there's a world of difference between transplanting something and uprooting it to send off to New York City. I don't know what gets into people to make them take and tear things up."

I had been silent for so long that I felt obliged to speak, and I said, "Mr. Oliphant, this trailing arbutus reminds me of a flower I used to know as a child. Have you ever seen lippia?"

"Lippia? No'm, I've never heard of it." He allowed his eyes to rest on my face for the briefest moment as though a sudden curiosity about me had stirred in him. But he immediately looked away. "I reckon a hundred and fifty years ago my kin were coming here for salt."

On our walk, he had told me that the deer, the Indians and the pioneers had been drawn here by the excrescences of salt in the gorge, from which the name, Deer Lick, had been taken. To our right, the chasm dropped a hundred feet. At the head of it, to our left, the waterfall, almost as high, crashed down, furious and swollen with heavy spring rains.

We were on a triangular promontory halfway between the walls. Mr. Oliphant had said that here had been found the thighbone of a prehistoric animal that had been big enough to be used as a tent pole. Colossal, aged hemlocks crowded the wild slopes.

I would have asked the old man about his pioneer ancestors, but he had already reverted to the arbutus. "Hard as it is to get it to grow, I just had the feeling this spring I'd succeed. If I was younger, I'd look for that other patch I was telling you about."

His voice was so senile that, although I knew he was as nimble almost as I, I got to my feet and said, "If you'll tell me the way, I'll try to find it for you, Mr. Oliphant."

"That's mighty obliging of you," he said with a smile. "You follow the path through the laurel and go a little beyond a big flat rock. You start going down there, and that arbutus used to grow under a ledge just beyond the first hemlock."

I took the knife and trowel he offered me and set out. Long thorny vines clutched at my dress and stockings and the laurel branches whipped my face. The path was obscure and, though it was only March, the brush was green enough for midsummer. But the autumn leaves, blackened by the winter's wetness, were still deep. I found the flat rock, surrounded by blueberry bushes on which the last year's fruit was dry and rusty. From here, the roar of the waterfall was thunderous, and from here I could see far down into the lower chasm. A straight wall of gray and pinkish rock rose sheer to the cloudless sky, and against it were patterned the blue-green feathers of the hemlocks.

After the rock, the going was difficult, and twice I slipped on the wet leaves and only kept my balance by seizing old roots and rocks. Mr. Oliphant's directions had been precise. I stooped under the low-hanging branch of the first hemlock and, when I straightened up again, I saw the arbutus growing in a shelf, shadowed by a roof of violet stone. The fragile flowers, nudging clean dark leaves, were refined, like something painted on china.

When I knelt down to uproot the plant, though, I found I was dealing with nothing frail. Its long, tough sinews branched under the ground far in every direction, grasping the earth so tightly that when I tugged at the main root, no more than the subsidiary tentacles came loose, and with them came great clods of black earth, leaving triangular gouges in the ground. The root did not go deep; instead, it crept just under the surface, but it was so long that my fingertips could not even guess where it ended, and the vine was confused with fern and low weeds, making it impossible to trace the stubborn filament so as to dig around it with the knife and trowel. I pulled again. It was as though the root was instinct with will. There was something so monstrous in its determination to remain where it grew that sweat, not from exertion but from alarm, streamed from my face, and the broken leaves were pasted to my wet fingers. Something prevented me from cutting it, not only my fear that this was the incorrect procedure, but a sort of inexplicable revulsion at the thought that the knife might not cleave through.

My labor was barely visible when I stood up. I knew that when I told Mr. Oliphant it was gone, I should be obliged to hear his droning tantrum all the way home. But I neither could nor would carry back to him that violent artery and its deceptively dainty flowers.

It was a little cooler now, and the sun was beginning to go down. Narrowing my eyes to shut out from their corners the chasm and the trees, I had a last look at the trailing arbutus and saw that it hardly resembled the lippia at all, or rather, that the lippia had faded away so completely that its name

225

was all I could remember. As though I were being watched, as though some alert ear were cocked to the slightest noise I should make, swiftly, as quietly as possible, I ascended the path. When I had passed the rock, I ran through the blueberries. Halfway through the laurel thicket I stopped and rested, then went slowly so that Mr. Oliphant would not see I was out of breath.

He was lying where I had left him. His wiry old legs in blue jeans were set on the needle-littered ground, bent at the knee, with the long feet in sneakers resting firmly in the pockets he had scooped out for them. Although his eyes were closed, his face wore an attentive look as if all his other senses were still active. As I stepped forward into the clearing, he at once sprang up, not at the sound of my footfall but at the low grunting of a lubberly black boar that came trotting along the path, its snout close to the ground. Mr. Oliphant flung up his arms and screamed imprecations at the creature that came on, oblivious. He reached down and picked up a stone, hurled it, and the hog, clipped on the shoulder, turned and ran squealing, its coiled tail bobbing.

The rout, though it was complete, did not satisfy the old man, and for some minutes he gesticulated and cried out, seemed actually to dance with rage. My gaze descended to his feet. They had not moved from the holds prepared for them, as if they shared the zealous intelligence of their master and of the trailing arbutus and of all beings that resist upheaval and defy invasion. Flushed and shaking, he cried out to me, "It's a crime, I tell you! When I was a boy this place was Eden!"

With quick, juvenile blue eyes he glanced around, and I knew that in that moment he was seeing the place as it had been when he first came here, sixty years ago. I envied him the clarity of his vision. I envied him his past when, pacified for a moment, he said gently, "Anyhow, a man can call the old things to mind."

He turned and led the way down the path. In the silence that had fallen upon us, his words repeated themselves to my disquieted mind, like a phrase of music once admired and now detested.

MEIR SHALEV

A NIGHT IN
THE GARDEN

FROM MY
WILD GARDEN

Translated by Joanna Chen

I HAVE WRITTEN here of the big old pear tree in the garden, whose blossoms are lovely but whose fruit is inedible. The time has come to admit that this is my own opinion, and there are others who really love the taste: once a year a colony of fruit bats descends upon the garden, and they, unlike me, have no interest in pear blossoms but are partial to the fruit and come to gorge themselves. The pear tree stands close to the house, and as soon as they appear I rush to the balcony, sit down, switch on the light, and use a bright flashlight in order to watch them lunging toward their nighttime feast.

These bats are not permanent fixtures in my garden. They come from afar, perhaps from the Carmel caves, for only one or two nights in the year, when the fruit ripens. Their visit is a unique and wondrous spectacle, different from any other spectacle offered by the garden. Since I also know how to identify ripe pears, I prepare myself for these flying dinner guests: incline my ear, peer into the dark – Are they here? Not yet? And I wonder, How do they know it is time? Do they send scouts and spies? How do they navigate through the darkness to the specific coordinate of a tree? Do they remember the route from previous years? Either way, I am happy at their arrival, because they cast an atmosphere of authentic savagery and wildness over my garden.

Although they are vegetarians, bats possess a predatory quality. They are large, nimble, and noiseless. They lunge at the fruit-laden tree like birds of prey. Each time a bat dives, it collects a pear and carries it to the nearby oak to consume it. I suppose this habit is designed to avoid overcrowding, collisions, and squabbles on the tree itself and to enable each bat to eat undisturbed, but I have no way of corroborating this hypothesis. I sit and watch them for hours and eventually thank them and say good night, and the next morning there are neither bats nor pears, and the garden resumes a restful pose until the bats return the following year.

Porcupines are additional nocturnal visitors to my garden. I have never seen them here, but sometimes they leave traces of digging, a few black-and-white quills, and easily identifiable droppings. Here and there I see hedgehogs, endearing creatures I like a lot and who, I am sorry to say, visit infrequently and are becoming increasingly rare. On summer nights, jackals and wild boars also venture into the garden. These are real pests, who have learned to dig up irrigation pipes to quench their thirst by biting into them. The wild boars also cause alarm. I was once forced to stand on my germination table after suddenly hearing the furious snorting of a female arriving with her offspring and already planning to charge at me. We stood facing each other for some minutes, me on the table and she on the ground. We cursed, snorted, spoke without mincing our words, and were generally boorish to each other. Finally, she came to the conclusion that I am a bad role model for her children. She called to them, and took off.

Nighttime is the kingdom of sound, and most nocturnal occurrences are detected aurally. Darkness descends with the blackbird's final calls and continues with the jackal's yelping, sometimes very close to home. The jackals come back much later to yelp some more, and occasionally return for a midnight encore. In my humble opinion, this is how the packs tell one another where they are in order not to waste time

232

and energy on arguments and skirmishes. I am certain of this because I already understand some of their words, and others I infer. This is how I translate some of their nightly exchanges:

"We're at the dumpster tonight. How about you?"

"We're down at the chicken coop on the kibbutz."

"Howww ... Howwww ... did you manage to get inside?"

"That's a secret."

And sometimes I hear the jackals when the muezzin from the nearby village calls, and they join in. All this is good. They are God's creatures, too, and were created by His will and His word, and they also have the right to supplicate and to jack up God's glory. Who knows, perhaps "jackal" and "jack" share the same linguistic root?

Other nocturnal poets are toads and crickets. The toads live in the neighbors' small ornamental pond, and their crooning is pleasant, but the crickets in my own garden cause me sleepless nights and almost drive me out of my mind. "So humble, and hidden, concealed 'mongst the dishes, / Lamenting in crannies, at home in dark fissures" – so Bialik described the cricket in his father's house. But I have looked into this and found that during the day the cricket hides close to the trunks of the same trees it frequents at night. This is how I discovered this "poet of poverty" and relocated it to another part of the moshav, and the problem was solved.

There are other insufferable sounds, first and foremost the barking of dogs left outside by their owners at night. These dogs stand by the dark forest and bark with fear and trembling, hackles raised. Since I live right by the forest, this wakes me up. On the one hand, I am as angry as the next person at being woken up. On the other hand, I am amused at the absurdity of the whole situation: These dogs are not the wild animals their ancestors were. They are domestic creatures created by man for his own use and pleasure with selective crossbreeding. Food is served to them, and clean water is readily available. They have a roof over their heads and medical insurance. But the real animal kingdom is in the forest, a kingdom of real animals who live real lives, devouring and being devoured in a real forest. Consequently, their nocturnal barking not only expresses fear but a respect for fear.

It really is absurd, but sometimes it dawns on me that my garden is not that different from those dogs. After all, the garden is not really one hundred percent wild. It is true that domesticated dogs are comparable to ornamental plants and, like them, were created by humans, whereas in my garden there are authentic wild plants whose genetics I have not meddled with. But I do help them along by weeding, and I sow them in the right places at the right times. I pamper my garden with extra water when there is a particularly severe heat wave. If I am not mistaken, the garden sometimes stands and barks at the forest, realizing that uncompromising nature is over there, a battle for survival is over there, and the real wild, too.

HUMOR IN
THE GARDEN

"Earth laughs in flowers."

– Ralph Waldo Emerson

SAKI

THE OCCASIONAL
GARDEN

"DON'T TALK TO me about town gardens," said Elinor Rapsley; "which means, of course, that I want you to listen to me for an hour or so while I talk about nothing else. 'What a nice-sized garden you've got,' people said to us when we first moved here. What I suppose they meant to say was what a nice-sized site for a garden we'd got. As a matter of fact, the size is all against it; it's too large to be ignored altogether and treated as a yard, and it's too small to keep giraffes in. You see, if we could keep giraffes or reindeer or some other species of browsing animal there we could explain the general absence of vegetation by a reference to the fauna of the garden: 'You can't have wapiti *and* Darwin tulips, you know, so we didn't put down any bulbs last year.' As it is, we haven't got the wapiti, and the Darwin tulips haven't survived the fact that most of the cats of the neighbourhood hold a parliament in the centre of the tulip bed; that rather forlorn-looking strip that we intended to be a border of alternating geranium and spiræa has been utilized by the cat-parliament as a division lobby. Snap divisions seem to have been rather frequent of late, far more frequent than the geranium blooms are likely to be. I shouldn't object so much to ordinary cats, but I do complain of having a congress of vegetarian cats in my garden; they must be vegetarians, my dear, because, whatever ravages they may commit among the sweet-pea seedlings, they never seem to touch the sparrows; there are always just as many adult sparrows in the garden

239

on Saturday as there were on Monday, not to mention newly fledged additions. There seems to have been an irreconcilable difference of opinion between sparrows and Providence since the beginning of time as to whether a crocus looks best standing upright with its roots in the earth or in a recumbent posture with its stem neatly severed; the sparrows always have the last word in the matter, at least in our garden they do. I fancy that Providence must have originally intended to bring in an amending Act, or whatever it's called, providing either for a less destructive sparrow or a more indestructible crocus. The one consoling point about our garden is that it's not visible from the drawing-room or the smoking-room, so unless people are dining or lunching with us they can't spy out the nakedness of the land. That is why I am so furious with Gwenda Pottingdon, who has practically forced herself on me for lunch on Wednesday next; she heard me offer the Paulcote girl lunch if she was up shopping on that day, and, of course, she asked if she might come too. She is only coming to gloat over my bedraggled and flowerless borders and to sing the praises of her own detestably over-cultivated garden. I'm sick of being told that it's the envy of the neighbourhood; it's like everything else that belongs to her – her car, her dinner-parties, even her headaches, they are all superlative; no one else ever had anything like them. When her eldest child was confirmed it was such a sensational event, according to her account of it, that one almost expected questions to be asked about it in the House of Commons, and now she's coming on purpose to stare at my few miserable pansies and the gaps in my sweet-pea border, and to give me a glowing, full-length description of the rare and sumptuous blooms in her rose-garden."

"My dear Elinor," said the Baroness, "you would save yourself all this heart-burning and a lot of gardener's bills, not to mention sparrow anxieties, simply by paying an annual subscription to the O.O.S.A."

"Never heard of it," said Elinor; "what is it?"

"The Occasional-Oasis Supply Association," said the Baroness; "it exists to meet cases exactly like yours, cases of backyards that are of no practical use for gardening purposes, but are required to blossom into decorative scenic backgrounds at stated intervals, when a luncheon or dinner-party is contemplated. Supposing, for instance, you have people coming to lunch at one-thirty; you just ring up the Association at about ten o'clock the same morning, and say, 'Lunch garden.' That is all the trouble you have to take. By twelve forty-five your yard is carpeted with a strip of velvety turf, with a hedge of lilac or red may, or whatever happens to be in season, as a background, one or two cherry trees in blossom, and clumps of heavily flowered rhododendrons filling in the odd corners; in the foreground you have a blaze of carnations or Shirley poppies, or tiger lilies in full bloom. As soon as the lunch is over and your guests have departed the garden departs also, and all the cats in Christendom can sit in council in your yard without causing you a moment's anxiety. If you have a bishop or an antiquary or something of that sort coming to lunch you just mention the fact when you are ordering the garden, and you get an old-world pleasaunce, with clipped yew hedges and a sun-dial and hollyhocks, and perhaps a mulberry tree, and borders of sweet-williams and Canterbury bells, and an old-fashioned beehive or two tucked away in a corner. Those are the ordinary lines of supply that the Oasis Association undertakes, but by paying a few guineas a year extra you are entitled to its emergency E.O.N. service."

"What on earth is an E.O.N. service?"

"It's just like a conventional signal to indicate special cases like the incursion of Gwenda Pottingdon. It means you've got some one coming to lunch or dinner whose garden is alleged to be 'the envy of the neighbourhood'."

"Yes," exclaimed Elinor, with some excitement, "and what happens then?"

"Something that sounds like a miracle out of the Arabian Nights. Your backyard becomes voluptuous with pomegranate and almond trees, lemon groves, and hedges of flowering cactus, dazzling banks of azaleas, marble-basined fountains, in which chestnut-and-white pond-herons step daintily amid exotic water-lilies, while golden pheasants strut about on alabaster terraces. The whole effect rather suggests the idea that Providence and Norman Wilkinson have dropped mutual jealousies and collaborated to produce a background for an open-air Russian Ballet; in point of fact, it is merely the background to your luncheon party. If there is any kick left in Gwenda Pottingdon, or whoever your E.O.N. guest of the moment may be, just mention carelessly that your climbing putella is the only one in England, since the one at Chatsworth died last winter. There isn't such a thing as a climbing putella, but Gwenda Pottingdon and her kind don't usually know one flower from another without prompting."

"Quick," said Elinor, "the address of the Association."

Gwenda Pottingdon did not enjoy her lunch. It was a simple yet elegant meal, excellently cooked and daintily served, but the piquant sauce of her own conversation was notably lacking. She had prepared a long succession of eulogistic comments on the wonders of her town garden, with its unrivalled effects of horticultural magnificence, and, behold, her theme was shut in on every side by the luxuriant hedge of Siberian berberis that formed a glowing background to Elinor's bewildering fragment of fairyland. The pomegranate and lemon trees, the terraced fountain, where golden carp slithered and wriggled amid the roots of gorgeous-hued irises, the banked masses of exotic blooms, the pagoda-like enclosure, where Japanese sand-badgers disported themselves, all these contributed to take away Gwenda's appetite and moderate her desire to talk about gardening matters.

"I can't say I admire the climbing putella," she observed shortly, "and anyway it's not the only one of its kind in England; I happen to know of one in Hampshire. How gardening is going out of fashion. I suppose people haven't the time for it nowadays."

Altogether it was quite one of Elinor's most successful luncheon parties.

It was distinctly an unforeseen catastrophe that Gwenda should have burst in on the household four days later at lunch-time and made her way unbidden into the dining-room.

"I thought I must tell you that my Elaine has had a water-colour sketch accepted by the Latent Talent Art Guild; it's to be exhibited at their summer exhibition at the Hackney Gallery. It will be the sensation of the moment in the art world – Hullo, what on earth has happened to your garden? It's not there!"

"Suffragettes," said Elinor promptly; "didn't you hear about it? They broke in and made hay of the whole thing in about ten minutes. I was so heartbroken at the havoc that I had the whole place cleared out; I shall have it laid out again on rather more elaborate lines."

"That," she said to the Baroness afterwards, "is what I call having an emergency brain."

W. W. JACOBS

A GARDEN PLOT

THE ABLE-BODIED MEN of the village were at work, the children were at school singing the multiplication-table lullaby, while the wives and mothers at home nursed the baby with one hand and did the housework with the other. At the end of the village an old man past work sat at a rough deal table under the creaking signboard of the Cauliflower, gratefully drinking from a mug of ale supplied by a chance traveller who sat opposite him.

The shade of the elms was pleasant and the ale good. The traveller filled his pipe and, glancing at the dusty hedges and the white road baking in the sun, called for the mugs to be refilled, and pushed his pouch towards his companion. After which he paid a compliment to the appearance of the village.

"It ain't what it was when I was a boy," quavered the old man, filling his pipe with trembling fingers. "I mind when the grindstone was stuck just outside the winder o' the forge instead o' being one side as it now is; and as for the shop winder – it's twice the size it was when I was a young 'un."

He lit his pipe with the scientific accuracy of a smoker of sixty years' standing, and shook his head solemnly as he regarded his altered birthplace. Then his colour heightened and his dim eyes flashed.

"It's the people about 'ere 'as changed more than the place 'as," he said, with sudden fierceness; "there's a set o' men about here nowadays as are no good to anybody; reg'lar

247

raskels. And if you've the mind to listen *I* can tell you of one or two as couldn't be beat in London itself.

"There's Tom Adams for one, he went and started wot 'e called a Benevolent Club. Threepence a week each we paid agin sickness or accident, and Tom was secretary. Three weeks arter the club was started he caught a chill and was laid up for a month. He got back to work a week, and then 'e sprained something in 'is leg; and arter that was well 'is inside went wrong. We didn't think much of it at first, not understanding figures; but at the end o' six months the club hadn't got a farthing, and they was in Tom's debt one pound seventeen-and-six.

"He isn't the only one o' that sort in the place, either. There was Herbert Richardson. He went to town, and came back with the idea of a Goose Club for Christmas. We paid twopence a week into that for pretty near ten months, and then Herbert went back to town again, and all we 'ear of 'im, through his sister, is that he's still there and doing well, and don't know when he'll be back.

"But the artfullest and worst man in this place – and that's saying a good deal, mind you – is Bob Pretty. Deep is no word for 'im. There's no way of being up to 'im. It's through 'im that we lost our Flower Show; and, if you'd like to 'ear the rights o' that, I don't suppose there's anybody in this place as knows as much about it as I do – barring Bob hisself that is, but 'e wouldn't tell it to you as plain as I can.

"We'd only 'ad the Flower Show one year, and little any-body thought that the next one was to be the last. The first year you might smell the place a mile off in the summer and on the day of the show people came from a long way round, and brought money to spend at the Cauliflower and other places.

"It was started just after we got our new parson, and Mrs.

Pawlett, the parson's wife, 'is name being Pawlett, thought as she'd encourage men to love their 'omes and be better 'usbands by giving a prize every year for the best cottage garden. Three pounds was the prize, and a metal teapot with writing on it.

"As I said, we only 'ad it two years. The fust year the garden as got it was a picter, and Bill Chambers, 'im as won the prize, used to say as 'e was out o' pocket by it, taking 'is time and the money 'e spent on flowers. Not as we believed that, you understand, 'specially as Bill did 'is very best to get it the next year, too. 'E didn't get it, and though p'r'aps most of us was glad 'e didn't, we was all very surprised at the way it turned out in the end.

"The Flower Show was to be 'eld on the 5th o' July, just as a'most everything about here was at its best. On the 15th of June Bill Chambers's garden seemed to be leading, but Peter Smith and Joe Gubbins and Sam Jones and Henery Walker was almost as good, and it was understood that more than one of 'em had got a surprise which they'd produce at the last moment, too late for the others to copy. We used to sit up here of an evening at this Cauliflower public-house and put money on it. I put mine on Henery Walker, and the time I spent in 'is garden 'elping 'im is a sin and a shame to think of.

"Of course some of 'em used to make fun of it, and Bob Pretty was the worst of 'em all. He was always a lazy, good-for-nothing man, and 'is garden was a disgrace. He'd chuck down any rubbish in it: old bones, old tins, bits of an old bucket, anything to make it untidy. He used to larf at 'em awful about their gardens and about being took up by the parson's wife. Nobody ever see 'im do any work, real 'ard work, but the smell from 'is place at dinner-time was always nice, and I believe that he knew more about game than the parson hisself did.

249

"It was the day arter this one I'm speaking about, the 16th o' June, that the trouble all began, and it came about in a very eggstrordinary way. George English, a quiet man getting into years, who used when 'e was younger to foller the sea, and whose only misfortin was that 'e was a brother-in-law o' Bob Pretty's, his sister marrying Bob while 'e was at sea and knowing nothing about it, 'ad a letter come from a mate of his who 'ad gone to Australia to live. He'd 'ad letters from Australia before, as we all knew from Miss Wicks at the post office, but this one upset him altogether. He didn't seem like to know what to do about it.

"While he was wondering Bill Chambers passed. He always did pass George's house about that time in the evening, it being on 'is way 'ome, and he saw George standing at 'is gate with a letter in 'is 'and looking very puzzled.

" 'Evenin', George,' ses Bill.

" 'Evenin',' ses George.

" 'Not bad news, I 'ope?' ses Bill, noticing 'is manner, and thinking it was strange.

" 'No,' ses George. 'I've just 'ad a very eggstrordinary letter from Australia,' he ses, 'that's all.'

"Bill Chambers was always a very inquisitive sort o' man, and he stayed and talked to George until George, arter fust making him swear oaths that 'e wouldn't tell a soul, took 'im inside and showed 'im the letter.

"It was more like a story-book than a letter. George's mate, John Biggs by name, wrote to say that an uncle of his who had just died, on 'is deathbed told him that thirty years ago he 'ad been in this very village, staying at this 'ere very Cauliflower, whose beer we're drinking now. In the night, when everybody was asleep, he got up and went quiet-like and buried a bag of five hundred and seventeen sovereigns and one half-sovereign in one of the cottage gardens till 'e could come for it agin. He didn't say 'ow he come by the money, and, when Bill spoke about that, George English said that, knowing the man, he was afraid 'e 'adn't come by it honest, but anyway his friend John Biggs wanted it, and, wot was more, 'ad asked 'im in the letter to get it for 'im.

" 'And wot I'm to do about it, Bill,' he ses, 'I don't know. All the directions he gives is, that 'e thinks it was the tenth cottage on the right-'and side of the road, coming down from the Cauliflower. He thinks it's the tenth, but 'e's not quite sure. Do you think I'd better make it known and offer a reward of ten shillings, say, to any one who finds it?'

" 'No,' ses Bill, shaking 'is 'ead. 'I should hold on a bit if I was you, and think it over. I shouldn't tell another single soul, if I was you.'

" 'I b'lieve you're right,' ses George. 'John Biggs would never forgive me if I lost that money for 'im. You'll remember about it keeping secret, Bill?'

"Bill swore he wouldn't tell a soul, and 'e went off 'ome and 'ad his supper, and then 'e walked up the road to the Cauliflower and back, and then up and back again, thinking over what George 'ad been telling 'im, and noticing, what 'e'd never taken the trouble to notice before, that 'is very house was the tenth one from the Cauliflower.

"Mrs. Chambers woke up at two o'clock next morning and told Bill to get up farther, and then found 'e wasn't there. She was rather surprised at first, but she didn't think much of it, and thought, what happened to be true, that 'e was busy in the garden, it being a light night. She turned over and went to sleep again, and at five when she woke up she could distinctly 'ear Bill working 'is 'ardest. Then she went to the winder and nearly dropped as she saw Bill in his shirt and trousers digging away like mad. A quarter of the garden was all dug up, and she shoved open the winder and screamed out to know what 'e was doing.

"Bill stood up straight and wiped 'is face with his shirt-sleeve and started digging again, and then his wife just put something on and rushed downstairs as fast as she could go.

" 'What on earth are you a-doing of, Bill?' she screams.

" 'Go indoors,' ses Bill, still digging.

" 'Have you gone mad?' she ses, half crying.

"Bill just stopped to throw a lump of mould at her, and then went on digging till Henery Walker who also thought 'e 'ad gone mad, and didn't want to stop 'im too soon, put 'is 'ead over the 'edge and asked 'im the same thing.

" 'Ask no questions and you'll 'ear no lies, and keep your ugly face your own side of the 'edge,' ses Bill. 'Take it indoors and frighten the children with,' he ses. 'I don't want it staring at me.'

"Henery walked off offended, and Bill went on with his digging. He wouldn't go to work, and 'e 'ad his breakfast in the garden, and his wife spent all the morning in the front answering the neighbours' questions and begging of 'em to go in and say something to Bill. One of 'em did go, and came back a'most directly and stood there for hours telling diff'rent people wot Bill 'ad said to *'er*, and asking whether 'e couldn't be locked up for it.

"By tea-time Bill was dead-beat, and that stiff he could 'ardly raise 'is bread and butter to his mouth. Several o' the chaps looked in in the evening, but all they could get out of 'im was, that it was a new way o' cultivating 'is garden 'e 'ad just 'eard of, and that those who lived the longest would see the most. By night-time 'e'd nearly finished the job, and 'is garden was just ruined.

"Afore people 'ad done talking about Bill, I'm blest if Peter Smith didn't go and cultivate 'is garden in exactly the same way. The parson and 'is wife was away on their 'oliday, and nobody could say a word. The curate who 'ad come over to take 'is place for a time, and who took the names of people for the Flower Show, did point out to 'im that he was spoiling 'is chances, but Peter was so rude to 'im that he didn't stay long enough to say much.

"When Joe Gubbins started digging up 'is garden people began to think they were all bewitched, and I went round to see Henery Walker to tell 'im wot a fine chance 'e'd got, and to remind 'im that I'd put another ninepence on 'im the night before. All 'e said was: 'More fool you,' and went on digging a 'ole in his garden big enough to put a 'ouse in.

"In a fortnight's time there wasn't a garden worth looking at in the place, and it was quite clear there'd be no Flower Show that year, and of all the silly, bad-tempered men in the place them as 'ad dug up their pretty gardens was the wust.

"It was just a few days before the day fixed for the Flower Show, and I was walking up the road when I see Joe and Henery Walker and one or two more leaning over Bob Pretty's fence and talking to 'im. I stopped too, to see what they were looking at and found they was watching Bob's two boys a-weeding of 'is garden, it was a disgraceful, untidy sort of place, as I said before, with a few marigolds and nasturtiums, and sich-like put in anywhere, and Bob was walking up and down smoking of 'is pipe and watching 'is wife hoe atween the plants and cut off dead marigold blooms.

" 'That's a pretty garden you've got there, Bob,' ses Joe, grinning.

" 'I've seen wuss,' ses Bob.

" 'Going in for the Flower Show, Bob?' ses Henery, with a wink at us.

" 'O' course I am,' ses Bob, 'olding 'is 'ead up; 'my marigolds ought to pull me through,' he ses.

"Henery wouldn't believe it at fust, but when he saw Bob show 'is missus 'ow to pat the path down with the back o' the spade and hold the nails for 'er while she nailed a climbing nasturtium to the fence, he went off and fetched Bill Chambers and one or two others, and they all leaned over the fence breathing their 'ardest and a-saying of all the nasty things to Bob they could think of.

" 'It's the best-kep' garden in the place,' ses Bob. 'I ain't afraid o' your new way o' cultivating flowers, Bill Chambers. Old-fashioned ways suit me best; I learnt 'ow to grow flowers from my father.'

" 'You ain't 'ad the cheek to give your name in, Bob?' ses Sam Jones, staring.

"Bob didn't answer 'im. 'Pick those bits o' grass out o' the path, old gal,' he ses to 'is wife; 'they look untidy, and untidiness I can't abear.'

"He walked up and down smoking 'is pipe and pretending not to notice Henery Walker, wot 'ad moved farther along the fence, and was staring at some drabble-tailed-looking geraniums as if 'e'd seen 'em afore but wasn't quite sure where.

" 'Admiring my geraniums, Henery?' ses Bob at last.

" 'Where'd you get 'em?' ses Henery, 'ardly able to speak.

" 'My florist's,' says Bob in a off-hand manner.

" 'Your *wot*?' asks Henery.

" 'My florist,' ses Bob.

" 'And who might 'e be when 'e's at home?' asked Henery.

" 'Tain't so likely I'm going to tell you that,' ses Bob. 'Be reasonable, Henery, and ask yourself whether it's likely I should tell you 'is name. Why, I've never seen sich fine geraniums afore. I've been nursing 'em inside all the summer, and just planted 'em out.'

" 'About two days arter I threw mine over my back fence,' ses Henery Walker, speaking very slowly.

" 'Ho,' ses Bob, surprised. 'I didn't know you 'ad any geraniums, Henery. I thought you was digging for gravel this year.'

"Henery didn't answer him. Not because 'e didn't want to, mind you, but because he couldn't.

" 'That one,' ses Bob, pointing to a broken geranium with the stem of 'is pipe, 'is a "Dook o' Wellington," and that white one there is wot I'm going to call "Pretty's Pride." That fine marigold over there, wot looks like a sunflower, is called "Golden Dreams." '

" 'Come along, Henery,' ses Bill Chambers, bursting, 'come and get something to take the taste out of your mouth.'

" 'I'm sorry I can't offer you a flower for your button-'ole,' ses Bob, perlitely, 'but it's getting so near the Flower Show now I can't afford it. If you chaps only knew wot pleasure was to be 'ad sitting among your innercent flowers, you wouldn't want to go to the public-house so often.'

"He shook 'is 'ead at 'em, and telling his wife to give the 'Dook o' Wellington' a mug of water, sat down in the chair agin and wiped the sweat off 'is brow.

"Bill Chambers did a bit o' thinking as they walked up the road, and by and by 'e turns to Joe Gubbins and 'e ses:

" 'Seen anything o' George English lately, Joe?'

" '*Yes*,' ses Joe.

" 'Seems to me we all 'ave,' ses Sam Jones.

"None of 'em liked to say wot was in their minds, 'aving all seen George English and swore pretty strong not to tell his secret, and none of 'em liking to own up that they'd been digging up their gardens to get money as 'e'd told 'em about. But presently Bill Chambers ses: 'Without telling no secrets or breaking no promises, Joe, supposing a certain 'ouse was mentioned in a certain letter from forrin parts, wot 'ouse was it?'

" 'Supposing it was so,' ses Joe, careful, too; 'the second 'ouse, counting the Cauliflower.'

" 'The ninth 'ouse, you mean,' ses Henery Walker sharply.

" 'Second 'ouse in Mill Lane, you mean,' ses Sam Jones, wot lived there.

"Then they all see 'ow they'd been done, and that they wasn't, in a manner o' speaking, referring to the same letter. They came up and sat 'ere where we're sitting now, all dazed-like. It wasn't only the chance o' losing the prize that upset 'em, but they'd wasted their time and ruined their gardens and got called mad by the other folks. Henery Walker's state o' mind was dreadful for to see, and he kep' thinking of 'orrible things to say to George English, and then being afraid they wasn't strong enough.

"While they was talking who should come along but George English hisself! He came right up to the table, and they all sat back on the bench and stared at 'im fierce, and Henery Walker crinkled 'is nose at him.

" 'Evening,' he ses, but none of 'em answered 'im; they all looked at Henery to see wot 'e was going to say.

" 'Wot's up?' ses George in surprise.

" '*Gardens*,' ses Henery.

" 'So I've 'eard,' ses George.

"He shook his 'ead and looked at them sorrowful and severe at the same time.

" 'So I 'eard, and I couldn't believe my ears till I went and looked for myself,' he ses, 'and wot I want to say is this: you know wot I'm referring to. If any man 'as found wot don't belong to him 'e knows who to give it to. It ain't wot I should 'ave expected of men wot's lived in the same place as *me* for years. Talk about honesty,' 'e ses, shaking 'is 'ead agin, 'I should like to see a little of it.'

"Peter Smith opened his mouth to speak, and 'ardly knowing wot 'e was doing took a pull at 'is beer at the same time, and if Sam Jones 'adn't been by to thump 'im on the back I b'lieve he'd ha' died there and then.

" 'Mark my words,' ses George English, speaking very slow and solemn, 'there'll be no blessing on it. Whoever's made 'is fortune by getting up and digging 'is garden over won't get no real benefit from it. He may wear a black coat and new trousers on Sunday, but 'e won't be 'appy. I'll go and get my little taste 'o beer somewhere else,' 'e ses. 'I can't breathe here.'

"He walked off before any one could say a word; Bill Chambers dropped 'is pipe and smashed it. Henery Walker sat staring after 'im with 'is mouth wide open, and Sam Jones, who was always one to take advantage, drank 'is own beer under the firm belief that it was Joe's.

" 'I shall take care that Mrs. Pawlett 'ears o' this,' ses Henery at last.

" 'And be asked wot you dug your garden up for,' ses Joe, 'and 'ave to explain that you broke your promise to George. Why, she'd talk at us for years and years.'

" 'And parson 'ud preach a sermon about it,' ses Sam; 'where's your sense, Henery?'

" 'We should be the larfing-stock for miles round,' ses Bill Chambers. 'If anybody wants to know, I dug my garden up to enrich the soil for next year, and also to give some other chap a chance of the prize.'

"Peter Smith 'as always been a unfortunit man; he's got the name for it. He was just 'aving another drink as Bill said that, and this time we all thought 'e'd gorn. He did hisself.

"Mrs. Pawlett and the parson came 'ome next day, an'

'er voice got that squeaky with surprise it was painful to listen to her. All the chaps stuck to the tale that they'd dug their garden up to give the others a chance, and Henery Walker, 'e went farther and said it was owing to a sermon on unselfishness wot the curate 'ad preached three weeks afore. He 'ad a nice little red-covered 'ymnbook the next day with 'From a friend' wrote in it.

"All things considered, Mrs. Pawlett was for doing away with the Flower Show that year and giving two prizes next year instead, but one or two other chaps, encouraged by Bob's example, 'ad given in their names too, and they said it wouldn't be fair to their wives. All the gardens but one was worse than Bob's, the men not having started till later than wot 'e did, and not being able to get their geraniums from 'is florist. The only better garden was Ralph Thomson's, who lived next door to 'im, but two nights afore the Flower Show 'is pig got walking in its sleep. Ralph said it was a mystery to 'im 'ow the pig could ha' got out; it must ha' put its foot through a hole too small for it, and turned the button of its door, and then climbed over a four-foot fence. He told Bob 'e wished the pig could speak, but Bob said that that was sinful and unchristian of 'im, and that most likely if it could, it would only call 'im a lot o' bad names, and ask 'im why he didn't feed it properly.

"There was quite a crowd on Flower Show day following the judges. First of all, to Bill Chambers's astonishment and surprise, they went to 'is place and stood on the 'eaps in 'is garden judging 'em, while Bill peeped at 'em through the kitchen winder 'arf crazy. They went to every garden in the place, until one of the young ladies got tired of it, and asked Mrs. Pawlett whether they was there to judge cottage gardens or earthquakes.

"Everybody 'eld their breaths that evening in the schoolroom when Mrs. Pawlett got up on the platform and took a slip of paper from one of the judges. She stood a moment waiting for silence, and then 'eld up her 'and to stop what she thought was clapping at the back, but which was two or three wimmin who 'ad 'ad to take their crying babies out, trying to quiet 'em in the porch. Then Mrs. Pawlett put 'er glasses on her nose and just read out, short and sweet, that the prize of three sovereigns and a metal teapot for the best-kept cottage garden 'ad been won by Mr. Robert Pretty.

"One or two people patted Bob on the back as 'e walked up the middle to take the prize; then one or two more did, and Bill Chambers's pat was the 'eartiest of 'em all. Bob stopped and spoke to 'im about it.

"You would 'ardly think that Bob 'ud have the cheek to stand up there and make a speech, but 'e did. He said it gave 'im great pleasure to take the teapot and the money, and the more pleasure because 'e felt that 'e had earned 'em. He said that if 'e told 'em all 'e'd done to make sure o' the prize they'd be surprised. He said that 'e'd been like Ralph Thomson's pig, up early and late.

"He stood up there talking as though 'e was never going to leave off, and said that 'e hoped as 'is example would be a benefit to 'is neighbours. Some of 'em seemed to think that digging was everything, but 'e could say with pride that 'e 'adn't put a spade to 'is garden for three years until a week ago, and then not much.

"He finished 'is remarks by saying that 'e was going to give a tea-party up at the Cauliflower to christen the teapot, where 'e'd be pleased to welcome all friends. Quite a crowd got up and followed 'im out then, instead o' waiting for the dissolving views, and came back 'arf an hour arterwards, saying that until they'd got as far as the Cauliflower they'd no idea as Bob was so pertickier who 'e mixed with.

"That was the last Flower Show we ever 'ad in Claybury, Mrs. Pawlett and the judges meeting the tea-party coming 'ome, and 'aving to get over a gate into a field, to let it pass. What with that and Mrs. Pawlett tumbling over something farther up the road, which turned out to be the teapot, smelling strongly of beer, the Flower Show was given up, and the parson preached three Sundays running on the sin of beer-drinking to children who'd never 'ad any and wimmen who couldn't get it."

O. HENRY

ROSES, RUSES
AND ROMANCE

RAVENEL — RAVENEL, the traveller, artist and poet, threw his magazine to the floor. Sammy Brown, broker's clerk, who sat by the window, jumped.

"What is it, Ravvy?" he asked. "The critics been hammering your stock down?"

"Romance is dead," said Ravenel, lightly. When Ravenel spoke lightly he was generally serious. He picked up the magazine and fluttered its leaves.

"Even a Philistine, like you, Sammy," said Ravenel, seriously (a tone that ensured him to be speaking lightly), "ought to understand. Now, here is a magazine that once printed Poe and Lowell and Whitman and Bret Harte and Du Maurier and Lanier and – well, that gives you the idea. The current number has this literary feast to set before you: an article on the stokers and coal bunkers of battleships, an exposé of the methods employed in making liverwurst, a continued story of a Standard Preferred International Baking Powder deal in Wall Street, a 'poem' on the bear that the President missed, another 'story' by a young woman who spent a week as a spy making overalls on the East Side, another 'fiction' story that reeks of the 'garage' and a certain make of automobile. Of course, the title contains the words 'Cupid' and 'Chauffeur' – an article on naval strategy, illustrated with cuts of the Spanish Armada, and the new Staten Island ferry-boats; another story of a political boss who won the love of a Fifth Avenue belle by blackening her eye and refusing to vote for an iniquitous ordinance (it doesn't say whether it was in the Street-Cleaning Department or Congress), and nineteen pages by the editors bragging about the circulation. The whole thing, Sammy, is an obituary on Romance."

Sammy Brown sat comfortably in the leather armchair by the open window. His suit was a vehement brown with visible checks, beautifully matched in shade by the ends of four cigars that his vest pocket poorly concealed. Light tan were his shoes, gray his socks, sky-blue his apparent linen, snowy and high and adamantine his collar, against which a black butterfly had alighted and spread his wings. Sammy's face – least important – was round and pleasant and pinkish, and in his eyes you saw no haven for fleeing Romance.

That window of Ravenel's apartment opened upon an old garden full of ancient trees and shrubbery. The apartment-house towered above one side of it; a high brick wall fended it from the street; opposite Ravenel's window an old, old mansion stood, half-hidden in the shade of the summer foliage. The house was a castle besieged. The city howled and roared and shrieked and beat upon its double doors, and shook white, fluttering checks above the wall, offering terms of surrender. The gray dust settled upon the trees; the siege was pressed hotter, but the drawbridge was not lowered. No further will the language of chivalry serve. Inside lived an old gentleman who loved his home and did not wish to sell it. That is all the romance of the besieged castle.

Three or four times every week came Sammy Brown to Ravenel's apartment. He belonged to the poet's club, for the former Browns had been conspicuous, though Sammy had been vulgarized by Business. He had no tears for departed Romance. The song of the ticker was the one that reached his heart, and when it came to matters equine and batting scores he was something of a pink edition. He loved to sit in the leather armchair by Ravenel's window. And Ravenel didn't mind particularly. Sammy seemed to enjoy his talk; and then the broker's clerk was such a perfect embodiment of modernity and the day's sordid practicality that Ravenel rather liked to use him as a scapegoat.

"I'll tell you what's the matter with you," said Sammy, with the shrewdness that business had taught him. "The magazine has turned down some of your poetry stunts. That's why you are sore at it."

"That would be a good guess in Wall Street or in a campaign for the presidency of a woman's club," said Ravenel, quietly. "Now, there is a poem – if you will allow me to call it that – of my own in this number of the magazine."

"Read it to me," said Sammy, watching a cloud of pipe-smoke he had just blown out the window.

Ravenel was no greater than Achilles. No one is. There is bound to be a spot. The Somebody-or-Other must take hold of us somewhere when she dips us in the Something-or-Other that makes us invulnerable. He read aloud this verse in the magazine:

THE FOUR ROSES

> "One rose I twined within your hair –
> (White rose, that spake of worth);
> And one you placed upon your breast –
> (Red rose, love's seal of birth).
> You plucked another from its stem –
> (Tea rose, that means for aye);
> And one you gave – that bore for me
> The thorns of memory."

"That's a crackerjack," said Sammy, admiringly.

"There are five more verses," said Ravenel, patiently sardonic. "One naturally pauses at the end of each. Of course –"

"Oh, let's have the rest, old man," shouted Sammy, contritely, "I didn't mean to cut you off. I'm not much of a poetry expert, you know. I never saw a poem that didn't look like it ought to have terminal facilities at the end of every verse. Reel off the rest of it."

Ravenel sighed, and laid the magazine down. "All right," said Sammy, cheerfully, "we'll have it next time. I'll be off now. Got a date at five o'clock."

He took a last look at the shaded green garden and left, whistling in an off key an untuneful air from a roofless farce comedy.

The next afternoon Ravenel, while polishing a ragged line of a new sonnet, reclined by the window overlooking the besieged garden of the unmercenary baron. Suddenly he sat up, spilling two rhymes and a syllable or two.

Through the trees one window of the old mansion could be seen clearly. In its window, draped in flowing white, leaned the angel of all his dreams of romance and poesy. Young, fresh as a drop of dew, graceful as a spray of clematis, conferring upon the garden hemmed in by the roaring traffic the air of a princess's bower, beautiful as any flower sung by poet – thus Ravenel saw her for the first time. She lingered for a while, and then disappeared within, leaving a few notes of a birdlike ripple of song to reach his entranced ears through the rattle of cabs and the snarling of the electric cars.

Thus, as if to challenge the poet's flaunt at romance and to punish him for his recreancy to the undying spirit of youth and beauty, this vision had dawned upon him with a thrilling and accusive power. And so metabolic was the power that in an instant the atoms of Ravenel's entire world were redistributed. The laden drays that passed the house in which she lived rumbled a deep double-bass to the tune of love. The newsboys' shouts were the notes of singing birds; that garden was the pleasance of the Capulets; the janitor was an ogre; himself a knight, ready with sword, lance or lute.

Thus does romance show herself amid forests of brick and stone when she gets lost in the city, and there has to be sent out a general alarm to find her again.

At four in the afternoon Ravenel looked out across the garden. In the window of his hopes were set four small vases, each containing a great, full-blown rose – red and white. And, as he gazed, she leaned above them, shaming them with her loveliness and seeming to direct her eyes pensively toward his own window. And then, as though she had caught his respectful but ardent regard, she melted away, leaving the fragrant emblems on the windowsill.

Yes, emblems! – he would be unworthy if he had not understood. She had read his poem, "The Four Roses"; it had reached her heart; and this was its romantic answer. Of course she must know that Ravenel, the poet, lived there across her garden. His picture, too, she must have seen in the magazines. The delicate, tender, modest, flattering message could not be ignored.

Ravenel noticed beside the roses a small flowering-pot containing a plant. Without shame he brought his opera-glasses and employed them from the cover of his window-curtain. A nutmeg geranium!

With the true poetic instinct he dragged a book of useless information from his shelves, and tore open the leaves at "The Language of Flowers."

"Geranium, Nutmeg – I expect a meeting."

So! Romance never does things by halves. If she comes back to you she brings gifts and her knitting, and will sit in your chimney-corner if you will let her.

And now Ravenel smiled. The lover smiles when he thinks he has won. The woman who loves ceases to smile with victory. He ends a battle; she begins hers. What a pretty idea to set the four roses in her window for him to see! She must have a sweet, poetic soul. And now to contrive the meeting.

A whistling and slamming of doors preluded the coming of Sammy Brown.

Ravenel smiled again. Even Sammy Brown was shone upon by the far-flung rays of the renaissance. Sammy, with his ultra clothes, his horseshoe pin, his plump face, his trite slang, his uncomprehending admiration of Ravenel – the broker's clerk made an excellent foil to the new, bright unseen visitor to the poet's sombre apartment.

Sammy went to his old seat by the window, and looked out over the dusty green foliage in the garden. Then he looked at his watch, and rose hastily.

"By grabs!" he exclaimed. "Twenty after four! I can't stay, old man; I've got a date at 4:30."

"Why did you come, then?" asked Ravenel, with sarcastic jocularity, "if you had an engagement at that time. I thought you business men kept better account of your minutes and seconds than that."

Sammy hesitated in the doorway and turned pinker.

"Fact is, Ravvy," he explained, as to a customer whose margin is exhausted, "I didn't know I had it till I came. I'll tell you, old man – there's a dandy girl in that old house next door that I'm dead gone on. I put it straight – we're engaged. The old man says 'nit' but that don't go. He keeps her pretty close. I can see Edith's window from yours here. She gives me a tip when she's going shopping, and I meet her. It's 4:30 to-day. Maybe I ought to have explained sooner, but I know it's all right with you – so long."

"How do you get your 'tip,' as you call it?" asked Ravenel, losing a little spontaneity from his smile.

"Roses," said Sammy, briefly. "Four of 'em to-day. Means four o'clock at the corner of Broadway and Twenty-third."

"But the geranium?" persisted Ravenel, clutching at the end of flying Romance's trailing robe.

"Means half-past five," shouted Sammy from the hall. "See you to-morrow."

JOAN AIKEN

THE SERIAL GARDEN

"COLD RICE PUDDING for breakfast?" said Mark, looking at it with disfavour.

"Don't be fussy," said his mother. "You're the only one who's complaining." This was unfair, for she and Mark were the only members of the family at table, Harriet having developed measles while staying with a school friend, while Mr. Armitage had somehow managed to lock himself in the larder. Mrs. Armitage never had anything but toast and marmalade for breakfast anyway.

Mark went on scowling at the chilly-looking pudding. It had come straight out of the fridge, which was not in the larder.

"If you don't like it," said Mrs. Armitage, "unless you want Daddy to pass you cornflakes through the larder ventilator, flake by flake, you'd better run down to Miss Pride and get a small packet of cereal. She opens at eight; Hickmans doesn't open till nine. It's no use waiting until the blacksmith comes to let your father out; I'm sure he won't be here for hours yet."

There came a gloomy banging from the direction of the larder, just to remind them that Mr. Armitage was alive and suffering in there.

"*You're* all right," shouted Mark heartlessly as he passed the larder door. "There's nothing to stop *you* having cornflakes. Oh, I forgot, the milk's in the fridge. Well, have cheese and pickles then. Or treacle tart."

Even through the zinc grating on the door he could hear his father shudder at the thought of treacle tart and pickles for breakfast. Mr. Armitage's imprisonment was his own fault, though; he had sworn that he was going to find out where the mouse had got into the larder if it took him all night, watching and waiting. He had shut himself in, so that no member of the family should come bursting in and disturb his vigil. The larder door had a spring catch that sometimes jammed; it was bad luck that this turned out to be one of the times.

Mark ran across the fields to Miss Pride's shop at Sticks Corner and asked if she had any cornflakes.

"Oh, I don't think I have any left, dear," Miss Pride said woefully. "I'll have a look . . . I think I sold the last packet a week ago Tuesday."

"What about the one in the window?"

"That's a dummy, dear."

Miss Pride's shop window was full of nasty, dingy old cardboard cartons with nothing inside them, and several empty display stands which had fallen down and never been propped up again. Inside the shop were a few, small, tired-looking tins and jars, which had a worn and scratched appearance as if mice had tried them and given up. Miss Pride herself was small and wan, with yellowish grey hair; she rooted rather hopelessly in a pile of empty boxes. Mark's mother never bought any groceries from Miss Pride's if she could help it, since the day when she had found a label inside the foil wrapping of a cream cheese saying, "This cheese should be eaten before May 11, 1899."

"No cornflakes I'm afraid, dear."

"Any wheat crispies? Puffed corn? Rice nuts?"

"No, dear. Nothing left, only Brekkfast Brikks."

"Never heard of *them*," Mark said doubtfully.

"Or I have a jar of Ovo here. You spread it on bread. That's nice for breakfast," said Miss Pride, with a sudden burst of salesmanship. Mark thought the Ovo looked beastly, like yellow paint, so he took the packet of Brekkfast Brikks. At least it wasn't very big. . . . On the front of the box was a picture of a fat, repulsive, fair-haired boy, rather like the chubby Augustus, banging on his plate with his spoon.

"They look like tiny doormats," said Mrs. Armitage, as Mark shoveled some Brikks into the bowl.

"They taste like them, too. Gosh," said Mark, "I must hurry or I'll be late for school. There's rather a nice cut-out garden on the back of the packet though; don't throw it away when it's empty, Mother. Good-bye, Daddy," he shouted through the larder door, "hope Mr. Ellis comes soon to let you out." And he dashed off to catch the school bus.

At breakfast next morning Mark had a huge helping of Brekkfast Brikks and persuaded his father to try them.

"They taste just like esparto grass," said Mr. Armitage fretfully.

"Yes, I know, but do take some more, Daddy. I want to cut out the model garden, it's so lovely."

"Rather pleasant, I must say. It looks like an eighteenth-century German engraving," his father agreed. "It certainly was a stroke of genius putting it on the packet. No one would ever buy these things to eat for pleasure. Pass me the sugar, please. And the cream. And the strawberries."

It was the half-term holiday, so after breakfast Mark was able to take the empty packet away to the playroom and get on with the job of cutting out the stone walls, the row of little trees, the fountain, the yew arch, the two green lawns, and the tiny clumps of brilliant flowers. He knew better than to "stick tabs in slots and secure with paste", as the directions suggested; he had made models from packets

275

before and knew they always fell to pieces unless they were firmly bound together with sticky tape.

It was a long, fiddling, pleasurable job.

Nobody interrupted him. Mrs. Armitage only cleaned the playroom once every six months or so, when she made a ferocious descent on it and tidied up the tape recorders, roller skates, meteorological sets, and dismantled railway engines, and threw away countless old magazines, stringless tennis rackets, abandoned paintings, and unsuccessful models. There were always bitter complaints from Mark and Harriet; then they forgot and things piled up again till next time.

As Mark worked, his eye was caught by a verse on the outside of the packet:

"Brekkfast Brikks to start the day
Make you fit in every way.
Children bang their plates with glee
At Brekkfast Brikks for lunch and tea!
Brekkfast Brikks for supper too
Give peaceful sleep the whole night through."

"Blimey," thought Mark, sticking a cedar tree into the middle of the lawn and then bending a stone wall round at the dotted lines A, B, C, and D. "I wouldn't want anything for breakfast, lunch, tea, and supper, not even Christmas pudding. Certainly not Brekkfast Brikks."

He propped a clump of gaudy scarlet flowers against the wall and stuck them in place.

The words of the rhyme kept coming into his head as he worked, and presently he found that they went rather well to a tune that was running through his mind, and he began to hum, and then to sing; Mark often did this when he was alone and busy.

> "Brekkfast Brikks to sta-art the day,
> Ma-ake you fit in every way –

"Blow, where did I put that little bit of sticky tape? Oh, there it is.

> "Children bang their pla-ates with glee
> At Brekkfast Brikks for lunch and tea

"Slit gate with razor blade, it says, but it'll have to be a penknife.

> "Brekkfast Brikks for supper toohoo
> Give peaceful sleep the whole night throughoo. . . .

"Hullo. That's funny," said Mark.

It was funny. The openwork iron gate he had just stuck in position now suddenly towered above him. On either side, to right and left, ran the high stone wall, stretching away into foggy distance. Over the top of the wall he could see tall trees, yews and cypresses and others he didn't know.

"Well, that's the neatest trick I ever saw," said Mark. "I wonder if the gate will open?"

He chuckled as he tried it, thinking of the larder door. The gate did open, and he went through into the garden.

One of the things that had already struck him as he cut them out was that the flowers were not at all in the right proportions. But they were all the nicer for that. There were huge velvety violets and pansies the size of saucers; the holly-hocks were as big as dinner plates and the turf was sprinkled with enormous daisies. The roses, on the other hand, were miniature, no bigger than cuff buttons. There were real fish in the fountain, bright pink.

"*I* made all this," thought Mark, strolling along the mossy path to the yew arch. "Won't Harriet be surprised when she sees it. I wish she could see it now. I wonder what made it come alive like that?"

He passed through the yew arch as he said this and discovered that on the other side there was nothing but grey, foggy blankness. This, of course, was where his cardboard garden had ended. He turned back through the archway and gazed with pride at a border of huge scarlet tropical flowers that were perhaps supposed to be geraniums but certainly hadn't turned out that way. "I know! Of course, it was the rhyme, the rhyme on the packet."

He recited it. Nothing happened. "Perhaps you have to sing it," he thought and (feeling a little foolish) he sang it through to the tune that fitted so well. At once, faster than blowing out a match, the garden drew itself together and shrank into its cardboard again, leaving Mark outside.

"What a marvellous hiding place it'll make when I don't want people to come bothering," he thought. He sang the spell once more, just to make sure that it worked, and there was the high mossy wall, the stately iron gate, and the tree-tops. He stepped in and looked back. No playroom to be seen, only grey blankness.

At that moment he was startled by a tremendous clanging, the sort of sound the Trump of Doom would make if it was a dinner bell. "Blow," he thought, "I suppose that's lunch." He sang the spell for the fourth time; immediately he was in the playroom, and the garden was on the floor beside him, and Agnes was still ringing the dinner bell outside the door.

"All right, I heard," he shouted. "Just coming."

He glanced hurriedly over the remains of the packet to see if it bore any mention of the fact that the cut-out garden had magic properties. It did not. He did, however, learn that this was Section Three of the Beautiful Brekkfast Brikk Garden Series, and that Sections One, Two, Four, Five, and Six would be found on other packets. In case of difficulty in obtaining supplies, please write to Fruhstucksgeschirrziegelsteinindustrie (Great Britain), Lily Road, Shepherds Bush.

"Elevenpence a packet," Mark murmured to himself, going to lunch with unwashed hands. "Five elevens are thirty-five. Thirty-five pennies are – no, that's wrong. Fifty-five pence are four-and-sevenpence. Father, if I mow the lawn and carry coal every day for a month, can I have four shillings and sevenpence?"

"You don't want to buy another space gun, do you?" said Mr. Armitage looking at him suspiciously. "Because one is quite enough in this family."

"No, it's not for a space gun, I swear."

"Oh, very well."

"And can I have the four-and-seven now?"

Mr. Armitage gave it reluctantly. "But that lawn has to be like velvet, mind," he said. "And if there's any falling off in the coal supply, I shall demand my money back."

"No, no, there won't be," Mark promised in reply. As soon as lunch was over, he dashed down to Miss Pride's. Was there a chance that she would have sections One, Two, Four, Five, and Six? He felt certain that no other shop had even heard of Brekkfast Brikks, so she was his only hope, apart from the address in Shepherds Bush.

"Oh, I don't know, I'm sure," Miss Pride said, sounding very doubtful – and more than a little surprised. "There might just be a couple on the bottom shelf – yes, here we are."

They were sections Four and Five, bent and dusty, but intact, Mark saw with relief. "Don't you suppose you have any more anywhere?" he pleaded.

"I'll look in the cellar but I can't promise. I haven't had deliveries of any of these for a long time. Made by some foreign firm they were; people didn't seem very keen on them," Miss Pride said aggrievedly. She opened a door revealing a flight of damp stone stairs. Mark followed her down them like a bloodhound on the trail.

The cellar was a fearful confusion of mildewed, tattered, and toppling cartons, some full, some empty. Mark was nearly knocked cold by a shower of pilchards in tins, which he dislodged on to himself from the top of a heap of boxes. At last Miss Pride, with a cry of triumph, unearthed a little cache of Brekkfast Brikks, three packets which turned out to be the remaining sections, Six, One, and Two.

"There, isn't that a piece of luck now!" she said, looking quite faint with all the excitement. It was indeed rare for Miss Pride to sell as many as five packets of the same thing at one time.

Mark galloped home with his booty and met his father on the porch. Mr. Armitage let out a groan of dismay.

"I'd almost rather you'd bought a space gun," he said. Mark chanted in reply:

"Brekkfast Brikks for supper too
Give peaceful sleep the whole night through."

"I don't want peaceful sleep," Mr. Armitage said. "I intend to spend tonight mouse-watching again. I'm tired of finding footprints in the Stilton."

During the next few days Mark's parents watched anxiously to see, Mr. Armitage said, whether Mark would start to sprout esparto grass instead of hair. For he doggedly ate Brekkfast Brikks for lunch, with soup, or sprinkled over his pudding; for tea, with jam, and for supper lightly fried in dripping, not to mention, of course, the immense helpings he had for breakfast with sugar and milk. Mr. Armitage for his part soon gave out; he said he wouldn't taste another Brekkfast Brikk even if it were wrapped in an inch-thick layer of *pâté de foie gras*. Mark regretted that Harriet, who was a handy and uncritical eater, was still away, convalescing from her measles with an aunt.

In two days, the second packet was finished (sundial, paved garden, and espaliers). Mark cut it out, fastened it together, and joined it onto Section Three with trembling hands. Would the spell work for this section, too? He sang the rhyme in rather a quavering voice, but luckily the playroom door was shut and there was no one to hear him. Yes! The gate grew again above him, and when he opened it and ran across the lawn through the yew arch, he found himself in a flagged garden full of flowers like huge blue cabbages.

Mark stood hugging himself with satisfaction, and then began to wander about smelling the flowers, which had a spicy perfume most unlike any flower he could think of. Suddenly he pricked up his ears. Had he caught a sound? There! It was like somebody crying and seemed to come from the other side of the hedge. He ran to the next opening and looked through. Nothing, only grey mist and empti-ness. But, unless he had imagined it, just before he got there, he thought his eye had caught the flash of white-and-gold draperies swishing past the gateway.

"Do you think Mark's all right?" Mrs. Armitage said to her husband next day. "He seems to be in such a dream all the time."

"Boy's gone clean off his rocker if you ask me," grumbled Mr. Armitage. "It's all these doormats he's eating. Can't be good to stuff your insides with mouldy jute. Still I'm bound to say he's cut the lawn very decently and seems to be remembering the coal. I'd better take a day off from the office and drive you over to the shore for a picnic; sea air will do him good."

Mrs. Armitage suggested to Mark that he should slack off on the Brekkfast Brikks, but he was so horrified that she had to abandon the idea. But, she said, he was to run four times round the garden every morning before breakfast. Mark almost said, "Which garden?" but stopped just in time. He had cut out and completed another large lawn, with a lake and weeping willows, and on the far side of the lake had a tantalizing glimpse of a figure dressed in white and gold who moved away and was lost before he could get there.

After munching his way through the fourth packet, he was able to add on a broad grass walk bordered by curiously clipped trees. At the end of the walk he could see the white-and-gold person, but when he ran to the spot, no one was there – the walk ended in the usual grey mist.

When he had finished and had cut out the fifth packet (an orchard), a terrible thing happened to him. For two days he could not remember the tune that worked the spell. He tried other tunes, but they were no use. He sat in the playroom singing till he was hoarse or silent with despair. Suppose he never remembered it again?

His mother shook her head at him that evening and said he looked as if he needed a dose. "It's lucky we're going to Shinglemud Bay for the day tomorrow," she said. "That ought to do you good."

"Oh, *blow*. I'd forgotten about that," Mark said. "Need I go?"

His mother stared at him in utter astonishment.

But in the middle of the night he remembered the right tune, leaped out of bed in a tremendous hurry, and ran down

282

to the playroom without even waiting to put on his dressing-gown and slippers.

The orchard was most wonderful, for instead of mere apples its trees bore oranges, lemons, limes, and all sorts of tropical fruits whose names he did not know, and there were melons and pineapples growing and plantains and avocados. Better still, he saw the lady in her white and gold waiting at the end of an alley and was able to draw near enough to speak to her.

"Who are you?" she asked. She seemed very much astonished at the sight of him.

"My name's Mark Armitage," he said politely. "Is this your garden?"

Close to, he saw that she was really very grand indeed. Her dress was white satin embroidered with pearls, and swept the ground; she had a gold scarf and her hair, dressed high and powdered, was confined in a small gold-and-pearl tiara. Her face was rather plain, pink with a long nose, but she had a kind expression and beautiful grey eyes.

"Indeed it is," she announced with hauteur. "I am Princess Sophia Maria Louisa of Saxe-Hoffenpoffen-und-Hamster. What are you doing here, pray?"

"Well," Mark explained cautiously, "it seemed to come about through singing a tune."

"Indeed. That is very interesting. Did the tune, perhaps, go like this?"

The princess hummed a few bars.

"That's it! How did you know?"

"Why, you foolish boy, it was I who put that spell on the garden, to make it come alive when the tune is played or sung."

"I say!" Mark was full of admiration. "Can you do spells as well as being a princess?"

She drew herself up. "Naturally! At the court of Saxe-Hoffenpoffen, where I was educated, all princesses were taught a little magic, not so much as to be vulgar, just enough to get out of social difficulties."

"Jolly useful," Mark said. "How did you work the spell for the garden, then?"

"Why, you see" (the princess was obviously delighted to have somebody to talk to; she sat on a stone seat and patted it, inviting Mark to do likewise), "I had the misfortune to fall in love with Herr Rudolf, the Court Kapellmeister, who taught me music. Oh, he was so kind and handsome! And he was most talented, but my father, of course, would not hear of my marrying him because he was only a common person."

"So what did you do?"

"I arranged to vanish, of course. Rudi had given me a beautiful book with many pictures of gardens. My father kept strict watch to see I did not run away, so I used to slip between the pages of the book when I wanted to be alone. Then, when we decided to marry, I asked my maid to take the book to Rudi. And I sent him a note telling him to play the tune when he received the book. But I believe that spiteful Gertrud must have played me false and never taken the book, for more than fifty years have now passed and I have been here all alone, waiting in the garden, and Rudi has never come. Oh, Rudi, Rudi," she exclaimed, wringing her hands and crying a little, "where can you be? It is so long – so long!"

"Fifty years," Mark said kindly, reckoning that must make her nearly seventy. "I must say you don't look it."

"Of course I do not, dumbhead. For me, I make it that time does not touch me. But tell me, how did you know the tune that works the spell? It was taught me by my dear Rudi."

"I'm not sure where I picked it up," Mark confessed. "For all I know it may be one of the Top Ten. I'll have to ask my music teacher, he's sure to know. Perhaps he'll have heard of your Rudolf, too."

Privately Mark feared that Rudolf might very well have died by now, but he did not like to depress Princess Sophia Maria by such a suggestion, so he bade her a polite good night, promising to come back as soon as he could with another section of the garden and any news he could pick up.

He planned to go and see Mr. Johansen, his music teacher, next morning, but he had forgotten the family trip to the beach. There was just time to scribble a hasty postcard to the British office of Fruhstucksgeschirrziegelsteinindustrie, asking if they could inform him from what source they had obtained the pictures used on the packets of Brekkfast Brikks. Then Mr. Armitage drove his wife and son to Shinglemud Bay, gloomily prophesying wet weather.

In fact, the weather turned out fine, and Mark found it quite restful to swim and play beach cricket and eat ham sandwiches and lie in the sun. For he had been struck by a horrid thought: suppose he should forget the tune again while he was inside the garden – would he be stuck there, like Father in the larder? It was a lovely place to go and wander at will, but somehow he didn't fancy spending the next fifty years there with Princess Sophia Maria. Would she oblige him by singing the spell if he forgot it, or would she be too keen on company to let him go? He was not inclined to take any chances.

It was late when they arrived home, too late, Mark thought, to disturb Mr. Johansen, who was elderly and kept early hours. Mark ate a huge helping of Brekkfast Brikks for supper – he was dying to finish Section Six – but did not visit the garden that night.

Next morning's breakfast (Brikks with hot milk, for a change) finished the last packet – and just as well, for the larder mouse, which Mr. Armitage still had not caught, was discovered to have nibbled the bottom left-hand corner of the packet, slightly damaging an ornamental grotto in a grove of lime trees. Rather worried about this, Mark decided to make up the last section straightaway, in case the magic had been affected. By now he was becoming very skilled at the tiny fiddling task of cutting out the little tabs and slipping them into the little slots; the job did not take long to finish. Mark attached Section Six to Section Five and then, drawing a deep breath, sang the incantation once more. With immense relief he watched the mossy wall and rusty gate grow out of the playroom floor; all was well.

He raced across the lawn, round the lake, along the avenue, through the orchard, and into the lime grove. The scent of the lime flowers was sweeter than a cake baking.

Princess Sophia Maria came towards him from the grotto, looking slightly put out.

"Good morning!" she greeted Mark. "Do you bring me any news?"

"I haven't been to see my music teacher yet," Mark confessed. "I was a bit anxious because there was a hole –"

"Ach, yes, a hole in the grotto! I have just been looking. Some wild beast must have made its way in, and I am afraid it may come again. See, it has made tracks like those of a big bear." She showed him some enormous footprints in the soft sand of the grotto floor. Mark stopped up the hole with prickly branches and promised to bring a dog when he next came, though he felt fairly sure the mouse would not return.

"I can borrow a dog from my teacher – he has plenty. I'll be back in an hour or so – see you then," he said.

"*Auf Wiedersehen*, my dear young friend."

Mark ran along the village street to Mr. Johansen's house, Houndshaven Cottage. He knew better than to knock at the door, because Mr. Johansen would be either practicing his violin or out in the barn at the back, and in any case the sound of barking was generally loud enough to drown any noise short of gunfire.

Besides giving music lessons at Mark's school, Mr. Johansen kept a guest house for dogs whose owners were abroad or on holiday. He was extremely kind to the guests and did his best to make them feel at home in every way, finding out from their owners what were their favourite foods, and letting them sleep on his own bed, turn about. He spent all his spare time with them, talking to them and playing either his violin or long-playing records of domestic sounds likely to appeal to the canine fancy – such as knives being sharpened, cars starting up, and children playing ball games.

Mark could hear Mr. Johansen playing Brahms's lullaby in the barn, so he went out there; the music was making some of the more susceptible inmates feel homesick: howls, sympathetic moans, and long, shuddering sighs came from the numerous comfortably carpeted cubicles all the way down the barn.

Mr. Johansen reached the end of the piece as Mark entered. He put down his fiddle and smiled welcomingly.

"Ach, how *gut*! It is the young Mark."

"Hullo, sir."

"You know," confided Mr. Johansen, "I play to many audiences in my life all over the world, but never anywhere do I get such a response as from zese dear doggies – it is really remarkable. But come in, come into ze house and have some coffee cake."

Mr. Johansen was a gentle, white-haired elderly man; he

walked slowly with a slight stoop and had a kindly, sad face with large dark eyes. He looked rather like some sort of dog himself, Mark always thought, perhaps a collie or a long-haired dachshund.

"Sir," Mark said, "if I whistle a tune to you, can you write it down for me?"

"Why, yes, I shall be most happy," Mr. Johansen said, pouring coffee for both of them.

So Mark whistled his tune once more; as he came to the end, he was surprised to see the music master's eyes fill with tears, which slowly began to trickle down his thin cheeks.

"It recalls my youth, zat piece," he explained, wiping the tears away and rapidly scribbling crotchets and minims on a piece of music paper. "Many times I am whistling it myself – it is wissout doubt from me you learn it – but always it is reminding me of how happy I was long ago when I wrote it."

"You *wrote* that tune?" Mark said, much excited.

"Why, yes. What is so strange in zat? Many, many tunes haf I written."

"Well –" Mark said, "I won't tell you just yet in case I'm mistaken – I'll have to see somebody else first. Do you mind if I dash off right away? Oh, and might I borrow a dog – preferably a good ratter?"

"In zat case, better have my dear Lotta – alzough she is so old, she is ze best of zem all," Mr. Johansen said proudly. Lotta was his own dog, an enormous shaggy lumbering animal with a tail like a palm tree and feet the size of electric polishers; she was reputed to be of incalculable age; Mr. Johansen called her his strudel-hound. She knew Mark well and came along with him quite biddably, though it was rather like leading a mammoth.

Luckily his mother, refreshed by her day at the sea, was

heavily engaged with Agnes the maid in spring cleaning. Furniture was being shoved about, and everyone was too busy to notice Mark and Lotta slip into the playroom.

A letter addressed to Mark lay among the clutter on the table; he opened and read it while Lotta foraged happily among the piles of magazines and tennis nets and cricket bats and rusting electronic equipment, managing to upset several things and increase the general state of hugger-mugger in the room.

Dear Sir, (the letter said – it was from Messrs. Digit, Digit & Rule, a firm of chartered accountants) – We are in receipt of your inquiry as to the source of pictures on packets of Brekkfast Brikks. We are pleased to inform you that these were reproduced from the illustrations of a little-known 18th-century German work, *Steinbergen's Gartenbuch*. Unfortunately the only known remaining copy of this book was burnt in the disastrous fire which destroyed the factory and premises of Messrs. Fruhstucksgeschirrziegel-steinindustrie two months ago. The firm has now gone into liquidation and we are winding up their effects. Yours faithfully, P. J. Zero, Gen. Sec.

"*Steinbergen's Gartenbuch*," Mark thought. "That must have been the book that Princess Sophia Maria used for the spell – probably the same copy. Oh, well, since it's burned, it's lucky the pictures were reproduced on the Brekkfast Brikks packets. Come on, Lotta, let's go and find a nice princess then. Good girl! Rats! Chase 'em!"

He sang the spell and Lotta, all enthusiasm, followed him into the garden.

They did not have to go far before they saw the princess – she was sitting sunning herself on the rim of the fountain. But what happened then was unexpected. Lotta let out the most extraordinary cry – whine, bark, and howl all in one – and hurled herself towards the princess like a rocket.

"Hey! Look out! Lotta! *Heel!*" Mark shouted in alarm. But Lotta, with her great paws on the princess's shoulders, had about a yard of salmon-pink tongue out, and was washing the princess's face all over with frantic affection.

The princess was just as excited. "Lotta. Lotta! She knows me, it's dear Lotta, it must be! Where did you get her?" she cried to Mark, hugging the enormous dog, whose tail was going round faster than a turbo prop.

"Why, she belongs to my music master, Mr. Johansen, and it's he who made up the tune," Mark said.

The princess turned quite white and had to sit down on the fountain's rim again.

"*Johansen*? Rudolf Johansen? My Rudi! At last! After all these years! Oh, run, run, and fetch him immediately, please! Immediately!"

Mark hesitated just a moment.

"Please make haste!" she besought him. "Why do you wait?"

"It's only – well, you won't be surprised if he's quite *old*, will you? Remember he hasn't been in a garden keeping young like you."

"All that will change," the princess said confidently. "He has only to eat the fruit of the garden. Why, look at Lotta – when she was a puppy, for a joke I gave her a fig from this tree, and you can see she is a puppy still, though she must be older than any other dog in the world! Oh, please hurry to bring Rudi here."

"Why don't you come with me to his house?"

"That would not be correct etiquette," she said with dignity. "After all, I *am* royal."

"Okay," Mark said. "I'll fetch him. Hope he doesn't think I'm crackers."

"Give him this." The princess took off a locket on a gold chain. It had a miniature of a romantically handsome young man with dark curling hair. "My Rudi," she explained fondly. Mark could just trace a faint resemblance to Mr. Johansen.

He took the locket and hurried away. At the gate something made him look back: the princess and Lotta were sitting at the edge of the fountain, side by side. The princess had an arm round Lotta's neck; with the other hand she waved to him, just a little.

"Hurry!" she called again.

Mark made his way out of the house, through the spring-cleaning chaos, and flew down the village to Houndshaven Cottage. Mr. Johansen was in the house this time, boiling up a noisome mass of meat and bones for the dogs' dinner. Mark said nothing at all, just handed him the locket. He took one look at it and staggered, putting his hand to his heart; anxiously, Mark led him to a chair.

"Are you all right, sir?"

"Yes, yes! It was only ze shock. Where did you get ziss, my boy?"

So Mark told him.

Surprisingly, Mr. Johansen did not find anything odd about the story; he nodded his head several times as Mark related the various points.

"Yes, yes, her letter, I have it still" – he pulled out a worn little scrap of paper – "but ze *Gartenbuch* it reached me never. Zat wicked Gertrud must haf sold it to some bookseller who sold it to Fruhstucksgeschirrziegelsteinindustrie. And so she has been waiting all ziss time! My poor little Sophie!"

"Are you strong enough to come to her now?" Mark asked.

"*Naturlich!* But first we must give ze dogs zeir dinner; zey must not go hungry."

So they fed the dogs, which was a long job as there were at least sixty and each had a different diet, including some very odd preferences like Swiss roll spread with Marmite and yeast pills wrapped in slices of caramel. Privately, Mark thought the dogs were a bit spoiled, but Mr. Johansen was very careful to see that each visitor had just what it fancied.

"After all, zey are not mine! Must I not take good care of zem?"

At least two hours had gone by before the last willow-pattern plate was licked clean, and they were free to go. Mark made rings around Mr. Johansen all the way up the village; the music master limped quietly along, smiling a little; from time to time he said, "Gently, my friend. We do not run a race. Remember I am an old man."

That was just what Mark did remember. He longed to see Mr. Johansen young and happy once more.

The chaos in the Armitage house had changed its location: the front hall was now clean, tidy, and damp; the rumpus of vacuuming had shifted to the playroom. With a black hollow of apprehension in his middle, Mark ran through the open door and stopped, aghast. All the toys, tools, weapons, boxes, magazines, and bits of machinery had been rammed into the cupboards; the floor where his garden had been laid out was bare. Mrs. Armitage was in the playroom taking down the curtains.

"*Mother!* Where's my Brekkfast Brikks garden?"

"Oh, darling, you didn't want it, did you? It was all dusty, I thought you'd finished it. I'm afraid I've burned it in the furnace. Really, you *must* try not to let this room get into such a clutter, it's perfectly disgraceful. Why, hullo, Mr. Johansen, I'm afraid you've called at the worst possible moment. But I'm sure you'll understand how it is at spring-cleaning time."

She rolled up her bundle of curtains, glancing worriedly at Mr. Johansen; he looked rather odd, she thought. But he gave her his tired, gentle smile, and said,

"Why, yes, Mrs. Armitage, I understand, I understand very well. Come, Mark. We have no business here, you can see."

Speechlessly, Mark followed him. What was there to say?

"Never mind," Mrs. Armitage called after Mark. "The Rice Nuts pack has a helicopter on it."

Every week in *The Times* newspaper you will see this advertisement:

> BREKKFAST BRIKKS PACKETS. £100
> offered for any in good condition,
> whether empty or full.

So if you have any, you know where to send them.

But Mark is growing anxious; none have come in yet, and every day Mr. Johansen seems a little thinner and more elderly. Besides, what will the princess be thinking?

JOHN COLLIER

GREEN THOUGHTS

Annihilating all that's made
To a green thought in a green shade.
MARVELL

THE ORCHID HAD been sent among the effects of his friend, who had come by a lonely and mysterious death on the expedition. Or he had bought it among a miscellaneous lot, "unclassified," at the close of the auction. I forget which it was, but it was certainly one or the other of these. Moreover, even in its dry, brown, dormant root state, this orchid had a certain sinister quality. It looked, with its bunched and ragged projections, like a rigid yet a gripping hand, hideously gnarled, or a grotesquely whiskered, threatening face. Would you not have known what sort of an orchid it was?

Mr. Mannering did not know. He read nothing but catalogues and books on fertilizers. He unpacked the new acquisition with a solicitude absurd enough in any case toward any orchid, or primrose either, in the twentieth century, but idiotic, foolhardy, doom-eager, when extended to an orchid thus come by, in appearance thus. And in his traditional obtuseness he at once planted it in what he called the "Observation Ward," a hothouse built against the south wall of his dumpy red dwelling. Here he set always the most interesting additions to his collection, and especially weak and sickly plants, for there was a glass door in his study wall through which he could see into this hothouse, so that the weak and sickly plants could encounter no crisis without his immediate knowledge and his tender care.

This plant, however, proved hardy enough. At the ends of thick and stringy stalks it opened out bunches of darkly shining leaves, and soon it spread in every direction, usurping so much space that first one, then another, then all its neighbours had to be removed to a hothouse at the end of the garden. It was, Cousin Jane said, a regular hopvine. At the ends of the stalks, just before the leaves began, were set groups of tendrils, which hung idly, serving no apparent purpose. Mr. Mannering thought that very probably these were vestigial organs, a heritage from some period when the plant had been a climber. But when were the vestigial tendrils of an ex-climber half or quarter so thick and strong?

After a long time sets of tiny buds appeared here and there among the extravagant foliage. Soon they opened into small flowers, miserable little things; they looked like flies' heads. One naturally expects a large, garish, sinister bloom, like a sea anemone, or a Chinese lantern, or a hippopotamus yawning, on any important orchid; and should it be an unclassified one as well, I think one has every right to insist on a sickly and overpowering scent into the bargain.

Mr. Mannering did not mind at all. Indeed, apart from his joy and happiness in being the discoverer and godfather of a new sort of orchid, he felt only a mild and scientific interest in the fact that the paltry blossoms were so very much like flies' heads. Could it be to attract other flies for food or as fertilizers? But then, why like their heads?

It was a few days later that Cousin Jane's cat disappeared. This was a great blow to Cousin Jane, but Mr. Mannering was not, in his heart of hearts, greatly sorry. He was not fond of the cat, for he could not open the smallest chink in a glass roof for ventilation but the creature would squeeze through somehow to enjoy the warmth, and in this way it had broken many a tender shoot. But before poor Cousin Jane had lamented two days something happened which so engrossed Mr. Mannering that he had no mind left at all with which to sympathize with her affliction, or to make at breakfast kind and hypocritical inquiries after the lost cat. A strange new bud appeared on the orchid. It was clearly evident that there would be two quite different sorts of bloom on this one plant, as sometimes happens in such fantastic corners of the vegetable world, and that the new flower would be very different in size and structure from the earlier ones. It grew bigger and bigger, till it was as big as one's fist.

And just then – it could never have been more inopportune – an affair of the most unpleasant, the most distressing nature summoned Mr. Mannering to town. It was his wretched nephew, in trouble again, and this time so deeply and so very disgracefully that it took all Mr. Mannering's generosity, and all his influence, too, to extricate the worthless young man. Indeed, as soon as he saw the state of affairs, he told the prodigal that this was the very last time he might expect assistance, that his vices and his ingratitude had long ago cancelled all affection between them, and that for this last helping hand he was indebted only to his mother's memory, and to no faith on the part of his uncle either in his repentance or his reformation. He wrote, moreover, to Cousin Jane, to relieve his feelings, telling her of the whole business, and adding that the only thing left to do was to cut the young man off entirely.

When he got back to Torquay, Cousin Jane was nowhere to be found. The situation was extremely annoying. Their only servant was a cook who was very old and very stupid and very deaf. She suffered besides from an obsession, owing to the fact that for many years Mr. Mannering had had no conversation with her in which he had not included an impressive reminder that she must always, no matter what might happen, keep the big kitchen stove up to a certain pitch of activity. For this stove, besides supplying the house with hot water, heated the pipes in the "Observation Ward," to which the daily gardener who had charge of the other hothouses had no access. By this time she had come to regard her duties as stoker as her chief *raison d'être*, and it was difficult to penetrate her deafness with any question which her stupidity and her obsession did not somehow transmute into an inquiry after the stove, and this, of course, was especially the case when Mr. Mannering spoke to her. All he could disentangle was what she had volunteered on first seeing him, that his cousin had not been seen for three days, that she had left without saying a word. Mr. Mannering was perplexed and annoyed, but, being a man of method, he thought it best to postpone further inquiries until he had refreshed himself a little after his long and tiring journey. A full supply of energy was necessary to extract any information from the old cook; besides, there was probably a note somewhere. It was only natural that before he went to his room Mr. Mannering should peep into the hothouse, just to make sure that the wonderful orchid had come to no harm during the inconsiderate absence of Cousin Jane. As soon as he opened the door his eyes fell upon the bud; it had now changed in shape very considerably, and had increased in size to the bigness of a human head. It is no exaggeration to state that Mr. Mannering remained rooted to the spot, with his eyes fixed upon this wonderful bud, for fully five minutes.

But, you will ask, why did he not see her clothes on the floor? Well, as a matter of fact (it is a delicate point), there were no clothes on the floor. Cousin Jane, though of course she was entirely estimable in every respect, though she was well over forty, too, was given to the practice of the very latest ideas on the dual culture of the soul and body – Swedish, German, neo-Greek and all that. And the orchid house was the warmest place available. I must proceed with the order of events.

Mr. Mannering at length withdrew his eyes from this stupendous bud, and decided that he must devote his attention to the grey exigencies of everyday life. But although his body dutifully ascended the stairs, heart, mind, and soul all remained in adoration of the plant. Although he was philosophical to the point of insensibility over the miserable smallness of the earlier flowers, yet he was now as much gratified by the magnitude of the great new bud as you or I might be. Hence it was not unnatural that Mr. Mannering while in his bath should be full of the most exalted visions of the blossoming of his heart's darling, his vegetable godchild. It would be by far the largest known, complex as a dream, or dazzlingly simple. It would open like a dancer, or like the sun rising. Why, it might be opening at this very moment! Mr. Mannering could restrain himself no longer; he rose from the steamy water, and, wrapping his bathrobe about him, hurried down to the hothouse, scarcely staying to dry himself, though he was subject to colds.

The bud had not yet opened; it still reared its unbroken head among the glossy, fleshy foliage, and he now saw, what he had had no eyes for previously, how very exuberant that foliage had grown. Suddenly he realized with astonishment that this huge bud was not the one which had appeared before he went away. That one had been lower down on the plant. Where was it now, then? Why, this new thrust and spread of foliage concealed it from him. He walked across, and discovered it. It had opened into a bloom. And as he looked at this bloom his astonishment grew to stupefaction, one might say to petrification, for it is a fact that Mr. Mannering remained rooted to the spot, with his eyes fixed on the flower, for fully fifteen minutes. The flower was an exact replica of the head of Cousin Jane's lost cat. The similitude was so exact, so life-like, that Mr. Mannering's first movement, after the fifteen minutes, was to seize his bathrobe and draw it about him, for he was a modest man, and the cat, though bought for a Tom, had proved to be quite the reverse. I relate this to show how much character, spirit, *presence* – call it what you will – there was upon this floral cat's face. But although he made to seize his bathrobe, it was too late. He could not move. The new lusty foliage had closed in unperceived; the too lightly dismissed tendrils were everywhere upon him; he gave a few weak cries and sank to the ground, and there, as the Mr. Mannering of ordinary life, he passes out of this story.

Mr. Mannering sank into a coma, into an insensibility so deep that a black eternity passed before the first faint elements of his consciousness reassembled themselves in his brain. For of his brain was the centre of a new bud being made. Indeed, it was two or three days before this at first almost hopeless and quite primitive lump of organic matter had become sufficiently mature to be called Mr. Mannering at all. These days, which passed quickly enough, in a certain mild, not unpleasant excitement, in the outer world, seemed to the dimly working mind within the bud to resume the whole history of the development of our species, in a great many epochal parts.

A process analogous to the mutations of the embryo was being enacted here. At last the entity which was thus being rushed down an absurdly foreshortened vista of the ages slowed up and came almost to a stop in the present.

It became recognizable. The Seven Ages of Mr. Mannering were presented, as it were, in a series of close-ups, as in an educational film; his consciousness settled and cleared. The bud was mature, ready to open. At this point, I believe, Mr. Mannering's state of mind was exactly that of a patient who, wakening from under an anaesthetic, struggling up from vague dreams, asks plaintively, "Where am I?" Then the bud opened, and he knew.

There was the hothouse, but seen from an unfamiliar angle. There, through the glass door, was his study. There below him was the cat's head, and there – there beside him was Cousin Jane. He could not say a word, but then, neither could she. Perhaps it was as well. At the very least, he would have been forced to own that she had been in the right in an argument of long standing; she had always maintained that in the end no good would come of his preoccupation with "those unnatural flowers."

It must be admitted that Mr. Mannering was not at first greatly upset by this extraordinary upheaval in his daily life. This, I think, was because he was interested, not only in private and personal matters, but in the wider and more general, one might say the biological, aspects of his metamorphosis. For the rest, simply because he *was* now a vegetable, he responded with a vegetable reaction. The impossibility of locomotion, for example, did not trouble him in the least, or even the absence of body and limbs, any more than the cessation of that stream of rashers and tea, biscuits and glasses of milk, luncheon cutlets, and so forth, that had flowed in at his mouth for over fifty years, but which had now been reversed to a gentle, continuous, scarcely noticeable feeding from below. All the powerful influence of the physical upon the mental, therefore, inclined him to tranquillity. But the physical is not all. Although no longer

303

a man, he was still Mr. Mannering. And from this anomaly, as soon as his scientific interest had subsided, issued a host of woes, mainly subjective in origin.

He was fretted, for instance, by the thought that he would now have no opportunity to name his orchid, or to write a paper upon it, and, still worse, there grew up in his mind the abominable conviction that, as soon as his plight was discovered, it was he who would be named and classified, and that he himself would be the subject of a paper, possibly even of comment and criticism in the lay press. Like all orchid collectors, he was excessively shy and sensitive, and in his present situation these qualities were very naturally exaggerated, so that the bare idea of such attentions brought him to the verge of wilting. Worse yet was the fear of being transplanted, thrust into some unfamiliar, draughty, probably public place. Being dug up! Ugh! A violent shudder pulsated through all the heavy foliage that sprang from Mr. Mannering's division of the plant. He became conscious of ghostly and remote sensations in the stem below, and in certain tufts of leaves that sprouted from it; they were somehow reminiscent of spine and heart and limbs. He felt quite a dryad.

In spite of all, however, the sunshine was very pleasant. The rich odour of hot, spicy earth filled the hothouse. From a special fixture on the hot-water pipes a little warm steam oozed into the air. Mr. Mannering began to abandon himself of a feeling of *laissez-aller*. Just then, up in a corner of the glass roof, at the ventilator, he heard a persistent buzzing. Soon the note changed from one of irritation to a more complacent sound; a bee had managed, after some difficulty, to find his way through one of the tiny chinks in the metal work. The visitor came drifting down and down through the still, green air, as if into some subaqueous world, and he came to rest on one of those petals which were Mr. Mannering's eyebrows. Thence he commenced to explore one feature after another, and at last he settled heavily on the lower lip, which drooped under his weight and allowed him to crawl right into Mr. Mannering's mouth. This was quite a considerable shock, of course, but on the whole the sensation was neither as alarming nor as unpleasant as might have been expected. "Indeed," thought the vegetable gentleman, "it seems quite agreeable."

But Mr. Mannering soon ceased the drowsy analysis of his sensations when he saw the departed bee, after one or two lazy circlings, settle directly upon the maiden lip of Cousin Jane. Ominous as lightning, a simple botanical principle flashed across the mind of her wretched relative. Cousin Jane was aware of it also, although, being the product of an earlier age, she might have remained still blessedly ignorant had not her cousin – vain, garrulous, proselytizing fool! – attempted for years past to interest her in the rudiments of botany. How the miserable man upbraided himself now! He saw two bunches of leaves just below the flower tremble and flutter, and rear themselves painfully upwards into the very likeness of two shocked and protesting hands. He saw the soft and orderly petals of his cousin's face ruffle and incarnadine with rage and embarrassment, then turn sickly as a gardenia with horror and dismay. But what was he to do? All the rectitude implanted by his careful training, all the chivalry proper to an orchid-collector, boiled and surged beneath a paralytically calm exterior. He positively travailed in the effort to activate the muscles of his face, to assume an expression of grief, manly contrition, helplessness in the face of fate, willingness to make honourable amends, all suffused with the light of a vague but solacing optimism; but it was in vain. When he had strained till his nerves seemed likely to tear under the tension, the only movement he could achieve was a trivial flutter of the left eyelid – worse than nothing.

This incident completely aroused Mr. Mannering from his vegetable lethargy. He rebelled against the limitations of the form into which he had thus been cast while subjectively he remained all too human. Was he not still at heart a man, with a man's hopes, ideals, aspirations – and capacity for suffering?

When dusk came, and the opulent and sinister shapes of the great plant dimmed to a suggestiveness more powerfully impressive than had been its bright noonday luxuriance, and the atmosphere of a tropical forest filled the orchid-house like an exile's dream or the nostalgia of the saxophone; when the cat's whiskers drooped, and even Cousin Jane's eyes slowly closed, the unhappy man remained wide awake, staring into the gathering darkness. Suddenly the light in the study was switched on. Two men entered the room. One of them was his lawyer, the other was his nephew.

"This is his study, as you know, of course," said the wicked nephew. "There's nothing here. I looked when I came over on Wednesday."

"I've sat in this room many an evening," said the lawyer with an expression of distaste. "I'd sit on this side of the fireplace and he on that. 'Mannering,' I'd think to myself, 'I wonder how you'll end up. Drugs? Sexual perversion? Or murder?' Well, maybe we'll soon know the answer. Until we do, I suppose you, as next of kin, had better take charge here."

Saying this, the lawyer turned, about to go, and Mr. Mannering saw a malicious smile overspread the young man's face. The uneasiness which had overcome him at first sight of his nephew was intensified to fear and trembling at the sight of this smile.

When he had shown the lawyer out, the nephew returned to the study and looked round him with lively and sinister satisfaction. Then he cut a caper on the hearth-rug. Mr. Mannering thought he had never seen anything so diabolical as this solitary expression of the glee of a venomous nature at the prospect of unchecked sway, here whence he had been outcast. How vulgar petty triumph appeared, beheld thus; how disgusting petty spite, how appalling revengefulness and hardness of heart! He remembered suddenly that his nephew had been notable, in his repulsive childhood, for his cruelty to flies, tearing their wings off, and for his barbarity toward cats. A sort of dew might have been noticed upon the good man's forehead. It seemed to him that his nephew had only to glance that way, and all would be discovered, although he might have remembered that it was impossible to see from the lighted room into the darkness of the hothouse.

On the mantelpiece stood a large unframed photograph of Mr. Mannering. His nephew soon caught sight of this, and strode across to confront it with a triumphant and insolent sneer. "What? You old Pharisee," said he, "taken her off for a trip to Brighton, have you? My God! How I hope you'll never come back! How I hope you've fallen over the cliffs, or got swept off by the tide or something! Anyway – I'll make hay while the sun shines. Ugh! you old skinflint, you!" And he reached forward his hand, and bestowed a contemptuous fillip upon the nose in the photograph. Then the usurping rascal left the room, leaving all the lights on, presumably preferring the dining-room with its cellarette to the scholarly austerities of the study.

All night long the glare of electric light from the study fell upon Mr. Mannering and his Cousin Jane, like the glare of a cheap and artificial sun. You who have seen at midnight in the park a few insomniac asters standing stiff and startled under an arc light, all their weak colour bleached out of them by the drenching chemical radiance, neither asleep nor awake, but held fast in a tense, a neurasthenic trance, you can form an idea of how the night passed with this unhappy pair.

And toward morning an incident occurred, trivial in itself no doubt, but sufficient then and there to add the last drop to poor Cousin Jane's discomfiture and to her relative's embarrassment and remorse. Along the edge of the great earthbox in which the orchid was planted, ran a small black mouse. It had wicked red eyes, a naked, evil snout, and huge, repellent ears, queer as a bat's. This creature ran straight over the lower leaves of Cousin Jane's part of the plant. It was simply appalling. The stringy main stem writhed like a hair on a coal-fire, the leaves contracted in an agonized spasm, like seared mimosa; the terrified lady nearly uprooted herself in her convulsive horror. I think she would actually have done so, had not the mouse hurried on past her.

But it had not gone more than a foot or so when it looked up and saw, bending over it, and seeming positively to bristle with life, that flower which had once been called Tib. There was a breathless pause. The mouse was obviously paralysed with terror, the cat could only look and long. Suddenly the more human watchers saw a sly frond of foliage curve softly outward and close in behind the hypnotized creature. Cousin Jane, who had been thinking exultantly, "Well, now it'll go away and never, never, never come back," suddenly became aware of hideous possibilities. Summoning all her energy, she achieved a spasmodic flutter, enough to break the trance that held the mouse, so that, like a clock-work toy, it swung round and fled. But already the fell arm of the orchid had cut off its retreat. The mouse leaped straight at it. Like a flash five tendrils at the end caught the fugitive and held it fast, and soon its body dwindled and was gone. Now the heart of Cousin Jane was troubled with horrid fears, and slowly and painfully she turned her weary face first to one side, then to the other, in a fever of anxiety as to where the new bud would appear. A sort of sucker, green and sappy, which twisted lightly about her main stem, and reared a blunt head, much like a tip of asparagus, close to her own, suddenly began to swell in the most suspicious manner. She squinted at it, fascinated and appalled. Could it be her imagination? It was not.

Next evening the door opened again, and again the nephew entered the study. This time he was alone, and it was evident that he had come straight from table. He carried in his hand a decanter of whiskey capped by an inverted glass. Under his arm was a siphon. His face was distinctly flushed, and such a smile as is often seen in saloon bars played about his lips. He put down his burdens and, turning to Mr. Mannering's cigar cabinet, produced a bunch of keys, which he proceeded to try upon the lock, muttering vindictively at each abortive attempt, until it opened, when he helped himself from the best of its contents. Annoying as it was to witness this insolent appropriation of his property, and mortifying to see the contempt with which the cigar was smoked, the good gentleman found deeper cause for uneasiness in the thought that, with the possession of the keys, his abominable nephew had access to every private corner that was his.

At present, however, the usurper seemed indisposed to carry on investigations; he splashed a great deal of whiskey into the tumbler and relaxed into an attitude of extravagant comfort. But after a while the young man began to tire of his own company. He had not yet had time to gather any of his pothouse companions into his uncle's home, and repeated recourse to the whiskey bottle only increased his longing for something to relieve the monotony. His eye fell upon the door of the orchid-house. Sooner or later it was bound to have happened. Does this thought greatly console the condemned man when the fatal knock sounds upon the door of his cell? No. Nor were the hearts of the trembling pair in the hothouse at all comforted by the reflection.

As the nephew fumbled with the handle of the glass door, Cousin Jane slowly raised two fronds of leaves that grew on each side, high upon her stem, and sank her troubled head behind them. Mr. Mannering observed, in a sudden rapture of hope, that by this device she was fairly well concealed from any casual glance. Hastily he strove to follow her example. Unfortunately, he had not yet gained sufficient control of his – his *limbs*? – and all his tortured efforts could not raise them beyond an agonized horizontal. The door had opened, the nephew was feeling for the electric light switch just inside. It was a moment for one of the superlative achievements of panic. Mr. Mannering was well equipped for the occasion. Suddenly, at the cost of indescribable effort, he succeeded in raising the right frond, not straight upwards, it is true, but in a series of painful jerks along a curve outward and backward, and ascending by slow degrees till it attained the position of an arm held over the possessor's head from behind. Then, as the light flashed on, a spray of leaves at the very end of this frond spread out into a fan, rather like a very fleshy horse-chestnut leaf in structure, and covered the anxious face below. What a relief! And now the nephew advanced into the orchid-house, and now the hidden pair simultaneously remembered the fatal presence of the cat. Simultaneously also, their very sap stood still in their veins. The nephew was walking along by the plant. The cat, a sagacious beast, "knew" with the infallible intuition of its kind that this was an idler, a parasite, a sensualist, gross and brutal, disrespectful of age, insolent to weakness, barbarous to cats. Therefore it remained very still, trusting to its low and somewhat retired position on the plant, and to protective mimicry and such things, and to the half-drunken condition of the nephew, to avoid his notice. But all in vain.

"What?" said the nephew. "What, a cat?" And he raised his hand to offer a blow at the harmless creature. Something in the dignified and unflinching demeanour of his victim must have penetrated into his besotted mind, for the blow never fell, and the bully, a coward at heart, as bullies invariably are, shifted his gaze from side to side to escape the steady, contemptuous stare of the courageous cat. Alas! His eye fell on something glimmering whitely behind the dark foliage. He brushed aside the intervening leaves that he might see what it was. It was Cousin Jane.

"Oh! Ah!" said the young man, in great confusion. "*You're* back. But what are you hiding there for?"

His sheepish stare became fixed, his mouth opened in bewilderment; then the true condition of things dawned upon his mind. Most of us would have at once instituted some attempt at communication, or at assistance of some kind, or at least have knelt down to thank our Creator that we had, by His grace, been spared such a fate, or perhaps have made haste from the orchid-house to ensure against accidents. But alcohol had so inflamed the young man's hardened nature that he felt neither fear, nor awe, nor gratitude. As he grasped the situation a devilish smile overspread his face.

"Ha! Ha! Ha!" said he. "But where's the old man?"

He peered about the plant, looking eagerly for his uncle. In a moment he had located him and, raising the inadequate visor of leaves, discovered beneath it the face of our hero, troubled with a hundred bitter emotions.

"Hullo, Narcissus!" said the nephew.

A long silence ensued. The spiteful wretch was so pleased that he could not say a word. He rubbed his hands together, and licked his lips, and stared and stared as a child might at a new toy.

"Well, you're properly up a tree," he said. "Yes, the tables are turned now all right, aren't they? Do you remember the last time we met?"

A flicker of emotion passed over the face of the suffering blossom, betraying consciousness.

"Yes, you can hear what I say," added the tormentor. "Feel, too, I expect. What about that?"

As he spoke, he stretched out his hand and, seizing a delicate frill of fine, silvery filaments that grew as whiskers grow around the lower half of the flower, he administered a sharp tug. Without pausing to note, even in the interests of science, the subtler shades of his uncle's reaction, content with the general effort of that devastating wince, the wretch chuckled with satisfaction and, taking a long pull from the reeking butt of the stolen cigar, puffed the vile fumes straight into his victim's centre. The brute!

"How do you like that, John the Baptist?" he asked with a leer. "Good for the blight, you know. Just what you want!"

Something rustled upon his coat sleeve. Looking down, he saw a long stalk, well adorned with the fatal tendrils, groping its way over the arid and unsatisfactory surface. In a moment it had reached his wrist, he felt it fasten, but knocked it off as one would a leech, before it had time to establish its hold.

"Ugh!" said he. "So that's how it happens, is it? I think I'll keep outside till I get the hang of things a bit. I don't want to be made an Aunt Sally of. Though I shouldn't think they could get you with your clothes on." Struck by a sudden thought, he looked from his uncle to Cousin Jane, and from

Cousin Jane back to his uncle again. He scanned the floor, and saw a single crumpled bathrobe lying in the shadow.

"Why!" he said. "*Well!* – Haw! Haw! Haw!" And with an odious backward leer, he made his way out of the orchid-house.

Mr. Mannering felt that his suffering was capable of no increase. Yet he dreaded the morrow. His fevered imagination patterned the long night with waking nightmares, utterly fantastic visions of humiliation and torture. Torture! It was absurd, of course, for him to fear cold-blooded atrocities on the part of his nephew, but how he dreaded some outrageous whim that might tickle the youth's sense of humour, and lead him to *any* wanton freak, especially if he were drunk at the time. He thought of slugs and snails, espaliers and topiary. If only the monster would rest content with insulting jests, with wasting his substance, ravaging his cherished possessions before his eyes, with occasional pulling at the whiskers, even! Then it might be possible to turn gradually from all that still remained in him of man, to subdue the passions, no longer to admire or desire, to go native as it were, relapsing into the Nirvana of a vegetable dream. But in the morning he found this was not so easy.

In came the nephew and, pausing only to utter the most perfunctory of jeers at his relatives in the glass house, he sat at the desk and unlocked the top drawer. He was evidently in search of money, his eagerness betrayed that; no doubt he had run through all he had filched from his uncle's pockets, and had not yet worked out a scheme for getting direct control of his bank account. However, the drawer held enough to cause the scoundrel to rub his hands with satisfaction and, summoning the housekeeper, to bellow into her ear a reckless order upon the wine and spirits merchant.

"Get along with you!" he shouted, when he had at last

made her understand. "I shall have to get someone a bit more on the spot to wait on me; I can tell you that. Yes," he added to himself as the poor old woman hobbled away, deeply hurt by his bullying manner, "yes, a nice little parlour-maid."

He hunted in the telephone book for the number of the local registry office. That afternoon he interviewed a succession of maidservants in his uncle's study. Those that happened to be plain, or too obviously respectable, he treated curtly and coldly; they soon made way for others. It was only when a girl was attractive (according to the young man's depraved tastes, that is) and also bore herself in a fast or brazen manner, that the interview was at all prolonged. In these cases the nephew would conclude in a fashion that left no doubt in the minds of any of his auditors as to his real intentions. Once, for example, leaning forward, he took the girl by the chin, saying with an odious smirk, "There's no one else but me, and so you'd be treated just like one of the family, d'you see, my dear?" To another he would say, slipping his arm round her waist, "Do you think we shall get on well together?"

After this conduct had sent two or three in confusion from the room, there entered a young person of the most regrettable description; one whose character, betrayed as it was in her meretricious finery, her crude cosmetics, and her tinted hair, showed yet more clearly in florid gesture and too facile smile. The nephew lost no time in coming to an arrangement with this creature. Indeed, her true nature was so obvious that the depraved young man only went through the farce of an ordinary interview as a sauce to his anticipations, enjoying the contrast between conventional dialogue and unbridled glances. She was to come next day. Mr. Mannering feared more for his unhappy cousin than for himself. "What scenes may she not have to witness," he thought, "that yellow cheek of hers to incarnadine?" If only he could have said a few words!

But that evening, when the nephew came to take his ease in the study, it was obvious that he was far more under the influence of liquor than he had been before. His face, flushed patchily by the action of the spirits, wore a sullen sneer; an ominous light burned in that bleared eye; he muttered savagely under his breath. Clearly this fiend in human shape was what is known as "fighting drunk"; clearly some trifle had set his vile temper in a blaze.

It is interesting to note, even at this stage, a sudden change in Mr. Mannering's reactions. They now seemed entirely egotistical, and were to be elicited only by stimuli directly associated with physical matters. The nephew kicked a hole in a screen in his drunken fury, he flung a burning cigar-end down on the carpet, he scratched matches on the polished table. His uncle witnessed this with the calm of one whose sense of property and of dignity has become numbed and paralysed; he felt neither fury nor mortification. Had he, by one of those sudden strides by which all such development takes place, approached much nearer to his goal, complete vegetation? His concern for the threatened modesty of Cousin Jane, which had moved him so strongly only a few hours earlier, must have been the last dying flicker of exhausted altruism; that most human characteristic had faded from him. The change, however, in its present stage, was not an unmixed blessing. Narrowing in from the wider and more expressly human regions of his being, his consciousness now left outside its focus not only pride and altruism, which had been responsible for much of his woe, but fortitude and detachment also, which, with quotations from the Greek, had been his support before the whole battery of his distresses. Moreover, within its constricted circle, his ego was not reduced but concentrated; his serene, flower-like indifference toward the ill-usage of his furniture was balanced by the absorbed, flower-like single-mindedness of his terror at the thought of similar ill-usage directed toward himself.

Inside the study the nephew still fumed and swore. On the mantelpiece stood an envelope, addressed in Mr. Mannering's handwriting to Cousin Jane. In it was the letter he had written from town, describing his nephew's disgraceful conduct. The young man's eye fell upon this and, unscrupulous, impelled by idle curiosity, he took it up and drew out the letter. As he read, his face grew a hundred times blacker than before.

"What," he muttered, " 'a mere race-course cad . . . a worthless vulgarian . . . a scoundrel of the sneaking sort' . . . and what's this? '. . . cut him off absolutely . . .' What?" said he, with a horrifying oath. "*Would* you cut me off absolutely? Two can play at that game, you old devil!"

And he snatched up a large pair of scissors that lay on the desk, and burst into the hothouse –

Among fish, the dory, they say, screams when it is seized upon by man; among insects, the caterpillar of the death's-head moth is capable of a still, small shriek of terror; in the vegetable world, only the mandrake could voice its agony – till now.

GARDENS OF THE IMAGINATION

"The soul cannot thrive in the absence of a garden."

– Sir Thomas More

NATHANIEL HAWTHORNE

RAPPACCINI'S
DAUGHTER

A YOUNG MAN, named Giovanni Guasconti, came, very long ago, from the more southern region of Italy, to pursue his studies at the University of Padua. Giovanni, who had but a scanty supply of gold ducats in his pocket, took lodgings in a high and gloomy chamber of an old edifice which looked not unworthy to have been the palace of a Paduan noble, and which, in fact, exhibited over its entrance the armorial bearings of a family long since extinct. The young stranger, who was not unstudied in the great poem of his country, recollected that one of the ancestors of this family, and perhaps an occupant of this very mansion, had been pictured by Dante as a partaker of the immortal agonies of his Inferno. These reminiscences and associations, together with the tendency to heartbreak natural to a young man for the first time out of his native sphere, caused Giovanni to sigh heavily as he looked around the desolate and ill-furnished apartment.

"Holy Virgin, signor!" cried old Dame Lisabetta, who, won by the youth's remarkable beauty of person, was kindly endeavoring to give the chamber a habitable air, "what a sigh was that to come out of a young man's heart! Do you find this old mansion gloomy? For the love of Heaven, then, put your head out of the window, and you will see as bright sunshine as you have left in Naples."

Guasconti mechanically did as the old woman advised, but could not quite agree with her that the Paduan sunshine was as cheerful as that of southern Italy. Such as it was, however, it fell upon a garden beneath the window and expended its fostering influences on a variety of plants, which seemed to have been cultivated with exceeding care.

"Does this garden belong to the house?" asked Giovanni.

"Heaven forbid, signor, unless it were fruitful of better pot herbs than any that grow there now," answered old Lisabetta. "No; that garden is cultivated by the own hands of Signor Giacomo Rappaccini, the famous doctor, who, I warrant him, has been heard of as far as Naples. It is said that he distils these plants into medicines that are as potent as a charm. Oftentimes you may see the signor doctor at work, and perchance the signora, his daughter, too, gathering the strange flowers that grow in the garden."

The old woman had now done what she could for the aspect of the chamber; and, commending the young man to the protection of the saints, took her departure.

Giovanni still found no better occupation than to look down into the garden beneath his window. From its appearance, he judged it to be one of those botanic gardens which were of earlier date in Padua than elsewhere in Italy or in the world. Or, not improbably, it might once have been the pleasure-place of an opulent family; for there was the ruin of a marble fountain in the centre, sculptured with rare art, but so woefully shattered that it was impossible to trace the original design from the chaos of remaining fragments. The water, however, continued to gush and sparkle into the sunbeams as cheerfully as ever. A little gurgling sound ascended to the young man's window, and made him feel as if the fountain were an immortal spirit that sung its song unceasingly and without heeding the vicissitudes around it, while one century imbodied it in marble and another scattered the perishable garniture on the soil. All about the pool into which the water subsided grew various plants, that seemed to require a plentiful supply of moisture for the nourishment of gigantic leaves, and, in some instances, flowers gorgeously magnificent. There was one shrub in particular, set in a marble vase in the midst of the pool, that bore a profusion of purple blossoms, each of which had the lustre and richness of a gem; and the whole together made a show so resplendent that it seemed enough to illuminate the garden, even had there been no sunshine. Every portion of the soil was peopled with plants and herbs, which, if less beautiful, still bore tokens of assiduous care, as if all had their individual virtues, known to the scientific mind that fostered them. Some were placed in urns, rich with old carving, and others in common garden pots; some crept serpent-like along the ground or climbed on high, using whatever means of ascent was offered them. One plant had wreathed itself round a statue of Vertumnus, which was thus quite veiled and shrouded in a drapery of hanging foliage, so happily arranged that it might have served a sculptor for a study.

While Giovanni stood at the window he heard a rustling behind a screen of leaves, and became aware that a person was at work in the garden. His figure soon emerged into view, and showed itself to be that of no common laborer, but a tall, emaciated, sallow, and sickly-looking man, dressed in a scholar's garb of black. He was beyond the middle term of life, with gray hair, a thin, gray beard, and a face singularly marked with intellect and cultivation, but which could never, even in his more youthful days, have expressed much warmth of heart.

Nothing could exceed the intentness with which this scientific gardener examined every shrub which grew in his path: it seemed as if he was looking into their inmost nature, making observations in regard to their creative essence, and discovering why one leaf grew in this shape and another in that, and wherefore such and such flowers differed among themselves in hue and perfume. Nevertheless, in spite of this deep intelligence on his part, there was no approach to intimacy between himself and these vegetable existences. On the contrary, he avoided their actual touch or the direct inhaling of their odors with a caution that impressed Giovanni most disagreeably; for the man's demeanor was that of one walking among malignant influences, such as savage beasts, or deadly snakes, or evil spirits, which, should he allow them one moment of license, would wreak upon him some terrible fatality. It was strangely frightful to the young man's imagination to see this air of insecurity in a person cultivating a garden, that most simple and innocent of human toils, and which had been alike the joy and labor of the unfallen parents of the race. Was this garden, then, the Eden of the present world? And this man, with such a perception of harm in what his own hands caused to grow, – was he the Adam?

The distrustful gardener, while plucking away the dead leaves or pruning the too luxuriant growth of the shrubs, defended his hands with a pair of thick gloves. Nor were these his only armor. When, in his walk through the garden, he came to the magnificent plant that hung its purple gems beside the marble fountain, he placed a kind of mask over his mouth and nostrils, as if all this beauty did but conceal a deadlier malice; but, finding his task still too dangerous, he drew back, removed the mask, and called loudly, but in the infirm voice of a person affected with inward disease, –

"Beatrice! Beatrice!"

"Here am I, my father. What would you?" cried a rich and youthful voice from the window of the opposite house – a voice as rich as a tropical sunset, and which made Giovanni, though he knew not why, think of deep hues of purple or crimson and of perfumes heavily delectable. "Are you in the garden?"

"Yes, Beatrice," answered the gardener, "and I need your help."

Soon there emerged from under a sculptured portal the figure of a young girl, arrayed with as much richness of taste as the most splendid of the flowers, beautiful as the day, and with a bloom so deep and vivid that one shade more would have been too much. She looked redundant with life, health, and energy; all of which attributes were bound down and compressed, as it were, and girdled tensely, in their luxuriance, by her virgin zone. Yet Giovanni's fancy must have grown morbid while he looked down into the garden; for the impression which the fair stranger made upon him was as if here were another flower, the human sister of those vegetable ones, as beautiful as they, more beautiful than the richest of them, but still to be touched only with a glove, nor to be approached without a mask. As Beatrice came down the garden path, it was observable that she handled and inhaled the odor of several of the plants which her father had most sedulously avoided.

"Here, Beatrice," said the latter, "see how many needful offices require to be done to our chief treasure. Yet, shattered as I am, my life might pay the penalty of approaching it so closely as circumstances demand. Henceforth, I fear, this plant must be consigned to your sole charge."

"And gladly will I undertake it," cried again the rich tones of the young lady, as she bent towards the magnificent plant and opened her arms as if to embrace it. "Yes, my sister, my splendor, it shall be Beatrice's task to nurse and serve thee; and thou shalt reward her with thy kisses and perfumed breath, which to her is as the breath of life."

Then, with all the tenderness in her manner that was so strikingly expressed in her words, she busied herself with such attentions as the plant seemed to require; and Giovanni, at his lofty window, rubbed his eyes and almost doubted whether it were a girl tending her favorite flower, or one sister performing the duties of affection to another. The scene soon terminated. Whether Dr. Rappaccini had finished his labors in the garden, or that his watchful eye had caught the stranger's face, he now took his daughter's arm and retired. Night was already closing in; oppressive exhalations seemed to proceed from the plants and steal upward past the open window; and Giovanni, closing the lattice, went to his couch and dreamed of a rich flower and beautiful girl. Flower and maiden were different, and yet the same, and fraught with some strange peril in either shape.

But there is an influence in the light of morning that tends to rectify whatever errors of fancy, or even of judgment, we may have incurred during the sun's decline, or among the shadows of the night, or in the less wholesome glow of moonshine. Giovanni's first movement, on starting from sleep, was to throw open the window and gaze down into the garden which his dreams had made so fertile of mysteries. He was surprised and a little ashamed to find how real and matter-of-fact an affair it proved to be, in the first rays of the sun which gilded the dew-drops that hung upon leaf and blossom, and, while giving a brighter beauty to each rare flower, brought everything within the limits of ordinary experience. The young man rejoiced that, in the heart of the barren city, he had the privilege of overlooking this spot of lovely and luxuriant vegetation. It would serve, he said to himself, as a symbolic language to keep him in communion with Nature. Neither the sickly and thoughtworn Dr. Giacomo Rappaccini, it is true, nor his brilliant daughter, were now visible; so that Giovanni could not determine how much of the singularity which he attributed to both was due to their own qualities and how much to his wonder-working fancy; but he was inclined to take a most rational view of the whole matter. In the course of the day he paid his respects to Signor Pietro Baglioni, professor of medicine in the university, a physician of eminent repute, to whom Giovanni had brought a letter of introduction. The professor was an elderly personage, apparently of genial nature, and habits that might almost be called jovial. He kept the young man to dinner, and made himself very agreeable by the freedom and liveliness of his conversation, especially when warmed by a flask or two of Tuscan wine. Giovanni, conceiving that men of science, inhabitants of the same city, must needs be on familiar terms with one another, took an opportunity to mention the name of Dr. Rappaccini. But the professor did not respond with so much cordiality as he had anticipated.

"Ill would it become a teacher of the divine art of medicine," said Professor Pietro Baglioni, in answer to a question of Giovanni, "to withhold due and well-considered praise of a physician so eminently skilled as Rappaccini; but, on the other hand, I should answer it but scantily to my conscience were I to permit a worthy youth like yourself, Signor Giovanni, the son of an ancient friend, to imbibe erroneous ideas respecting a man who might hereafter chance to hold your life and death in his hands. The truth is, our worshipful Dr. Rappaccini has as much science as any member of the faculty – with perhaps one single exception – in Padua, or all Italy; but there are certain grave objections to his professional character."

"And what are they?" asked the young man.

"Has my friend Giovanni any disease of body or heart, that he is so inquisitive about physicians?" said the professor, with a smile. "But as for Rappaccini, it is said of him – and I, who know the man well, can answer for its truth – that he cares infinitely more for science than for mankind. His patients are interesting to him only as subjects for some new experiment. He would sacrifice human life, his own among the rest, or whatever else was dearest to him, for the sake of adding so much as a grain of mustard seed to the great heap of his accumulated knowledge."

"Methinks he is an awful man indeed," remarked Guasconti, mentally recalling the cold and purely intellectual aspect of Rappaccini. "And yet, worshipful professor, is it not a noble spirit? Are there many men capable of so spiritual a love of science?"

"God forbid," answered the professor, somewhat testily; "at least, unless they take sounder views of the healing art than those adopted by Rappaccini. It is his theory that all medicinal virtues are comprised within those substances which we term vegetable poisons. These he cultivates with his own hands, and is said even to have produced new varieties of poison, more horribly deleterious than Nature, without the assistance of this learned person, would ever have plagued the world withal. That the signor doctor does less mischief than might be expected with such dangerous substances is undeniable. Now and then, it must be owned, he has effected, or seemed to effect, a marvellous cure; but, to tell you my private mind, Signor Giovanni, he should receive little credit for such instances of success, – they being probably the work of chance, – but should be held strictly accountable for his failures, which may justly be considered his own work."

The youth might have taken Baglioni's opinions with many grains of allowance had he known that there was a professional warfare of long continuance between him and

Dr. Rappaccini, in which the latter was generally thought to have gained the advantage. If the reader be inclined to judge for himself, we refer him to certain black-letter tracts on both sides, preserved in the medical department of the University of Padua.

"I know not, most learned professor," returned Giovanni, after musing on what had been said of Rappaccini's exclusive zeal for science, – "I know not how dearly this physician may love his art; but surely there is one object more dear to him. He has a daughter."

"Aha!" cried the professor, with a laugh. "So now our friend Giovanni's secret is out. You have heard of this daughter, whom all the young men in Padua are wild about, though not half a dozen have ever had the good hap to see her face. I know little of the Signora Beatrice save that Rappaccini is said to have instructed her deeply in his science, and that, young and beautiful as fame reports her, she is already qualified to fill a professor's chair. Perchance her father destines her for mine! Other absurd rumors there be, not worth talking about or listening to. So now, Signor Giovanni, drink off your glass of lachryma."

Guasconti returned to his lodgings somewhat heated with the wine he had quaffed, and which caused his brain to swim with strange fantasies in reference to Dr. Rappaccini and the beautiful Beatrice. On his way, happening to pass by a florist's, he bought a fresh bouquet of flowers.

Ascending to his chamber, he seated himself near the window, but within the shadow thrown by the depth of the wall, so that he could look down into the garden with little risk of being discovered. All beneath his eye was a solitude. The strange plants were basking in the sunshine, and now and then nodding gently to one another, as if in acknowledgment of sympathy and kindred. In the midst, by the shattered fountain, grew the magnificent shrub, with its purple gems clustering all over it; they glowed in the air, and gleamed back again out of the depths of the pool, which thus seemed to overflow with colored radiance from the rich reflection that was steeped in it. At first, as we have said, the garden was a solitude. Soon, however, – as Giovanni had half hoped, half feared, would be the case, – a figure appeared beneath the antique sculptured portal, and came down between the rows of plants, inhaling their various perfumes as if she were one of those beings of old classic fable that lived upon sweet odors. On again beholding Beatrice, the young man was even startled to perceive how much her beauty exceeded his recollection of it; so brilliant, so vivid, was its character, that she glowed amid the sunlight, and, as Giovanni whispered to himself, positively illuminated the more shadowy intervals of the garden path. Her face being now more revealed than on the former occasion, he was struck by its expression of simplicity and sweetness, – qualities that had not entered into his idea of her character, and which made him ask anew what manner of mortal she might be. Nor did he fail again to observe, or imagine, an analogy between the beautiful girl and the gorgeous shrub that hung its gemlike flowers over the fountain, – a resemblance which Beatrice seemed to have indulged a fantastic humor in heightening, both by the arrangement of her dress and the selection of its hues.

Approaching the shrub, she threw open her arms, as with a passionate ardor, and drew its branches into an intimate embrace – so intimate that her features were hidden in its leafy bosom and her glistening ringlets all intermingled with the flowers.

"Give me thy breath, my sister," exclaimed Beatrice; "for I am faint with common air. And give me this flower of thine, which I separate with gentlest fingers from the stem and place it close beside my heart."

With these words the beautiful daughter of Rappaccini plucked one of the richest blossoms of the shrub, and was about to fasten it in her bosom. But now, unless Giovanni's draughts of wine had bewildered his senses, a singular incident occurred. A small orange-colored reptile, of the lizard or chameleon species, chanced to be creeping along the path, just at the feet of Beatrice. It appeared to Giovanni, – but, at the distance from which he gazed, he could scarcely have seen anything so minute, – it appeared to him, however, that a drop or two of moisture from the broken stem of the flower descended upon the lizard's head. For an instant the reptile contorted itself violently, and then lay motionless in the sunshine. Beatrice observed this remarkable phenomenon, and crossed herself, sadly, but without surprise; nor did she therefore hesitate to arrange the fatal flower in her bosom. There it blushed, and almost glimmered with the dazzling effect of a precious stone, adding to her dress and aspect the one appropriate charm which nothing else in the world could have supplied. But Giovanni, out of the shadow of his window, bent forward and shrank back, and murmured and trembled.

"Am I awake? Have I my senses?" said he to himself. "What is this being? Beautiful shall I call her, or inexpressibly terrible?"

Beatrice now strayed carelessly through the garden, approaching closer beneath Giovanni's window, so that he was compelled to thrust his head quite out of its concealment in order to gratify the intense and painful curiosity which she excited. At this moment there came a beautiful insect over the garden wall; it had, perhaps, wandered through the city, and found no flowers of verdure among those antique haunts of men until the heavy perfumes of Dr. Rappaccini's shrubs had lured it from afar. Without alighting on the flowers, this winged brightness seemed to be attracted by Beatrice, and lingered in the air and fluttered about her head. Now, here it could not be but that Giovanni Guasconti's eyes deceived him. Be that as it might, he fancied that, while Beatrice was gazing at the insect with childish delight, it grew faint and fell at her feet; its bright wings shivered; it was dead – from no cause that he could discern, unless it were the atmosphere of her breath. Again Beatrice crossed herself and sighed heavily as she bent over the dead insect.

An impulsive movement of Giovanni drew her eyes to the window. There she beheld the beautiful head of the young man – rather a Grecian than an Italian head, with fair, regular features, and a glistening of gold among his ringlets – gazing down upon her like a being that hovered in mid air. Scarcely knowing what he did, Giovanni threw down the bouquet which he had hitherto held in his hand.

"Signora," said he, "there are pure and healthful flowers. Wear them for the sake of Giovanni Guasconti."

"Thanks, signor," replied Beatrice, with her rich voice, that came forth as it were like a gush of music, and with a mirthful expression half childish and half woman-like. "I accept your gift, and would fain recompense it with this precious purple flower; but if I toss it into the air it will not reach you. So Signor Guasconti must even content himself with my thanks."

She lifted the bouquet from the ground, and then, as if inwardly ashamed at having stepped aside from her maidenly reserve to respond to a stranger's greeting, passed swiftly homeward through the garden. But few as the moments were, it seemed to Giovanni, when she was on the point of vanishing beneath the sculptured portal, that his beautiful bouquet was already beginning to wither in her grasp. It was an idle thought; there could be no possibility of distinguishing a faded flower from a fresh one at so great a distance.

For many days after this incident the young man avoided the window that looked into Dr. Rappaccini's garden, as if something ugly and monstrous would have blasted his eyesight had he been betrayed into a glance. He felt conscious of having put himself, to a certain extent, within the influence of an unintelligible power by the communication which he had opened with Beatrice. The wisest course would have been, if his heart were in any real danger, to quit his lodgings and Padua itself at once; the next wiser, to have accustomed himself, as far as possible, to the familiar and daylight view of Beatrice – thus bringing her rigidly and systematically within the limits of ordinary experience. Least of all, while avoiding her sight, ought Giovanni to have remained so near this extraordinary being that the proximity and possibility even of intercourse should give a kind of substance and reality to the wild vagaries which his imagination ran riot continually in producing. Guasconti had not a deep heart – or, at all events, its depths were not sounded now; but he had a quick fancy, and an ardent southern temperament, which rose every instant to a higher fever pitch. Whether or no Beatrice possessed those terrible attributes, that fatal breath, the affinity with those so beautiful and deadly flowers which were indicated by what Giovanni had witnessed, she had at least instilled a fierce and subtle poison into his system. It was not love, although her rich beauty was a madness to him; nor horror, even while he fancied her spirit to be imbued with the same baneful essence that seemed to pervade her physical frame; but a wild offspring of both love and horror that had each parent in it, and burned like one and shivered like the other. Giovanni knew not what to dread; still less did

333

he know what to hope; yet hope and dread kept a continual warfare in his breast, alternately vanquishing one another and starting up afresh to renew the contest. Blessed are all simple emotions, be they dark or bright! It is the lurid intermixture of the two that produces the illuminating blaze of the infernal regions.

Sometimes he endeavored to assuage the fever of his spirit by a rapid walk through the streets of Padua or beyond its gates: his footsteps kept time with the throbbings of his brain, so that the walk was apt to accelerate itself to a race. One day he found himself arrested; his arm was seized by a portly personage, who had turned back on recognizing the young man and expended much breath in overtaking him.

"Signor Giovanni! Stay, my young friend!" cried he. "Have you forgotten me? That might well be the case if I were as much altered as yourself."

It was Baglioni, whom Giovanni had avoided ever since their first meeting, from a doubt that the professor's sagacity would look too deeply into his secrets. Endeavoring to recover himself, he stared forth wildly from his inner world into the outer one and spoke like a man in a dream.

"Yes; I am Giovanni Guasconti. You are Professor Pietro Baglioni. Now let me pass!"

"Not yet, not yet, Signor Giovanni Guasconti," said the professor, smiling, but at the same time scrutinizing the youth with an earnest glance. "What! did I grow up side by side with your father? and shall his son pass me like a stranger in these old streets of Padua? Stand still, Signor Giovanni; for we must have a word or two before we part."

"Speedily, then, most worshipful professor, speedily," said Giovanni, with feverish impatience. "Does not your worship see that I am in haste?"

Now, while he was speaking there came a man in black

along the street, stooping and moving feebly like a person in inferior health. His face was all overspread with a most sickly and sallow hue, but yet so pervaded with an expression of piercing and active intellect that an observer might easily have overlooked the merely physical attributes and have seen only this wonderful energy. As he passed, this person exchanged a cold and distant salutation with Baglioni, but fixed his eyes upon Giovanni with an intentness that seemed to bring out whatever was within him worthy of notice. Nevertheless, there was a peculiar quietness in the look, as if taking merely a speculative, not a human, interest in the young man.

"It is Dr. Rappaccini!" whispered the professor when the stranger had passed. "Has he ever seen your face before?"

"Not that I know," answered Giovanni, starting at the name.

"He *has* seen you! he must have seen you!" said Baglioni, hastily. "For some purpose or other, this man of science is making a study of you. I know that look of his! It is the same that coldly illuminates his face as he bends over a bird, a mouse, or a butterfly, which, in pursuance of some experiment, he has killed by the perfume of a flower; a look as deep as Nature itself, but without Nature's warmth of love. Signor Giovanni, I will stake my life upon it, you are the subject of one of Rappaccini's experiments!"

"Will you make a fool of me?" cried Giovanni, passionately. "*That*, signor professor, were an untoward experiment."

"Patience! patience!" replied the imperturbable professor. "I tell thee, my poor Giovanni, that Rappaccini has a scientific interest in thee. Thou hast fallen into fearful hands! And the Signora Beatrice, – what part does she act in this mystery?"

But Guasconti, finding Baglioni's pertinacity intolerable,

here broke away, and was gone before the professor could again seize his arm. He looked after the young man intently and shook his head.

"This must not be," said Baglioni to himself. "The youth is the son of my old friend, and shall not come to any harm from which the arcana of medical science can preserve him. Besides, it is too insufferable an impertinence in Rappaccini, thus to snatch the lad out of my own hands, as I may say, and make use of him for his infernal experiments. This daughter of his! It shall be looked to. Perchance, most learned Rappaccini, I may foil you where you little dream of it!"

Meanwhile Giovanni had pursued a circuitous route, and at length found himself at the door of his lodgings. As he crossed the threshold he was met by old Lisabetta, who smirked and smiled, and was evidently desirous to attract his attention; vainly, however, as the ebullition of his feelings had momentarily subsided into a cold and dull vacuity. He turned his eyes full upon the withered face that was puckering itself into a smile, but seemed to behold it not. The old dame, therefore, laid her grasp upon his cloak.

"Signor! signor!" whispered she, still with a smile over the whole breadth of her visage, so that it looked not unlike a grotesque carving in wood, darkened by centuries. "Listen, signor! There is a private entrance into the garden!"

"What do you say?" exclaimed Giovanni, turning quickly about, as if an inanimate thing should start into feverish life. "A private entrance into Dr. Rappaccini's garden?"

"Hush! hush! not so loud!" whispered Lisabetta, putting her hand over his mouth. "Yes; into the worshipful doctor's garden, where you may see all his fine shrubbery. Many a young man in Padua would give gold to be admitted among those flowers."

Giovanni put a piece of gold into her hand.

"Show me the way," said he.

A surmise, probably excited by his conversation with Baglioni, crossed his mind, that this interposition of old Lisabetta might perchance be connected with the intrigue, whatever were its nature, in which the professor seemed to suppose that Dr. Rappaccini was involving him. But such a suspicion, though it disturbed Giovanni, was inadequate to restrain him. The instant that he was aware of the possibility of approaching Beatrice, it seemed an absolute necessity of his existence to do so. It mattered not whether she were angel or demon; he was irrevocably within her sphere, and must obey the law that whirled him onward, in ever-lessening circles, towards a result which he did not attempt to fore-shadow; and yet, strange to say, there came across him a sudden doubt whether this intense interest on his part were not delusory; whether it were really of so deep and positive a nature as to justify him in now thrusting himself into an incalculable position; whether it were not merely the fantasy of a young man's brain, only slightly or not at all connected with his heart.

He paused, hesitated, turned half about, but again went on. His withered guide led him along several obscure passages, and finally undid a door, through which, as it was opened, there came the sight and sound of rustling leaves, with the broken sunshine glimmering among them. Giovanni stepped forth, and, forcing himself through the entanglement of a shrub that wreathed its tendrils over the hidden entrance, stood beneath his own window in the open area of Dr. Rappaccini's garden.

How often is it the case that, when impossibilities have come to pass and dreams have condensed their misty sub-stance into tangible realities, we find ourselves calm, and even coldly self-possessed, amid circumstances which it

337

would have been a delirium of joy or agony to anticipate! Fate delights to thwart us thus. Passion will choose his own time to rush upon the scene, and lingers sluggishly behind when an appropriate adjustment of events would seem to summon his appearance. So was it now with Giovanni. Day after day his pulses had throbbed with feverish blood at the improbable idea of an interview with Beatrice, and of standing with her, face to face, in this very garden, basking in the Oriental sunshine of her beauty, and snatching from her full gaze the mystery which he deemed the riddle of his own existence. But now there was a singular and untimely equanimity within his breast. He threw a glance around the garden to discover if Beatrice or her father were present, and, perceiving that he was alone, began a critical observation of the plants.

The aspect of one and all of them dissatisfied him; their gorgeousness seemed fierce, passionate, and even unnatural. There was hardly an individual shrub which a wanderer, straying by himself through a forest, would not have been startled to find growing wild, as if an unearthly face had glared at him out of the thicket. Several also would have shocked a delicate instinct by an appearance of artificialness indicating that there had been such commixture, and, as it were, adultery, of various vegetable species, that the production was no longer of God's making, but the monstrous offspring of man's depraved fancy, glowing with only an evil mockery of beauty. They were probably the result of experiment, which in one or two cases had succeeded in mingling plants individually lovely into a compound possessing the questionable and ominous character that distinguished the whole growth of the garden. In fine, Giovanni recognized but two or three plants in the collection, and those of a kind that he well knew to be poisonous. While busy with these contemplations he heard the rustling of a silken garment, and, turning, beheld Beatrice emerging from beneath the sculptured portal.

Giovanni had not considered with himself what should be his deportment; whether he should apologize for his intrusion into the garden, or assume that he was there with the privity at least, if not by the desire, of Dr. Rappaccini or his daughter; but Beatrice's manner placed him at his ease, though leaving him still in doubt by what agency he had gained admittance. She came lightly along the path and met him near the broken fountain. There was surprise in her face, but brightened by a simple and kind expression of pleasure.

"You are a connoisseur in flowers, signor," said Beatrice, with a smile, alluding to the bouquet which he had flung her from the window. "It is no marvel, therefore, if the sight of my father's rare collection has tempted you to take a nearer view. If he were here, he could tell you many strange and interesting facts as to the nature and habits of these shrubs; for he has spent a lifetime in such studies, and this garden is his world."

"And yourself, lady," observed Giovanni, "if fame says true, – you likewise are deeply skilled in the virtues indicated by these rich blossoms and these spicy perfumes. Would you deign to be my instructress, I should prove an apter scholar than if taught by Signor Rappaccini himself."

"Are there such idle rumors?" asked Beatrice, with the music of a pleasant laugh. "Do people say that I am skilled in my father's science of plants? What a jest is there! No; though I have grown up among these flowers, I know no more of them than their hues and perfume; and sometimes methinks I would fain rid myself of even that small knowledge. There are many flowers here, and those not the least brilliant, that shock and offend me when they meet my eye. But pray, signor, do not believe these stories about my science. Believe nothing of me save what you see with your own eyes."

"And must I believe all that I have seen with my own eyes?" asked Giovanni, pointedly, while the recollection of former scenes made him shrink. "No, signora; you demand too little of me. Bid me believe nothing save what comes from your own lips."

It would appear that Beatrice understood him. There came a deep flush to her cheek; but she looked full into Giovanni's eyes, and responded to his gaze of uneasy suspicion with a queenlike haughtiness.

"I do so bid you, signor," she replied. "Forget whatever you may have fancied in regard to me. If true to the outward senses, still it may be false in its essence; but the words of Beatrice Rappaccini's lips are true from the depths of the heart outward. Those you may believe."

A fervor glowed in her whole aspect and beamed upon Giovanni's consciousness like the light of truth itself; but while she spoke there was a fragrance in the atmosphere around her, rich and delightful, though evanescent, yet which the young man, from an indefinable reluctance, scarcely dared to draw into his lungs. It might be the odor of the flowers. Could it be Beatrice's breath which thus embalmed her words with a strange richness, as if by steeping them in her heart? A faintness passed like a shadow over Giovanni and flitted away; he seemed to gaze through the beautiful girl's eyes into her transparent soul, and felt no more doubt or fear.

The tinge of passion that had colored Beatrice's manner vanished; she became gay, and appeared to derive a pure delight from her communion with the youth not unlike what the maiden of a lonely island might have felt conversing with a voyager from the civilized world. Evidently her experience of life had been confined within the limits of that garden. She talked now about matters as simple as the daylight or summer clouds, and now asked questions in reference to the city, or Giovanni's distant home, his friends, his mother, and his sisters – questions indicating such seclusion, and such lack of familiarity with modes and forms, that Giovanni responded as if to an infant. Her spirit gushed out before him like a fresh rill that was just catching its first glimpse of the sunlight and wondering at the reflections of earth and sky which were flung into its bosom. There came thoughts, too, from a deep source, and fantasies of a gemlike brilliancy, as if diamonds and rubies sparkled upward among the bubbles of the fountain. Ever and anon there gleamed across the young man's mind a sense of wonder that he should be walking side by side with the being who had so wrought upon his imagination, whom he had idealized in such hues of terror, in whom he had positively witnessed such manifestations of dreadful attributes, – that he should be conversing with Beatrice like a brother, and should find her so human and so maidenlike. But such reflections were only momentary; the effect of her character was too real not to make itself familiar at once.

In this free intercourse they had strayed through the garden, and now, after many turns among its avenues, were come to the shattered fountain, beside which grew the magnificent shrub, with its treasury of glowing blossoms. A fragrance was diffused from it which Giovanni recognized as identical with that which he had attributed to Beatrice's breath, but incomparably more powerful. As her eyes fell upon it, Giovanni beheld her press her hand to her bosom as if her heart were throbbing suddenly and painfully.

"For the first time in my life," murmured she, addressing the shrub, "I had forgotten thee."

"I remember, signora," said Giovanni, "that you once promised to reward me with one of these living gems for the bouquet which I had the happy boldness to fling at your feet. Permit me now to pluck it as a memorial of this interview."

He made a step towards the shrub with extended hand; but Beatrice darted forward, uttering a shriek that went through his heart like a dagger. She caught his hand and drew it back with the whole force of her slender figure. Giovanni felt her touch thrilling through his fibres.

"Touch it not!" exclaimed she, in a voice of agony. "Not for thy life! It is fatal!"

Then, hiding her face, she fled from him and vanished beneath the sculptured portal. As Giovanni followed her with his eyes, he beheld the emaciated figure and pale intelligence of Dr. Rappaccini, who had been watching the scene, he knew not how long, within the shadow of the entrance.

No sooner was Guasconti alone in his chamber than the image of Beatrice came back to his passionate musings, invested with all the witchery that had been gathering around it ever since his first glimpse of her, and now likewise imbued with a tender warmth of girlish womanhood. She was human; her nature was endowed with all gentle and feminine qualities; she was worthiest to be worshipped; she was capable, surely, on her part, of the height and heroism of love. Those tokens which he had hitherto considered as proofs of a frightful peculiarity in her physical and moral system were now either forgotten, or, by the subtle sophistry of passion transmitted into a golden crown of enchantment, rendering Beatrice the more admirable by so much as she was the more unique. Whatever had looked ugly was now beautiful; or, if incapable of such a change, it stole away and hid itself among those shapeless half ideas which throng the dim region beyond the daylight of our perfect consciousness.

Thus did he spend the night, nor fell asleep until the dawn had begun to awake the slumbering flowers in Dr. Rappaccini's garden, whither Giovanni's dreams doubtless led him. Up rose the sun in his due season, and, flinging his beams upon the young man's eyelids, awoke him to a sense of pain. When thoroughly aroused, he became sensible of a burning and tingling agony in his hand – in his right hand – the very hand which Beatrice had grasped in her own when he was on the point of plucking one of the gemlike flowers. On the back of that hand there was now a purple print like that of four small fingers, and the likeness of a slender thumb upon his wrist.

Oh, how stubbornly does love, – or even that cunning semblance of love which flourishes in the imagination, but strikes no depth of root into the heart, – how stubbornly does it hold its faith until the moment comes when it is doomed to vanish into thin mist! Giovanni wrapped a handkerchief about his hand and wondered what evil thing had stung him, and soon forgot his pain in a reverie of Beatrice.

After the first interview, a second was in the inevitable course of what we call fate. A third; a fourth; and a meeting with Beatrice in the garden was no longer an incident in Giovanni's daily life, but the whole space in which he might be said to live; for the anticipation and memory of that ecstatic hour made up the remainder. Nor was it otherwise with the daughter of Rappaccini. She watched for the youth's appearance, and flew to his side with confidence as unreserved as if they had been playmates from early infancy – as if they were such playmates still. If, by any unwonted chance, he failed to come at the appointed moment, she stood beneath the window and sent up the rich sweetness of her tones to float around him in his chamber and echo and reverberate throughout his heart: "Giovanni! Giovanni!

Why tarriest thou? Come down!" And down he hastened into that Eden of poisonous flowers.

But, with all this intimate familiarity, there was still a reserve in Beatrice's demeanor, so rigidly and invariably sustained that the idea of infringing it scarcely occurred to his imagination. By all appreciable signs, they loved; they had looked love with eyes that conveyed the holy secret from the depths of one soul into the depths of the other, as if it were too sacred to be whispered by the way; they had even spoken love in those gushes of passion when their spirits darted forth in articulated breath like tongues of long-hidden flame; and yet there had been no seal of lips, no clasp of hands, nor any slightest caress such as love claims and hallows. He had never touched one of the gleaming ringlets of her hair; her garment – so marked was the physical barrier between them – had never been waved against him by a breeze. On the few occasions when Giovanni had seemed tempted to overstep the limit, Beatrice grew so sad, so stern, and withal wore such a look of desolate separation, shuddering at itself, that not a spoken word was requisite to repel him. At such times he was startled at the horrible suspicions that rose, monster-like, out of the caverns of his heart and stared him in the face; his love grew thin and faint as the morning mist, his doubts alone had substance. But, when Beatrice's face brightened again after the momentary shadow, she was transformed at once from the mysterious, questionable being whom he had watched with so much awe and horror; she was now the beautiful and unsophisticated girl whom he felt that his spirit knew with a certainty beyond all other knowledge.

A considerable time had now passed since Giovanni's last meeting with Baglioni. One morning, however, he was disagreeably surprised by a visit from the professor, whom he had scarcely thought of for whole weeks, and would willingly have forgotten still longer. Given up as he had long been to a pervading excitement, he could tolerate no companions except upon condition of their perfect sympathy with his present state of feeling. Such sympathy was not to be expected from Professor Baglioni.

The visitor chatted carelessly for a few moments about the gossip of the city and the university, and then took up another topic.

"I have been reading an old classic author lately," said he, "and met with a story that strangely interested me. Possibly you may remember it. It is of an Indian prince, who sent a beautiful woman as a present to Alexander the Great. She was as lovely as the dawn and gorgeous as the sunset; but what especially distinguished her was a certain rich perfume in her breath – richer than a garden of Persian roses. Alexander, as was natural to a youthful conqueror, fell in love at first sight with this magnificent stranger; but a certain sage physician, happening to be present, discovered a terrible secret in regard to her."

"And what was that?" asked Giovanni, turning his eyes downward to avoid those of the professor.

"That this lovely woman," continued Baglioni, with emphasis, "had been nourished with poisons from her birth upward, until her whole nature was so imbued with them that she herself had become the deadliest poison in existence. Poison was her element of life. With that rich perfume of her breath she blasted the very air. Her love would have been poison – her embrace death. Is not this a marvellous tale?"

"A childish fable," answered Giovanni, nervously starting from his chair. "I marvel how your worship finds time to read such nonsense among your graver studies."

"By the by," said the professor, looking uneasily about him, "what singular fragrance is this in your apartment? Is

345

it the perfume of your gloves? It is faint, but delicious; and yet, after all, by no means agreeable. Were I to breathe it long, methinks it would make me ill. It is like the breath of a flower; but I see no flowers in the chamber."

"Nor are there any," replied Giovanni, who had turned pale as the professor spoke; "nor, I think, is there any fragrance except in your worship's imagination. Odors, being a sort of element combined of the sensual and the spiritual, are apt to deceive us in this manner. The recollection of a perfume, the bare idea of it, may easily be mistaken for a present reality."

"Ay; but my sober imagination does not often play such tricks," said Baglioni; "and, were I to fancy any kind of odor, it would be that of some vile apothecary drug, wherewith my fingers are likely enough to be imbued. Our worshipful friend Rappaccini, as I have heard, tinctures his medicaments with odors richer than those of Araby. Doubtless, likewise, the fair and learned Signora Beatrice would minister to her patients with draughts as sweet as a maiden's breath; but woe to him that sips them!"

Giovanni's face evinced many contending emotions. The tone in which the professor alluded to the pure and lovely daughter of Rappaccini was a torture to his soul; and yet the intimation of a view of her character, opposite to his own, gave instantaneous distinctness to a thousand dim suspicions, which now grinned at him like so many demons. But he strove hard to quell them and to respond to Baglioni with a true lover's perfect faith.

"Signor professor," said he, "you were my father's friend; perchance, too, it is your purpose to act a friendly part towards his son. I would fain feel nothing towards you save respect and deference; but I pray you to observe, signor, that there is one subject on which we must not speak. You know not the Signora Beatrice. You cannot, therefore, estimate the wrong – the blasphemy, I may even say – that is offered to her character by a light or injurious word."

"Giovanni! my poor Giovanni!" answered the professor, with a calm expression of pity, "I know this wretched girl far better than yourself. You shall hear the truth in respect to the poisoner Rappaccini and his poisonous daughter; yes, poisonous as she is beautiful. Listen; for, even should you do violence to my gray hairs, it shall not silence me. That old fable of the Indian woman has become a truth by the deep and deadly science of Rappaccini and in the person of the lovely Beatrice."

Giovanni groaned and hid his face.

"Her father," continued Baglioni, "was not restrained by natural affection from offering up his child in this horrible manner as the victim of his insane zeal for science; for, let us do him justice, he is as true a man of science as ever distilled his own heart in an alembic. What, then, will be your fate? Beyond a doubt you are selected as the material of some new experiment. Perhaps the result is to be death; perhaps a fate more awful still. Rappaccini, with what he calls the interest of science before his eyes, will hesitate at nothing."

"It is a dream," muttered Giovanni to himself; "surely it is a dream."

"But," resumed the professor, "be of good cheer, son of my friend. It is not yet too late for the rescue. Possibly we may even succeed in bringing back this miserable child within the limits of ordinary nature, from which her father's madness has estranged her. Behold this little silver vase! It was wrought by the hands of the renowned Benvenuto Cellini, and is well worthy to be a love gift to the fairest dame in Italy. But its contents are invaluable. One little sip of this antidote would have rendered the most virulent poisons of

the Borgias innocuous. Doubt not that it will be as effica-
cious against those of Rappaccini. Bestow the vase, and the
precious liquid within it, on your Beatrice, and hopefully
await the result."

Baglioni laid a small, exquisitely wrought silver vial on the
table and withdrew, leaving what he had said to produce its
effect upon the young man's mind.

"We will thwart Rappaccini yet," thought he, chuckling
to himself, as he descended the stairs; "but, let us confess
the truth of him, he is a wonderful man – a wonderful man
indeed; a vile empiric, however, in his practice, and therefore
not to be tolerated by those who respect the good old rules
of the medical profession."

Throughout Giovanni's whole acquaintance with Beatrice,
he had occasionally, as we have said, been haunted by dark
surmises as to her character; yet so thoroughly had she made
herself felt by him as a simple, natural, most affectionate,
and guileless creature, that the image now held up by Professor Baglioni looked as strange and incredible as if it were not
in accordance with his own original conception. True, there
were ugly recollections connected with his first glimpses of
the beautiful girl; he could not quite forget the bouquet that
withered in her grasp, and the insect that perished amid the
sunny air, by no ostensible agency save the fragrance of her
breath. These incidents, however, dissolving in the pure light
of her character, had no longer the efficacy of facts, but were
acknowledged as mistaken fantasies, by whatever testimony
of the senses they might appear to be substantiated. There
is something truer and more real than what we can see with
the eyes and touch with the finger. On such better evidence
had Giovanni founded his confidence in Beatrice, though
rather by the necessary force of her high attributes than by
any deep and generous faith on his part. But now his spirit

was incapable of sustaining itself at the height to which the early enthusiasm of passion had exalted it; he fell down, grovelling among earthly doubts, and defiled therewith the pure whiteness of Beatrice's image. Not that he gave her up; he did but distrust. He resolved to institute some decisive test that should satisfy him, once for all, whether there were those dreadful peculiarities in her physical nature which could not be supposed to exist without some corresponding monstrosity of soul. His eyes, gazing down afar, might have deceived him as to the lizard, the insect, and the flowers; but if he could witness, at the distance of a few paces, the sudden blight of one fresh and healthful flower in Beatrice's hand, there would be room for no further question. With this idea he hastened to the florist's and purchased a bouquet that was still gemmed with the morning dew-drops.

It was now the customary hour of his daily interview with Beatrice. Before descending into the garden, Giovanni failed not to look at his figure in the mirror, – a vanity to be expected in a beautiful young man, yet, as displaying itself at that troubled and feverish moment, the token of a certain shallowness of feeling and insincerity of character. He did gaze, however, and said to himself that his features had never before possessed so rich a grace, nor his eyes such vivacity, nor his cheeks so warm a hue of superabundant life.

"At least," thought he, "her poison has not yet insinuated itself into my system. I am no flower to perish in her grasp."

With that thought he turned his eyes on the bouquet, which he had never once laid aside from his hand. A thrill of indefinable horror shot through his frame on perceiving that those dewy flowers were already beginning to droop; they wore the aspect of things that had been fresh and lovely yesterday. Giovanni grew white as marble, and stood motionless before the mirror, staring at his own reflection there as at the likeness of something frightful. He remembered Baglioni's remark about the fragrance that seemed to pervade the chamber. It must have been the poison in his breath! Then he shuddered – shuddered at himself. Recovering from his stupor, he began to watch with curious eye a spider that was busily at work hanging its web from the antique cornice of the apartment, crossing and recrossing the artful system of interwoven lines – as vigorous and active a spider as ever dangled from an old ceiling. Giovanni bent towards the insect, and emitted a deep, long breath. The spider suddenly ceased its toil; the web vibrated with a tremor originating in the body of the small artisan. Again Giovanni sent forth a breath, deeper, longer, and imbued with a venomous feeling out of his heart: he knew not whether he were wicked, or only desperate. The spider made a convulsive gripe with his limbs and hung dead across the window.

"Accursed! accursed!" muttered Giovanni, addressing himself. "Hast thou grown so poisonous that this deadly insect perishes by thy breath?"

At that moment a rich, sweet voice came floating up from the garden.

"Giovanni! Giovanni! It is past the hour! Why tarriest thou? Come down!"

"Yes," muttered Giovanni again. "She is the only being whom my breath may not slay! Would that it might!"

He rushed down, and in an instant was standing before the bright and loving eyes of Beatrice. A moment ago his wrath and despair had been so fierce that he could have desired nothing so much as to wither her by a glance; but with her actual presence there came influences which had too real an existence to be at once shaken off: recollections of the delicate and benign power of her feminine nature, which had so often enveloped him in a religious calm; recollections of many a holy and passionate out-gush of her heart, when the pure fountain had been unsealed from its depths and made visible in its transparency to his mental eye; recollections which, had Giovanni known how to estimate them, would have assured him that all this ugly mystery was but an earthly illusion, and that, whatever mist of evil might seem to have gathered over her, the real Beatrice was a heavenly angel. Incapable as he was of such high faith, still her presence had not utterly lost its magic. Giovanni's rage was quelled into an aspect of sullen insensibility. Beatrice, with a quick spiritual sense, immediately felt that there was a gulf of blackness between them which neither he nor she could pass. They walked on together, sad and silent, and came thus to the marble fountain and to its pool of water on the ground, in the midst of which grew the shrub that bore gemlike blossoms. Giovanni was affrighted at the eager enjoyment – the appetite, as it were – with which he found himself inhaling the fragrance of the flowers.

"Beatrice," asked he, abruptly, "whence came this shrub?"

"My father created it," answered she, with simplicity.

"Created it! created it!" repeated Giovanni. "What mean you, Beatrice?"

"He is a man fearfully acquainted with the secrets of Nature," replied Beatrice; "and, at the hour when I first drew breath, this plant sprang from the soil, the offspring of his science, of his intellect, while I was but his earthly child. Approach it not!" continued she, observing with terror that Giovanni was drawing nearer to the shrub. "It has qualities that you little dream of. But I, dearest Giovanni, – I grew up and blossomed with the plant and was nourished with its breath. It was my sister, and I loved it with a human affection; for, alas! – hast thou not suspected it? – there was an awful doom."

Here Giovanni frowned so darkly upon her that Beatrice paused and trembled. But her faith in his tenderness reassured her, and made her blush that she had doubted for an instant.

"There was an awful doom," she continued, "the effect of my father's fatal love of science, which estranged me from all society of my kind. Until Heaven sent thee, dearest Giovanni, oh, how lonely was thy poor Beatrice!"

"Was it a hard doom?" asked Giovanni, fixing his eyes upon her.

"Only of late have I known how hard it was," answered she, tenderly. "Oh, yes; but my heart was torpid, and therefore quiet."

Giovanni's rage broke forth from his sullen gloom like a lightning flash out of a dark cloud.

"Accursed one!" cried he, with venomous scorn and anger. "And, finding thy solitude wearisome, thou hast severed me likewise from all the warmth of life and enticed me into thy region of unspeakable horror!"

"Giovanni!" exclaimed Beatrice, turning her large bright eyes upon his face. The force of his words had not found its way into her mind; she was merely thunderstruck.

"Yes, poisonous thing!" repeated Giovanni, beside himself with passion. "Thou hast done it! Thou hast blasted me! Thou hast filled my veins with poison! Thou hast made me as hateful, as ugly, as loathsome and deadly a creature as thyself – a world's wonder of hideous monstrosity! Now, if our breath be happily as fatal to ourselves as to all others, let us join our lips in one kiss of unutterable hatred, and so die!"

"What has befallen me?" murmured Beatrice, with a low moan out of her heart. "Holy Virgin, pity me, a poor heart-broken child!"

"Thou, – dost thou pray?" cried Giovanni, still with the same fiendish scorn. "Thy very prayers, as they come from thy lips, taint the atmosphere with death. Yes, yes; let us pray! Let us to church and dip our fingers in the holy water at the portal! They that come after us will perish as by a pestilence! Let us sign crosses in the air! It will be scattering curses abroad in the likeness of holy symbols!"

"Giovanni," said Beatrice, calmly, for her grief was beyond passion, "why dost thou join thyself with me thus in those terrible words? I, it is true, am the horrible thing thou namest me. But thou, – what hast thou to do, save with one other shudder at my hideous misery to go forth out of the garden and mingle with thy race, and forget that there ever crawled on earth such a monster as poor Beatrice?"

"Dost thou pretend ignorance?" asked Giovanni, scowling upon her. "Behold! this power have I gained from the pure daughter of Rappaccini."

There was a swarm of summer insects flitting through the air in search of the food promised by the flower odors of the fatal garden. They circled round Giovanni's head, and were evidently attracted towards him by the same influence which had drawn them for an instant within the sphere of several of the shrubs. He sent forth a breath among them, and smiled bitterly at Beatrice as at least a score of the insects fell dead upon the ground.

"I see it! I see it!" shrieked Beatrice. "It is my father's fatal science! No, no, Giovanni; it was not I! Never! never! I dreamed only to love thee and be with thee a little time, and so to let thee pass away, leaving but thine image in mine heart; for, Giovanni, believe it, though my body be nourished with poison, my spirit is God's creature, and craves love as its daily food. But my father, – he has united us in this fearful sympathy. Yes; spurn me, tread upon me, kill me!

Oh, what is death after such words as thine? But it was not I. Not for a world of bliss would I have done it."

Giovanni's passion had exhausted itself in its outburst from his lips. There now came across him a sense, mournful, and not without tenderness, of the intimate and peculiar relationship between Beatrice and himself. They stood, as it were, in an utter solitude, which would be made none the less solitary by the densest throng of human life. Ought not, then, the desert of humanity around them to press this insulated pair closer together? If they should be cruel to one another, who was there to be kind to them? Besides, thought Giovanni, might there not still be a hope of his returning within the limits of ordinary nature, and leading Beatrice, the redeemed Beatrice, by the hand? O, weak, and selfish, and unworthy spirit, that could dream of an earthly union and earthly happiness as possible, after such deep love had been so bitterly wronged as was Beatrice's love by Giovanni's blighting words! No, no; there could be no such hope. She must pass heavily, with that broken heart, across the borders of Time – she must bathe her hurts in some fount of paradise, and forget her grief in the light of immortality, and *there* be well.

But Giovanni did not know it.

"Dear Beatrice," said he, approaching her, while she shrank away as always at his approach, but now with a different impulse, "dearest Beatrice, our fate is not yet so desperate. Behold! there is a medicine, potent, as a wise physician has assured me, and almost divine in its efficacy. It is composed of ingredients the most opposite to those by which thy awful father has brought this calamity upon thee and me. It is distilled of blessed herbs. Shall we not quaff it together, and thus be purified from evil?"

"Give it me!" said Beatrice, extending her hand to receive

the little silver vial which Giovanni took from his bosom. She added, with a peculiar emphasis, "I will drink; but do thou await the result."

She put Baglioni's antidote to her lips; and, at the same moment, the figure of Rappaccini emerged from the portal and came slowly towards the marble fountain. As he drew near, the pale man of science seemed to gaze with a triumphant expression at the beautiful youth and maiden, as might an artist who should spend his life in achieving a picture or a group of statuary and finally be satisfied with his success. He paused; his bent form grew erect with conscious power; he spread out his hands over them in the attitude of a father imploring a blessing upon his children; but those were the same hands that had thrown poison into the stream of their lives. Giovanni trembled. Beatrice shuddered nervously, and pressed her hand upon her heart.

"My daughter," said Rappaccini, "thou art no longer lonely in the world. Pluck one of those precious gems from thy sister shrub and bid thy bridegroom wear it in his bosom. It will not harm him now. My science and the sympathy between thee and him have so wrought within his system that he now stands apart from common men, as thou dost, daughter of my pride and triumph, from ordinary women. Pass on, then, through the world, most dear to one another and dreadful to all besides!"

"My father," said Beatrice, feebly, – and still as she spoke she kept her hand upon her heart, – "wherefore didst thou inflict this miserable doom upon thy child?"

"Miserable!" exclaimed Rappaccini. "What mean you, foolish girl? Dost thou deem it misery to be endowed with marvellous gifts against which no power nor strength could avail an enemy – misery, to be able to quell the mightiest with a breath – misery, to be as terrible as thou art beautiful?

Wouldst thou, then, have preferred the condition of a weak woman, exposed to all evil and capable of none?"

"I would fain have been loved, not feared," murmured Beatrice, sinking down upon the ground. "But now it matters not. I am going, father, where the evil which thou hast striven to mingle with my being will pass away like a dream – like the fragrance of these poisonous flowers, which will no longer taint my breath among the flowers of Eden. Farewell, Giovanni! Thy words of hatred are like lead within my heart; but they, too, will fall away as I ascend. Oh, was there not, from the first, more poison in thy nature than in mine?"

To Beatrice, – so radically had her earthly part been wrought upon by Rappaccini's skill, – as poison had been life, so the powerful antidote was death; and thus the poor victim of man's ingenuity and of thwarted nature, and of the fatality that attends all such efforts of perverted wisdom, perished there, at the feet of her father and Giovanni. Just at that moment Professor Pietro Baglioni looked forth from the window, and called loudly, in a tone of triumph mixed with horror, to the thunder-stricken man of science, –

"Rappaccini! Rappaccini! and is *this* the upshot of your experiment!"

ITALO CALVINO

THE ENCHANTED GARDEN

Translated by Archibald Colquhoun and Peggy Wright

GIOVANNINO AND SERENELLA were strolling along the railway lines. Below was a scaly sea of sombre, clear blue; above, a sky lightly streaked with white clouds. The railway lines were shimmering and burning hot. It was fun going along the railway, there were so many games to play – he balancing on one rail and holding her hand while she walked along on the other, or else both jumping from one sleeper to the next without ever letting their feet touch the stones in between. Giovannino and Serenella had been out looking for crabs, and now they had decided to explore the railway lines as far as the tunnel. He liked playing with Serenella, for she did not behave as all the other little girls did, forever getting frightened or bursting into tears at every joke. Whenever Giovannino said, "Let's go there" or "Let's do this," Serenella followed without a word.

Ping! They both gave a start and looked up. A telephone wire had snapped off the top of the pole. It sounded like an iron stork shutting its beak in a hurry. They stood with their noses in the air and watched. What a pity not to have seen it! Now it would never happen again.

"There's a train coming," said Giovannino.

Serenella did not move from the rail. "Where from?" she asked.

Giovannino looked around in a knowledgeable way. He pointed at the black hole of the tunnel, which showed clear one moment, then misty the next, through the invisible heat haze rising from the stony track.

"From there," he said. It was as though they could already hear a snort from the darkness of the tunnel and see the train suddenly appear, belching out fire and smoke, the wheels mercilessly eating up the rails as it hurtled toward them.

"Where shall we go, Giovannino?"

There were big grey aloes down by the sea, surrounded by dense, impenetrable nettles, while up the hillside ran a rambling hedge with thick leaves but no flowers. There was still no sign of the train; perhaps it was coasting, with the engine cut off, and would jump out at them all of a sudden. But Giovannino had now found an opening in the hedge. "This way," he called.

The fence under the rambling hedge was an old bent rail. At one point it twisted about on the ground like the corner of a sheet of paper. Giovannino had slipped into the hole and already half vanished.

"Give me a hand, Giovannino."

They found themselves in the corner of a garden, on all fours in a flower bed, with their hair full of dry leaves and moss. Everything was quiet; not a leaf was stirring.

"Come on," said Giovannino, and Serenella nodded in reply.

There were big old flesh-coloured eucalyptus trees and winding gravel paths. Giovannino and Serenella tiptoed along the paths, taking care not to crunch the gravel. Suppose the owners appeared now?

Everything was so beautiful: sharp bends in the path and high, curling eucalyptus leaves and patches of sky. But there was always the worrying thought that it was not their garden, and that they might be chased away any moment. Yet not a sound could be heard. A flight of chattering sparrows rose from a clump of arbutus at a turn in the path. Then all was silent again. Perhaps it was an abandoned garden?

But the shade of the big trees came to an end, and they found themselves under the open sky facing flower beds filled with neat rows of petunias and convolvulus, and paths and balustrades and rows of box trees. And up at the end of the garden was a large villa with flashing windowpanes and yellow-and-orange curtains.

And it was all quite deserted. The two children crept forward, treading carefully over the gravel: perhaps the windows would suddenly be flung open, and angry ladies and gentlemen appear on the terraces to unleash great dogs down the paths. Now they found a wheelbarrow standing near a ditch. Giovannino picked it up by the handles and began pushing it along: it creaked like a whistle at every turn. Serenella seated herself in it and they moved slowly forward, Giovannino pushing the barrow with her on top, beside the flower beds and fountains.

Every now and then Serenella would point to a flower and say in a low voice, "That one," and Giovannino would put the barrow down, pluck it, and give it to her. Soon she had a lovely bouquet.

Eventually the gravel ended and they reached an open space paved in bricks and mortar. In the middle of this space was a big empty rectangle: a swimming pool. They crept up to the edge; it was lined with blue tiles and filled to the brim with clear water. How lovely it would be to swim in!

"Shall we go for a dip?" Giovannino asked Serenella. The idea must have been quite dangerous if he asked her instead of just saying, "In we go!" But the water was so clear and blue, and Serenella was never afraid. She jumped off the barrow and put her bunch of flowers in it. They were already in bathing suits, since they'd been out for crabs before. Giovannino plunged in – not from the diving board, because the splash would have made too much noise, but from the edge of the pool. Down and down he went with his eyes wide open, seeing only the blue from the tiles and his pink hands like goldfish; it was not the same as under the sea, full of shapeless green-black shadows. A pink form appeared above him: Serenella! He took her hand and they swam up to the surface, a bit anxiously. No, there was no one watching them at all. But it was not so nice as they'd thought it would be; they always had that uncomfortable feeling that they had no right to any of this and might be chased out at any moment.

They scrambled out of the water, and there beside the swimming pool they found a Ping-Pong table. Instantly Giovannino picked up a paddle and hit the ball, and Serenella, on the other side, was quick to return his shot. And so they went on playing, though only lightly tapping the ball, in case someone in the villa heard them. Then Giovannino, in trying to parry a shot that had bounced high, sent the ball sailing away through the air and smack against a gong hanging in a pergola. There was a long, sombre boom. The two children crouched down behind a clump of ranunculus. At once two menservants in white coats appeared, carrying big trays; when they had put the trays down on a round table under an orange-and-yellow-striped umbrella, off they went.

Giovannino and Serenella crept up to the table. There was tea, milk, and sponge cake. They had only to sit down and help themselves. They poured out two cups of tea and cut two slices of cake. But somehow they did not feel at all at ease, and sat perched on the edge of their chairs, their knees shaking. And they could not really enjoy the tea and cake, for nothing seemed to have any taste. Everything in the garden was like that: lovely but impossible to enjoy properly, with that worrying feeling inside that they were only there through an odd stroke of luck, and the fear that they'd soon have to give an account of themselves.

Very quietly they tiptoed up to the villa. Between the slits of a Venetian blind they saw a beautiful shady room, with collections of butterflies hanging on the walls. And in the room was a pale little boy. Lucky boy, he must be the owner of this villa and garden. He was stretched out on a chaise longue, turning the pages of a large book filled with figures. He had big white hands and wore pyjamas buttoned up to the neck, though it was summer.

As the two children went on peeping through the slits, the pounding of their hearts gradually subsided. Why, the little rich boy seemed to be sitting there and turning the pages and glancing around with more anxiety and worry than their own. Then he got up and tiptoed around, as if he were afraid that at any moment someone would come and turn him out, as if he felt that that book, that chaise longue, and those butterflies framed on the wall, the garden and games and tea trays, the swimming pool and paths, were only granted to him by some enormous mistake, as if he were incapable of enjoying them and felt the bitterness of the mistake as his own fault.

The pale boy was wandering about his shady room furtively, touching with his white fingers the edges of the cases studded with butterflies; then he stopped to listen. Giovannino's and Serenella's hearts, which had returned to a regular beat, now pounded harder than ever. Perhaps it was the fear of a spell that hung over this villa and garden and over all these lovely, comfortable things, the residue of some injustice committed long ago.

Clouds darkened the sun. Very quietly Giovannino and

Serenella crept away. They went back along the same paths they had come on, stepping fast but never at a run. And they went through the hedge again on all fours. Between the aloes they found a path leading down to the small stony beach, with banks of seaweed along the shore. Then they invented a wonderful new game: a seaweed fight. They threw great handfuls of it in each other's faces till late in the afternoon. And Serenella never once cried.

J. G. BALLARD

THE GARDEN OF TIME

TOWARD EVENING, WHEN the great shadow of the Palladian villa filled the terrace, Count Axel left his library and walked down the wide rococo steps among the time flowers. A tall, imperious figure in a black velvet jacket, a gold tiepin glinting below his George V beard, cane held stiffly in a white-gloved hand, he surveyed the exquisite crystal flowers without emotion, listening to the sounds of his wife's harpsichord, as she played a Mozart rondo in the music room, echo and vibrate through the translucent petals.

The garden of the villa extended for some two hundred yards below the terrace, sloping down to a miniature lake spanned by a white bridge, a slender pavilion on the opposite bank. Axel rarely ventured as far as the lake; most of the time flowers grew in a small grove just below the terrace, sheltered by the high wall which encircled the estate. From the terrace he could see over the wall to the plain beyond, a continuous expanse of open ground that rolled in great swells to the horizon, where it rose slightly before finally dipping from sight. The plain surrounded the house on all sides, its drab emptiness emphasizing the seclusion and mellowed magnificence of the villa. Here, in the garden, the air seemed brighter, the sun warmer, while the plain was always dull and remote.

As was his custom before beginning his evening stroll, Count Axel looked out across the plain to the final rise, where the horizon was illuminated like a distant stage by the fading sun. As the Mozart chimed delicately around him, flowing from his wife's graceful hands, he saw that the advance column of an enormous army was moving slowly over the horizon. At first glance, the long ranks seemed to be progressing in orderly lines, but on closer inspection, it was apparent that, like the obscured detail of a Goya landscape, the army was composed of a vast throng of people, men and women, interspersed with a few soldiers in ragged uniforms, pressing forward in a disorganized tide. Some laboured under heavy loads suspended from crude yokes around their necks, others struggled with cumbersome wooden carts, their hands wrenching at the wheel spokes, a few trudged on alone, but all moved on at the same pace, bowed backs illuminated in the fleeting sun.

The advancing throng was almost too far away to be visible, but even as Axel watched, his expression aloof yet observant, it came perceptibly nearer, the vanguard of an immense rabble appearing from below the horizon. At last, as the daylight began to fade, the front edge of the throng reached the crest of the first swell below the horizon, and Axel turned from the terrace and walked down among the time flowers.

The flowers grew to a height of about six feet, their slender stems, like rods of glass, bearing a dozen leaves, the once transparent fronds frosted by the fossilized veins. At the peak of each stem was the time flower, the size of a goblet, the opaque outer petals enclosing the crystal heart. Their diamond brilliance contained a thousand faces, the crystal seeming to drain the air of its light and motion. As the flowers swayed slightly in the evening air, they glowed like flame-tipped spears.

Many of the stems no longer bore flowers, and Axel examined them all carefully, a note of hope now and then crossing

his eyes as he searched for any further buds. Finally he selected a large flower on the stem nearest the wall, removed his
gloves, and with his strong fingers snapped it off.

As he carried the flower back onto the terrace, it began to
sparkle and deliquesce, the light trapped within the core at
last released. Gradually the crystal dissolved, only the outer
petals remaining intact, and the air around Axel became
bright and vivid, charged with slanting rays that flared away
into the waning sunlight. Strange shifts momentarily transformed the evening, subtly altering its dimensions of time
and space. The darkened portico of the house, its patina of
age stripped away, loomed with a curious spectral whiteness
as if suddenly remembered in a dream.

Raising his head, Axel peered over the wall again. Only
the farthest rim of the horizon was lit by the sun, and the
great throng, which before had stretched almost a quarter of
the way across the plain, had now receded to the horizon, the
entire concourse abruptly flung back in a reversal of time,
and appeared to be stationary.

The flower in Axel's hand had shrunk to the size of a glass
thimble, the petals contracting around the vanishing core.
A faint sparkle flickered from the centre and extinguished
itself, and Axel felt the flower melt like an ice-cold bead of
dew in his hand.

Dusk closed across the house, sweeping its long shadows over the plain, the horizon merging into the sky. The
harpsichord was silent, and the time flowers, no longer
reflecting its music, stood motionlessly, like an embalmed
forest.

For a few minutes Axel looked down at them counting
the flowers which remained, then greeted his wife as she
crossed the terrace, her brocade evening dress rustling over
the ornamental tiles.

"What a beautiful evening, Axel." She spoke feelingly, as if she were thanking her husband personally for the great ornate shadow across the lawn and the dark brilliant air. Her face was serene and intelligent, her hair, swept back behind her head into a jewelled clasp, touched with silver. She wore her dress low across her breast, revealing a long slender neck and high chin. Axel surveyed her with fond pride. He gave her his arm and together they walked down the steps into the garden.

"One of the longest evenings this summer," Axel confirmed, adding, "I picked a perfect flower, my dear, a jewel. With luck it should last us for several days." A frown touched his brow, and he glanced involuntarily at the wall. "Each time now they seem to come nearer."

His wife smiled at him encouragingly and held his arm more tightly.

Both of them knew that the time garden was dying.

Three evenings later, as he had estimated (though sooner than he secretly hoped), Count Axel plucked another flower from the time garden.

When he first looked over the wall the approaching rabble filled the distant half of the plain, stretching across the horizon in an unbroken mass. He thought he could hear the low, fragmentary sounds of voices carried across the empty air, a sullen murmur punctuated by cries and shouts, but quickly told himself that he had imagined them. Luckily, his wife was at the harpsichord, and the rich contrapuntal patterns of a Bach fugue cascaded lightly across the terrace, masking any other noises.

Between the house and the horizon the plain was divided into four huge swells, the crest of each one clearly visible in the slanting light. Axel had promised himself that he would never count them, but the number was too small to remain unobserved, particularly when it so obviously marked the progress of the advancing army. By now the forward line had passed the first crest and was well on its way to the second; the main bulk of the throng pressed behind it, hiding the crest and the even vaster concourse spreading from the horizon. Looking to left and right of the central body, Axel could see the apparently limitless extent of the army. What had seemed at first to be the central mass was no more than a minor advance guard, one of many similar arms reaching across the plain. The true centre had not yet emerged, but from the rate of extension, Axel estimated that when it finally reached the plain it would completely cover every foot of ground.

Axel searched for any large vehicles or machines, but all was amorphous and uncoordinated as ever. There were no banners or flags, no mascots or pike bearers. Heads bowed, the multitude pressed on, unaware of the sky.

Suddenly, just before Axel turned away, the forward edge of the throng appeared on top of the second crest, and swarmed down across the plain. What astounded Axel was the incredible distance it had covered while out of sight. The figures were now twice the size, each one clearly within sight.

Quickly, Axel stepped from the terrace, selected a time flower from the garden, and tore it from the stem. As it released its compacted light, he returned to the terrace. When the flower had shrunk to a frozen pearl in his palm he looked out at the plain, with relief saw that the army had retreated to the horizon again.

Then he realized that the horizon was much nearer than previously, and that what he assumed to be the horizon was the first crest.

* * *

When he joined the Countess on their evening walk he told her nothing of this, but she could see behind his casual unconcern and did what she could to dispel his worry.

Walking down the steps, she pointed to the time garden. "What a wonderful display, Axel. There are so many flowers still."

Axel nodded, smiling to himself at his wife's attempt to reassure him. Her use of *still* had revealed her own unconscious anticipation of the end. In fact a mere dozen flowers remained of the many hundred that had grown in the garden, and several of these were little more than buds – only three or four were fully grown. As they walked down to the lake, the Countess's dress rustling across the cool turf, he tried to decide whether to pick the larger flowers first or leave them to the end. Strictly, it would be better to give the smaller flowers additional time to grow and mature, and this advantage would be lost if he retained the larger flowers to the end, as he wished to do, for the final repulse. However, he realized that it mattered little either way; the garden would soon die and the smaller flowers required far longer than he could give them to accumulate their compressed cores of time. During his entire lifetime he had failed to notice a single evidence of growth among the flowers. The larger blooms had always been mature, and none of the buds had shown the slightest development.

Crossing the lake, he and his wife looked down at their reflections in the still black water. Shielded by the pavilion on one side and the high garden wall on the other, the villa in the distance, Axel felt composed and secure, the plain with its encroaching multitude a nightmare from which he had safely awakened. He put one arm around his wife's smooth waist and pressed her affectionately to his shoulder, realizing that he had not embraced her for several years, though their lives together had been timeless and he could remember as if yesterday when he first brought her to live in the villa.

"Axel," his wife asked with sudden seriousness, "before the garden dies . . . may I pick the last flower?"

Understanding her request, he nodded slowly.

One by one over the succeeding evenings, he picked the remaining flowers, leaving a single small bud which grew just below the terrace for his wife. He took the flowers at random, refusing to count or ration them, plucking two or three of the smaller buds at the same time when necessary. The approaching horde had now reached the second and third crests, a vast concourse of labouring humanity that blotted out the horizon. From the terrace Axel could see clearly the shuffling, straining ranks moving down into the hollow toward the final crest, and occasionally the sounds of their voices carried across to him, interspersed with cries of anger and the cracking of whips. The wooden carts lurched from side to side on tilting wheels, their drivers struggling to control them. As far as Axel could tell, not a single member of the throng was aware of its overall direction. Rather, each one blindly moved forward across the ground directly below the heels of the person in front of him, and the only unity was that of the cumulative compass. Pointlessly, Axel hoped that the true centre, far below the horizon, might be moving in a different direction, and that gradually the multitude would alter course, swing away from the villa, and recede from the plain like a turning tide.

On the last evening but one, as he plucked the time flower, the forward edge of the rabble had reached the third crest, and was swarming past it. While he waited for the Countess, Axel looked at the two flowers left, both small buds which would carry them back through only a few minutes of the next evening. The glass stems of the dead flowers reared up stiffly into the air, but the whole garden had lost its bloom.

Axel passed the next morning quietly in his library, sealing the rarer of his manuscripts into the glass-topped cases between the galleries. He walked slowly down the portrait corridor, polishing each of the pictures carefully, then tidied his desk and locked the door behind him. During the afternoon he busied himself in the drawing rooms, unobtrusively assisting his wife as she cleaned their ornaments and straightened the vases and busts.

By evening, as the sun fell behind the house, they were both tired and dusty, and neither had spoken to the other all day. When his wife moved toward the music room, Axel called her back.

"Tonight we'll pick the flowers together, my dear," he said to her evenly. "One for each of us."

He peered only briefly over the wall. They could hear, less than half a mile away, the great dull roar of the ragged army, the ring of iron and lash, pressing on toward the house.

Quickly, Axel plucked his flower, a bud no bigger than a sapphire. As it flickered softly, the tumult outside momentarily receded, then began to gather again.

Shutting his ears to the clamour, Axel looked around at the villa, counting the six columns in the portico, then gazed out across the lawn at the silver disk of the lake, its bowl reflecting the last evening light, and at the shadows moving between the tall trees, lengthening across the crisp turf. He lingered over the bridge where he and his wife had stood arm in arm for so many summers—

"Axel!"

The tumult outside roared into the air, a thousand voices bellowed only twenty or thirty yards away. A stone flew

374

over the wall and landed among the time flowers, snapping several of the brittle stems. The Countess ran toward him as a further barrage rattled along the wall. Then a heavy tile whirled through the air over their heads and crashed into one of the conservatory windows.

"Axel!" He put his arms around her, straightening his silk cravat when her shoulder brushed it between his lapels.

"Quickly, my dear, the last flower!" He led her down the steps and through the garden. Taking the stem between her jewelled fingers, she snapped it cleanly, then cradled it within her palms.

For a moment the tumult lessened slightly and Axel collected himself. In the vivid light sparkling from the flower he saw his wife's white, frightened eyes. "Hold it as long as you can, my dear, until the last grain dies."

Together they stood on the terrace, the Countess clasping the brilliant dying jewel, the air closing in upon them as the voices outside mounted again. The mob was battering at the heavy iron gates, and the whole villa shook with the impact.

While the final glimmer of light sped away, the Countess raised her palms to the air, as if releasing an invisible bird, then in a final access of courage put her hands in her husband's, her smile as radiant as the vanished flower.

"Oh, Axel!" she cried.

Like a sword, the darkness swooped down across them.

Heaving and swearing, the outer edges of the mob reached the knee-high remains of the wall enclosing the ruined estate, hauled their carts over it and along the dry ruts of what once had been an ornate drive. The ruin, formerly a spacious villa, barely interrupted the ceaseless tide of humanity. The lake was empty, fallen trees rotting at its bottom, an old bridge rusting into it. Weeds flourished among the long grass in the lawn, overrunning the ornamental pathways and carved stone screens.

Much of the terrace had crumbled, and the main section of the mob cut straight across the lawn, bypassing the gutted villa, but one or two of the more curious climbed up and searched among the shell. The doors had rotted from their hinges and the floors had fallen through. In the music room an ancient harpsichord had been chopped into firewood, but a few keys still lay among the dust. All the books had been toppled from the shelves in the library, the canvases had been slashed, and gilt frames littered the floor.

As the main body of the mob reached the house, it began to cross the wall at all points along its length. Jostled together, the people stumbled into the dry lake, swarmed over the terrace, and pressed through the house toward the open doors on the north side.

One area alone withstood the endless wave. Just below the terrace, between the wrecked balcony and the wall, was a dense, six-foot-high growth of heavy thornbushes. The barbed foliage formed an impenetrable mass, and the people passing stepped around it carefully, noticing the belladonna entwined among the branches. Most of them were too busy finding their footing among the upturned flagstones to look up into the centre of the thornbushes, where two stone statues stood side by side, gazing out over the grounds from their protected vantage point. The larger of the figures was the effigy of a bearded man in a high-collared jacket, a cane under one arm. Beside him was a woman in an elaborate full-skirted dress, her slim, serene face unmarked by the wind and rain. In her left hand she lightly clasped a single rose, the delicately formed petals so thin as to be almost transparent.

As the sun died away behind the house a single ray of

light glanced through a shattered cornice and struck the rose, reflected off the whorl of petals onto the statues, lighting up the grey stone so that for a fleeting moment it was indistinguishable from the long-vanished flesh of the statues' originals.

MATSUDA AOKO

PLANTING

Translated by Angus Turvill

MARGUERITE PLANTED. She planted roses. She planted violets. She planted lilies of the valley. She planted
clover. And, of course, she planted marguerites. When she
found marguerites in the box, she would smile. "We meet
again!" she would say softly. The gentle curves etched lightly by the years around her mouth and eyes would dance.
Marguerite planted. She planted balloons of pretty colours.
She planted lip cream, its smell tingling in her nose. She
planted thick ceramic mugs. She planted cashmere socks.
It was Marguerite's job to plant. And so she planted. She
planted lovely things, but nothing grand. She planted
things one wouldn't tire of. She planted clothes that
would make one feel happy all day. She planted soft, gentle
colours. She planted soft, gentle textures. Marguerite planted every day. She planted a heart that knew each day was
precious. She planted a heart that kept things it liked and
used them time and again. She planted a heart that treated things with care. Marguerite didn't hurry. She planted
slowly. It was fine to plant slowly here. How long had she
been planting slowly? It was hard to say. Marguerite – her
glasses unfashionable but delicate, cardigan and trousers of
pure cotton, simple curls at the tips of her white-tinged,
light brown hair. Marguerite and her garden, wrapped in the
faint light of evening – to a passer-by it would have seemed
like Heaven.

*　　*　　*

381

Marguerite was turning the pages of *Townwork*. She looked tired. Her clothes itched. She didn't care about them, didn't even notice the material was artificial. She was in a Doutor coffee shop, upstairs, in the seat nearest the toilet. Normally she drank her iced coffee quickly. If she waited for the ice to melt, the outside of the glass would become wet with condensation and droplets would seep down through the thin paper napkin on which it rested and wet the table. She hated that. But on Mondays she let the water spread messily on the table. Goodness knows how many futile days she had spent like this, week after week, waiting for the next issue of *Townwork*. She picked up a copy at the FamilyMart convenience store every Monday, crossed the road to Doutor and started turning the pages. Before looking inside the thin magazine, she could never suppress a momentary hope – perhaps this week there would be the perfect job. But by the time she came to close the magazine, this hope had always turned to dejection, dejection mixed with resignation. Every single time. It was too much – Marguerite felt as though she might faint. The jobs were updated every week. There were always new positions advertised. What struck her most were the dental nurse ads. They gushed out of the pages like water from a spring – it was hard to believe there could be so many dental surgeries in the world. Looking through the ads in *Townwork* was interesting. But the fact was Marguerite never felt like applying for any of the jobs. "A friendly workplace" – that was no good. She didn't think she could work with friendly people. "We'll help your dream come true!" declared a restaurant manager beside a photograph of cheerful young staff, bandanas around their heads. That was no good. She didn't think that she could work with people who had dreams. And she couldn't work in a place where the staff would have to clap and sing if they found out it was a customer's birthday. "Supportive colleagues" were no good either. Marguerite had never come across a colleague she could rely on. Basically, Marguerite was tired. She was tired of involvement with people, tired of working with people. But she didn't think she was yet tired of work itself. She wanted a job working alone, without having to speak to anyone. There had never been any jobs like that. But one week she found one – on a flimsy page in a small square-framed ad.

The first thing to come out of the box was a pure white shirt. Marguerite planted the shirt nervously, but in accordance with the manual. She was relieved when she had successfully planted it. And after that she planted, carefully, one by one, each of the other items that came out of the box. A box arrived every day. Some days from Yamato Transport, some days from Sagawa Express. Working time was nine to six – eight hours, allowing for breaks – nine hundred yen an hour. No work at weekends. At first, she thought the rate of pay was rather low, but she soon decided she couldn't help that. After all, the job was only planting. And she didn't have to meet anyone or speak to anyone apart from the deliverymen who gave her the boxes. There were no performance targets. If she couldn't plant everything from the box one day, she could plant them the next. So Marguerite planted slowly. Lovely tinkling ceramic bells. Macarons of many colours. Figurines of fighter girls. Band T-shirts. One after another they came out of the box. And Marguerite planted each one slowly, so that she would not forget any of the wonderful objects, beautiful objects that came to her. Marguerite cherished everything that came out of the box. That above all was what made her happy.

* * *

Marguerite was surprised to see the dead rat that came out of the box. She planted the dead rat, holding it away from her between forefinger and thumb. A crumpled handkerchief came out of the box. Marguerite planted the crumpled handkerchief. Muddy water came out. Marguerite planted the muddy water. She went to a nearby supermarket on her break and bought some rubber gloves. Rubber gloves on, she planted. She planted a soaking-wet cuddly toy. She planted shrivelled vegetables. She planted a bird with its wings pulled off. She planted a carpet stained red-black with blood. She could not bear to look directly at what came out of the box. She didn't understand what had happened. As soon as a thought came out of the box, the exact opposite thought would follow. As soon as a feeling came out, the exact opposite feeling would follow. Marguerite was confused. Confused, she planted. She planted a broken cup. She planted a tongue cut out of a mouth. She planted a heart that could love nobody. She planted hatred. She planted anger. She planted, though she wanted to bury. She wanted to bury everything that came out of the box. She wanted to bury them so deep in the earth that no shoot could ever reach the surface. It was only Marguerite who could bury them. But Marguerite had to plant, and so she planted. She wished what she planted would wither quickly away. "Wither, wither, wither," she muttered. That is what her job had become. She didn't plant slowly any more. Her heart sank when each new box arrived. She tried to deal with them as quickly as she could. But however many she dealt with, nothing wonderful now came out, nothing now to warm the heart. Marguerite planted sadness. She planted anxiety. She planted regret. She planted fear. She planted fear. She planted fear. She planted fear. She planted fear. Day after day she planted fear, as though in a game of forfeit. Instead of relaxing with a home-made lunch, she now ate as she worked, gnawing at a rice ball from a convenience store. Marguerite stopped breathing deeply. Her field of vision narrowed. She took fear from the box and it slipped from her hands. She gasped. As if waking from a trance, she picked up the fear and planted it quickly. She noticed she was sticky with sweat. It was uncomfortable. She felt sick. She took off her wig, releasing trapped heat and, with it, stiff black hair. She took off her non-prescription spectacles and rubbed her face. Her wrinkles, drawn in eyebrow pencil, smudged diagonally and disappeared. What do you mean "Marguerite"? A stupid girl, not yet thirty, pretending to be washed out. A girl who can only plant what she wants to bury. A coward, incapable of anything. Makiko cried. Makiko stood crying stupidly in the middle of the garden.

Some time ago there was an author named Mori Mari, who called herself Maria. Makiko loved Mori Mari. She thought that if Mari could call herself Maria, then she, Makiko, could call herself Marguerite. It wouldn't harm anyone, would it? She knew that the men who delivered the boxes looked at her with mystified expressions, mystified feelings, but in this workplace she would be "Marguerite". She had decided this on the first day, when she planted the shirt.

Makiko looked around the garden as she cried. Fear hung low in the air, like fog. The pitch-black garden was like a mire, sucking Makiko down. Like a black hole. The place she stood was nowhere. Where is this? she thought. Then she realized – she had never had a choice. There is no way she could have chosen. Of course there wasn't. Makiko smiled faintly. Her tears stopped. She put her wig back on. She put on her glasses. She wiped her face with a handkerchief and took a make-up pouch from her bag. Looking in her hand mirror, she redrew the wrinkles. I will plant. I will plant, she thought. She put her hand in the box. Fear appeared. Marguerite did not look away. She fixed her gaze on fear. Then she slowly planted it. She planted it neatly. Marguerite resolved: I do not have the right to choose. But I can wait. If I carry on planting here like this, one day wonderful things may come out of the box again, things it warms the heart just to see. So I will wait here. Keep planting and wait. Marguerite planted fear. She planted fear. She took a deep breath. She planted fear. She stretched a little to relieve the tension in her body. She relaxed for a while with some nice-smelling herb tea from her flask. She planted fear. She planted fear. The man from Yamato Transport brought the next box. Marguerite took it, smiling. The man thought this was the first time he had seen her smile. What was in the box, she did not know. Her watch, a men's-style watch that would never go out of fashion, told her that her working hours were up. She decided she would open tomorrow's box tomorrow. Marguerite will be planting again tomorrow.

ACKNOWLEDGMENTS

JOAN AIKEN: "The Serial Garden" published in *The Serial Garden: The Complete Armitage Family Stories.* Virago/ Brandt & Hochman Literary Agents, Inc.

MATSUDA AOKO: "Planting" from *Heaven's Wind*, translated by Angus Turvill, published by The Japan Society. Reprinted with permission. Translation copyright © Angus Turvill. Reprinted with permission from the translator.

J. G. BALLARD: "The Garden of Time" from J. G. Ballard: *The Complete Short Stories* (vol. 1), HarperCollins UK. The Wylie Agency.

ITALO CALVINO: "The Enchanted Garden": from *Difficult Loves* by Italo Calvino, translated by William Weaver, Archibald Colquhoun and Peggy Wright (Harcourt Brace Jovanovich, 1984). Copyright © 1949 by Giulio Einaudi editore, Torino. Copyright © 1958 by Giulio Einaudi editore, s.p.a., Torino. English translation copyright © 1983, 1984 by HarperCollins Publishers PLC. Reprinted by permission of Mariner Books, an imprint of HarperCollins Publishers LLC. All rights reserved. "The Enchanted Garden" first published in Italo Calvino: *Adam, One Afternoon*, translated by Archibald Colquhoun and Peggy Wright, Collins, 1957, reprinted Secker & Warburg, 1983 (Penguin Random House UK).

SANDRA CISNEROS: "The Monkey Garden" from *The House on Mango Street.* Copyright © 1984 by Sandra Cisneros. Published by Vintage Books, a division of Random House, Inc., and in hardcover by Alfred A. Knopf

Titles in Everyman's Library
Pocket Classics

Bedtime Stories
Selected by Diana Secker Tesdell

Berlin Stories
Selected by Philip Hensher

The Best Medicine: Stories of Healing
Selected by Theodore Dalrymple

Cat Stories
Selected by Diana Secker Tesdell

Christmas Stories
Selected by Diana Secker Tesdell

Detective Stories
Selected by Peter Washington

Dog Stories
Selected by Diana Secker Tesdell

Erotic Stories
Selected by Rowan Pelling

Fishing Stories
Selected by Henry Hughes

Florence Stories
Selected by Ella Carr

Garden Stories
Selected by Diana Secker Tesdell

Ghost Stories
Selected by Peter Washington

Golf Stories
Selected by Charles McGrath

Horse Stories
Selected by Diana Secker Tesdell

London Stories
Selected by Jerry White

Love Stories
Selected by Diana Secker Tesdell

New York Stories
Selected by Diana Secker Tesdell

Paris Stories
Selected by Shaun Whiteside

Prague Stories
Selected by Richard Bassett

Rome Stories
Selected by Jonathan Keates

Shaken and Stirred: Intoxicating Stories
Selected by Diana Secker Tesdell